François Marie Arouet De Voltaire

FRANÇOIS MARIE AROUET DE VOLTAIRE
was born in 1694 into a Parisian bourgeois family.
Educated by Jesuits, he was an excellent pupil but
one quickly enraged by dogma. An early rift with his
father—who wished him to study law—led to his
choice of letters as a career. Insinuating himself into
court circles, he became notorious for lampoons on
leading notables and was twice imprisoned in the
Bastille. By his mid-thirties his diplomatic activities
precipitated a four-year exile in England where he
won the praise of Swift and Pope for his political
tracts. His publication, three years later in France,
of *Lettres philosophiques sur les Anglais* (1733)
—an attack on French Church and State—forced
him to flee again. For twenty years Voltaire lived
chiefly away from France. In this, his most prolific
period, he wrote such satirical tales as "Zadig"
(1747) and "Candide" (1759). His old age at Ferney, outside Geneva, was made bright by his adopted
daughter, "Belle et Bonne," and marked by his in-
tercessions in behalf of victims of political injustice.
Sharp-witted and lean in his white wig, impatient
with all appropriate rituals, he died in Paris in 1778
—the foremost French author of his day.

VOLTAIRE

Candide, Zadig

and Selected Stories

Translated and with an intro-
duction, by Donald M. Frame
Revised and Updated Bibliography

A SIGNET CLASSIC

SIGNET CLASSIC
Published by New American Library, a division of
Penguin Putnam Inc., 375 Hudson Street,
New York, New York 10014, U.S.A.
Penguin Books Ltd, 27 Wrights Lane,
London W8 5TZ, England
Penguin Books Australia Ltd, Ringwood,
Victoria, Australia
Penguin Books Canada Ltd, 10 Alcorn Avenue,
Toronto, Ontario, Canada M4V 3B2
Penguin Books (N.Z.) Ltd, 182–190 Wairau Road,
Auckland 10, New Zealand

Penguin Books Ltd, Registered Offices:
Harmondsworth, Middlesex, England

Published by Signet Classic, an imprint of New American Library,
a division of Penguin Putnam Inc.

A hardbound edition of this book is published
by Indiana University Press.

First Signet Classic Printing, May 1961
43 42 41 40 39 38 37 36 35

Cover painting, "Louis XV leaving the Lit de Justice held
at the Palace September 12, 1775" (detail), by Pierre Deno
Martin, Paris: Carnavelet. Courtesy of Hubert Josse Art Resource.

Printed in the United States of America

CONTENTS

INTRODUCTION

CHARACTERISTIC of all Voltaire's life were the acclaim and harassment that marked its close. At the age of eighty-three he returned to his native Paris for a triumph such as few authors have ever enjoyed. Delegations from the Académie Française and the Comédie Française, personages as diverse as Mme du Barry and Mme Necker, Diderot and Franklin, Gluck and the English ambassador, came to pay him their respects. Crowds cheered him in the streets. At the sixth performance of his tragedy *Irène,* he in his box and later his bust on the stage were crowned with wreaths amid wild acclaim. Yet he had come to Paris with no clear authorization after twenty-four years of exile. When he died there ten weeks later (May 30, 1778) the religious authorities denied him burial, and his body was removed secretly at night to be interred in the abbey of Scellières in Champagne.

The oppressive power of Voltaire's opponents must be kept in mind if his tales are to appear in their true perspective. Great satire creates the illusion that its targets are more comic than sinister. Imprisonments, exiles, a beating had whetted Voltaire's will to fight; the longer he lived the more constantly he used his wit to forge weapons of war. His tales, all written after he was fifty, are the weapons that have worn best. Their luster must not blind us, however, to the fact that when Voltaire died his long battle for liberty and justice was not won.

The acclaim, like the harassment, came to Voltaire early as well as late. François-Marie Arouet, who adopted the nobiliary pen name "de Voltaire" at twenty-three, was born in 1694 of an intelligent, ambitious bourgeois family and given a strong classical education at the distinguished Collège Louis-le-Grand, where his Jesuit masters enjoyed his precocity and rated him as "a talented boy, but a notable scamp." He resisted his father's pressure to follow him into the law, and devoted himself early to literature. In the hedonistic society of the Regency after the death of Louis XIV (1715) he won renown—also imprisonment and brief exile—for his wit. In his twenty-fourth year he scored his first success as a tragedian with *Oedipe* (1718). Though even his best trage- dies, such as *Zaïre* (1732), *Mahomet* (1742), and *Mérope* (1743), are little more than documents today, for much of his life Voltaire's greatest fame was as the leading successor to Corneille and Racine in classical French verse tragedy, which he spiced with themes from Shakespeare and the East, colorful and violent visual effects, and thinly veiled social and religious criticism.

Five years later he made another successful debut in the epic with *La Henriade*, today quite dated but enormously popular in its time, and still probably the best French epic in the classical mode. His subject was a lifelong hero, Henry IV, fighter for religious peace and tolerance in France and author (1598) of the Edict of Nantes.

In 1725 a sneer at Voltaire by the Chevalier de Rohan led to a sharp reply, and this to a beating by lackeys directed by Rohan under the indifferent eyes of other aristocrats whom Voltaire had thought his friends. He challenged Rohan, who accepted; but on the morning set for the duel Voltaire was arrested and put in the Bastille, which he was allowed to leave two weeks later for an exile of over two years (1726–1729) in England.

His exposure to English freedoms in his early thirties, following the harsh awakening to his lack of status in the eyes of French nobles, turned his mind to social inequalities as never before. He studied English hard and learned it rather well, made friends with Swift, Pope, Congreve, Bolingbroke, and others, and hailed English freedom of worship, thought, and speech, as well as the Quakers, Shakespeare, Bacon, Locke, Newton, and the parliamentary system, in his *Philo- sophical Letters*, or *Letters Concerning the English Nation*, whose long-delayed publication in 1734 brought about the burning of the book and a warrant for the author's arrest. The openness and power of his ironic attack on French abuses and inequities give this date great importance.

Meanwhile Voltaire had triumphed in another field with his *History of Charles XII* (1731). Less important than two later works, *The Century of Louis XIV* (1751) and the *Essay on the Manners and the Spirit of Nations* (1756), which brought all civilization and all civilizations into the purview of history, his account of the Swedish warrior-king showed what harm such a man can do even to his own country, and demonstrated Voltaire's mastery at shaping masses of material into a clear and enjoyable story.

The persecution brought on by the *Philosophical Letters* found Voltaire prepared. Financially secure since his early thirties after studious and successful investment, he had a safe asylum in the independent duchy of Lorraine at the Château of Cirey with his beloved mistress Emilie, Marquise du Châtelet. Here he settled down for eleven years (1733–1744) with Emilie and her accommodating husband, writing indefatigably, delving deeply, though as an amateur, into the science of his time, especially that of Newton. An even greater lover of science than Voltaire, Mme du Châtelet also loved the philosophical optimism of Leibniz and Wolff, which Voltaire treated gently until her death but ridiculed ten years later in *Candide*.

In his early fifties (1744–1750) Voltaire was mainly occupied at court, with some success: appointment as historiographer-royal and as gentleman of the King's chamber, election to the Académie Française. His uneasiness and his disgust with this life, however, appear already in his first philosophical tale, *Zadig* (1747). The death of Mme du Châtelet in 1749 left him sad and unsettled. For ten years Frederick the Great of Prussia, culturally an ardent Francophile, had been urging Voltaire to come to his "German Versailles" in Potsdam, near Berlin. Hoping to find a philosopher-king, Voltaire at last accepted.

His stay in Berlin (1750–1753) started like a honeymoon and ended in a violent though not permanent break. Frederick was no comfortable master for a spirited subordinate, nor Voltaire a comfortable courtier for an authoritarian monarch. Both were better at using than at supporting irony. French courtiers aroused Voltaire's jealousy and fomented bad feeling. Voltaire's shady speculation with a Jew named Hirschel led to a squalid lawsuit that angered Frederick. The last straw came when Maupertuis, president of the Academy of Berlin, by sheer force of authority had the mathematician and philosopher Koenig condemned as a forger and dismissed from the Academy in disgrace. Voltaire, convinced that Koenig was in the right, protested; Frederick sided with his President. When Maupertuis published some inept *Letters,* Voltaire ridiculed him scathingly in his *Diatribe of Doctor*

Akakia. Frederick had this burned and Voltaire arrested, and subjected him on his departure later to another humiliating arrest and detainment—not without reason—in Frankfort.

Back in France, Voltaire was soon in trouble over a pirated edition of the *Essay on the Manners*, and permission to return to Paris was not granted. Needing a safe retreat with Cirey gone, he chose Lake Geneva, renting a house between Lausanne and the lake and buying another just outside Geneva which he named Les Délices. To Voltaire, now sixty, this was a happy home, which could comfortably accommodate his niece—and mistress—Mme Denis, a considerable household, and many visitors. Here, at his own private theater, he could indulge a favorite passion by directing his own plays and acting in them with his guests. Since stage performances were banned in Calvinist Geneva, he was presently required to move his to Lausanne. In return he encouraged his friend D'Alembert to criticize the ban in his article on Geneva in the *Encyclopédie*, which led Jean-Jacques Rousseau to answer the article and Voltaire with his eloquent *Letter to D'Alembert* (1758). Voltaire and Rousseau, friendly at first, were now at odds for good. When other matters in D'Alembert's article worsened Voltaire's relations with the Genevans, he started looking for a home outside Genevan territory. In 1758 he bought the large property of Ferney on French soil but still on Lake Geneva and only four miles from the town.

The Patriarch of Ferney, as he came to be called, now added to his many other activities those of a country gentleman. He took a strong paternal interest in his village, planting trees, raising wheat and cows, developing pasture land, a stone quarry, a tile works, a tannery, factories of silk stockings, lace, and Swiss watches, obtaining lighter and more equitable taxes for the whole region, establishing a school and a hospital, even building a church. He took many unfortunates into his home: victims of injustice like the Calas and Sirven families; others who provided him a chance for matchmaking, such as a grandniece of Corneille, for whose dowry he published a critical edition of that playwright's works; and later a particular favorite, Mlle Varicourt, destined for a convent for economy's sake and in despair until Voltaire took her in, nicknamed her "Belle et Bonne," and eventually married her to the Marquis de Villette. Visitors of great distinction flocked to Ferney as to a capital of letters. Meanwhile Voltaire worked as tirelessly as ever, usually in bed, on his enormous and fascinating correspondence, on some plays, but mainly on keen, satiric, short pieces of all sorts including his witty *Philosophical Dictionary* and most of his tales. The great philosophic struggle was on in earnest, with Voltaire the main leader of the fight to *"écraser l'infâme*—crush infamy": the infamy of intolerance and authoritarian suppression of freedom in thought and word. Publication of that great secular monument the *Encyclopédie* was completed, after much opposition and repeated suspensions, in 1765. Voltaire contributed considerably to it by writing and soliciting articles, by encouragement and spirited defense.

Nor was the old warrior content to seek justice simply in the abstract. Again and again he fought tirelessly for the victims of judicial injustice and religious intolerance: Jean Calas, Protestant of Toulouse, condemned and executed for the murder of his son, unanimously rehabilitated (1765); Sirven, another Protestant of Toulouse, condemned for killing his daughter (1764), fleeing arrest with his wife and two remaining daughters, exonerated (1771); Lally, a former commander in India, executed in 1766, rehabilitated in 1778; the Perra family, Martin, Montbailli; La Barre, whose torture and death were a bitter blow; La Barre's friend d'Etallonde, whom Voltaire greatly helped. This unsparing dedication to the victims of persecution led to the final transfiguration of Voltaire's public image: in Paris on his final visit, as in Geneva two years before, enthusiastic crowds hailed him as the defender of Calas.

Voltaire was always a man of action. Highly volatile, sensitive, ambitious, emotional, irascible and generous, vindictive and compassionate, he found his greatest satisfaction and release in work. But work, to satisfy him, must act on others. He once complained that Rousseau wrote for the sake of writing, while he himself wrote in the interest of action. Hence his lack of fondness for meditation or speculation. When Martin, in the conclusion of *Candide,* recommends work without reasoning as the only way of making life endurable, he is not challenging the priority of reason like Rousseau; he is condemning the *libido ratiocinandi* of Pangloss, displayed perhaps most clearly in Chapter 5. There

Candide, lying injured in the ruins of Lisbon, begged Pangloss for oil and wine, and was treated to a theory of the origin of the earthquake.

" 'Nothing is more probable,' said Candide, 'but for the love of God, a little oil and wine.'

" 'What do you mean, probable?' replied the philosopher. 'I maintain that the matter is proved.' Candide lost consciousness. . . ." What Voltaire, like Martin, condemns is impractical reasoning and theorizing not leading to action.

Thus Voltaire is not a philosopher in any usual sense. Convinced like Descartes that clarity and distinctness are the prime criteria of truth; convinced that man, an insect living a few seconds on an atom of mud, cannot understand the grand designs of his infinite Creator, that systems claiming to explain the unfathomable are imposture and vanity, he is equally convinced that there is much worth knowing and worth doing. Science, which had given men some certain knowledge of the measurable, he found useful; but since science was impeded by repressive dogmatism, even here action for freedom was as necessary as research. The most vital study, for Voltaire, was that of the means and the obstacles to human betterment; the most vital action was to remove those obstacles. In the France of his time the chief obstacles seemed to be social injustice and religious intolerance; these were the infamy that he strove to crush.

His main weapon was wit, wit prompted but not controlled by emotion. Passion, as the angel points out in *Zadig* (Chapter 20), is necessary but dangerous, the wind that moves our vessel but may sink it. Voltaire put his faith in reason as the test of truth. Abuses must be exposed to the light of reason clearly, satirically, in the nakedness of their absurdity; the reader must see that the emperor has no clothes.

This being the main purpose of Voltaire's tales, they must not seek fully to reproduce the rich texture of human nature, motive, or situation; we must neither believe in his characters, nor be involved with them, too completely; the ideas must be dominant and clear. There is no harm, in *Candide*, in bringing the Baron and Pangloss back to life; they have useful roles to play later, and their apparent deaths are further proof that human misfortune is universal. Despite Voltaire's debt to Swift, the two are very different. Voltaire never makes the same pretense of truth about his tales that Swift, with his utterly veracious narrator and his precise physical measurements, does about *Gulliver's Travels;* he does not seek the richness of ambiguity and texture that Swift derives in part from this dead-pan humor of his; his points must be unmistakable and full of impact. Uncertainties in Voltaire—the relative importance of Jesrad's assertions and of Zadig's "But . . . ," the precise scope of Candide's "cultivate our garden"—are of another order than in Swift: the rarity of happiness for the good, the futility of idle reasoning are crystal clear.

The ideas, of course, are not everything. Voltaire's best tales sweep along on lively plots, often Oriental, often both exploiting and parodying contemporary romances of sentiment and adventure, often using travel to give the protagonist experience of the world. This experience he must gain, and his gain is ours. Along the way we are treated to ever-varied pyrotechnics as an anecdote here, a comment there, sheds the light of ridicule on Voltaire's favorite abuses. Always the movement is rapid, the style lean and sparkling. Always the story, however entertaining, is ancillary to the ideas.

In some tales the ideas are simple. *Memnon* (1749) teaches us the folly of aspiring to perfect wisdom; *Bababec* (1750), that good deeds are better than useless asceticism; *Scarmentado* (1756), that intolerance is universal; *The World as It Is* (1748) and *Plato's Dream* (1756), that we and our globe might be worse; *Berthier* (1759), that most Jesuits are proud, some boring; *Story of a Good Brahman* (1761), that man does not want happiness at the price of imbecility; *Jeannot and Colin* (1764), that vanity is profitless; *An Indian Adventure* (1766), that all creatures are cruel to one another; *The One-Eyed Porter* (1774), that happiness is in the eye of the beholder; *Memory's Adventure* (1775), that man would be lost without memory and the senses.

In others the themes are complex. *Count Chesterfield's Ears* (1775) ranges from the inanity of the concept *soul* through the beauty of Tahitian love festivals to picturesque theories of human motivation. *Ingenuous* (1767) hits at the folly of sectarians, the cruelty of oppressors, and the evils of arbitrary power, while presenting the noble savage as a good-natured brute needing education to become truly a man. *Micromegas* (1752) is a lesson in relativity, the presumption of puny man, and the dignity that scientific knowledge gives him. The two greatest tales, *Candide* and *Zadig,* focus on the problem of evil, which most of the others touch upon. In *Zadig* (1747), probably because of Mme du Châtelet, Voltaire gives the hermit a strong argument for a beneficent Providence whose ways are beyond us, and the story ends happily. However, Zadig still argues as the hermit-angel flies off, and the story suggests that goodness, wisdom, and valor rarely lead to happiness. *Candide* (1759), written at white heat after Emilie's death, disillusionment with Frederick, and the Lisbon earthquake, demonstrates that our life is either suffering or boredom, philosophical optimism is the acme of folly, the concept of Providence is wishful thinking, and our sole salvation lies in fruitful work cultivating our garden.

This is a new translation, coming after many others. I have found myself very often in agreement with Richard Aldington's version of *Candide,* and found value in the translations of Robert Bruce Boswell (as revised by Haskell M. Block) and of H. I. Woolf. My main departure even from Aldington has been in following Voltaire more resolutely in quest of spareness and surprise—suppressing connectives, moving back and forth between past and historical present, and the like— because these effects seem to me clearly deliberate, personal, and as noticeable in the language Voltaire used as in ours. I have steadfastly tried to keep out of Voltaire's way, for I find that he speaks very good English.

My debt to the work of many scholars, notably Georges Ascoli, George R. Havens, Gustave Lanson, André Morize, Raymond Naves, Norman L. Torrey, and Ira O. Wade, is very great.

To reduce the number of footnotes, I have placed in the Notes and Glossary at the end two kinds of notes: (1) those that otherwise would need to appear more than once and (2) those I consider not essential to an adequate understanding of the text.

References to the Notes and Glossary are designated by the sign *.

DONALD M. FRAME
Columbia University

Candide

or OPTIMISM

Translated from the German of DR. RALPH [1]

With the Additions Found in the Doctor's Pocket When He Died at Minden
in the Year of Our Lord 1759

[1759]

1 *How Candide Was Brought Up in a Fine Castle, and How He Was Expelled Therefrom*

IN WESTPHALIA, in the castle of My Lord the Baron of Thunder-ten-tronckh, there was a young man whom nature had endowed with the gentlest of characters. His face bespoke his soul. His judgment was rather sound and his mind of the simplest; this is the reason, I think, why he was named Candide. The old servants of the house suspected that he was the son of My Lord the Baron's sister and of a good and honorable gentleman of the neighborhood whom that lady never would marry because he could prove only seventy-one quarterings [2] and the rest of his genealogical tree had been lost by the injuries of time.

My Lord the Baron was one of the most powerful lords in

1   For some weeks after its publication Voltaire denied authorship of *Candide*, as he often did with works potentially dangerous to himself.
2   Divisions on a coat of arms indicating degrees of nobility. Sixty-four was considered the maximum.

Westphalia, for his castle had a door and windows. His great hall was even adorned with a piece of tapestry. All the dogs of his stable yards formed a pack of hounds when necessary; his grooms were his huntsmen; the village vicar was his Grand Almoner. They all called him My Lord, and they laughed at the stories he told.

My Lady the Baroness, who weighed about three hundred and fifty pounds, attracted very great consideration by that fact, and did the honors of the house with a dignity that made her even more respectable. Her daughter Cunégonde, aged seventeen, was rosy-complexioned, fresh, plump, appetizing. The Baron's son appeared in all respects worthy of his father. The tutor Pangloss [3] was the oracle of the house, and little Candide listened to his lessons with all the candor of his age and character.

Pangloss taught metaphysico-theologo-cosmolo-nigology.[4] He proved admirably that there is no effect without a cause and that, in this best of all possible worlds,[5] My Lord the Baron's castle was the finest of castles, and My Lady the best of all possible Baronesses.

"It is demonstrated," he said, "that things cannot be otherwise, for, everything being made for an end, everything is necessarily for the best end. Note that noses were made to wear spectacles, and so we have spectacles. Legs were visibly instituted to be breeched, and we have breeches. Stones were formed to be cut and to make into castles; so My Lord has a very handsome castle; the greatest baron in the province should be the best housed; and, pigs being made to be eaten, we eat pork all year round: consequently, those who have asserted that all is well have said a foolish thing; they should have said that all is for the best."

Candide listened attentively and believed innocently; for he thought Mademoiselle Cunégonde extremely beautiful, though he never made bold to tell her so. He concluded that after the happiness of being born Baron of Thunder-ten-tronckh, the second degree of happiness was to be Mademoiselle Cunégonde; the third, to see her every day; and the

3   From the Greek: "all tongue."
4   The "-nigo-" suggests the French *nigaud*, "booby."
5   The systematic optimism ridiculed throughout *Candide* is a caricature of that of Leibniz (1646–1716), popularized by Alexander Pope in his *Essay on Man* (1733–1734), and systematized by Christian Wolff (1679–1754).

fourth, to listen to Doctor Pangloss, the greatest philosopher in the province and consequently in the whole world.

One day Cunégonde, walking near the castle in the little wood they called The Park, saw in the bushes Doctor Pangloss giving a lesson in experimental physics to her mother's chambermaid, a very pretty and very docile little brunette. Since Mademoiselle Cunégonde had much inclination for the sciences, she observed breathlessly the repeated experiments of which she was a witness; she clearly saw the Doctor's sufficient reason, the effects and the causes, and returned home all agitated, all pensive, all filled with the desire to be learned, thinking that she might well be the sufficient reason of young Candide, who might equally well be hers.

She met Candide on the way back to the castle, and blushed; Candide blushed too; she said good morning to him in a faltering voice; and Candide spoke to her without knowing what he was saying. The next day, after dinner, as everyone was leaving the table, Cunégonde and Candide found themselves behind a screen; Cunégonde dropped her handkerchief, Candide picked it up, she innocently took his hand, the young man innocently kissed the young lady's hand with a very special vivacity, sensibility, and grace; their lips met, their eyes glowed, their knees trembled, their hands wandered. My Lord the Baron of Thunder-ten-tronckh passed near the screen and, seeing this cause and this effect, expelled Candide from the castle with great kicks in the behind; Cunégonde swooned; she was slapped in the face by My Lady the Baroness as soon as she had come to herself; and all was in consternation in the finest and most agreeable of all possible castles.

2 What Became of Candide among the Bulgarians[1]

CANDIDE, expelled from the earthly paradise, walked for a long time without knowing where, weeping, raising his eyes to

1   Voltaire chose this name to represent the Prussians of Frederick the Great because he had reason to think that Frederick was a pederast and because the French *bougre*, like the English "bugger," comes from *Bulgare* (Bulgarian). Note the treatment of the Baron's son in Chapter 4 and his adventures narrated in Chapters 15 and 28.

heaven, turning them often toward the finest of castles, which
enclosed the most beautiful of future Baronesses; he lay down
to sleep without supper in the midst of the fields between two
furrows; the snow was falling in fat flakes. The next day
Candide, frozen, dragged himself toward the neighboring town,
which was named Valdberghoff-trarbk-dikdorff, with no
money, dying of hunger and fatigue. He stopped sadly at the
door of an inn. Two men dressed in blue noticed him.

"Comrade," said one, "there's a very well-built young man,
and he's of the right height."

They advanced toward Candide and very civilly invited him
to dinner.

"Gentlemen," said Candide with charming modesty, "you
do me great honor, but I haven't the money to pay my bill."

"Ah, sir," said one of the men in blue, "persons of your
figure and merit never pay for anything; aren't you five feet
five?"

"Yes, gentlemen, that is my height," he said with a bow.

"Ah, sir, sit down to table; not only will we pay your
expenses, but we will never allow a man like you to lack
money; men are made only to help one another."

"You are right," said Candide. "That is what Monsieur
Pangloss always told me, and I clearly see that all is for the
best."

They urge him to accept a few crowns, he takes them and
wants to make out a promissory note; they want none, they
all sit down to table.

"Don't you love tenderly . . . ?"

"Oh yes," he replied, "I love Mademoiselle Cunégonde
tenderly."

"No," said one of the gentlemen, "we are asking you
whether you do not tenderly love the King of the Bulgarians."

"Not at all," he said, "for I have never seen him."

"What! He is the most charming of Kings, and you must
drink his health."

"Oh! most gladly, gentlemen"; and he drinks.

"That is sufficient," they say to him, "you are now the prop,
the support, the defender, the hero of the Bulgarians; your
fortune is made, and your glory is assured."

They immediately put irons on his legs and they take him
to the regiment. They make him turn right, turn left, raise
the ramrod, return the ramrod, take aim, fire, march on the

double, and they give him thirty strokes with a stick; the next
day he drills a little less badly and he gets only twenty strokes;
the day after they give him only ten, and he is regarded as a
prodigy by his comrades.

Candide, completely stupefied, could not yet understand too
well how he was a hero. He took it into his head one fine
spring day to go for a stroll, walking straight ahead, believing
that it was a privilege of the race of humans, as of the race
of animals, to use their legs as they please.[2] He had not gone
two leagues when up came four other heroes, six feet tall; they
overtake him, they bind him, they put him in a dungeon. He
was asked, juridically, which he liked better, to be beaten
thirty-six times by the whole regiment, or to receive twelve lead
bullets at once in his brain. In vain he told them that the will
is free and that he wanted neither of these; he had to make
a choice. By virtue of the gift of God that is called *liberty*, he
decided to run the gantlet thirty-six times; he did it twice.
The regiment was made up of two thousand men. That gave
him four thousand strokes of the ramrod, which laid open his
muscles and nerves from the nape of his neck to his rump.
As they were about to proceed to the third run, Candide, at
the end of his rope, asked them as a favor to be kind enough
to smash in his head; he obtained this favor. They bandage
his eyes; they make him kneel; at that moment the King of the
Bulgarians passes, inquires about the victim's crime; and since
this King was a man of great genius, he understood, from all
he learned about Candide, that this was a young metaphysician
very ignorant of the ways of this world, and he granted him
his pardon with a clemency that will be praised in all newspapers and in all ages. A worthy surgeon cured Candide in
three weeks with the emollients prescribed by Dioscorides. He
already had a little bit of skin, and could walk, when the King
of the Bulgarians gave battle to the King of the Abarians.[3]

2   This whole chapter satirizes the drillmastership of Frederick
the Great. The desertion is suggested by Voltaire's memory of a
Frenchman named Courtilz, whose release from prison into a hospital Voltaire had procured from Frederick.
3   This name, which designates a Scythian tribe, represents
the French, who were involved in the Seven Years' War (1756–
1763) opposite the Prussians.

3 How Candide Escaped from among the Bulgarians, and What Became of Him

NOTHING COULD BE SO BEAUTIFUL, so smart, so brilliant, so well drilled as the two armies. Trumpets, fifes, oboes, drums, cannons formed a harmony such as was never heard even in hell. First the cannons felled about six thousand men on each side; then the musketry removed from the best of worlds some nine or ten thousand scoundrels who infected its surface. The bayonet also was the sufficient reason for the death of some thousands of men. The whole might well amount to about thirty thousand souls. Candide, trembling like a philosopher, hid himself as best he could during this heroic butchery.

Finally, while both kings were having *Te Deums* sung, each in his own camp, he decided to go reason elsewhere about effects and causes. He passed over heaps of dead and dying and first reached a neighboring village; it was in ashes; it was an Abarian village which the Bulgarians had burned in accordance with the rules of international law. Here, old men riddled with wounds watched their wives die, with their throats cut, holding their children to their bleeding breasts; there, girls, disemboweled after satisfying the natural needs of a few heroes, were gasping their last sighs; others, half-burned, screamed to be given the *coup de grâce*. Brains were spattered over the ground beside severed arms and legs.

Candide fled full speed to another village; it belonged to some Bulgarians, and the Abarian heroes had treated it in the same way. Candide, still treading on quivering limbs or through ruins, arrived at last outside the theater of war, carrying a few small provisions in his knapsack, and never forgetting Mademoiselle Cunégonde. His provisions ran out when he was in Holland; but having heard that everyone in that country was rich, and that they were Christians, he had no doubt that he would be treated as well as he had been in the castle of My Lord the Baron before he had been expelled from it on account of the lovely eyes of Mademoiselle Cunégonde.

He asked alms of several grave personages, who all replied that if he continued that practice he would be shut up in a house of correction to teach him how to live.

He then addressed a man who had just talked about charity for one solid hour unaided in a large assembly. This orator, looking askance at him, said to him: "What brings you here? Are you here for the good cause?"

"There is no effect without a cause," replied Candide modestly, "everything is linked by necessity and arranged for the best. It was necessary for me to be expelled from the presence of Mademoiselle Cunégonde and to run the gantlet, and now to beg my bread until I can earn it; all this could not happen differently."

"My friend," said the orator to him, "do you believe that the Pope is antichrist?"

"I had never heard that before," replied Candide; "but whether he is or not, I have no bread."

"You do not deserve to eat any," said the other. "Hence, scoundrel; hence, wretch; never come near me again in your life."

The orator's wife, who had put her head out the window, seeing a man who doubted that the Pope was antichrist, poured out on his head a full . . . O Heavens! to what excess is religious zeal carried in ladies!

A man who had not been baptized, a good Anabaptist* named Jacques, saw the cruel and ignominious treatment accorded to one of his brethren, a two-footed featherless creature with a soul; [1] he took him home, cleaned him up, gave him some bread and some beer, made him a present of two florins, and even volunteered to teach him to work in his factories of Persian cloth that is made in Holland. Candide, wanting to fall prostrate at his feet, cried:

"Doctor Pangloss was certainly right to tell me that all is for the best in this world, for I am infinitely more touched by your extreme generosity than by the harshness of that gentleman in the black coat and of my lady his wife."

The next day on a walk he met a beggar all covered with sores, his eyes dull as death, the end of his nose eaten away, his mouth awry, his teeth black, talking out of his throat, tormented with a violent cough, and spitting out a tooth at each spasm.

1   The phrase goes back to Plato's so-called *Definitions*.

4 How Candide Met His Old Philosophy Teacher, Doctor Pangloss, and What Happened

CANDIDE, moved even more by compassion than by horror, gave this frightful beggar the two florins he had received from his honest Anabaptist Jacques. The phantom gazed fixedly at him, shed tears, and threw his arms around his neck. Candide recoiled in terror.

"Alas!" said the wretch to the other wretch, "don't you recognize your dear Pangloss any more?"

"What do I hear? You, my dear master! You in this horrible state! Why, what misfortune has happened to you? Why are you no longer in the finest of castles? What has become of Mademoiselle Cunégonde, the pearl of young ladies, the masterpiece of nature?"

"I am exhausted," said Pangloss.

Immediately Candide took him into the Anabaptist's stable, where he had him eat a little bread; and when Pangloss had recovered: "Well," he said, "Cunégonde?"

"She is dead," the other replied.

Candide swooned at these words; his friend restored him to his senses with a little bad vinegar that happened to be in the stable. Candide opened his eyes.

"Cunégonde is dead! Ah, best of worlds, where are you? But what illness did she die of? Could it have been for having seen me expelled with great kicks from the fine castle of My Lord, her father?"

"No," said Pangloss, "she was disemboweled by Bulgarian soldiers after being raped as much as anyone can be; they smashed in the head of My Lord the Baron, who tried to defend her; My Lady the Baroness was cut to pieces; my poor pupil was treated precisely like his sister; and as for the castle, not a stone is left standing upon another, not a barn, not a sheep, not a duck, not a tree; but we have been well avenged, for the Abarians did as much in a neighboring barony that belonged to a Bulgarian lord."

At this account Candide swooned again; but having come back to his senses and said all that was appropriate, he inquired about the cause and effect, had put Pangloss in such a piteous

"Alas!" said Pangloss, "it is love; love human race, the preserver of the univers emotional beings, tender love."

"Alas!" said Candide, "I have known this love, of hearts, this soul of our soul; all it has ever broug as one kiss and twenty kicks in the ass. How could this beautiful cause produce in you so abominable an effect?"

Pangloss answered in these terms:

"O my dear Candide! You knew Paquette, that pretty attendant upon our august Baroness; I tasted in her arms the delights of paradise, which produced these torments of hell by which you see me devoured; she was infected and she may have died of it. Paquette had received this present from a very learned Franciscan, who had gone back to the source; for he had got it from an old countess, who had received it from a cavalry captain, who owed it to a marquise, who had it from a page, who had received it from a Jesuit, who as a novice had got it in a direct line from one of the companions of Christopher Columbus. For my part I shall give it to no one, for I am dying."

"O Pangloss!" exclaimed Candide, "that is a strange genealogy! Wasn't the devil the root of it?"

"Not at all," replied the great man. "It was an indispensable thing in the best of worlds, a necessary ingredient; for if Columbus had not caught, in an island in America, this disease which poisons the source of generation, which often even prevents generation, and which is obviously opposed to the great purpose of nature, we would not have either chocolate or cochineal. It should also be noted that to this day this malady is peculiar to us in our continent, like religious controversy. The Turks, the Indians, the Persians, the Chinese, the Siamese, the Japanese are not yet acquainted with it; but there is sufficient reason for their making its acquaintance, in their turn, within a few centuries. Meanwhile it has made marvelous progress among us, and especially in those great armies composed of decent, well-brought-up mercenaries, which decide the destiny of states; one may confidently assert that when thirty thousand men fight a pitched battle against an equal number of troops, there are about twenty thousand on each side with the pox."

admirable," said Candide, "but we must get you

"How can I be?" said Pangloss. "I haven't a sou, my friend; and in the whole area of this globe you cannot be bled or given an enema without paying, or without someone paying for you."

This last speech made up Candide's mind; he went and threw himself at the feet of his charitable Anabaptist Jacques and painted him such a touching picture of the state to which his friend was reduced that the good man had no hesitation in taking in Doctor Pangloss; he had him cured at his own expense. In the cure Pangloss lost only one eye and one ear. He wrote a good hand and knew arithmetic perfectly. The Anabaptist Jacques made him his bookkeeper.

Two months later, having to go to Lisbon on business, he took his two philosophers on his ship with him. Pangloss explained to him how everything was for the very best. Jacques was not of this opinion.

"Surely," he said, "men must have corrupted nature a little, for they were not born wolves, and they have become wolves; God gave them neither twenty-four-pounder cannon nor bayonets, and they have made bayonets and cannon to destroy one another. I could put bankruptcies into account, and the justice which seizes the goods of the bankrupt to defraud their creditors of them."

"All that was indispensable," replied the one-eyed Doctor, "and private misfortunes make up the general good; so that the more private misfortunes there are, the more all is well."

While he was reasoning, the air darkened, the winds blew from the four corners of the world, and the ship was assaulted by the most horrible tempest in sight of the port of Lisbon.

5 *Tempest, Shipwreck, Earthquake, and What Happened to Doctor Pangloss, Candide, and the Anabaptist Jacques*

HALF THE PASSENGERS, weakened, nearly dying of those inconceivable tortures that the rolling of a ship imparts to the nerves and all the humors of a body tossed in opposite directions, had not even the strength to worry about the danger.

The other half were uttering screams and prayers; the sails were torn, the masts shattered, the vessel split open. Those who could worked, no one co-operated, no one commanded. The Anabaptist was helping a little with the work; he was on the main deck; a frenzied sailor struck him a hard blow and stretched him on the planks, but got such a jolt from the blow he gave him that he fell out of the ship headfirst. He was caught on a piece of broken mast and remained dangling from it. The good Jacques runs to his aid, helps him to climb back up, and by this effort is flung headfirst into the sea in full view of the sailor, who lets him perish without even deigning to look at him. Candide approaches, sees his benefactor come up again for a moment and then be swallowed up forever. He wants to throw himself into the sea after him; the philosopher Pangloss stops him, proving to him that the Lisbon roads had been formed expressly for this Anabaptist to be drowned in. While he was proving this a priori, the ship splits open and everyone perishes with the exception of Pangloss, Candide, and that brute of a sailor who had drowned the virtuous Anabaptist; the scoundrel swam successfully ashore and Pangloss and Candide were carried there on a plank.

When they had recovered themselves a little, they walked toward Lisbon; they had a little money left, with which they hoped to be saved from hunger after escaping from the tempest.

Hardly have they set foot in the city, weeping over the death of their benefactor, when they feel the earth tremble under their feet; the sea rises boiling in the port and shatters the vessels that are at anchor.[1] Whirlwinds of flame and ashes cover the streets and public squares, the houses crumble, the roofs are tumbled down upon the foundations, and the foundations disintegrate; thirty thousand inhabitants of every age and of either sex are crushed beneath the ruins. Said the sailor, whistling and swearing: "There'll be something to pick up here." Said Pangloss: "What can be the sufficient reason for this phenomenon?" "It is the end of the world," exclaimed Candide.

1   The Lisbon earthquake and fire (November 1, 1755), which killed over 30,000 people and reduced the city to ruins, led Voltaire to make strong attacks on philosophical optimism, especially in his *Poem on the Lisbon Disaster* (written in 1755) and in *Candide*.

The sailor runs headlong into the midst of the debris, braves death to find money, finds some, seizes it, gets drunk, and when he has slept it off buys the favors of the first girl of good will he meets upon the ruins of demolished houses and in the midst of the dying and the dead. Pangloss meanwhile was tugging at his sleeve: "My friend," he said, "this is not good, you are departing from universal reason, you are choosing your time badly."

" 'Sblood and zounds!" the other replied. "I am a sailor, and born in Batavia; I have stamped on the crucifix four times on four trips to Japan;* you certainly picked the right man, you and your universal reason!"

Candide had been wounded by some splinters of stone; he was stretched out in the street and covered with debris. He said to Pangloss: "Alas! get me a little wine and oil, I am dying."

"This earthquake is not a new thing," replied Pangloss. "The town of Lima suffered the same shocks in America last year; same causes, same effects; there is certainly a vein of sulfur underground from Lima to Lisbon."

"Nothing is more probable," said Candide, "but for the love of God, a little oil and wine."

"What do you mean, probable?" replied the philosopher. "I maintain that the matter is proved." Candide lost consciousness, and Pangloss brought him a little water from a neighboring fountain.

The next day, having found a few victuals as they slipped through the ruins, they restored their strength a bit. Then they worked like the rest to relieve the inhabitants who had escaped death. A few citizens whom they had helped gave them as good a dinner as could be provided in such a disaster. True, the meal was sad, the guests watered their bread with their tears; but Pangloss consoled them by assuring them that things could not be otherwise.

"For," he said, "all this is for the very best. For if there is a volcano in Lisbon, it could not be anywhere else. For it is impossible that things should not be where they are. For all is well."

A little dark man, a familiar of the Inquisition, who was beside him, spoke up politely and said: "Apparently the gentleman does not believe in original sin; for, if all is for the best, then there has been neither fall nor punishment."

"I very humbly beg Your Excellency's pardon," replied Pangloss still more politely, "for the fall of man and the curse necessarily entered into the best of possible worlds."

"Then the gentleman does not believe in free will?" said the familiar.

"Your Excellency will excuse me," said Pangloss; "free will can coexist with absolute necessity, for it was necessary that we should be free; for after all, predetermined will . . ."

Pangloss was in the middle of his sentence when the familiar gave a nod to his armed attendant, who was pouring him out some port, or Oporto, wine.

6 How They Held a Fine Auto-da-Fé to Prevent Earthquakes, and How Candide Was Flogged

AFTER THE EARTHQUAKE, which had destroyed three-quarters of Lisbon, the country's wise men had found no more efficacious means of preventing total ruin than to give the people a fine auto-da-fé;* it was decided by the University of Coimbra that the spectacle of a few persons burned by a slow fire in great ceremony is an infallible secret for keeping the earth from quaking.

They had consequently seized a Biscayan convicted of having married his godchild's godmother, and two Portuguese who when eating a chicken had taken out the bacon;[1] after dinner they came and bound Doctor Pangloss and his disciple Candide, the one for having spoken, and the other for having listened with an air of approbation; both were taken separately into extremely cool apartments in which one was never bothered by the sun;[2] a week later they were each clad in a sanbenito,* and their heads were adorned with paper miters; Candide's miter and sanbenito were painted with flames upside down and with devils that had neither tails nor claws; but Pangloss's devils wore claws and tails, and his flames were right side up.

Thus dressed, they marched in procession and heard a very pathetic sermon followed by some beautiful music in a

[1] Thus showing that they were Jews still secretly faithful to Judaism.
[2] Prison cells.

droning plain song. Candide was flogged in time to the singing, the Biscayan and the two men who wouldn't eat the
bacon were burned; and Pangloss was hanged although this
is not the custom. On the same day the earth quaked again
with a fearful crash.

Candide, terrified, dumfounded, bewildered, bleeding and
quivering all over, said to himself:

"If this is the best of all possible worlds, then what are
the others? I could let it pass if I had only been flogged, that
happened also with the Bulgarians; but, O my dear Pangloss,
greatest of philosophers, was it necessary that I see you
hanged without knowing why! O my dear Anabaptist, best of
men, was it necessary that you be drowned in the port! O
Mademoiselle Cunégonde, pearl of young ladies, was it
necessary that your belly be slit open!"

He was going back, barely supporting himself, preached at,
flogged, absolved and blessed, when an old woman accosted
him and said: "My son, take courage, follow me."

7 How an Old Woman Took Care of Candide, and How He Recovered That Which He Loved

CANDIDE DID NOT TAKE COURAGE, but he followed the old
woman into a hovel; she gave him a jar of ointment to rub
on and left him food and drink; she showed him a fairly clean
little bed; beside the bed there was a suit of clothes.

"Eat, drink, sleep," she said, "and may Our Lady of Atocha,
My Lord Saint Anthony of Padua, and My Lord Saint James
of Compostela take care of you. I shall come back tomorrow."

Candide, still astounded at all he had seen, at all he had
suffered, and even more at the old woman's charity, tried to
kiss her hand.

"It is not my hand you should kiss," said the old woman.
"I shall come back tomorrow. Rub yourself with ointment,
eat, and sleep."

Candide for all his misfortunes ate and slept. The next day
the old woman brings him some breakfast, examines his back,
rubs it herself with another ointment; later she brings him
dinner; she returns toward evening and brings supper. The
day after, she again performed the same ceremonies.

"Who are you?" Candide kept asking her. "Who has inspired you with such kindness? How can I possibly thank you?"

The good woman never made any answer; she returned toward evening and brought no supper. "Come with me," she said, "and don't say a word."

She takes him by the arm and walks with him into the country for about a quarter of a mile; they arrive at an isolated house surrounded with gardens and canals. The old woman knocks on a little door. It is opened; she takes Candide by a hidden staircase into a gilded boudoir, leaves him on a brocaded sofa, closes the door, and goes away. Candide thought he was dreaming and considered his whole life as a sinister dream and the present moment as a sweet dream.

The old woman soon reappeared; she was supporting with difficulty a trembling woman of majestic stature, gleaming with precious stones and covered with a veil. "Remove that veil," said the old woman to Candide. The young man approaches, he lifts the veil with a timid hand. What a moment! What a surprise! He thinks he sees Mademoiselle Cunégonde, he did indeed see her, it was she herself. His strength fails him, he cannot utter a word, he falls at her feet. Cunégonde falls on the sofa. The old woman plies them copiously with aromatic spirits; they regain their senses, they speak to each other; at first it is only disconnected words, questions and answers at cross purposes, sighs, tears, cries. The old woman recommends that they make less noise, and leaves them by themselves.

"What! Is it you?" said Candide. "You are alive! I find you again here in Portugal! Then you were not raped? Your belly was not slit open, as the philosopher Pangloss had assured me?"

"Oh yes," said the fair Cunégonde, "but people do not always die of those two accidents."

"But were your father and mother killed?"

"'Tis only too true," said Cunégonde, weeping.

"And your brother?"

"My brother was killed too."

"And why are you in Portugal, and how did you learn I was here, and by what strange adventure did you have me brought to this house?"

"I will tell you all that," replied the lady; "but first you must tell me everything that has happened to you since the innocent kiss that you gave me and the kicks that you received."

Candide obeyed her with profound respect; and though he was dumfounded, though his voice was weak and trembling, though his spine still hurt a little, he told her in the most naïve manner all that he had undergone since the moment of their separation. Cunégonde kept raising her eyes to heaven; she shed tears at the death of the good Anabaptist and of Pangloss; after which she spoke in these terms to Candide, who did not miss a word and devoured her with his eyes.

8   *Cunégonde's Story*

"I WAS IN BED and fast asleep when it pleased Heaven to send the Bulgarians to our fine castle of Thunder-ten-tronckh; they slaughtered my father and brother and cut my mother into pieces. A big Bulgarian six feet tall, seeing that I had lost consciousness at the sight of this, set about raping me; this brought me to, I regained my senses, I screamed, I struggled, I bit, I scratched, I tried to tear that big Bulgarian's eyes out, not knowing that all that was happening in my father's castle was a matter of custom; the brute stabbed me with a knife in the left side and I still bear the mark." "Alas! I certainly hope I shall see it," said the naïve Candide. "You shall see it," said Cunégonde, "but let me go on." "Go on," said Candide. She took up the thread of her story thus:

"A Bulgarian captain came in, he saw me all bleeding, and the soldier did not disturb himself. The captain grew angry at the lack of respect this brute showed him, and killed him upon my body. Then he had my wounds dressed and took me to his quarters as a prisoner of war. I laundered the few shirts he had, I did his cooking; he found me very pretty, I must admit; and I shall not deny that he was very well built and had soft white skin; for the rest little wit, little philosophy; it was easy to see that he had not been brought up by Doctor Pangloss. After three months, having lost all his money as well as his taste for me, he sold me to a Jew named Don Issachar, who traded in Holland and Portugal and had a passionate love of women. This Jew grew much attached to my person but could not triumph over it; I resisted him better than I did the Bulgarian soldier. A person of honor may have been raped once, but her virtue gains strength from it. The Jew, to tame me, brought me to this country house that you see. I had thought until then that there was nothing on earth so splendid as the castle of Thunder-ten-tronckh. I was undeceived.

"The Grand Inquisitor noticed me one day at Mass; he eyed me a great deal, and sent word to me that he had secret affairs to speak to me about. I was taken to his palace, I informed him of my birth; he pointed out to me how much it was beneath my rank to belong to an Israelite. On his behalf it was proposed to Don Issachar to yield me to His Lordship. Don Issachar, who is the court banker and a man of influence, would do no such thing. The Inquisitor threatened him with an auto-da-fé. Finally my Jew, intimidated, made a bargain by which the house and I would belong to them both in common, the Jew would have Monday, Wednesday, and the Sabbath day for him, and the Inquisitor would have the other days of the week. This agreement has lasted for six months. It has not been without quarrels, for it has often been undecided whether the night between Saturday and Sunday belongs to the old law or the new. For my part, thus far I have resisted them both, and I think that is the reason why I have still been loved.

"Finally, to turn aside the scourge of earthquakes and to intimidate Don Issachar, My Lord the Inquisitor was pleased to celebrate an auto-da-fé. He did me the honor of inviting me. I had a very good seat; they served the ladies with refreshments between the Mass and the execution. Truly I was seized with horror on seeing them burn those two Jews and that worthy Biscayan who had married the godmother of his godchild; but what was my surprise, my fright, my distress, when I saw, in a sanbenito and under a miter, a face resembling that of Pangloss! I rubbed my eyes, I looked attentively, I saw him hanged; I fell into a faint; hardly was I regaining my senses when I saw you stripped stark naked; that was the height of horror, consternation, grief, despair. I will tell you truthfully that your skin is even whiter and more perfectly rosy than that of my Bulgarian captain. This sight redoubled all the feelings that crushed me, that devoured me. I cried out, I tried to say 'Stop, barbarians!' but my voice failed me, and my cries would have been useless. When you had been well

flogged, I said: 'How can it be that the charming Candide
and the wise Pangloss are in Lisbon, one to receive a hundred
lashes, and the other to be hanged by order of My Lord the
Inquisitor, whose dearly beloved I am? Then Pangloss deceived me most cruelly when he told me that all is for the very
best.'

"Agitated, bewildered, now beside myself and now ready
to die of faintness, I had my mind filled with the massacre of
my father, mother, and brother, the insolence of my horrid
Bulgarian soldier, the stab he gave me, my slavery, my work
as a cook, my Bulgarian captain, my horrid Don Issachar, my
abominable Inquisitor, the hanging of Doctor Pangloss, that
long *miserere* in droning plain song during which they were
whipping you, and above all the kiss I gave you behind a
screen the day I saw you for the last time. I praised God, who
was bringing you back to me through so many trials. I charged
my old woman to take care of you and to bring you here as
soon as she could. She has carried out my commission very
well; I have enjoyed the inexpressible pleasure of seeing you
again, hearing you, speaking to you. You must be ravenously
hungry; my appetite is good; let's begin with supper."

So they both sit down to table, and after supper resume
their places on that handsome sofa that has been already
mentioned; they were there when Señor Don Issachar, one of
the masters of the house, arrived. It was the Sabbath day.
He was coming to enjoy his rights and expound his tender
love.

9 What Happened to Cunégonde, Candide, the Grand Inquisitor, and a Jew

THIS ISSACHAR was the most choleric Hebrew ever seen in
Israel since the Babylonian captivity.

"What!" he said. "Bitch of a Galilean, My Lord the Inquisitor isn't enough? This scoundrel must share with me too?"

So saying, he draws a long dagger which he always carried
and, not thinking that his adversary was armed, throws himself upon Candide; but our good Westphalian had received a
fine sword from the old woman together with the suit. He
draws his sword, although he had a very gentle character, and

stretches out the Israelite stone dead on the floor at the feet of the fair Cunégonde.

"Holy Virgin!" she cried, "what is to become of us? A man killed in my house! If the law comes, we are lost."

"If Pangloss had not been hanged," said Candide, "he would give us good advice in this extremity, for he was a great philosopher. Failing him, let us consult the old woman."

She was very prudent, and was beginning to state her advice, when another little door opened. It was one hour after midnight, it was the beginning of Sunday. That day belonged to My Lord the Inquisitor. He came in and saw the flogged Candide sword in hand, a dead man stretched on the floor, Cunégonde terrified, and the old woman giving advice.

Here is what went on in that moment in Candide's soul, and how he reasoned: "If this holy man calls for help, he will have me burned without fail; he may do as much to Cunégonde; he has had me pitilessly whipped; he is my rival; I have started killing, there is no hesitating."

This reasoning was clear-cut and swift, and without giving the Inquisitor the time to recover from his surprise, he pierces him through and through and tosses him beside the Jew.

"Now here's another one," said Cunégonde; "there is no more chance of pardon; we are excommunicated, our last hour is come. How could you, who were born so mild, manage to kill one Jew and one Inquisitor in two minutes?"

"My fair lady," replied Candide, "when a man is in love, jealous, and whipped by the Inquisition, he is out of his mind."

The old woman then spoke up and said: "There are three Andalusian horses in the stable with their saddles and bridles; let the brave Candide prepare them; My Lady has moidores* and diamonds; let us mount quickly, although I can ride on only one buttock, and let us go to Cádiz; the weather could not be finer, and it is a great pleasure to travel in the cool of the night."

Immediately Candide saddles the three horses. Cunégonde, the old woman, and he do thirty miles at one stretch. While they were riding away, the Holy Hermandad [1] arrives in the house; they bury His Lordship in a beautiful church and they toss Don Issachar on the dump.

Candide, Cunégonde, and the old woman were already in

1   The Holy Brotherhood, an association formed in Spain with a police force to track down criminals.

the little town of Avacena in the midst of the mountains of the Sierra Morena; and they were talking as follows in an inn.

10 In What Distress Candide, Cunégonde, and the Old Woman Arrive at Cádiz; and About Their Embarkation

"NOW WHO CAN have stolen my pistoles* and my diamonds?" said Cunégonde, weeping. "What shall we live on? What shall we do? Where shall we find Inquisitors and Jews to give me others?"

"Alas!" said the old woman. "I strongly suspect a reverend Franciscan father who slept in the same inn with us yesterday at Badajoz; God keep me from forming a rash judgment, but he came into our room twice and he left long before us."

"Alas!" said Candide, "the good Pangloss had often proved to me that the goods of the earth are common to all men, that each has an equal right to them. That Franciscan, according to these principles, should certainly have left us enough to complete our trip. Have you nothing at all left then, my fair Cunégonde?"

"Not a maravedi,"* said she. "What should we do?" said Candide. "Let's sell one of the horses," said the old woman. "I'll ride on the crupper behind my lady, although I can ride on only one buttock, and we will get to Cádiz."

In the same hostelry there was a Benedictine prior; he bought the horse at a bargain. Candide, Cunégonde, and the old woman passed through Lucena, Chillas, Lebrixa, and at last reached Cádiz. There a fleet was being equipped and troops assembled to bring to terms the reverend Jesuit Fathers in Paraguay, who were accused of causing one of their tribes, near the town of San Sacramento, to revolt against the kings of Spain and Portugal.[1] Candide, having served with the Bulgarians, performed the Bulgarian drill before the general of the little army with so much grace, celerity, skill, pride, and agility, that they gave him an infantry company to command. Here he is a captain; he embarks with Mademoiselle Cunégonde, the old woman, two valets, and the two Andalusian horses that had belonged to His Lordship the Grand Inquisitor of Portugal.

1   This revolt occurred in 1756.

During the whole crossing they reasoned a great deal about the philosophy of poor Pangloss.

"We are going to another universe," said Candide; "no doubt it is in that one that all is well. For it must be admitted that one might groan a little over what happens in the physical and the moral domain in ours."

"I love you with all my heart," said Cunégonde, "but my soul is still frightened by what I have seen, what I have undergone."

"All will be well," replied Candide; "the sea of this new world is already better than the seas of our Europe; it is calmer, the winds are more constant. It is certainly the new world that is the best of possible universes."

"God grant it," said Cunégonde; "but I have been so horribly unhappy in mine that my heart is almost closed to hope."

"You complain," the old woman said to them. "Alas! You have not undergone misfortunes such as mine."

Cunégonde almost burst out laughing, and thought this good woman very comical to claim to be more unfortunate than herself.

"Alas!" she said to her, "my dear woman, unless you have been raped by two Bulgarians, been stabbed twice in the belly, had two of your castles demolished and two mothers and two fathers slaughtered before your eyes, and seen two of your beloveds flogged in an auto-da-fé, I don't see that you can outdo me; plus the fact that I was born a Baroness with seventy-two quarterings, and now I have been a cook."

"My Lady," replied the old woman, "you do not know my birth, and if I showed you my bottom you would not speak as you do and you would suspend your judgment."

This speech aroused extreme curiosity in the minds of Cunégonde and Candide. The old woman spoke to them in these terms.

11 *The Old Woman's Story*

"MY EYES WERE not always bloodshot and red-rimmed; my nose did not always touch my chin, and I was not always a servant. I am the daughter of Pope Urban X and the Princess of Palestrina.[1] Until the age of fourteen I was brought up in a palace to which all the castles of your German barons would not have served as stables, and one of my dresses was worth more than all the magnificence of Westphalia. I grew in beauty, graces, and talents, in the midst of pleasures, respect, and hopes. Already I inspired love, my bosom was forming; and what a bosom! White, firm, sculptured like that of the Venus de' Medici. And what eyes! What eyelids! What black eyebrows! What flames shone in my two irises and dimmed the glistening of the stars, as the neighborhood poets used to tell me. The women who dressed and undressed me fell into ecstasies when they looked at me in front and behind, and all the men would have liked to be in their place.

"I was betrothed to a sovereign prince of Massa-Carrara. What a prince! As handsome as I, formed of sweetness and charms, agleam with wit and afire with love. I loved him as one loves for the first time, with idolatrous frenzy. The nuptials were prepared. The pomp, the magnificence were unheard of; there were continual festivities, tournaments, comic operas, and all Italy composed for me sonnets not one of which was passable.

"The moment of my happiness was at hand when an old marquise who had been my prince's mistress invited him to have some chocolate at her house. He died in less than two hours in frightful convulsions. But that is only a trifle. My mother, in despair, yet much less afflicted than I, decided to tear herself away for a time from such a fateful place. She had a very beautiful estate near Gaeta.* We embarked on a local galley, gilded like the altar of St. Peter's in Rome. Suddenly a pirate from Salé* swoops down on us and boards us. Our soldiers defended themselves like soldiers of the Pope; they all fell on their knees, throwing away their arms, and begging the pirates for absolution *in articulo mortis.*[2]

"Immediately they stripped them naked as monkeys, and my mother too, our ladies of honor too, and me too. The diligence with which those gentlemen undress people is a wonderful thing. But what surprised me more was that they put

1   Author's posthumous note: "Observe the author's extreme discretion. There has been up to now no Pope named Urban X. The author fears to assign a bastard daughter to a known Pope. What circumspection! What delicacy of conscience!"
2   At the point of death.

their fingers in a place in all of us where we women ordinarily admit only the nozzle of a syringe. This ceremony seemed quite strange to me; that is how one judges of everything when one has never been out of one's country. I soon learned that this was to see whether we had not hidden some diamonds there; it is a custom established from time immemorial among the civilized nations that roam the seas. I learned that My Lords the religious Knights of Malta never fail to do this when they capture Turkish men and women; it is a rule of international law that has never been broken.

"I shall not tell you how hard it is for a young princess to be taken to Morocco as a slave with her mother. You can imagine well enough all that we had to suffer in the pirate ship. My mother was still very beautiful; our ladies of honor, our mere chambermaids had more charms than can be found in all Africa. As for me, I was ravishing, I was beauty and grace itself, and I was a virgin. I was not so for long: that flower that had been reserved for the handsome Prince of Massa-Carrara was ravished from me by the pirate captain. He was an abominable Negro who yet thought he was doing me much honor. Indeed My Lady the Princess of Palestrina and I had to be very strong to endure all we underwent until we arrived in Morocco. But let's get on; these are things so common that they are not worth speaking of.

"Morocco was swimming in blood when we arrived. Fifty sons of the Emperor Muley Ismael each had a faction; which produced in effect fifty civil wars, of blacks against blacks, blacks against tans, tans against tans, mulattoes against mulattoes. It was a continual carnage over the whole extent of the empire.

"Hardly had we landed when some blacks, of a faction hostile to that of my pirate, came up to take his booty from him. After the diamonds and the gold, we were the most precious thing he had. I was witness to a combat such as you never see in your European climates. The blood of the northern peoples is not ardent enough. They are not mad about women to the point that is common in Africa. It seems as though your Europeans have milk in their veins; it is vitriol, it is fire that flows in those of the inhabitants of Mount Atlas and the neighboring countries. They fought with the fury of the lions, tigers, and snakes of the country to see who should have us. One Moor seized my mother by the right arm, my captain's lieutenant held her back by the left arm; a Moorish soldier took her by one leg, one of our pirates held her by the other. In a moment nearly all our girls found themselves pulled in this way by four soldiers. My captain kept me hidden behind him. He had his scimitar in hand, and was killing everything that opposed his rage. Finally I saw all our Italian women and my mother torn, cut, massacred by the monsters who were fighting over them. My fellow captives, those who had captured them, soldiers, sailors, blacks, tans, whites, mulattoes, and finally my captain—all were killed, and I remained dying on a heap of dead. Similar scenes were taking place, as everyone knows, over an area of more than three hundred square leagues, without anyone failing to say the five prayers a day ordained by Mohammed.

"I extricated myself with great difficulty from the press of so many heaped-up bleeding corpses, and I dragged myself beneath a big orange tree at the edge of a nearby stream; there I fell down from fright, weariness, horror, despair, and hunger. Soon afterward my exhausted senses gave themselves up to a sleep that was more like a swoon than a rest. I was in this state of weakness and insensibility, between life and death, when I felt something pressing on me and moving on my body. I opened my eyes and saw a white man of good appearance who was sighing and muttering between his teeth: *'O che sciagura d'essere senza coglioni!'* " [3]

12   *Continuation of the Old Woman's Misfortunes*

"ASTOUNDED AND DELIGHTED to hear the language of my homeland, and no less surprised at the words this man was uttering, I replied that there were worse misfortunes than the one he was complaining of. I informed him in a few words of the horrors I had suffered, and I fell back into a faint. He took me into a neighboring house, had me put to bed and given food, served me, consoled me, flattered me, told me he had never seen anything as beautiful as I and that he had never so much regretted what no one could restore to him.

" 'I was born in Naples,' he told me; 'there they caponize

3   "Oh, what an affliction to be without testicles!"

two or three thousand boys every year; some die of it, others acquire a voice more beautiful than a woman's, others go and govern states. This operation was performed on me with great success, and I was a musician in the chapel of My Lady the Princess of Palestrina.'

" 'Of my mother!' I cried out.

" 'Of your mother!' he exclaimed, weeping. 'What! Can you be that young princess that I brought up until the age of six, and who already then promised to be as beautiful as you are?'

" 'I am indeed; my mother is four hundred yards from here, cut into quarters under a heap of dead.'

"I told him everything that had happened to me; he too told me his adventures, and informed me that he had been sent by a Christian power to the King of Morocco to conclude a treaty with that monarch by which he would be furnished with gunpowder, cannon, and ships to help him to exterminate the commerce of the other Christians. 'My mission is performed,' this honest eunuch said; 'I am going to embark at Ceuta and I will take you back to Italy. *Ma che sciagura d'essere senza coglioni!'*

"I thanked him with tears of emotion, and instead of taking me to Italy he conducted me to Algiers and sold me to the Dey of that province. Hardly was I sold when that plague which has spread all over Africa, Asia, and Europe broke out furiously in Algiers. You have seen earthquakes; but, My Lady, have you ever had the plague?"

"Never," replied the Baroness.

"If you had had it," the old woman went on, "you would admit that it is far worse than an earthquake. It is very common in Africa; I was struck with it. Imagine what a situation for the daughter of a Pope, aged fifteen, who in three months' time had undergone poverty and slavery, had been raped almost every day, had seen her mother cut into quarters, had endured hunger and war, and was now dying of the plague in Algiers. However, I did not die of it; but my eunuch and the Dey and almost all the seraglio of Algiers perished.

"When the first ravages of this frightful plague were over, the Dey's slaves were sold. A merchant bought me and took me to Tunis. He sold me to another merchant, who resold me at Tripoli; from Tripoli I was resold to Alexandria, from Alexandria resold to Smyrna, from Smyrna to Constantinople.

I finally belonged to an Aga of the Janizaries,[1] who was soon ordered to go and defend Azov against the Russians who were besieging it.

"The Aga, who was a very gallant man, took his whole seraglio with him and lodged us in a little fort on the Maeotian Marsh,* guarded by two black eunuchs and twenty soldiers. They killed a prodigious number of Russians, but these repaid us with interest. Azov was put to fire and sword, and there was no pardon for sex nor for age; nothing remained but our little fort; the enemy tried to take us by famine. The twenty Janizaries had sworn never to surrender. The extremities of hunger to which they were reduced forced them to eat our two eunuchs, for fear of violating their oath. A few days later they resolved to eat the women.

"We had with us a very pious and very compassionate imam,* who preached them a fine sermon by which he persuaded them not to kill us completely. 'Just cut off one buttock from each of these ladies,' he said, 'you will make very good cheer; if you have to come back, you will have as much again in a few days; heaven will be pleased with you for so charitable an action, and you will be rescued.'

"He had great eloquence; he persuaded them. They performed this horrible operation on us. The imam applied to us the same balm that they put on children who have just been circumcised. We were all at the point of death.

"Scarcely had the Janizaries eaten the meal we had furnished them when the Russians arrived in flat-bottomed boats; not one Janizary escaped. The Russians paid no attention to the state we were in. There are French surgeons everywhere; one of them, who was very skillful, took care of us; he cured us; and I shall remember all my life that when my wounds were fully closed, he made propositions to me. For the rest, he told us all to console ourselves; he assured us that the same sort of thing had happened in many sieges and that it was a law of war.

"As soon as my companions could walk, they were sent to Moscow. I fell to the lot of a Boyar,[2] who made me his gardener and gave me twenty lashes a day. But when this lord was broken on the wheel two years later with some thirty other Boyars for some petty fuss at court, I profited by this

1   A high officer of the guards of the Turkish Sultan.
2   Russian nobleman.

adventure; I fled; I crossed the whole of Russia; I was long a servant in an inn at Riga, then at Rostock, at Wismar, at Leipzig, Cassel, Utrecht, Leyden, the Hague, Rotterdam; I have grown old in misery and opprobrium, having only half a backside, always remembering that I was the daughter of a Pope; a hundred times I wanted to kill myself, but I still loved life. This ridiculous foible is perhaps one of our most disastrous inclinations. For is there anything more stupid than to want to bear continually a burden that we always want to throw to the ground? To regard our being with horror, and to cling to our being? In fine, to caress the serpent that devours us until it has eaten up our heart?

"I have seen, in the countries that fate has driven me through and in the inns where I have served, a prodigious number of persons who loathed their existence; but I have seen only twelve who voluntarily put an end to their misery: three Negroes, four Englishmen, four Genevans, and a German professor named Robeck.[3] I ended up by being a servant to the Jew Don Issachar; he put me in your service, my fair young lady; I have attached myself to your destiny, and I have been more occupied with your adventures than with mine. I would never even have spoken to you of my misfortunes if you had not piqued me a little and if it were not customary on shipboard to tell stories to conquer boredom. In short, My Lady, I have experience, I know the world; have some fun, get each passenger to tell you his story; and if there is a single one who has not often cursed his life, who has not often said to himself that he was the unhappiest of men, throw me into the sea headfirst."

13 How Candide Was Obliged to Part from the Fair Cunégonde and the Old Woman

THE FAIR CUNÉGONDE, having heard the old woman's story, showed her all the courtesy due to a person of her rank and merit. She accepted the proposition and got all the passengers one after the other to tell her their adventures; Candide and she admitted that the old woman was right.

3   Author of theses on the folly of loving life, who drowned himself in 1739 at the age of sixty-seven.

"It is a great pity," said Candide, "that the wise Pangloss
was hanged contrary to custom in an auto-da-fé; he would
tell us wonderful things about the physical evil and the moral
evil that cover earth and sea, and I would feel strong enough
to dare to offer him, respectfully, a few objections."

As each one was telling his story the vessel moved on. They
landed in Buenos Aires. Cunégonde, Captain Candide, and
the old woman called on the governor, Don Fernando
d'Ibaraa y Figueora y Mascarenes y Lampourdos y Souza.
This lord had the pride befitting a man who bore so many
names. He spoke to men with the noblest disdain, bearing his
nose so high, raising his voice so pitilessly, assuming so imposing a tone, affecting so lofty a bearing, that all who addressed him were tempted to give him a beating. He loved
women with a frenzy. Cunégonde seemed to him the most
beautiful thing he had ever seen. The first thing he did was
ask if she were not the Captain's wife. The air with which he
asked this question alarmed Candide; he did not dare say
she was his wife because in fact she was not; he did not dare
say she was his sister, because she was not that either; and
although this diplomatic lie was once very fashionable among
the ancients [1] and might be useful to the moderns, his soul
was too pure to be disloyal to the truth. "Mademoiselle Cunégonde," he said, "is to do me the honor of marrying me, and
we beseech Your Excellency to deign to perform our wedding
ceremony."

Don Fernando d'Ibaraa y Figueora y Mascarenes y Lampourdos y Souza, twirling his mustache, smiled bitterly and
ordered Captain Candide to go pass his company in review.
Candide obeyed; the governor remained with Mademoiselle
Cunégonde. He declared his passion to her, protested that the
next day he would marry her publicly in church, or otherwise,
as it might please her charms. Cunégonde asked him for a
quarter of an hour to collect herself, to consult the old
woman, and to make up her mind.

The old woman said to Cunégonde:

"My Lady, you have seventy-two quarterings and not a
penny; it depends on you alone to be the wife of the greatest
lord in South America, who has a very handsome mustache;
is it for you to pride yourself on an invincible fidelity? You

1   A reference to Abraham and Sarah (Genesis 12:12–13 and
again 20:2–3) and to Isaac and Rebekah (Genesis 26:7–9).

have been raped by the Bulgarians; a Jew and an Inquisitor
have enjoyed your good graces. Misfortunes confer rights. I
admit that if I were in your place, I would have no scruple
over marrying My Lord the Governor and making the fortune
of Captain Candide."

While the old woman was speaking with all the prudence
that age and experience give, a little vessel was seen to enter
the port; it brought an alcaide and some alguazils,[2] and here
is what had happened.

The old woman had guessed correctly that it was a long-
sleeved Franciscan who stole Cunégonde's money and jewels
in the town of Badajoz when she was fleeing in haste with
Candide. This monk tried to sell some of the precious stones
to a jeweler. The merchant recognized them as belonging to
the Grand Inquisitor. The Franciscan, before being hanged,
admitted that he had stolen them; he indicated the persons
and the route they were taking. The flight of Cunégonde and
Candide was already known. They were followed to Cádiz;
with no loss of time a ship was sent in pursuit of them. The
ship was already in the port of Buenos Aires. The rumor
spread that an alcaide was about to land and that they were
pursuing the murderers of His Lordship the Grand Inquisitor.
The prudent old woman saw in an instant all that was to be
done.

"You cannot flee," she said to Cunégonde, "and you have
nothing to fear; it was not you that killed His Lordship; besides, the governor, who loves you, will not allow you to be
maltreated; stay."

She immediately ran to Candide. "Flee," she said, "or
you're going to be burned within an hour." There was not a
moment to lose; but how could he part with Cunégonde, and
where was he to take refuge?

14 *How Candide and Cacambo Were
Received by the Jesuits in Paraguay*

CANDIDE HAD BROUGHT from Cádiz a valet of a type often
found on the coasts of Spain and in the colonies. He was one-
quarter Spanish, born of a half-breed in Tucuman;* he had

2   A municipal officer and some police officers.

been a choirboy, sacristan, sailor, monk, merchant's represent-
ative, soldier, lackey. His name was Cacambo, and he loved
his master very much, because his master was a very good
man. He saddled the two Andalusian horses as fast as possible.

"Come, master, let us take the old woman's advice, leave,
and run for it without looking behind us."

Candide shed tears. "O my dear Cunégonde! Must I abandon
you just when My Lord the Governor is going to perform our
marriage! Cunégonde, brought here from so far, what will become of you?"

"She will get along as best she can," said Cacambo;
"women are never at a loss; God looks after them; let's run
for it."

"Where are you taking me? Where are we going? What
shall we do without Cunégonde?" said Candide.

"By St. James of Compostela," said Cacambo, "you were
going to make war on the Jesuits; let's make war for them;
I know the roads well enough, I will take you to their kingdom, they will be delighted to have a captain who can drill
Bulgarian style, you will make a prodigious fortune; when
you don't get your due in one world you find it in another. It
is a very great pleasure to see and do new things."

"Then you have already been in Paraguay?" said Candide.

"Oh yes indeed," said Cacambo, "I was a servant in the
College of the Assumption, and I know the government of
Los Padres [1] as well as I know the streets of Cádiz. It is an
admirable thing, this government. The kingdom is already
more than three hundred leagues in diameter; it is divided
into thirty provinces; *Los Padres* have everything and the people
nothing; it is the masterpiece of reason and justice. For my
part, I know nothing so divine as *Los Padres*, who here make
war on the King of Spain and the King of Portugal, and who
in Europe confess those Kings; who here kill Spaniards, and
in Madrid send them to heaven; this enchants me; let's get
on; you are going to be the happiest of men. What pleasure
Los Padres will have when they learn that a captain is coming
to them who knows the Bulgarian drill!"

As soon as they had reached the first barrier, Cacambo told
the outpost that a captain asked to speak to My Lord the
Commandant. They went to notify the main guard. A Para-

1   "The Fathers," i.e., the Jesuits.

guayan officer ran to the feet of the Commandant to impart the news to him. First Candide and Cacambo were disarmed; their two Andalusian horses were seized. The two strangers were brought in between two ranks of soldiers; the Commandant was at the end, three-cornered hat on head, gown tucked up, sword at side, and a half-pike in hand. He made a sign; and immediately twenty-four soldiers surround the two newcomers. A sergeant tells them that they must wait, that the Commandant cannot speak to them, that the Reverend Provincial Father does not permit any Spaniard to open his mouth except in his presence or to remain more than three hours in the country.

"And where is the Reverend Provincial Father?" said Cacambo.

"He is at the parade after having said Mass," replied the sergeant, "and you will not be able to kiss his spurs until three hours from now."

"But," said Cacambo, "the captain, who is dying of hunger as I am, is not a Spaniard, he is a German; mightn't we have breakfast while waiting for His Reverence?"

The sergeant immediately went and reported this statement to the Commandant.

"Praise God!" said this lord. "Since he is a German I can speak to him; let him be brought to my arbor."

Candide was taken immediately into a leafy bower adorned with a very pretty colonnade in green and gold marble and with trellises which enclosed parrots, two kinds of hummingbirds, guinea fowl, and all the rarest of birds. An excellent breakfast stood prepared in vessels of gold; and while the Paraguayans ate corn out of wooden bowls in the open fields in the blaze of the sun, the Reverend Father Commandant entered the arbor.

He was a very handsome young man, full-faced, rather white-skinned, high-colored, with arched eyebrows, keen eyes, red ears, vermilion lips, his manner proud, but with a pride that was neither that of a Spaniard nor that of a Jesuit. Candide and Cacambo were given back their arms, which had been taken from them, as well as their two Andalusian horses; Cacambo fed them oats near the arbor and kept his eye constantly on them for fear of a surprise.

Candide first kissed the hem of the Commandant's robe, then they sat down to table.

"So you are a German?" the Jesuit said to him in that language.

"Yes, Reverend Father," said Candide.

Each one, as he pronounced these words, looked at the other with extreme surprise and an emotion which they could not master.

"And what part of Germany are you from?" said the Jesuit.

"From the filthy province of Westphalia," said Candide; "I was born in the castle of Thunder-ten-tronckh."

"Heavens! Is it possible!" cried the Commandant.

"What a miracle!" cried Candide.

"Can it be you?" said the Commandant.

"That is not possible," said Candide. They both fall over backwards, they embrace, they shed torrents of tears.

"What! Can that be you, Reverend Father? You, the brother of the fair Cunégonde! You, who were killed by the Bulgarians! You, the son of My Lord the Baron! You a Jesuit in Paraguay! I must admit that this world is a strange thing. O Pangloss! Pangloss! How happy you would be if you had not been hanged!"

The Commandant sent away the Negro slaves and the Paraguayans who were serving drink in rock-crystal goblets. He thanked God and St. Ignatius a thousand times; he clasped Candide in his arms; their faces were bathed in tears.

"You would be even more astounded, more touched, more beside yourself," said Candide, "if I told you that Mademoiselle Cunégonde your sister, whom you thought disemboweled, is in full health."

"Where?"

"In your neighborhood, with My Lord the Governor of Buenos Aires; and I was coming to make war on you."

Each word they uttered in this long conversation piled prodigy upon prodigy. Their whole souls flew from their tongues, listened in their ears, sparkled in their eyes. Since they were Germans, they stayed long at table, waiting for the Reverend Father Provincial; and the Commandant spoke thus to his dear Candide.

15 How Candide Killed the Brother of His Dear Cunégonde

"ALL MY LIFE I shall have present in my memory the horrible day when I saw my father and mother killed and my sister raped. When the Bulgarians were withdrawn, that adorable sister was not found, and my mother, my father, and I, two serving girls and three little boys who had all been slaughtered were put into a cart to be taken and buried in a Jesuit chapel two leagues from the castle of my forefathers. A Jesuit threw holy water on us; it was horribly salt; a few drops got into my eyes; the father noticed a tiny movement in my eyelid; he put his hand on my heart and felt it beating; I was rescued, and after three weeks it was as if nothing had happened. You know, my dear Candide, that I was very pretty, I became even more so; so the Reverend Father Kroust,* superior of the house, conceived the most tender friendship for me; he gave me the dress of a novice; some time later I was sent to Rome. The Father General needed some young German Jesuit recruits. The sovereigns of Paraguay receive as few Spanish Jesuits as they can; they prefer foreigners, since they feel more their masters. I was judged fit by the Reverend Father General to go and labor in this vineyard. We set out, a Pole, a Tyrolese, and I. On arriving, I was honored with a subdeaconate and a lieutenancy; today I am a colonel and priest. We shall give the King of Spain's troops a vigorous reception; I warrant you they will be excommunicated and beaten. Providence sends you here to second us. But is it really true that my dear sister Cunégonde is in the neighborhood with the Governor of Buenos Aires?"

Candide assured him on his oath that nothing could be truer. Their tears began to flow again.

The Baron seemed unable to tire of embracing Candide; he kept calling him his brother, his savior.

"Ah!" he said, "my dear Candide, perhaps we can enter the city together as conquerors and regain my sister Cunégonde."

"That is all I wish for," said Candide; "for I was counting on marrying her, and I still hope to."

"You, insolent wretch!" replied the Baron. "You would have the impudence to marry my sister who has seventy-two quarterings! I am amazed at your effrontery in daring to speak to me of so rash a plan!"

Candide, petrified at such a speech, replied: "Reverend Father, all the quarterings in the world have nothing to do with it; I have saved your sister from the arms of a Jew and an Inquisitor; she has obligations enough toward me, she wants to marry me; Doctor Pangloss always told me that men are equal, and certainly I shall marry her."

"We'll see about that, you scoundrel!" said the Jesuit Baron of Thunder-ten-tronckh, and at the same time he struck him a great blow on the face with the flat of his sword. That same instant Candide drew his own and thrust it up to the hilt in the Jesuit Baron's belly; but as he drew it out all smoking he began to weep: "Alas! Good Lord!" he said. "I have killed my former master, my friend, my brother-in-law; I am the kindest man in the world, and here I am killing three men already, and two of the three are priests."

Cacambo, who was standing watch at the door to the arbor, ran up.

"There is nothing left for us but to sell our lives dear," said his master to him. "No doubt they will be coming into the arbor, we must die arms in hand."

Cacambo, who had seen the likes of this before, did not lose his head; he took the Jesuit robe worn by the Baron, put it over Candide's body, gave him the dead man's square bonnet, and got him to mount his horse. All this was done in the twinkling of an eye. "Let's gallop, master. Everyone will take you for a Jesuit on his way to give orders, and we will have passed the frontiers before they can come after us."

He was already in flight as he uttered these words, and shouted in Spanish: "Make way, make way for the Reverend Father Colonel."

16 What Happened to the Two Travelers with Two Girls, Two Monkeys, and the Savages Called Oreillons [1]

CANDIDE AND HIS VALET were beyond the barriers, and as yet no one in the camp knew of the death of the German Jesuit.

1   From the Spanish *Orejones*, suggesting "pierced ears" or "big ears." The French name likewise suggests *oreilles*, "ears."

The vigilant Cacambo had taken care to fill his bag with bread, chocolate, ham, fruit, and a few bottles of wine. On their Andalusian horses they plunged into an unknown land where they found no road. Finally there appeared before them a beautiful meadow interlaced with streams. Our two travelers give food to their mounts. Cacambo proposes to his master that they eat, and sets the example.

"How," said Candide, "can you expect me to eat ham, when I have killed the son of My Lord the Baron and find myself condemned never to see the fair Cunégonde again in my life? What will it profit me to prolong my wretched days, since I must drag them out far from her in remorse and despair? And what will the *Journal de Trévoux** say?"

As he spoke thus, he did not fail to eat. The sun was setting. The two wanderers heard a few little cries that seemed to be uttered by women. They did not know whether these were cries of pain or of joy; but they jumped to their feet hastily with the anxiety and alarm that everything inspires in an unknown country. These sounds came from two girls, stark naked, who were running lightly along the edge of the meadow, while two monkeys followed them and bit their buttocks. Candide was moved with pity; he had learned to shoot among the Bulgarians, and he could have knocked a nut off a bush without touching the leaves. He takes his double-barreled Spanish gun, fires, and kills the two monkeys.

"God be praised, my dear Cacambo, I have delivered these two poor creatures from great peril; if I committed a sin in killing an Inquisitor and a Jesuit, I have certainly made up for it by saving the lives of these two girls. Perhaps they are two young ladies of quality, and this adventure may earn us great advantages in this country."

He was going to continue, but his tongue was silenced when he saw these two girls tenderly embrace the two monkeys, burst into tears over their bodies, and fill the air with the most grievous cries.

"I was not expecting such goodness of soul," he said at last to Cacambo, who answered him: "You've done a fine piece of work there, my master; you have killed the two lovers of these young ladies."

"Their lovers! Can this be possible? You are making fun of me, Cacambo; how can I believe you?"

"My dear master," replied Cacambo, "you are always

astonished at everything; why do you find it so strange that in some countries there are monkeys who obtain the good graces of the ladies? They are one-quarter men as I am one-quarter Spaniard."

"Alas!" replied Candide, "I remember hearing Doctor Pangloss say that in other times similar accidents had happened and that these mixtures had produced Aegipans, fauns, and satyrs; that many great personages of antiquity had seen them; but I took that for fables."

"You ought to be convinced now," said Cacambo, "that it is the truth, and you see how people behave who have not received a certain education; all I fear is that these ladies may get us into bad trouble."

These solid reflections led Candide to leave the meadow and plunge into a wood. There he ate supper with Cacambo, and they both, after cursing the Inquisitor of Portugal, the Governor of Buenos Aires, and the Baron, fell asleep on some moss. When they woke up they found that they could not move; the reason was that during the night the Oreillons, the inhabitants of the country, to whom the two ladies had denounced them, had bound them with ropes of bark. They were surrounded by about fifty stark-naked Oreillons armed with arrows and stone clubs and hatchets; some were boiling up a great caldron, others were preparing spits; and all were shouting: "It's a Jesuit, it's a Jesuit; we shall be avenged and we shall have a good meal; let's eat Jesuit, let's eat Jesuit."

"I told you so, my dear master," exclaimed Cacambo sadly; "I said that those two girls would do us a bad turn."

Candide, perceiving the caldron and the spits, exclaimed: "We are certainly going to be roasted or boiled. Ah! what would Doctor Pangloss say if he saw what the pure state of nature is like? All is well; so be it; but I confess it is very cruel to have lost Mademoiselle Cunégonde and to be put on a spit by the Oreillons."

Cacambo never lost his head. "Do not despair about anything," he said to the disconsolate Candide; "I understand a bit of the lingo of these people, I'm going to speak to them."

"Do not fail," said Candide, "to point out to them what frightful inhumanity it is to cook men and how unchristian it is."

"Gentlemen," said Cacambo, "so you are counting on eating a Jesuit today; that is a very good thing to do; nothing

is more just than to treat one's enemies thus. In fact natural law teaches us to kill our neighbor, and this is how people behave all over the world. If we do not exercise our right to eat him, that is because we have other ingredients for a good meal; but you do not have the same resources as we do; certainly it is better to eat one's enemies than to abandon the fruits of victory to the crows and the ravens. But, gentlemen, you would not want to eat your friends. You think you are going to put a Jesuit on the spit, and it is your defender, it is the enemy of your enemies that you are about to roast. For my part I was born in your country; the gentleman you see here is my master; and far from being a Jesuit, he has just killed a Jesuit, he is wearing his spoils, that is the reason for your mistake. To verify what I am telling you, take his robe, carry it to the first barrier of the kingdom of *Los Padres,* find out whether my master has not killed a Jesuit officer. It won't take you long; you can still eat us if you find I have lied to you. But if I have told you the truth, you know the principles of international law, its customs and rules, too well not to spare us."

The Oreillons found this speech very reasonable; they deputized two notables to go with all diligence and find out the truth; the two deputies acquitted themselves of their commission like intelligent men and soon returned bearing good news. The Oreillons untied their two prisoners, paid them all sorts of courtesies, offered them girls, gave them refreshments, and conducted them all the way to the confines of their states, shouting joyfully: "He's not a Jesuit, he's not a Jesuit!"

Candide could not tire of wondering at the reason for his deliverance. "What a race!" he said. "What men! What customs! If I had not had the good fortune of giving a great sword thrust through the body of Mademoiselle Cunégonde's brother, I would have been eaten without mercy. But after all, the pure state of nature is good, since these people, instead of eating me, offered me a thousand courtesies as soon as they learned that I was not a Jesuit."

17 Arrival of Candide and His Valet in the Country of Eldorado,[1] and What They Saw There

WHEN THEY WERE at the frontiers of the Oreillons, Cacambo said to Candide: "You see, this hemisphere is no better than the other; take my word for it, let's go back to Europe by the shortest route."

"How can we go back there?" said Candide. "And where could we go? If I go to my own country, the Bulgarians and Abarians are slaughtering everyone; if I go back to Portugal I am burned; if we stay in this country we run the risk at any moment of being put on the spit. But how can one bring oneself to leave the part of the world where Mademoiselle Cunégonde lives?"

"Let's turn toward Cayenne," said Cacambo; "there we will find Frenchmen; they go all over the world; they may help us; perhaps God will have pity on us."

It was not easy to go to Cayenne. They knew about what direction they had to go; but mountains, rivers, precipices, brigands, savages, were terrible obstacles on all sides. Their horses died of fatigue; their provisions were used up. For a whole month they lived on wild fruits, and at last found themselves by a little river bordered with coconut trees, which supported their lives and hopes.

Cacambo, who always gave as good advice as the old woman, said to Candide: "We are at the end of our rope, we have walked far enough; I see an empty canoe on the bank, let us fill it with coconuts, cast ourselves into this little bark, and drift with the current; a river always leads to some inhabited spot. If we do not find pleasant things, at least we shall find new things."

"Let's go," said Candide, "let us recommend ourselves to Providence."

They drifted a few leagues between banks now flowery, now barren, now smooth, now rugged. The river kept getting wider; finally it disappeared under an arch of frightful rocks that rose to the heavens. The two travelers had the hardihood

1   "The Golden (Country)," which a lieutenant of Pizarro claimed to have discovered.

to abandon themselves to the waters underneath this arch.
The river, at this point narrowed, carried them along with
horrible rapidity and noise. After twenty-four hours they
saw daylight again, but their canoe smashed on the reefs. They
had to drag themselves from rock to rock for a whole league;
finally they discovered an immense horizon bordered by inaccessible mountains. The country was cultivated for pleasure
as well as for need; everywhere the useful was attractive. The
roads were covered, or rather adorned, with carriages brilliant
in form and material, bearing men and women of singular
beauty, and drawn rapidly by big red sheep which in swiftness
surpassed the finest horses of Andalusia, Tetuan,* and
Meknes.*

"All the same," said Candide, "here is a country that is
better than Westphalia." With Cacambo he set foot on land
near the first village he came upon. A few village children
covered with badly torn gold brocade were playing quoits at
the entrance to the village. Our two men from the other world
watched them with enjoyment. Their quoits were rather wide
round pieces, yellow, red, and green, which shone with singular brilliance. The travelers took a notion to pick up a few
of them; they were gold, emerald, and rubies, the least of
which would have been the greatest ornament of the Mogul's
throne.

"No doubt," said Cacambo, "these children are the sons
of the King of the country playing quoits."

The village schoolmaster appeared at that moment, to call
them back to school. "That," said Candide, "is the tutor of
the royal family."

The little beggars immediately left their game, leaving on
the ground their quoits and everything they had been playing
with. Candide picks them up, runs to the tutor, and humbly
presents them to him, giving him to understand by signs that
Their Royal Highnesses had forgotten their gold and their
precious stones. The village schoolmaster, smiling, threw them
on the ground, looked at Candide's face for a moment with
much surprise, and continued on his way.

The travelers did not fail to pick up the gold, the rubies,
and the emeralds. "Where are we?" exclaimed Candide.
"Kings' children must be well brought up in this country,
since they teach them to despise gold and jewels." Cacambo
was as surprised as Candide. Finally they approached the

first house in the village. It was built like a European palace. A crowd of people was bustling at the door, and even more inside the house. You could hear very pleasant music and smell a delicious odor of cooking. Cacambo approached the door and heard them speaking Peruvian; it was his mother tongue; for everyone knows that Cacambo was born in Tucuman* in a village where only that language was known. "I will serve as your interpreter," he said to Candide; "let's go in, this is an inn."

Instantly two boys and two girls of the hostelry, dressed in cloth of gold, their hair bound up with ribbons, invited them to sit at the host's table. They served four soups each garnished with two parrots, a boiled condor that weighed two hundred pounds, two roast monkeys of excellent flavor; three hundred colibri hummingbirds on one platter and six hundred other hummingbirds on another; exquisite stews, delicious pastries; all this on platters of a sort of rock crystal. The boys and girls of the inn poured several liquors made of sugar cane.

The guests were for the most part merchants and coachmen, all of the greatest politeness, who asked Cacambo many questions with the most circumspect discretion and who answered his in a wholly satisfactory manner.

When the meal was over, Cacambo, like Candide, thought to pay his bill full well by throwing on the host's table two of those big gold pieces that he had picked up; the host and hostess burst out laughing and held their sides for quite a while. Finally they recovered themselves.

"Gentlemen," said the host, "we can easily see that you are foreigners; we are not accustomed to see any. Pardon us if we began to laugh when you offered us in payment the pebbles of our highroads. No doubt you have none of this country's money, but it is not necessary to have any in order to dine here. All the hostelries established for the convenience of commerce are paid for by the government. You had a bad meal here because this is a poor village; but everywhere else you will be received as you deserve to be."

Cacambo explained to Candide all the host's remarks, and Candide listened to them with the same amazement and the same bewilderment with which his friend Cacambo reported them. "What kind of a country is this, then," they said to each other, "unknown to the rest of the world, and where all nature is of a sort so different from ours? Probably this is the country where all is well; for there absolutely must be one of that sort. And no matter what Doctor Pangloss said about it, I often noticed that all was pretty bad in Westphalia."

18 What They Saw in the Land of Eldorado

CACAMBO MANIFESTED all his curiosity to his host; the host said to him: "I am very ignorant, and I get along all right that way; but we have here an old man who has retired from the court, who is the most learned man in the kingdom and the most communicative." Immediately he took Cacambo to the old man. Candide was now playing only second fiddle and going along with his valet. They entered a house that was very simple, for the door was only of silver and the paneling in the apartments only of gold, but wrought with so much taste that the richest paneling did not eclipse it. True, the antechamber was encrusted only with rubies and emeralds, but the order in which everything was arranged fully made up for this extreme simplicity.

The old man received the two foreigners on a sofa stuffed with hummingbird feathers, and had them served liquors in diamond vases; after which he satisfied their curiosity in these terms:

"I am a hundred and seventy-two years old, and I learned from my late father, equerry to the King, of the astounding revolutions in Peru that he had witnessed. The kingdom we are in is the ancient homeland of the Incas, who left it very imprudently to go and subjugate part of the world, and who were finally destroyed by the Spaniards.

"The princes of their family who remained in their native country were wiser; they ordained, with the consent of the nation, that no inhabitant should ever leave our little kingdom; and that is what has preserved our innocence and happiness for us. The Spaniards gained some confused knowledge of this country; they called it El Dorado; and an Englishman named Lord Raleigh even came near it about a hundred years ago; but since we are surrounded by inaccessible rocks and precipices, we have up to now always been sheltered from the rapacity of the nations of Europe, who have an inconceivable rage for the pebbles and mud of our land, and who would kill us all to the last man to get some."

The conversation was long; it bore on the form of government, customs, women, public spectacles, arts. Finally Candide, who always had a taste for metaphysics, had Cacambo ask whether there was a religion in the country.

The old man blushed a little. "What," he said, "can you doubt it? Do you take us for ingrates?" Cacambo humbly asked what was the religion of Eldorado. The old man blushed again.

"Can there be two religions?" he said. "We have, I think, the religion of everyone; we worship God from morning till evening."

"Do you worship only one single God?" said Cacambo, who was still serving as interpreter for Candide's doubts.

"It appears," said the old man, "that there are not two, or three or four. I must admit that the people of your world ask very singular questions."

Candide could not tire of having this good old man questioned; he wanted to know how they prayed to God in Eldorado.

"We do not pray to him," said the good and respectable sage; "we have nothing to ask him for; he has given us all we need, we thank him without ceasing."

Candide had a curiosity to see some priests; he asked where they were. The good old man smiled.

"My friends," he said, "we are all priests; the King and all the heads of families solemnly sing hymns of thanksgiving every morning, and five or six thousand musicians accompany them."

"What! you have no monks to teach, to dispute, to govern, to intrigue, and to have people burned who are not of their opinion?"

"We would have to be crazy," said the old man; "we are all of the same opinion, and we do not understand what you mean with your monks."

At all these remarks Candide remained in ecstasy and said to himself:

"This is very different from Westphalia and the castle of My Lord the Baron; if our friend Pangloss had seen Eldorado, he would no longer have said that the castle of Thunder-ten-tronckh was the best thing on earth; travel is certainly necessary."

After this long conversation, the good old man had a carriage harnessed with six sheep and gave the two travelers twelve of his servants to take them to court. "Excuse me," he said to them, "if my age deprives me of the honor of accompanying you. The King will receive you in a way that will not leave you discontented, and you will doubtless pardon the customs of the country if there are some that displease you."

Candide and Cacambo climbed into the carriage, the six sheep flew, and in less than four hours they arrived at the King's palace, situated at one end of the capital. The portal was two hundred and twenty feet high and a hundred wide; it is impossible to describe what material it was. It is easy to see what prodigious superiority it must have had over those pebbles and sand that we call gold and precious stones.

Twenty beautiful girls of the watch received Candide and Cacambo as they got out of the carriage, took them to the baths, dressed them in robes woven from hummingbird down; after which the men and women grand officers of the crown took them to His Majesty's apartment between two files of a thousand musicians each, according to the ordinary custom. When they approached the throne room, Cacambo asked one grand officer how they should go about saluting His Majesty: whether you crawled on your knees or on your belly, whether you put your hands on your head or on your backside, whether you licked the dust of the room, in short what the ceremony was.

"The custom," said the grand officer, "is to embrace the King and kiss him on both cheeks."

Candide and Cacambo threw their arms around the neck of His Majesty, who received them with all the grace imaginable and politely asked them to supper.

While waiting, they were shown the town, the public buildings rising to the clouds, the market places adorned with a thousand columns, the fountains of pure water, those of rose water, and those of cane-sugar liquors, which flowed continually in great squares paved with a kind of precious stone which gave off a perfume like that of cloves and cinnamon.

Candide asked to see the law courts; they told him that there were none and that people never went to law. He inquired whether there were prisons, and they told him no. What surprised him even more and pleased him most was the Palace of Sciences, in which he saw a great gallery two thousand paces long all full of instruments for mathematics and physics.

After spending all afternoon touring about the thousandth part of the city, they were taken back to the King's palace; Candide sat down to table with His Majesty, his valet Cacambo, and several ladies. Never was better cheer made, and never had a man more wit at supper than His Majesty. Cacambo explained the King's witty remarks to Candide, and even when translated they still appeared witty. Of all that astounded Candide this was not what astounded him least.

They stayed a month in this hospitable place. Candide never stopped saying to Cacambo:

"It is true, my friend, once again, that the castle where I was born is not worth the country where we are now; but after all, Mademoiselle Cunégonde is not here, and no doubt you have some mistress in Europe. If we stay here, we shall only be like the others, whereas if we return to our own world with just twelve sheep laden with the pebbles of Eldorado, we shall be richer than all the Kings put together, we shall have no more Inquisitors to fear, and we shall easily be able to recover Mademoiselle Cunégonde."

Cacambo liked this idea; people are so fond of running about, showing off before the folks at home, and parading what they have seen on their travels, that the two happy men resolved to be so no longer and to ask His Majesty for leave to go.

"You are doing a foolish thing," the King said to them. "I know that my country is not much; but when a person is reasonably well off somewhere he should stay there. I certainly have no right to detain foreigners; that is a tyranny that does not exist either in our customs or in our laws; all men are free; leave when you will, but the way out is very difficult. It is impossible to go back up the rapid river on which by a miracle you came here and which runs under arches of rock. The mountains that surround my whole kingdom are ten thousand feet high and as perpendicular as walls; they are each more than ten leagues wide, you can descend them only by way of precipices. However, since you absolutely want to leave, I am going to give orders to the directors of machinery to make a machine that can transport you comfortably. When you have been taken to the other side of the mountains, no one will be able to accompany you farther; for my subjects have made a vow never to go beyond the mountain walls, and they are too wise to break their vow. Ask of me anything else you like."

"We ask of Your Majesty," said Cacambo, "only a few sheep loaded with victuals, pebbles, and some of the country's mud."

The King laughed. "I do not understand," he said, "the taste your people of Europe have for our yellow mud; but take as much as you want, and much good may it do you."

He immediately gave orders to his engineers to make a machine to hoist these two extraordinary men out of the kingdom. Three thousand good physicists worked on it; it was ready in two weeks and cost no more than twenty million pounds sterling in the money of the country. They put Candide and Cacambo on the machine; there were two big red sheep saddled and bridled to serve them as mounts when they had crossed the mountains; twenty pack sheep laden with victuals, thirty bearing presents of the most curious products of the country, and fifty laden with gold, precious stones, and diamonds. The King embraced the two wanderers tenderly.

A fine spectacle was their departure and the ingenious manner in which they and their sheep were hoisted to the top of the mountains. The physicists took leave of them after setting them down safely, and Candide was left with no other desire and object than to go and present his sheep to Mademoiselle Cunégonde.

"We have enough," he said, "to pay the Governor of Buenos Aires, if Mademoiselle Cunégonde can be ransomed. Let us head for Cayenne and take ship, and then we shall see what kingdom we can buy."

19 *What Happened to Them in Surinam, and How Candide Made the Acquaintance of Martin*

OUR TWO TRAVELERS' first day was rather pleasant. They were encouraged by the idea of finding themselves possessors of more treasures than Asia, Europe, and Africa could assemble. Candide in transport wrote Cunégonde's name on the trees. On the second day two of their sheep got stuck in marshes and went down with their loads; two other sheep died of fatigue a few days later; seven or eight then died of hunger in a desert; a few days later some others fell from precipices. Finally, after a hundred days of travel, they had only two sheep left.

Candide said to Cacambo: "My friend, you see how perishable are the riches of this world; there is nothing solid but virtue and the happiness of seeing Mademoiselle Cunégonde again."

"I admit it," said Cacambo, "but we still have two sheep left with more treasures than the King of Spain will ever have, and I see in the distance a town that I suspect is Surinam, which belongs to the Dutch. We are at the end of our troubles and the beginning of our happiness."

As they approached the town they met a Negro stretched on the ground, with only half his clothes left, that is to say a pair of blue cloth shorts; the poor man had his left leg and his right hand missing. "Oh, good Lord!" said Candide to him in Dutch. "What are you doing there, my friend, in that horrible state I see you in?"

"I am waiting for my master Monsieur Vanderdendur, the famous merchant," the Negro replied.

"Was it Monsieur Vanderdendur," said Candide, "who treated you this way?"

"Yes, sir," said the Negro, "it is the custom. They give us a pair of cloth shorts twice a year for all our clothing. When we work in the sugar mills and we catch our finger in the millstone, they cut off our hand; when we try to run away, they cut off a leg; both things have happened to me. It is at this price that you eat sugar in Europe. However, when my mother sold me for ten patacóns* on the Guinea coast, she said to me: 'My dear child, bless our fetishes, worship them always, they will make you live happily; you have the honor to be a slave to our lords the whites, and thereby you are making the fortune of your father and mother.' Alas! I don't know if I made their fortune, but they didn't make mine. Dogs, monkeys, parrots are a thousand times less miserable than we are. The Dutch fetishes who converted me tell me every Sunday that we are all, whites and blacks, children of Adam. I am no genealogist, but if those preachers are telling the truth, we are all second cousins. Now you must admit that no one could treat his relatives in a more horrible way."

"O Pangloss!" exclaimed Candide, "you had not guessed this abomination; this does it, at last I shall have to renounce your optimism."

"What is optimism?" said Cacambo.

"Alas," said Candide, "it is the mania of maintaining that all is well when we are miserable!" And he shed tears as he looked at his Negro, and he entered Surinam weeping.

The first thing they inquired about was whether there was not some ship in the port that could be sent to Buenos Aires. The man they addressed proved to be a Spanish ship's captain, who offered to make an honest bargain with them. He arranged to meet them at an inn. Candide and the faithful Cacambo went and waited for him there with their two sheep.

Candide, whose heart was on his lips, told the Spaniard all his adventures and admitted to him that he wanted to carry off Mademoiselle Cunégonde.

"I shall take good care not to take you to Buenos Aires," said the captain. "I would be hanged and you too. The fair Cunégonde is His Lordship's favorite mistress."

This was a bolt from the blue for Candide; he wept for a long time; finally he drew Cacambo aside.

"My dear friend," he said to him, "here is what you must do. We each have in our pockets five or six millions worth of diamonds; you are cleverer than I; go get Mademoiselle Cunégonde in Buenos Aires. If the Governor makes any difficulties, give him a million; if he still doesn't give in, give him two; you haven't killed an Inquisitor, they won't suspect you. I will fit out another ship; I will go to Venice and wait for you; it is a free country where there is nothing to fear either from Bulgarians, or Abarians, or Jews, or Inquisitors."

Cacambo applauded this wise resolution. He was in despair at parting from a good master who had become his intimate friend; but the pleasure of being useful to him overcame the grief of leaving him. They embraced, shedding tears. Candide recommended to him not to forget the good old woman. Cacambo left that very day. He was a very good man, this Cacambo.

Candide stayed on some time in Surinam and waited for another captain to be willing to take him to Italy, him and the two sheep he had left. He took servants and bought everything he needed for a long voyage. At last Monsieur Vanderdendur, master of a big ship, came to see him.

"How much do you want," he asked this man, "to take me straight to Venice, me, my men, my baggage, and the two sheep you see here?" The captain agreed to ten thousand piasters.* Candide did not hesitate.

"Oho!" said the prudent Vanderdendur to himself, "this foreigner gives ten thousand piasters right away! He must be very rich." Then, returning a moment later, he signified that he could not sail for less than twenty thousand. "Very well, you shall have them," said Candide.

"Whew!" said the merchant softly to himself, "this man gives twenty thousand piasters as easily as ten thousand." He came back again and said that he could not take him to Venice for less than thirty thousand piasters. "Then you shall have thirty thousand," said Candide.

"Oho!" said the Dutch merchant to himself again, "thirty thousand piasters means nothing to this man; no doubt the two sheep are carrying immense treasures; let's not insist any further; let's get the thirty thousand piasters paid first, and then we shall see."

Candide sold two little diamonds the smaller of which was worth more than all the money the captain was asking. He paid him in advance. The two sheep were put aboard. Candide was following in a little boat to join the ship in the roads; the captain seizes his chance, sets sail, weighs anchor; the wind favors him. Candide, bewildered and stupefied, soon loses sight of him. "Alas!" he cried, "that's a trick worthy of the Old World." He returns to shore sunk in grief, for after all he had lost enough to make the fortune of twenty monarchs.

He goes to see the Dutch judge; and since he was somewhat

upset, he knocks roughly on the door; he enters, expounds
his adventure, and exclaims a little louder than was fitting.
The judge began by making him pay ten thousand piasters
for the noise he had made. Then he listened to him patiently,
promised to look into his affair as soon as the merchant had
returned, and charged him another ten thousand piasters for
the costs of the hearing.

This procedure completed Candide's despair; true, he had
endured misfortunes a thousand times more painful; but the
cold-bloodedness of the judge, and of the captain by whom
he had been robbed, inflamed his bile and plunged him into
a black melancholy. The wickedness of men appeared to his
mind in all its ugliness; he fed only on sad ideas.

Finally when a French ship was on the point of leaving
for Bordeaux, since he had no more sheep laden with
diamonds to put on board, he hired a cabin at a proper price
and let it be known in the town that he would pay the passage
and food and two thousand piasters to a decent man who
would like to make the voyage with him, on condition that
this man should be the most disgusted with his lot, and the
most unfortunate in the province.

A throng of aspirants presented themselves that a fleet
could not have held. Candide, wanting to choose among the
most promising, picked out about twenty persons who seemed
to him sociable enough and who all claimed to deserve the
preference. He assembled them in his inn and gave them
supper on condition that each would take an oath to tell his
story faithfully; promising to choose the one who should seem
to him the most to be pitied and the most discontented
with his lot for the best reasons, and to give the others rewards.

The session lasted until four in the morning. Candide, as
he listened to all their adventures, remembered what the old
woman had said to him on the way to Buenos Aires, and the
wager she had made that there was no one on the ship to
whom very great misfortunes had not happened. At each
adventure that was told him he thought of Pangloss.

"That Pangloss," said he, "would be much embarrassed
to try to prove his system. I wish he were here. Certainly
if all is well it is in Eldorado and not in the rest of the
world."

Finally he made up his mind in favor of a poor scholar who

had worked ten years for the booksellers in Amsterdam.[1] He judged that there was no occupation in the world that a man should be more disgusted with.

This scholar, moreover, who was a good man, had been robbed by his wife, beaten by his son, and abandoned by his daughter, who had eloped with a Portuguese. He had just been deprived of a small job on which he lived, and the preachers of Surinam were persecuting him because they took him for a Socinian.* It must be admitted that the others were at least as unfortunate as he; but Candide hoped that the scholar would allay his boredom on the voyage. All his other rivals considered that Candide was doing them a great injustice, but he appeased them by giving them each a hundred piasters.

20 What Happened to Candide and Martin at Sea

SO THE OLD SCHOLAR, whose name was Martin, embarked with Candide for Bordeaux. Both had seen much, and suffered much; and if the ship had been scheduled to set sail from Surinam to Japan by the Cape of Good Hope, they would have had enough to say about moral and physical evil to last the whole voyage.

However, Candide had one great advantage over Martin: he still hoped to see Mademoiselle Cunégonde again, and Martin had nothing to hope for; furthermore, he had gold and diamonds; and though he had lost a hundred big red sheep laden with the greatest treasures on earth, though he still had the knavery of the Dutch captain on his mind, nevertheless, when he thought about what he had left in his pockets, and when he talked about Cunégonde, especially toward the end of a meal, he still leaned toward the system of Pangloss.

"But you, Monsieur Martin," he said to the scholar, "what

1   Because of French censorship, Dutch freedom of the press, and the lack of international copyright laws, many French books were published piratically in Holland. Voltaire, among others, had suffered much from this pirating.

do you think of all that? What is your idea about moral and physical evil?"

"Sir," replied Martin, "my priests accused me of being a Socinian; but the truth of the matter is that I am a Manichean."*

"You are making fun of me," said Candide, "there are no more Manicheans in the world."

"There's me," said Martin; "I don't know what to do about it, but I cannot think any other way."

"You must be full of the devil," said Candide.

"He takes so much part in the affairs of this world," said Martin, "that I might well be full of him, just like everything else; but I must admit that when I cast my eyes over this globe, or rather over this globule, I think that God has abandoned it to some maleficent being—always excepting Eldorado. I have hardly seen a town that did not desire the ruin of the neighboring town, never a family that did not want to exterminate some other family. Everywhere the weak loathe the powerful before whom they crawl, and the powerful treat them like flocks whose wool and flesh are for sale. A million regimented assassins, ranging from one end of Europe to the other, practice murder and brigandage with discipline to earn their bread, because there is no more honest occupation; and in the towns that seem to enjoy peace and where the arts flourish, men are devoured with more envy, cares, and anxieties than the scourges suffered by a town besieged. Secret griefs are even more cruel than public miseries. In a word, I have seen so much, and undergone so much, that I am a Manichean."

"Yet there is some good," said Candide.

"That may be," said Martin, "but I do not know it."

In the midst of this dispute they heard the sound of cannon. The noise redoubles each moment. Everyone takes his spyglass. They see two ships fighting about three miles away. The wind brought them both so near the French ship that they had the pleasure of seeing the combat quite at their ease. Finally one of the two ships sent the other a broadside so low and so accurate as to sink it. Candide and Martin distinctly saw a hundred men on the main deck of the sinking ship; they all raised their hands to heaven and uttered frightful screams; in a moment all was swallowed up.

"Well," said Martin, "that is how men treat each other."

"It is true," said Candide, "that there is something diabolical in this affair."

So saying, he spied something bright red swimming near his ship. They launched the ship's boat to see what it could be; it was one of his sheep. Candide felt more joy on finding this sheep again than he had felt grief on losing a hundred all laden with big diamonds from Eldorado.

The French captain soon perceived that the captain of the ship that sank the other was a Spaniard and that the captain of the ship that sank was a Dutch pirate; he was the very one who had robbed Candide. The immense riches that this scoundrel had stolen were buried with him in the sea, and nothing but one sheep was saved.

"You see," said Candide to Martin, "that crime is sometimes punished; that rascal of a Dutch captain met the fate he deserved."

"Yes," said Martin, "but was it necessary that the passengers on his ship should perish also? God punished that knave, the devil drowned the others."

Meanwhile the French ship and the Spaniard continued on their way, and Candide continued his conversations with Martin. They argued for two weeks without stopping, and after two weeks they were as far advanced as the first day. But after all they were talking, they were exchanging ideas, they were consoling each other. Candide kept stroking his sheep. "Since I have found you again," he said, "I may well find Cunégonde again."

21 Candide and Martin Approach the Coast of France, Reasoning

AT LAST they sighted the coast of France.

"Have you ever been in France, Monsieur Martin?" said Candide.

"Yes," said Martin, "I have been through several provinces. There are some where half the inhabitants are crazy, some where they are too tricky, others where they are usually rather gentle and rather stupid; others where they try to be witty; and in all of them the principal occupation is making love, the second talking slander, and the third talking nonsense."

"But, Monsieur Martin, have you seen Paris?"

"Yes, I have seen Paris; it is like all those kinds, it's a chaos, it's a crowd in which everyone seeks pleasure and in which almost no one finds it, at least so it appeared to me. I did not stay there long; on arrival I was robbed of all I had by pickpockets at the Saint-Germain fair. I was taken for a thief myself and I was in prison for a week; after which I became a printer's proofreader to earn enough to return on foot to Holland. I came to know the writing rabble, the intriguing rabble, and the convulsionary* rabble. They say there are some very polite persons in that city; I am willing to believe it."

"For my part, I have no curiosity to see France," said Candide. "You can easily guess that when a man has spent a month in Eldorado, he does not care about seeing anything else on earth, except Mademoiselle Cunégonde; I am going to wait for her in Venice; we will cross France on our way to Italy; won't you come along with me?"

"Very gladly," said Martin. "They say that Venice is good only for Venetian nobles, but that nevertheless they receive foreigners very well when they have a lot of money; I have none, you have, I will follow you anywhere."

"By the way," said Candide, "do you think that the earth was originally a sea, as we are assured in that big book [1] that belongs to the ship's captain?"

"I believe nothing of the sort," said Martin, "any more than all the daydreams that people have been trying to sell us for some time now."

"But then to what end was this world formed?" said Candide.

"To drive us mad," replied Martin.

"Aren't you quite astonished," Candide continued, "at the love of those two girls in the country of the Oreillons for those two monkeys, the adventure with whom I told you?"

"Not at all," said Martin, "I don't see what is strange about that passion; I have seen so many extraordinary things that there is nothing extraordinary left."

"Do you think," said Candide, "that men have always massacred each other as they do today, always been liars, cheats, faithbreakers, ingrates, brigands, weaklings, rovers,

1   The "big book" presumably is the Bible; the theory had recently been advanced again in Buffon's *Théorie de la terre* (1749).

cowards, enviers, gluttons, drunkards, misers, self-seekers, carnivores, calumniators, debauchees, fanatics, hypocrites, and fools?"

"Do you think," said Martin, "that sparrow hawks have always eaten pigeons when they found any?"

"Yes, no doubt," said Candide.

"Well," said Martin, "if sparrow hawks have always had the same character, why do you expect men to have changed theirs?"

"Oh!" said Candide, "there's a big difference, for free will . . ."

Reasoning thus, they arrived at Bordeaux.

22 What Happened to Candide and Martin in France

CANDIDE STOPPED in Bordeaux only as long as it took to sell a few pebbles from Eldorado and to provide himself with a good two-seated chaise; for he now could not do without his philosopher Martin; only he was very sorry to part with his sheep, which he left to the Bordeaux Academy of Science, which proposed, as the subject of that year's competition, to find out why this sheep's wool was red; and the prize was awarded to a scholar from the north, who proved by A plus B, minus C, divided by Z, that the sheep must be red and die of sheep pox.

Meanwhile all the travelers that Candide met in the inns on the road said to him: "We are going to Paris." This general eagerness finally gave him a hankering to see this capital; it was not much of a detour off the road to Venice.

He entered by the Faubourg Saint-Marceau [1] and thought he was in the ugliest village in Westphalia.

Hardly was Candide in his inn when he was attacked by a slight illness caused by his fatigue. Since he had an enormous diamond on his finger and a prodigiously heavy strongbox had been observed in his baggage, he immediately had at his side two doctors he had not called, some intimate friends who did not leave him, and two pious ladies heating up his broths.

1 In Voltaire's time an ugly, dirty suburb.

Martin said: "I remember having been sick in Paris too on my first trip; I was very poor, so I had neither friends, nor pious ladies, nor doctors; and I got well."

However, by dint of medicines and bloodlettings, Candide's illness became serious. A neighborhood priest came and asked him gently for a note payable to the bearer in the next world.[2] Candide wanted no part of it; the pious ladies assured him that it was a new fashion. Candide replied that he was not a man of fashion. Martin wanted to throw the priest out the window. The cleric swore that Candide should not be buried.[3] Martin swore that he would bury the cleric if he continued to bother them. The quarrel grew heated; Martin took him by the shoulders and pushed him out roughly, which caused a great scandal which led in turn to a legal report.

Candide got well, and during his convalescence he had very good company to supper with him. They gambled for high stakes. Candide was quite amazed that he never got any aces, and Martin was not amazed at this at all.

Among those who did the honors of the town for him was a little abbé from Périgord, one of those eager people, always alert, always obliging, brazen, fawning, complaisant, who lie in wait for strangers passing through, tell them the history of the town's scandals, and offer them pleasures at any price. This man first took Candide and Martin to the theater. They were playing a new tragedy. Candide found himself seated next to some wits. This did not keep him from weeping at certain perfectly played scenes. One of the reasoners beside him said to him during an intermission:

"You are very wrong to weep, for that actress is very bad, the actor playing opposite her even worse, the play is even worse than the actors: the author doesn't know a word of Arabic, and yet the scene is in Arabia; and besides, he is a man who doesn't believe in innate ideas;[4] tomorrow I will bring you twenty pamphlets against him."

2   A reference to the *billets de confession* required from 1746 on, on pain of refusal of absolution and the sacraments.
3   That is, buried in consecrated ground. See below, p. 70, note 7.
4   Voltaire followed Locke's view of the mind at birth as a blank slate, rather than Descartes' theory of innate ideas. Cf. *Memory's Adventure*, pp. 325–26.

"Sir,[5] how many plays do you have in France?" said Candide to the abbé, who replied: "Five or six thousand."

"That's a lot," said Candide. "How many of them are good?"

"Fifteen or sixteen," replied the other.

"That's a lot," said Martin.

Candide was very pleased with an actress who played Queen Elizabeth in a rather dull tragedy that is sometimes performed.[6]

"I like this actress very much," he said to Martin; "she reminds me of Mademoiselle Cunégonde; I would very much like to pay her my respects."

The abbé from Périgord offered to take him to meet her. Candide, brought up in Germany, asked what the proper etiquette was, and how they treated queens of England in France.

"You have to make a distinction," said the abbé. "In the provinces they take them to a tavern, in Paris they respect them when they are beautiful and throw them on the dump when they are dead."

"Queens on the dump!" said Candide.

"Yes, really," said Martin; "the abbé is right; I was in Paris when Mademoiselle Monime [7] passed on, as they say, from this life to the next; she was refused what those people call the honors of burial, that is to say, of rotting with all the beggars of the district in an ugly cemetery; alone of her troupe, she was buried at the corner of the Rue de Bourgogne; which must have pained her extremely, for she had a very noble mind."

"That was very impolite," said Candide.

"What do you expect?" said Martin. "These people are made that way. Imagine all possible contradictions and incompatibilities, you will see them in the government, the tribunals, the churches, the entertainments of this queer nation."

"Is it true that people are always laughing in Paris?" said Candide.

5   Here begins a long passage added by Voltaire in 1761, which ends below, p. 75.
6   Presumably Thomas Corneille, *Le Comte d'Essex.*
7   Adrienne Lecouvreur (1690–1730), a distinguished actress who made her debut at the Comédie Française as Monime in Racine's *Mithridate*. Being an actress at her death, she was refused burial in consecrated ground.

"Yes," said the abbé, "but it is with rage in their hearts; for here people complain about everything with great bursts of laughter, and they even perform the most detestable actions with a laugh."

"Who," said Candide, "is that fat pig who was telling me so many bad things about the play at which I wept so much and about the actors who gave me such pleasure?"

"He is a living disease," replied the abbé, "who makes his living by saying bad things about all plays and all books; he hates anyone who succeeds, as eunuchs hate those who can enjoy sex; he is one of those serpents of literature who feed on filth and venom; he is a foliferous pamphleteer. . . ."

"What do you mean by a foliferous pamphleteer?" said Candide.

"A producer of scribbled leaves," said the abbé, "a Fréron."*

That is how Candide, Martin, and the Perigordian were talking on the staircase as they watched people file out after the play.

"Although I am very eager to see Mademoiselle Cunégonde again," said Candide, "still I would like to have supper with Mademoiselle Clairon,[8] for she seemed admirable to me."

The abbé was not the man to approach Mademoiselle Clairon, for she saw only good company. "She is engaged for this evening," he said, "but I shall have the honor of taking you to the house of a lady of quality, and there you will come to know Paris as if you had been here four years."

Candide, who was naturally curious, let himself be taken to the lady's house, at the far end of the Faubourg Saint-Honoré;[9] they were busy playing faro; twelve sad punters [10] each held a small hand of cards, the foolish register of their misfortunes. A deep silence reigned, pallor sat on the punters' foreheads, anxiety on that of the banker; and the lady of the house, seated beside this pitiless banker, watched with a lynx's eyes all the underhand plays for double stakes or for three straight wins to pay seven times, for which each player turned up the corner of his cards;[11] she had them turned

8   A celebrated actress who played leading roles in many of Voltaire's plays.
9   An aristocratic quarter of Paris.
10   Faro is played by an unlimited number of punters against the banker.
11   To mark that he was making this bet—illegally, however.

back down with severe but polite attention, and did not show
any anger for fear of losing her customers; the lady called
herself the Marquise de Parolignac.[12] Her daughter, aged
fifteen, was one of the punters, and tipped her off with a
wink to the cheating of those who were trying to repair the
cruelties of fortune. The abbé from Périgord, Candide, and
Martin entered, no one got up, greeted them, or looked at
them; all were deeply preoccupied with their cards.

"My Lady the Baroness of Thunder-ten-tronckh was more
civil," said Candide.

However, the abbé got the ear of the Marquise, who half
rose, honored Candide with a gracious smile and Martin
with a truly noble nod; she saw to it that a seat and a hand
of cards were given to Candide, who lost fifty thousand
francs in two deals; after which they had supper most gaily,
and everyone was astounded that Candide was not moved
by his loss; the lackeys said to one another in their lackey
language: "He must be some English Milord."

The supper was like most suppers in Paris; first a silence;
then a noise of undistinguishable words; then jokes, most of
them insipid, false news, bad reasoning, a little politics, and
a lot of slander; there was even some talk about new books.

"Have you seen," said the abbé from Périgord, "the novel by
a certain Gauchat,* Doctor of Theology?"

"Yes," replied one of the guests, "but I could not finish it.
We have a host of nonsensical writings, but all of them together do not approach the nonsensicality of Gauchat, Doctor
of Theology; I am so surfeited with this immense number of
detestable books that inundate us that I have taken to punting
at faro. . . ."

"What about the *Mélanges* by Archdeacon Trublet?* What
do you say about them?" said the abbé.

"Oh!" said Madame de Parolignac, "what a tedious mortal!
How assiduously he tells you what everybody knows! How
ponderously he discusses what is not worth being noted
lightly! With what absence of wit he appropriates the wit of
others! How he spoils what he plunders! How he disgusts
me! But he will not disgust me any more; it is enough to have
read a few pages by the Archdeacon."

12   From *paroli*, the doubled stakes alluded to above, and the
-gnac ending common in the southwest of France, a great source
of impoverished and spurious nobility.

There was a learned man of taste at table who supported what the Marquise said. They talked of tragedies next; the lady asked why there were tragedies that were sometimes played and that could not be read. The man of taste explained very well how a play could have some interest and almost no merit; he proved in a few words that it was not enough to bring on one or two of those situations that you find in all novels and that always beguile the spectators, but that you have to be new without being bizarre, often sublime, and always natural, know the human heart and make it speak, be a great poet without letting any character in the play appear to be a poet, know the language perfectly, speak it with purity, with continual harmony, without ever rhyming at the expense of the sense.

"Anyone," he added, "who does not observe all these rules may compose one or two tragedies that win applause at the theater, but he will never be ranked among good writers; there are very few good tragedies; some are idyls in well-written and well-rhymed dialogue, others are political arguments that put you to sleep, or repulsive amplifications; still others are the dreams of enthusiasts, in a barbarous style; interrupted speeches, long apostrophes to the gods—because the author does not know how to speak to men—false maxims, bombastic commonplaces."

Candide listened attentively to this speech and formed a fine impression of the speaker; and since the Marquise had taken care to place him next to her, he got her ear and took the liberty of asking her who was that man who spoke so well.

"He is a learned man," said the lady, "who does not play faro and whom the abbé sometimes brings to supper with me; he is a perfect connoisseur of tragedies and books, and he has written a tragedy that was hissed and a book of which only one copy, which he dedicated to me, was ever seen outside his publisher's store."

"What a great man!" said Candide. "He is another Pangloss."

Then, turning toward him, he said to him:

"Sir, no doubt you think that all is for the best in the physical world and in the moral, and that nothing could have been otherwise?"

"I, sir," replied the scholar, "I think nothing of the sort;

I think that everything goes awry with us, that no one knows his rank or his job or what he is doing or what he should do, and that except for supper, which is rather gay and where there seems to be a good deal of agreement, all the rest of the time is spent in senseless quarrels: Jansenists* against Molinists,* lawyers against churchmen, men of letters against men of letters, courtiers against courtiers, financiers against the people, wives against husbands, relatives against relatives—it's an eternal war."

Candide replied: "I have seen worse; but a sage, who has since had the misfortune to be hanged, taught me that all this is wonderful: these are shadows in a beautiful picture."

"Your hanged man was making fun of everybody," said Martin; "your shadows are horrible stains."

"It is men who make the stains," said Candide, "and they can't help it."

"Then it isn't their fault," said Martin.

Most of the gamblers, who understood nothing of this kind of talk, were drinking; and Martin talked theory with the scholar, and Candide told the lady of the house part of his adventures.

After supper the Marquise took Candide into her boudoir and sat him down on a sofa.

"Well," she said to him, "so you are still madly in love with Mademoiselle Cunégonde of Thunder-ten-tronckh!"

"Yes, Madame," answered Candide.

The Marquise replied to him with a tender smile: "You answer me like a young man from Westphalia; a Frenchman would have said to me: 'It is true that I have been in love with Mademoiselle Cunégonde, but when I see you, Madame, I fear I no longer love her.'"

"Alas! Madame," said Candide, "I will answer as you wish."

"Your passion for her," said the Marquise, "began when you picked up her handkerchief; I want you to pick up my garter."

"With all my heart," said Candide, and he picked it up.

"But I want you to put it back on me," said the lady, and Candide put it back on her.

"You see," said the lady, "you are a foreigner; I sometimes make my Parisian lovers languish for two weeks, but I give myself to you on the very first night, because one must do the honors of one's country to a young man from Westphalia."

The beauty, having perceived two enormous diamonds on her young foreigner's two hands, praised them so sincerely that they passed from Candide's fingers to the fingers of the Marquise.

When Candide went home with his Perigordian abbé, he felt some remorse at having been unfaithful to Mademoiselle Cunégonde; the abbé took part in his grief; he had got only a small share of the fifty thousand francs lost at gambling by Candide and of the value of the two brilliants half given, half extorted from him. His plan was to make all the profit he could from the advantages that his acquaintance with Candide might procure him. He talked to him a lot about Cunégonde, and Candide told him that he would certainly beg that fair lady's pardon for his infidelity when he saw her in Venice.

The Perigordian redoubled his courtesies and attentions, and took a tender interest in everything Candide said, everything he did, everything he wanted to do.[13]

"So you have a rendezvous in Venice, sir?" he said.

"Yes, Mr. Abbé," said Candide; "I absolutely must go and find Mademoiselle Cunégonde."

Then, led on by the pleasure of talking about the one he loved, he related, as was his custom, a part of his adventures with that illustrious lady of Westphalia.

"I suppose," said the abbé, "that Mademoiselle Cunégonde has a great deal of wit and writes charming letters?"

"I have never received any from her," said Candide, "for you must realize that having been expelled from the castle for love of her, I could not write her; that soon afterward I learned that she was dead, then I found her again, and then lost her; and that I have sent her a dispatch by special messenger two thousand five hundred leagues from here and am awaiting her reply."

The abbé listened attentively and seemed a bit thoughtful. He soon took leave of the two foreigners after embracing them tenderly. The next day Candide, on waking, received a letter couched in these terms:

"Sir, my very dear lover, I have been ill in this city for a week; now I learn that you are here. I would fly into your arms if I could move. I heard that you had passed through Bordeaux, I left the faithful Cacambo and the old woman

13   Here ends the addition of 1761 that began on p. 70.

there, and they are to follow me soon. The Governor of Buenos Aires took everything, but I still have your heart. Come, your presence will restore me to life or make me die of pleasure."

This charming letter, this unhoped-for letter, transported Candide with inexpressible joy; and the illness of his dear Cunégonde overwhelmed him with grief. Torn between these two feelings, he takes his gold and his diamonds and has himself driven with Martin to the hotel where Mademoiselle Cunégonde was staying. He enters, trembling with emotion; his heart beats, his voice sobs; he wants to open the bed curtains, he wants to have a light brought.

"Don't do anything of the sort," says the waiting maid, "light is the death of her"; and promptly she closes the curtains again.

"My dear Cunégonde," says Candide, weeping, "how are you feeling? If you cannot see me, at least speak to me."

"She cannot speak," says the maid.

The lady then stretches out of the bed a plump hand which Candide waters at length with his tears and which he then fills with diamonds, leaving a bag full of gold on the armchair.

In the midst of these transports a police officer arrives followed by the Perigordian abbé and a squad.

"So these are those two suspicious foreigners?" he says.

He immediately has them arrested and orders his bravoes to drag them off to prison.

"This is not how they treat travelers in Eldorado," says Candide.

"I am more of a Manichean than ever," says Martin.

"But, sir, where are you taking us?" says Candide.

"To a deep dungeon," says the police officer.

Martin, having regained his coolness, decided that the lady who claimed to be Cunégonde was a fraud, the abbé from Périgord a fraud who had taken advantage of Candide's innocence as fast as he could, and the police officer another fraud of whom they could easily get rid.

Rather than expose himself to the processes of justice, Candide, enlightened by Martin's advice and moreover still impatient to see the real Mademoiselle Cunégonde again, suggests to the police officer three little diamonds worth about three thousand pistoles each.

"Ah, sir," says the man with the ivory baton, "even had you committed all the crimes imaginable, you are the finest man in the world. Three diamonds! Each worth three thousand pistoles! Sir, I would let myself be killed for you, instead of taking you to a dungeon. They arrest all foreigners here, but let me take care of things; I have a brother at Dieppe in Normandy, I'm going to take you there; and if you have an extra diamond to give him, he will take care of you just as I am doing myself."

"And why do they arrest all foreigners?" said Candide.

The abbé from Périgord then spoke up and said: "It is because a tramp from the region of Atrebatum [14] listened to foolish talk; this alone made him commit a parricide, not like that of May, 1610, but like that of December, 1594,[15] and like many others committed in other years and other months by other tramps who had listened to foolish talk."

The police officer then explained what it was all about.

"Oh, the monsters!" exclaimed Candide. "What! Such horrors in a nation that dances and sings! Can I not depart at once out of this country where monkeys incite tigers? I have seen bears in my own country; I have seen men only in Eldorado. In the name of God, Mr. Officer, take me to Venice, where I am to await Mademoiselle Cunégonde."

"I can take you only to Lower Normandy," said the officer.

Immediately he has his chains taken off, says he has made a mistake, sends his men away, and takes Candide and Martin to Dieppe and leaves them in the hands of his brother. There was a little Dutch ship in the roads. The Norman, having with the help of three other diamonds become the most obliging of men, embarks Candide and his men on the ship, which was about to set sail for Portsmouth in England. It was not the way to Venice; but Candide thought he was delivered from hell, and fully intended to get back on the way to Venice at the first opportunity.

14   Latin name for Arras, home of Damiens, who attempted to assassinate Louis XV in 1757.
15   Two attempts on the life of Henry IV were the unsuccessful one by Châtel in 1594 and the successful one by Ravaillac in 1610.

23 Candide and Martin Go to the Coast of England; What They See There

"O PANGLOSS, Pangloss! O Martin, Martin! O my dear Cunégonde! What sort of a world is this?" said Candide on the Dutch ship.

"Something very mad and very abominable," replied Martin.

"You know England; are they as mad there as in France?"

"It's another kind of madness," said Martin. "You know that these two nations are at war over a few acres of snow out around Canada, and that they are spending on that fine war much more than all of Canada is worth. As for telling you precisely whether there are more people who need to be locked up in one country than another, that is something that my poor lights do not allow me to do. I only know that in general the people we are on our way to see are very gloomy."

While chatting thus, they arrived at Portsmouth; a multitude of people covered the shore and looked attentively at a rather fat man who was on his knees, his eyes bandaged, on the main deck of one of the ships of the fleet; four soldiers posted facing this man shot three bullets each into his skull as peacefully as can be, and the whole assemblage went back home extremely satisfied.

"What in the world is all this?" said Candide. "And what demon is exercising his domination everywhere?" He asked who was that fat man who had just been ceremoniously killed.

"An admiral," [1] was the reply.

"And why kill this admiral?"

"Because," he was told, "he did not get enough people killed; he gave battle to a French admiral, and they decided that he was not close enough to him."

"But," said Candide, "the French admiral was as far from the English admiral as he was from him!"

"That is incontestable," was the reply; "but in this country

[1] Admiral Byng of England was executed on March 14, 1757, after a court-martial, for losing a naval battle to the French the year before. Voltaire had tried in vain to intervene to save his life.

it is a good thing to kill an admiral from time to time to encourage the others."

Candide was so stunned and so shocked at what he saw and what he heard that he would not even set foot on land, and made his bargain with the Dutch captain (even if he were to rob him like the one in Surinam) to take him to Venice without delay.

Two days later the captain was ready. They sailed along the coast of France. They passed in sight of Lisbon, and Candide shuddered. They entered the Strait [2] and the Mediterranean. Finally they landed in Venice. "God be praised," said Candide, embracing Martin, "here is where I shall see the fair Cunégonde again. I count on Cacambo as on myself. All is well, all goes well, all goes as well as it possibly could."

24   *Paquette and Friar Giroflée*

AS SOON as he was in Venice, he had a search made for Cacambo in all the taverns, all the cafés, and among all the ladies of pleasure, and did not find him. Every day he sent to investigate all the ships and boats: no news of Cacambo.

"What!" he said to Martin. "I have had time to cross from Surinam to Bordeaux, to go from Bordeaux to Paris, from Paris to Dieppe, from Dieppe to Portsmouth, to skirt the coasts of Portugal and Spain, to cross the whole Mediterranean, to spend a few months in Venice, and the fair Cunégonde has not arrived! Instead of her I have met only a tricky wench and an abbé from Périgord! Cunégonde is beyond doubt dead, there is nothing left for me to do but die. Ah! it would have been better to remain in the paradise of Eldorado than to return to this accursed Europe. How right you are, my dear Martin! All is but illusion and calamity."

He fell into a black melancholy and took no part in the opera *à la mode* or the other diversions of the carnival; not one lady caused him the least temptation. Martin said to him:

"Truly you are very simple to imagine that a half-breed valet who has five or six millions in his pockets will go find your mistress at the end of the world and bring her to you in

2   Of Gibraltar.

Venice. He will take her for himself if he finds her. If he does not find her, he will take another. I advise you to forget your valet Cacambo and your mistress Cunégonde."

Martin was not consoling. Candide's melancholy increased, and Martin never stopped proving to him that there was little virtue and little happiness on earth, except perhaps in Eldorado, where no one could go.

While arguing about this important matter and waiting for Cunégonde, Candide noticed a young Theatine* monk in the Piazza San Marco arm-in-arm with a girl. The Theatine looked fresh, plump, vigorous; his eyes were brilliant, his manner assured, his head erect, his bearing proud. The girl was very pretty and was singing; she looked lovingly at her Theatine, and from time to time pinched his plump cheeks.

"You will admit to me at least," said Candide to Martin, "that these people are happy; up to now I have found, in all the habitable earth except Eldorado, nothing but unfortunates; but as for that girl and that Theatine, I wager they are very happy creatures."

"I wager they're not," said Martin.

"We have only to ask them to dinner," said Candide, "and you'll see whether I'm wrong."

Immediately he accosts them, pays them his compliments, and invites them to come to his inn and eat macaroni, Lombardy partridges, and caviar, and drink Montepulciano, Lacryma Christi, Cyprus and Samos wine. The lady blushed, the Theatine accepted the invitation, and the girl followed him, looking at Candide with eyes full of surprise and confusion and dimmed with a few tears. Hardly had she entered Candide's room when she said to him: "What! Monsieur Candide no longer recognizes Paquette!"

At these words Candide, who had not looked at her with any attention until then, because he was preoccupied only with Cunégonde, said to her:

"Alas! my poor child, so it was you who put Doctor Pangloss in the fine state in which I saw him?"

"Alas! sir, I myself," said Paquette; "I see that you are informed about everything. I learned about the frightful misfortunes that happened to the whole household of My Lady the Baroness and to the fair Cunégonde. I swear to you that my destiny has been hardly less sad. I was very innocent when you knew me. A Franciscan who was my confessor easily

seduced me. The consequences were frightful; I was obliged
to leave the castle a little while after My Lord the Baron had
sent you away with great kicks in the backside. If a famous
doctor had not taken pity on me I would have died. For some
time out of gratitude I was that doctor's mistress. His wife,
who was madly jealous, used to beat me pitilessly every day,
she was a fury. This doctor was the ugliest of all men, and I
the unhappiest of all creatures at being beaten continually
because of a man I did not love. You know, sir, how dangerous it is for a shrewish woman to be a doctor's wife. This
man, outraged at his wife's ways, one day gave her, to cure
her of a little cold, a medicine so efficacious that she died of it
in two hours' time in horrible convulsions. My lady's relatives
brought a criminal suit against the gentleman; he took flight,
and I was put in prison. My innocence would not have saved
me if I had not been rather pretty. The judge turned me loose
on condition that he would succeed the doctor. I was soon
supplemented by a rival, tossed out with no compensation, and
obliged to continue this abominable occupation which seems
so amusing to you men and which for us is but an abyss of
misery. I went to Venice to practice the profession. Ah! sir,
if you could imagine what it is to be obliged to caress in-
discriminately an old merchant, a lawyer, a monk, a gondolier,
an abbé; to be exposed to every insult, every outrage; to be
often reduced to borrowing a skirt in order to go have it lifted
by some disgusting man; to be robbed by one of what you
have earned with the other; to be forced by the officers of the
law to buy protection, and to have in prospect nothing but
a frightful old age, a hospital, and a dunghill—you would
conclude that I am one of the unhappiest creatures in the
world."

Thus Paquette opened her heart to the good Candide in a
private room in the presence of Martin, who said to Candide:

"You see, I have already won half my wager."

Friar Giroflée had remained in the dining room and was
having a drink while waiting for dinner.

"But," said Candide to Paquette, "you looked so gay, so
happy, when I met you, you were singing, you were caressing
the Theatine with natural complaisance; you seemed to me as
happy as you claim to be unfortunate."

"Ah! sir," replied Paquette, "that is still another of the
miseries of the trade. Yesterday I was robbed and beaten by

an officer, and today I have to appear in a good humor to please a monk."

Candide had enough, he admitted that Martin was right. They sat down to table with Paquette and the Theatine; the meal was rather entertaining; and toward the end they talked to each other with some frankness.

"Father," said Candide to the monk, "you seem to me to enjoy a destiny that everyone must envy; the flower of health shines on your face,[1] your physiognomy bespeaks happiness, you have a very pretty girl for your recreation, and you seem very content with your condition as a Theatine."

"Faith, sir," said Friar Giroflée, "I wish all Theatines were at the bottom of the sea. I have been tempted a hundred times to set fire to the monastery and go turn Turk. My parents forced me at the age of fifteen to put on this detestable robe, in order to leave a greater fortune to an accursed older brother whom God confound! Jealousy, discord, rage inhabit the monastery. It is true, I have preached a few bad sermons that have brought me in a little money, half of which the prior steals from me; the rest serves me to keep girls; but when I go back to the monastery in the evening I am ready to smash my head against the dormitory walls; and all my colleagues are in the same state."

Martin, turning toward Candide with his customary coolness, said to him: "Well! Haven't I won the whole wager?"

Candide gave two thousand piasters to Paquette and a thousand piasters to Friar Giroflée. "I warrant you," he said, "with this they will be happy."

"I don't believe it in the very least," said Martin; "perhaps with these piasters you will make them much unhappier yet."

"That will be as it may," said Candide. "But one thing consoles me: I see that we often find people again whom we never thought to find; it may well be that having met up with my red sheep and Paquette, I shall also meet Cunégonde again."

"I hope," said Martin, "that she may someday be the making of your happiness; but that is something I strongly doubt."

"You are very hard," said Candide.

"That's because I have lived," said Martin.

1 In French, the monk's name means *gillyflower* or *wallflower*, while that of Paquette means *daisy*.

"But look at these gondoliers," said Candide. "Aren't they always singing?"

"You don't see them at home, with their wives and their brats of children," said Martin. "The Doge has his troubles, the gondoliers have theirs. It is true that taken all in all the lot of a gondolier is preferable to that of a doge; but I think the difference is so slight that it is not worth examining."

"They speak," said Candide, "of Senator Pococurante,[2] who lives in that handsome palace on the Brenta, and who receives foreigners rather well. They claim he is a man who has never known grief."

"I would like to see so rare a species," said Martin.

Candide immediately sent to ask Lord Pococurante for permission to come to see him the next day.

25 *Visit to the Venetian Nobleman, Lord Pococurante*

CANDIDE AND MARTIN took a gondola onto the Brenta and arrived at the palace of the noble Pococurante. The gardens were well conceived and adorned with handsome marble statues; the architecture of the palace was fine. The master of the house, a man of sixty, very rich, received the two sight-seers very politely but with very little enthusiasm, which disconcerted Candide and did not displease Martin.

First two pretty, neatly dressed girls served chocolate, well prepared with whipped cream. Candide could not refrain from praising them for their beauty, their grace, and their skill.

"They are pretty good creatures," said Senator Pococurante; "I sometimes take them to bed with me, for I am very tired of the town ladies, their coquetries, their jealousies, their quarrels, their humors, their pettinesses, their pride, their follies, and the sonnets one must compose on order for them; but after all, these two girls are beginning to bore me a lot."

Candide, walking after breakfast in a long gallery, was surprised by the beauty of the pictures. He asked what master had painted the first two.

"They are by Raphael," said the senator; "I bought them a few years ago at a very high price out of vanity; they say they are the finest things in Italy, but I do not like them at all;

2   From the Italian: "caring little."

their color has become very dark; the figures are not rounded enough and do not stand out enough; the draperies are not at all like cloth. In a word, no matter what they say, I do not find in them a true imitation of nature. I will like a picture only when I think I am seeing nature itself; and there are none of that kind. I have many pictures, but I no longer look at them."

While waiting for dinner, Pococurante had a concerto played for him. Candide found the music delightful.

"That noise," said Pococurante, "can be entertaining for half an hour, but if it lasts longer, it tires everyone, though no one dares admit it. Music today is merely the art of executing difficult things; and in the long run what is merely difficult is not pleasing. Perhaps I would like opera better, if they had not found the secret of making it a monster that revolts me. Let those who wish go to see bad tragedies set to music, where the scenes are composed only to bring in very clumsily two or three ridiculous songs which show off an actress's vocal cords. Let those who will, or who can, swoon with pleasure at seeing a eunuch hum the part of Caesar or Cato and tread the boards awkwardly. As for me, it has been a long time since I gave up these trivialities, which today are the glory of Italy and for which sovereigns pay so dear."

Candide argued a little, but with discretion. Martin was entirely in agreement with the senator.

They sat down to table, and after an excellent dinner they went into the library. Candide, seeing a magnificently bound Homer, praised the Illustrissimo on his good taste.

"That," he said, "is a book that was the delight of the great Pangloss, the best philosopher in Germany."

"It is no delight to me," said Pococurante coldly. "Once I was made to believe I took pleasure in reading it.[1] But that continual repetition of combats that are all alike, those gods that are always active and never do anything decisive, that Helen who is the subject of the war and who has hardly any part in the action, that Troy which is always besieged and never taken—all that caused me the most deadly boredom. I have sometimes asked learned men whether they were as

1 Pococurante's opinions are not to be taken for Voltaire's, but they often express Voltaire's sense of the weaknesses of the great. Virgil was generally much preferred to Homer until the nineteenth century. Ariosto and Tasso were favorites of Voltaire's.

bored as I was in reading it. All the sincere ones admitted to me that the book fell out of their hands, but that you always had to have it in your library, like an ancient monument, or like those rusty coins which cannot be used in commerce."

"Your Excellency does not think the same thing about Virgil?" said Candide.

"I admit," said Pococurante, "that the second, fourth, and sixth books of his *Aeneid* are excellent; but as for his pious Aeneas and strong Cloanthes and faithful Achates and little Ascanius and the imbecile King Latinus and middle-class Amata and insipid Lavinia, I do not believe there is anything so frigid or more disagreeable. I prefer Tasso and the fantastic fairy tales of Ariosto."

"Might I venture to ask you, sir," said Candide, "if you do not take great pleasure in reading Horace?"

"There are some maxims in him," said Pococurante, "that can profit a man of the world, and which, being compressed into energetic verses, engrave themselves the more easily on the memory. But I care very little about his journey to Brundisium or his description of a bad dinner, or the ruffians' quarrel between someone named Pupilus,[2] whose words, he said, were full of pus, and another whose words were vinegar. I have read only with extreme disgust his gross verses against old women and against witches; and I do not see what merit there can be in telling his friend Maecenas that if he is placed by him among the lyric poets he will strike the stars with his lofty brow. Fools admire everything in a noted author. I read only for myself, I like only what I have use for."

Candide, who had been brought up never to judge anything for himself, was greatly astonished at what he heard, and Martin considered Pococurante's way of thinking rather reasonable.

"Oh, here is a Cicero," said Candide. "Now as for that great man, I suppose you never tire of reading him?"

"I never read him," replied the Venetian. "What do I care whether he pleaded for Rabirius or for Cluentius? I have quite enough with the cases that I judge; I would have made out better with his philosophical works, but when I saw that he doubted everything, I concluded that I knew as much about it as he did, and that I did not need help from anyone in order to be ignorant."

2   Should be Rupilius. See *Satires*, I, vii.

"Ah, there are eighty volumes of proceedings of an Academy of Sciences," exclaimed Martin; "there may be something good there."

"There would be," said Pococurante, "if a single one of the authors of that rubbish had invented even the art of making pins; but in all those volumes there is nothing but empty systems and not a single useful thing."

"What a lot of plays I see here," said Candide, "in Italian, Spanish, and French!"

"Yes," said the senator, "there are three thousand of them and not three dozen good ones. As for these collections of sermons, which all together are not worth one page of Seneca, and all these great volumes of theology, you may well suppose that I never open them, not I nor anyone else."

Martin noticed some shelves loaded with English books. "I suppose," he said, "a republican must enjoy most of those works written with so much freedom."

"Yes," replied Pococurante, "it is fine to write what you think; that is the privilege of man. In all this Italy of ours people write only what they do not think; those who inhabit the land of the Caesars and the Antonines dare not have an idea without the permission of a Dominican.[3] I would be glad of the freedom that inspires English geniuses, if passion and factionalism did not corrupt all that is estimable in that precious freedom."

Candide, noticing a Milton,[4] asked him if he did not regard that author as a great man.

"Who?" said Pococurante. "That barbarian who writes a long commentary on the first chapter of Genesis in ten books of harsh verses? That crude imitator of the Greeks, who disfigures the Creation and who, whereas Moses represents the eternal Being as producing the world by the word, has the Messiah take a great compass from a cupboard in Heaven to trace out his work? I should esteem the man who spoiled Tasso's Hell and Devil, who disguises Lucifer now as a toad, now as a pygmy, who has him repeat the same remarks a hundred times, who has him argue about theology, who, imitating in all seriousness the comical invention of firearms

3 The Inquisition was in the hands of the Dominicans.
4 Voltaire had much admiration for Milton, as he did for Shakespeare, but as time passed he became more and more critical of what he considered the barbarism of both.

in Ariosto, has the devils fire cannon in Heaven? Not I, nor anyone in Italy has been able to enjoy all these sad eccentricities; and the marriage of Sin and Death, and the snakes that Sin gives birth to, make any man vomit who has a little delicacy of taste; and his long description of a hospital is good only for a gravedigger. This obscure, bizarre, and disgusting poem was despised at its birth; I treat it today as it was treated in its own country by its contemporaries. Besides, I say what I think, and I worry very little whether others think as I do."

Candide was distressed by these remarks. He respected Homer, and he rather liked Milton.

"Alas!" he whispered to Martin. "I'm very much afraid that this man may have a sovereign contempt for our German poets."

"There would be no great harm in that," said Martin.

"Oh, what a superior man!" said Candide under his breath. "What a great genius this Pococurante is! Nothing can please him."

After they had thus passed all the books in review, they went down into the garden. Candide praised all its beauties.

"I know of nothing in such bad taste," said the master; "we have nothing but trifles here; but tomorrow I am going to have one planted on a nobler plan."

When the two sight-seers had taken leave of His Excellency, Candide said to Martin: "Well now, you will agree that there is the happiest of all men; for he is above everything he possesses."

"Don't you see," said Martin, "that he is disgusted with everything he possesses? Plato said a long time ago that the best stomachs are not those which refuse all food."

"But," said Candide, "isn't there pleasure in criticizing everything, in sensing defects where other men think they see beauties?"

"That is to say," retorted Martin, "that there is pleasure in taking no pleasure?"

"Oh well!" said Candide, "then there is no one happy except me—when I see Mademoiselle Cunégonde again."

"It is always a good thing to hope," said Martin.

However, the days, the weeks passed by; Cacambo still did not come back, and Candide was so sunk in his sorrow that

he did not even notice that Paquette and Friar Giroflée had
not so much as come to thank him.

26 Of a Supper That Candide and Martin Had with Six Foreigners, and Who These Were

ONE EVENING when Candide, followed by Martin, was going
to sit down to table with the foreigners who were staying in
the same hotel, a man with a soot-colored face came up to
him from behind and, taking him by the arm, said: "Be ready
to leave with us, do not fail."

He turns around and sees Cacambo. Only the sight of Cunégonde could have astounded and pleased him more. He was
on the point of going mad with joy. He embraced his dear
friend.

"Then doubtless Cunégonde is here? Where is she? Take
me to her, let me die of joy with her."

"Cunégonde is not here," said Cacambo, "she is in Constantinople."

"Oh heavens! In Constantinople! But were she in China, I
fly to her, let's go."

"We will leave after supper," said Cacambo; "I cannot tell
you any more; I am a slave, my master is waiting for me, I
must go and serve him at table. Don't say a word; have supper
and be ready."

Candide, torn between joy and sorrow, charmed to see his
faithful agent again, astounded to see him a slave, full of the
idea of recovering his mistress, his heart agitated and his mind
topsy-turvy, sat down to table with Martin, who observed all
these adventures imperturbably, and with six foreigners who
had come to spend the Carnival in Venice.

Cacambo, who was pouring drink for one of these six foreigners, got his master's ear toward the end of the meal and
said to him: "Sire, Your Majesty will leave when you wish,
the vessel is ready." Having said these words he went out.

The guests, astonished, looked at each other without uttering a single word, when another servant, coming up to his
master, said to him: "Sire, Your Majesty's chaise is in Padua,
and the boat is ready." The master made a sign, and the
servant left.

All the guests looked at each other again, and the general surprise redoubled. A third valet, also approaching a third foreigner, said to him: "Sire, believe me, Your Majesty must not remain here any longer; I am going to prepare everything." And immediately he disappeared.

By now Candide and Martin had no doubt that this was a Carnival masquerade. A fourth servant said to the fourth master: "Your Majesty will leave when you please," and went out like the others. The fifth valet said as much to the fifth master. But the sixth valet spoke differently to the sixth foreigner who was sitting with Candide; he said to him: "Faith, Sire, they won't give Your Majesty credit any more, nor me either; and we could well be locked up tonight, you and me; I am going to see to my own affairs; farewell."

All the servants having disappeared, the six foreigners, Candide, and Martin remained in deep silence. Finally Candide broke it:

"Gentlemen," he said, "this is a singular jest. Why are you all kings? For myself, I admit that neither Martin nor I am."

Cacambo's master then spoke up gravely and said in Italian: "I am not jesting, my name is Ahmed III.[1] I was Grand Sultan for several years; I dethroned my brother; my nephew dethroned me; my viziers* had their heads cut off; I am ending my days in the old scraglio. My nephew, the Grand Sultan Mahmud, allows me to travel sometimes for my health, and I have come to spend the Carnival in Venice."

A young man who was next to Ahmed spoke after him and said: "My name is Ivan; I was Emperor of all the Russias; I was dethroned in my cradle; my father and mother were locked up; I was brought up in prison; I sometimes have permission to travel, accompanied by those who guard me, and I have come to spend the Carnival in Venice."

The third said: "I am Charles Edward, King of England; my father ceded me his rights to the kingdom. I fought to maintain them; they tore the hearts out of eight hundred of my supporters and dashed them in their faces. I was put in prison; I am going to Rome to pay a visit to the King my father, who is dethroned like my grandfather and me; and I have come to spend the Carnival in Venice."

The fourth then took the floor and said: "I am King of the Poles; the fortunes of war have deprived me of my hereditary

1   All these kings are real.

states; my father underwent the same reverses; I resign my-self to Providence like Sultan Ahmed, Emperor Ivan, and King Charles Edward, whom God give long life; and I have come to spend the Carnival in Venice."

The fifth said: "I too am King of the Poles; I have lost my kingdom twice; but Providence has given me another state,[2] in which I have done more good than all the kings of the Sarmatians together have ever been able to do on the banks of the Vistula; I too resign myself to Providence; and I have come to spend the Carnival in Venice."

It remained for the sixth monarch to speak. "Gentlemen," said he, "I am not as great a lord as you; but even so I have been a King like anyone else. I am Theodore; I was elected King of Corsica; I have been called Your Majesty, and at present I am hardly called Sir. I have coined money, and I do not have a penny; I have had two secretaries of state, and I have scarcely a valet. I was once on a throne, and I was in prison for a long time in London, on the straw. I am much afraid I shall be treated the same way here, although I have come, like Your Majesties, to spend the Carnival in Venice."

The five other Kings listened to this speech with noble com-passion. Each of them gave King Theodore twenty sequins* to get clothes and shirts; and Candide presented him with a diamond worth two thousand sequins. "Who is this man," said the five Kings, "who is in a position to give a hundred times as much as each of us, and who gives it? Are you a King too, sir?"

"No, gentlemen, and I have no desire to be." [3]

At the moment when they were leaving the table, there arrived in the same hotel four Most Serene Highnesses, who had also lost their states by the fortunes of war, and who were coming to spend the rest of the Carnival in Venice. But Candide did not even take note of these newcomers; he was preoccupied only with going to find his dear Cunégonde in Constantinople.

2 Stanislas Leszczynski (1677–1766), father of the Queen of France, abdicated the throne of Poland in 1736, was made Duke of Lorraine, and did much good in and around Lunéville. The Sarmatians are the Slavs.

3 These three sentences (from " 'Who is this man' " on) are the final form that Voltaire intended, replacing the following:

" 'Who is this ordinary citizen,' said the five Kings, 'who is in a position to give a hundred times as much as each of us, and who gives it?' "

27 Candide's Voyage to Constantinople

THE FAITHFUL CACAMBO had already obtained an agreement with the Turkish captain who was about to take Sultan Ahmed back to Constantinople that he would take Candide and Martin on his ship. Both came on board after having prostrated themselves before his miserable Highness. On the way, Candide said to Martin:

"But those were six dethroned Kings that we had supper with, and besides, among those six Kings there was one to whom I gave alms. Maybe there are many other princes still more unfortunate. As for me, I have lost only a hundred sheep, and I am flying to Cunégonde's arms. My dear Martin, once again, Pangloss was right, all is well."

"I hope so," said Martin.

"But," said Candide, "that was a most implausible adventure we had in Venice. No one ever saw or heard of six dethroned Kings having supper together in an inn."

"That is no more extraordinary," said Martin, "than most of the things that have happened to us. It is very common for Kings to be dethroned; and as for the honor we had in having supper with them, it is a thing that does not deserve our attention. What does it matter whom you sup with, provided you make good cheer?" [1]

Scarcely was Candide in the ship when he threw his arms around the neck of his former valet, his friend Cacambo.

"Well," he said, "what is Cunégonde doing? Is she still a prodigy of beauty? Does she still love me? How is she? No doubt you bought her a palace in Constantinople?"

"My dear master," replied Cacambo, "Cunégonde is washing dishes on the banks of Propontis* for a prince who has very few dishes; she is a slave in the household of a former sovereign named Ragotsky,[2] to whom the Grand Turk gives three crowns a day in his refuge; but what is much sadder is that she has lost her beauty and become horribly ugly."

"Ah! beautiful or ugly," said Candide, "I am an honorable

---

1 This passage, from "it is a thing" on, is another change intended by Voltaire (cf. previous page, note 3) to replace this: " 'it is a trifle that does not deserve our attention.' "
2 A former prince of Transylvania.

91

man, and my duty is to love her always. But how can she be reduced to so abject a state with the five or six millions you brought her?"

"Well," said Cacambo, "did I not have to give two millions to Señor Don Fernando d'Ibaraa y Figueora y Mascarenes y Lampourdos y Souza, Governor of Buenos Aires, for permission to take Mademoiselle Cunégonde back? And did not a pirate bravely despoil us of all the rest? And did not that pirate take us to Cape Matapan, to Milo, to Nicaria, to Samos, to Petra, to the Dardanelles, to Marmora, to Scutari? Cunégonde and the old woman are servants with that prince I spoke to you about, and I am a slave of the dethroned Sultan."

"What a chain of frightful calamities one after another!" said Candide. "But after all, I still have a few diamonds. I shall easily deliver Cunégonde. It is a great pity that she has become so ugly."

Then, turning toward Martin, he said: "Which one do you think is the most to be pitied, Emperor Ahmed, Emperor Ivan, King Charles Edward, or I?"

"I know nothing about that," said Martin; "I would have to be inside your hearts to know."

"Ah!" said Candide, "if Pangloss were here, he would know and would tell us."

"I do not know," said Martin, "with what scales your Pangloss could have weighed the misfortunes of men and estimated their sorrows. All I presume is that there are millions of men on earth a hundred times more to be pitied than King Charles Edward, Emperor Ivan, and Sultan Ahmed."

"That might well be," said Candide.

They arrived in a few days in the Bosporus. Candide began by buying back Cacambo at a very high price; and without wasting time he flung himself into a galley with his companions to go to the shores of Propontis and find Cunégonde, however ugly she might be.

In the convict crew there were two galley slaves who rowed very badly, and from time to time the Levantine captain applied a few strokes of a bull's pizzle to their bare shoulders; Candide, from a natural impulse, looked at them more attentively than at the other galley slaves and went up to them in pity. Some features of their disfigured faces seemed to him to have some resemblance to Pangloss and to that hapless

CANDIDE 93

Jesuit, the Baron, Mademoiselle Cunégonde's brother. This idea touched and saddened him. He looked at them even more attentively. "Truly," he said to Cacambo, "if I had not seen Doctor Pangloss hanged, and if I had not had the misfortune to kill the Baron, I would think it is they that are rowing in this galley."

At the names "Baron" and "Pangloss" the two convicts uttered a loud cry, sat still on their bench, and dropped their oars. The Levantine captain ran up to them, and the lashes with the bull's pizzle redoubled.

"Stop, stop, my lord," cried Candide, "I will give you as much money as you want."

"What! It's Candide!" said one of the convicts.

"What! It's Candide!" said the other.

"Is it a dream?" said Candide. "Am I really awake? Am I in this galley? Is that My Lord the Baron, whom I killed? Is that Doctor Pangloss, whom I saw hanged?"

"It is indeed, it is indeed," they replied.

"What! Is this that great philosopher?" said Martin.

"Oh! Master Levantine Captain," said Candide, "how much money do you want for the ransom of My Lord of Thunderten-tronckh, one of the first barons of the Empire, and for Monsieur Pangloss, the most profound metaphysician of Germany?"

"Dog of a Christian," replied the Levantine captain, "since these two dogs of Christian convicts are barons and metaphysicians, which is no doubt a great dignity in their country, you shall give me fifty thousand sequins for them."

"You shall have them, sir; take me back like a flash to Constantinople, and you shall be paid on the spot. But no, take me to Mademoiselle Cunégonde."

The Levantine captain, at Candide's first offer, had already turned his prow toward the city, and he was making the oarsmen row faster than a bird cleaves the air.

Candide embraced the Baron and Pangloss a hundred times. "And how is it that I did not kill you, my dear Baron? And my dear Pangloss, how is it that you are alive after being hanged? And why are you both in the galleys in Turkey?"

"Is it really true that my dear sister is in this country?" said the Baron.

"Yes," replied Cacambo.

"So I see my dear Candide again," exclaimed Pangloss.

Candide introduced Martin and Cacambo to them. They all embraced, they all talked at once. The galley flew, they were already in the port. They sent for a Jew, to whom Candide sold for fifty thousand sequins a diamond of the value of a hundred thousand, and who swore to him by Abraham that he could not give any more. Candide immediately paid the ransom of the Baron and Pangloss. The latter threw himself at the feet of his liberator and bathed them with tears; the other thanked him with a nod and promised to repay him the money at the first opportunity. "But is it really possible that my sister is in Turkey?" he said.

"Nothing is so possible," retorted Cacambo, "since she is scouring dishes for a prince of Transylvania."

Immediately they sent for two Jews; Candide sold some more diamonds; and they all set out again in another galley to go and deliver Cunégonde.

28 *What Happened to Candide, Cunégonde, Pangloss, Martin, et Al.*

"ONCE AGAIN, pardon," said Candide to the Baron, "pardon me, Reverend Father, for having given you a great sword thrust through the body."

"Let's say no more about it," said the Baron; "I was a little too hasty, I admit; but since you want to know by what chance you saw me in the galleys, I will tell you. After being cured of my wound by the brother apothecary of the College, I was attacked and carried off by a party of Spaniards; they put me in prison in Buenos Aires at the time when my sister had just left. I asked to return to the Father General in Rome. I was named to go to Constantinople and serve as almoner with My Lord the Ambassador of France. Not a week after I had taken up my duties, I met, toward evening, a very attractive ichoglan.[1] It was very hot; the young man wanted to bathe; I took the opportunity to bathe too. I did not know that it was a capital crime for a Christian to be found stark naked with a young Moslem. A cadi* had me given a hundred strokes on the soles of my feet and condemned me to the galleys. I do not think a more horrible injustice has ever been

1   Page to the Sultan.

done. But I would certainly like to know why my sister is in the kitchen of a sovereign of Transylvania who is a refugee among the Turks."

"But you, my dear Pangloss," said Candide, "how can it be that I see you again?"

"It is true," said Pangloss, "that you saw me hanged; naturally I was supposed to be burned; but you remember there was a heavy downpour just when they were going to cook me; the storm was so violent that they despaired of lighting the fire; I was hanged because they could do no better; a surgeon bought my body, took me home, and dissected me. First he made a cross-shaped incision in me from the navel to the clavicle. No one could have been worse hanged than I had been. The Holy Inquisition's Executor of High Operations, who was a subdeacon, did indeed burn people marvelously, but he was not accustomed to hanging them; the rope was wet and slipped badly, it became knotted; in short, I was still breathing. The cross-shaped incision made me utter such a loud scream that my surgeon fell over backward and, thinking that he was dissecting the devil, he fled, half-dead from fear, and he fell again on the staircase as he fled. His wife came running from a nearby room at the noise; she saw me stretched out on the table with my cross-shaped incision; she was even more afraid than her husband, fled, and fell over him. When they had recovered a little, I heard the surgeon's wife say to the surgeon: 'My dear, what are you thinking of, dissecting a heretic? Don't you know that the devil is always in those people? I am going quickly to get a priest to exorcise him.'

"I shuddered at these words and collected the little strength I had left to call out: 'Have pity on me!' Finally the Portuguese barber [2] grew bolder; he sewed up my skin; his wife even took care of me; in two weeks I was on my feet. The barber found me a job and made me lackey to a knight of Malta who was going to Venice; but as this master had no money to pay me, I entered the service of a Venetian merchant and followed him to Constantinople.

"One day I took a notion to enter a mosque; there was no one there but an old imam* and a very pretty young devotee who was saying her prayers. Her bosom was fully uncovered; between her breasts she had a beautiful bouquet of tulips,

2   The surgeon.

roses, anemones, buttercups, hyacinths, and yellow primroses;
she dropped her bouquet; I picked it up, and I replaced it for
her with the most respectful eagerness. I was so long in replacing it for her that the imam grew angry, and, seeing that I
was a Christian, called for help. I was taken before the cadi,
who had me given a hundred strokes on the soles of the feet
and sent me to the galleys. I was chained precisely in the same
galley and on the same bench as My Lord the Baron. In this
galley there were four young men from Marseilles, five
Neapolitan priests, and two monks from Corfu, who told us
that similar adventures occurred every day. My Lord the
Baron claimed that he had suffered a greater injustice than I;
for my part I claimed that it was much more permissible to
replace a bouquet on a woman's bosom than to be stark naked
with an ichoglan. We were arguing unceasingly and receiving
twenty strokes a day of the bull's pizzle, when the concatenation of the events of this universe brought you into our
galley and you ransomed us."

"Well, my dear Pangloss," said Candide, "when you were
hanged, dissected, racked with blows, and rowing in the
galleys, did you still think that all was for the very best?"

"I am still of my first opinion," replied Pangloss; "for after
all I am a philosopher, it is not fitting for me to recant, for
Leibniz cannot be wrong, and besides, pre-established harmony is the finest thing in the world, like the plenum and
subtle matter."

29 How Candide Found Cunégonde and the Old Woman Again

WHILE CANDIDE, the Baron, Pangloss, Martin, and Cacambo
were relating their adventures, reasoning on the contingent or
noncontingent events of this universe, arguing about effects
and causes, moral and physical evil, free will and necessity,
and the consolations that may be experienced when one is in
the galleys in Turkey, they landed on the shore of Propontis at
the house of the prince of Transylvania. The first objects that
met their eyes were Cunégonde and the old woman, who were
spreading out towels on lines to dry.

The Baron paled at this sight. The tender lover Candide, on

seeing his fair Cunégonde dark-skinned, eyes bloodshot, flat-bosomed, cheeks wrinkled, arms red and rough, recoiled three steps in horror, and then advanced out of good manners. She embraced Candide and her brother; they embraced the old woman; Candide ransomed them both.

There was a little farm in the neighborhood; the old woman proposed to Candide that he buy it while waiting for the entire group to enjoy a better destiny. Cunégonde did not know that she had grown ugly, no one had told her so; she reminded Candide of his promises in so positive a tone that the good Candide did not refuse her. So he notified the Baron that he was going to marry his sister.

"I shall never endure," said the Baron, "such baseness on her part and such insolence on yours; no one shall ever re-proach me with that infamy; my sister's children would not be able to enter the chapters [1] of Germany. No, never shall my sister marry anyone but a baron of the Empire."

Cunégonde threw herself at his feet and bathed them with tears; he was inflexible.

"You maddest of madmen," said Candide, "I rescued you from the galleys, I paid your ransom, I paid your sister's too; she was washing dishes here, she is ugly, I am kind enough to make her my wife, and you still presume to oppose it; I would kill you again if I heeded my anger."

"You may kill me again," said the Baron, "but you shall not marry my sister while I am alive."

1 Knightly assemblies.

30 *Conclusion*

AT THE BOTTOM of his heart, Candide had no desire to marry Cunégonde. But the Baron's extreme impertinence determined him to clinch the marriage, and Cunégonde urged him on so eagerly that he could not retract. He consulted Pangloss, Martin, and the faithful Cacambo. Pangloss composed a fine memoir by which he proved that the Baron had no rights over his sister, and that according to all the laws of the Empire she could make a left-handed marriage [1] with Candide. Martin's

1 A morganatic marriage, giving no equality to the party of lower rank.

judgment was to throw the Baron in the sea; Cacambo decided that he should be returned to the Levantine captain and put back in the galleys, after which he would be sent by the first ship to the Father General in Rome. The plan was considered very good; the old woman approved it; they said nothing about it to his sister; for a little money the thing was carried out, and they had the pleasure of trapping a Jesuit and punishing the pride of a German Baron.

It was quite natural to imagine that after so many disasters Candide, married to his mistress and living with the philosopher Pangloss, the philosopher Martin, the prudent Cacambo, and the old woman, moreover having brought back so many diamonds from the land of the ancient Incas, would lead the most pleasant life in the world. But he was so cheated by the Jews [2] that he had nothing left but his little farm; his wife, becoming uglier every day, became shrewish and intolerable; the old woman was an invalid and was even more bad-humored than Cunégonde. Cacambo, who worked in the garden and who went and sold vegetables at Constantinople, was worn out with work and cursed his destiny. Pangloss was in despair at not shining in some university in Germany. As for Martin, he was firmly persuaded that a man is equally badly off anywhere; he took things patiently.

Candide, Martin, and Pangloss sometimes argued about metaphysics and morality. They often saw passing under the windows of the farm boats loaded with effendis,* pashas,* and cadis who were being sent into exile at Lemnos, Mitylene, and Erzerum. They saw other cadis arriving, other pashas, other effendis, who took the place of the exiles and were exiled in their turn. They saw properly impaled heads on their way to be presented to the Sublime Porte.[3] These sights redoubled their discourses; and when they were not arguing, the boredom was so excessive that one day the old woman dared to say to them:

"I would like to know which is worse—to be raped a hundred times by Negro pirates, have a buttock cut off, run the gantlet among the Bulgarians, be flogged and hanged in

2   Voltaire had suffered financial losses from the bankruptcies of Jewish bankers.
3   Originally, the gate of the Sultan's palace, where justice was once administered; hence, his government.

an auto-da-fé, be dissected, row in the galleys, in short to undergo all the miseries we have all been through—or to stay here doing nothing?"

"It's a great question," said Candide.

These remarks engendered new reflections, and Martin above all concluded that man was born to live in the convulsions of anxiety or the lethargy of boredom. Candide did not agree, but he asserted nothing. Pangloss admitted that he had always suffered horribly; but having once maintained that everything was wonderful, he still maintained it and believed not a bit of it.

One thing completely confirmed Martin in his detestable principles, made Candide hesitate more than ever, and embarrassed Pangloss: one day they saw coming to their farm Paquette and Friar Giroflée, who were in the utmost misery; they had very quickly gone through their three thousand piasters, had parted, made it up, quarreled, been put in prison, escaped, and finally Friar Giroflée had turned Turk. Paquette continued to ply her trade everywhere, and no longer earned anything at it.

"I had quite foreseen," said Martin to Candide, "that your presents would soon be dissipated and would only make them more miserable. You and Cacambo were once glutted with millions of piasters, and you are no happier than Friar Giroflée and Paquette."

"Aha!" said Pangloss to Paquette, "so heaven brings you back among us here, my poor child! Do you realize that you cost me the end of my nose, an eye, and an ear? Look at you now! Ah! What a world is this!"

This new adventure led them to philosophize more than ever.

In the neighborhood there was a very famous dervish* who was considered the best philosopher in Turkey; they went to consult him; Pangloss was the spokesman and said to him: "Master, we have come to ask you to tell us why such a strange animal as man was ever created."

"What are you meddling in?" said the dervish. "Is that your business?"

"But, Reverend Father," said Candide, "there is a horrible amount of evil on earth."

"What does it matter," said the dervish, "whether there is evil or good? When His Highness sends a ship to Egypt, is he bothered about whether the mice in the ship are comfortable or not?"

"Then what should we do?" said Pangloss.

"Hold your tongue," said the dervish.

"I flattered myself," said Pangloss, "that you and I would reason a bit together about effects and causes, the best of all possible worlds, the origin of evil, the nature of the soul, and pre-established harmony." At these words the dervish shut the door in their faces.

During this conversation the news had gone round that in Constantinople they had just strangled two viziers of the Divan* and the mufti* and impaled several of their friends. This catastrophe caused a great stir everywhere for a few hours. Pangloss, Candide, and Martin, returning to the little farm, came upon a good old man enjoying the fresh air by his door under a bower of orange trees. Pangloss, whose curiosity was as great as his love of reasoning, asked him the name of the mufti who had just been strangled.

"I know nothing about it," replied the good man, "and I have never known the name of any mufti or any vizier. I am entirely ignorant of the adventure that you are telling me about; I presume that in general those who meddle with public affairs sometimes perish miserably, and that they deserve it; but I never inquire what is going on in Constantinople; I content myself with sending there for sale the fruits of the garden that I cultivate."

Having said these words, he had the strangers come into his house; his two daughters and his two sons presented them with several kinds of sherbets which they made themselves, Turkish cream flavored with candied citron peel, oranges, lemons, limes, pineapples, pistachios, and Mocha coffee that had not been mixed with the bad coffee from Batavia and the West Indies. After which the two daughters of this good Moslem perfumed the beards of Candide, Pangloss, and Martin.

"You must have a vast and magnificent estate?" said Candide to the Turk.

"I have only twenty acres," replied the Turk; "I cultivate them with my children; work keeps away three great evils: boredom, vice, and need."

As Candide went back to his farm, he reflected deeply on the Turk's remarks. He said to Pangloss and Martin: "That good old man seems to me to have made himself a life far preferable to that of the six Kings with whom we had the honor of having supper."

"Great eminence," said Pangloss, "is very dangerous, according to the report of all philosophers. For after all Eglon,[4] King of the Moabites, was assassinated by Ehud; Absalom was hanged by his hair and pierced with three darts; King Nadab son of Jeroboam was killed by Baasha, King Elah by Zimri, Ahaziah by Jehu, Athaliah by Jehoiada; Kings Jehoiakim, Jeconiah, and Zedekiah became slaves. You know how Croesus perished, Astyages, Darius, Dionysius of Syracuse, Pyrrhus, Perseus, Hannibal, Jugurtha, Ariovistus, Caesar, Pompey, Nero, Otho, Vitellius, Domitian, Richard II of England, Edward II, Henry VI, Richard III, Mary Stuart, Charles I, the three Henrys of France, the Emperor Henry IV? You know . . ."

"I also know," said Candide, "that we must cultivate our garden."

"You are right," said Pangloss, "for when man was put in the Garden of Eden, he was put there *ut operaretur eum,* to work; which proves that man was not born for rest."

"Let us work without reasoning," said Martin, "it is the only way to make life endurable."

All the little society entered into this laudable plan; each one began to exercise his talents. The little piece of land produced much. True, Cunégonde was very ugly; but she became an excellent pastry cook; Paquette embroidered; the old woman took care of the linen. No one, not even Friar Giroflée, failed to perform some service; he was a very good carpenter, and even became an honorable man; and Pangloss sometimes said to Candide: "All events are linked together in the best of all possible worlds; for after all, if you had not been expelled from a fine castle with great kicks in the backside for love of Mademoiselle Cunégonde, if you had not been subjected to the Inquisition, if you had not traveled about America on foot, if you had not given the Baron a great blow with your sword, if you had not lost all your sheep from the good country of Eldorado, you would not be here eating candied citrons and pistachios."

"That is well said," replied Candide, "but we must cultivate our garden."

4   For this first group, of Old Testament rulers, see Judges 3, II Samuel 18, and I and II Kings.

Zadig

or DESTINY

An Oriental Tale

[1747]

APPROBATION

I the undersigned, who have passed myself off as a man of learning and even of wit, have read this manuscript, which, in spite of myself, I have found curious, amusing, moral, philosophic, worthy of pleasing even those who hate novels. So I have disparaged it and assured My Lord the Cadilesker [1] that it is a detestable work.

---

1   Turkish chief judge in charge of religion and laws, originally of the army. This Approbation is a dig at the elder Crébillon (1674–1762), rival of Voltaire in tragedy, and royal censor from 1735.

Dedicatory Epistle
to the Sultana Sheraa [2]
by Sadi [3]

The 18th of the month of Shewal, the year 837 of the Hegira

Delight of the eyes, torment of hearts, light of the mind, I
do not kiss the dust off your feet, because you hardly
ever walk, or you walk on Persian carpets or on roses. I
offer you the translation of a book by an ancient sage, who,
having the good fortune to have nothing to do, had that of
amusing himself by writing the story of Zadig, a work that
says more than it seems to say. I beg you to read it and
judge it; for though you are in the springtime of your life,
though every pleasure seeks you out, though you are
beautiful, and your talents add to your beauty; though you
are praised from morn to eve, and though for all these
reasons you have the right to have no common sense;
nevertheless your mind is very wise and your taste very keen,
and I have heard you reason better than old dervishes* with
long beards and pointed caps; you are discreet and you are
not suspicious; you are gentle without being weak; you are
beneficent with discrimination; you love your friends and
you make no enemies. Your wit never borrows its charms
from the darts of slander; you neither say nor do evil, in spite
of the prodigious facility you would have for it. Lastly,
your soul has always seemed to me as pure as your beauty.
You even have a little fund of philosophy, which has led
me to believe that you would have more taste than the next
lady for this work of a sage.

It was written first in ancient Chaldean, which neither you
nor I understand. It was translated into Arabic to amuse
the famous Sultan Ulugh Beg.[4] This was in the time when
the Arabs and the Persians were beginning to write *The
Thousand and One Nights, The Thousand and One Days,*
etc. Ulugh preferred to read *Zadig;* but the sultanas preferred
the *Thousand and Ones.*

---

2   A possible reference to Madame de Pompadour, mistress of
Louis XV.
3   A famous thirteenth-century Persian didactic poet.
4   Persian ruler and astronomer (1394–1449), grandson of
Timur the Lame (Tamerlane).

"How can you prefer," said the wise Ulugh, "stories that make no sense and mean nothing?"

"That is precisely why we like them," replied the sultanas.

I flatter myself that you will not be like them and that you will be a true Ulugh. I even hope that when you grow tired of general conversations, which are rather like the *Thousand and Ones,* except that they are less amusing, I may have a minute to have the honor of talking sense with you. If you had been Thalestris,[5] in the time of Scander son of Philip, if you had been the Queen of Sheba in the time of Suleiman, it would have been those kings who would have traveled to see you.

I pray the celestial virtues that your pleasures may be unmixed, your beauty lasting, and your happiness unending.

Sadi

✳

1 *The One-Eyed Man*

IN THE TIME of King Moabdar there was a young man in Babylon named Zadig, whose fine native disposition had been strengthened by education. Though young and rich, he knew how to moderate his passions; he had no affectation; he did not insist on always being right, and was able to respect human frailty. People were astonished to see that with all his wit he never railed insultingly at the vague, incoherent, loud remarks, the reckless slander, the ignorant pronouncements, the crude puns, the empty clamor of words, that were called conversation in Babylon. He had learned in the first book of Zoroaster that self-love is a balloon inflated with wind, whence tempests emerge when it has been pricked. Above all, Zadig did not pride himself on scorning and conquering women. He was generous; he was not afraid to oblige ingrates, in accordance with Zoroaster's great precept: "When you eat, give some food to the dogs, even if they bite you." He was as wise as a man can be, for he sought to live with the wise. Instructed in the sciences of the ancient

---

5 Queen of the Amazons, who proposed to Alexander the Great that she have a child by him. Scander is the Arabic name for Alexander, as is Suleiman for Solomon.

Chaldeans, he was not ignorant of the physical principles of nature, such as were then known, and knew of metaphysics what has been known in every age, that is to say very little. He was firmly convinced that the year was composed of three hundred and sixty-five and a quarter days, in spite of the new philosophy of his time, and that the sun was in the center of the world; and when the leading magi told him, with insulting loftiness, that his sentiments were bad, and that to believe that the sun revolved on its axis and that the year had twelve months was to be an enemy of the state, he kept silent without anger and without disdain.

Zadig, having great riches, and consequently friends, as well as health, an attractive face, a just and moderate mind, a sincere and noble heart, thought he could be happy. He was to marry Semire, whose beauty, birth, and fortune made her the best match in Babylon. He had a solid and virtuous affection for her, and Semire loved him passionately. They were close to the happy moment that was to unite them, when, walking together toward one of the gates of Babylon, under the palm trees which adorned the bank of the Euphrates, they saw coming toward them some men armed with sabers and arrows. These were the satellites of young Orcan,[1] nephew of a minister, whom his uncle's courtiers had led to believe that he was permitted to do anything. He had none of the graces or virtues of Zadig; but, thinking himself a much better man, he was desperate at not being preferred to him. This jealousy, which came from his vanity alone, made him think he was madly in love with Semire. He wanted to abduct her. The ravishers seized her, and, in the frenzy of their violence, wounded her, shedding the blood of a person the sight of whom would have melted the hearts of the tigers of Mount Imaus.* She pierced the heavens with her lamentations. She cried out:

"My dear husband! They are tearing me from the one I adore!"

She was not concerned with her own danger; she thought only of her dear Zadig. He, meanwhile, was defending her with all the strength that love and valor give. With the help of only two slaves, he put the ravishers to flight and took

1 This Oriental name is a near anagram of Rohan, the nobleman who in 1726 had Voltaire beaten by servants because of a quarrel.

Semire home, unconscious and bleeding. On opening her eyes she saw her deliverer and said:

"O Zadig! I loved you as my husband, now I love you as the man to whom I owe my honor and my life."

Never was there a heart more filled with gratitude than Semire's. Never did a more enchanting mouth express more touching feelings with those words of fire that are inspired by the sense of the greatest of good deeds and by the tenderest transports of the most rightful love. Her wound was slight; she was soon cured. Zadig was hurt more dangerously; an arrow that struck him near the eye had made a deep wound. Semire asked the gods for nothing but the cure of her beloved. Night and day her eyes were bathed in tears; she longed for the moment when those of Zadig could enjoy her glances; but an abscess that formed on the wounded eye gave rise to fears for the worst. They sent all the way to Memphis for the great Doctor Hermes, who came with a numerous retinue. He examined the sick man and declared that he would lose his eye; he even predicted the day and the hour when this dire accident would happen.

"If it had been the right eye," he said, "I would have cured it; but wounds in the left eye are incurable."

All Babylon, while lamenting Zadig's destiny, marveled at the depth of Hermes' knowledge. Two days later the abscess burst by itself; Zadig was completely cured. Hermes wrote a book in which he proved to him that he should not have been cured. Zadig did not read it; but as soon as he could go out, he prepared to visit the one who was his hope for happiness in life, and for whom alone he wanted to have eyes. Semire had been in the country for three days. On his way he learned that this fair lady, having declared for all to hear that she had an insurmountable aversion for one-eyed men, had just married Orcan the night before. At this news he fell down unconscious; his grief brought him to the brink of the grave; he was ill for a long time; but at last reason prevailed over his affliction, and the atrocity of what he was suffering even served to console him.

"Since I have been subjected," he said, "to such a cruel caprice on the part of a girl brought up at court, I must marry one of the townspeople."

He chose Azora, the best-behaved and best-born girl in the city; he married her and lived with her for a month in the sweet enjoyments of the most tender of unions. Only he noticed in her a touch of frivolity and a strong inclination always to think that the best-looking young men were those who possessed the most intelligence and virtue.

2 *The Nose*

ONE DAY Azora came back from a walk in great anger and uttering loud exclamations.

"What is the matter with you, my dear wife?" he said to her. "What can be putting you so out of temper?"

"Alas!" she said, "you would be as indignant as I if you had seen the spectacle I have just witnessed. I went to console the young widow Cosrou, who just erected a tomb two days ago to her young husband beside the stream that borders this meadow. In her grief she promised the gods to stay beside that tomb as long as the water of the stream flowed by it."

"Well," said Zadig, "there is an estimable woman who truly loved her husband!"

"Ah," retorted Azora, "if you only knew what she was doing when I paid her my visit!"

"What then, beautiful Azora?"

"She was having the course of the stream changed."

Azora launched into such long invectives, burst into such violent reproaches against the young widow, that Zadig did not like this great display of virtue.

He had a friend named Cador, who was one of those young men in whom his wife found more integrity and merit than in others; he took him into his confidence and made sure of his fidelity, as far as he could, by a considerable present. Azora, having spent two days in the country at the house of one of her friends, on the third day returned home. Servants in tears announced to her that her husband had died suddenly the night before, that they had not dared bring her this dire news, and that they had just buried Zadig in the tomb of his forefathers at the end of the garden. She wept, tore her hair, and swore she would die. In the evening Cador asked permission to speak to her, and they both wept. The next day they wept less and dined together. Cador

confided to her that his friend had left him the greater part
of his estate and gave her to understand that it would be his
happiness to share his fortune with her. The lady wept,
grew angry, grew mild; the supper was longer than the dinner;
they talked more confidingly; Azora sang the praises of the
deceased, but she admitted that he had defects from which
Cador was free.

In the middle of supper, Cador complained of a violent
pain in the spleen; the lady, worried and attentive, sent for
all the perfumed essences that she used, to see if there was
not one of them that was good for a pain in the spleen; she
was very sorry that the great Hermes was not still in Babylon;
she even deigned to touch the side where Cador felt such
sharp pains.

"Are you subject to this cruel malady?" she said to him
with compassion.

"It sometimes brings me to the brink of the grave," replied
Cador, "and there is only one single remedy that can relieve
me: to apply to my side the nose of a man who has died
the day before."

"That is a strange remedy," said Azora.

"No more strange," he replied, "than the sachets of Master
Arnou [1] against apoplexy."

This reason, combined with the young man's extreme merit,
finally convinced the lady.

"After all," said she, "when my husband passes from the
world of yesterday into the world of tomorrow over the
bridge Tchinavar, will the angel Asrael grant him passage
any the less because his nose is a little less long in the second
life than in the first?"

So she took a razor; she went to her husband's tomb,
watered it with her tears, and approached to cut off the nose
of Zadig, whom she found stretched out full length in the
tomb. Zadig gets up, holding his nose in one hand and
checking the razor with the other.

"Madame," he says to her, "hereafter don't cry out so
much against young Cosrou; the plan of cutting off my nose
is fully a match for that of changing the course of a stream."

1   Author's note: "There was at that time a Babylonian
named Arnou, who cured and prevented every sort of apoplexy—
in the newspapers—by a sachet hung round the neck." The reference is to Voltaire's French contemporary Arnoult.

3 *The Dog and the Horse*

ZADIG FOUND by experience that the first month of marriage as it is written in the book of Zend, is the honeymoon, and the second is the wormwood-moon. After a time he was obliged to repudiate Azora, who had become too difficult to live with, and he sought his happiness in the study of nature.

"Nothing is happier," he said, "than a philosopher who reads in this great book that God has put under our eyes. The truths that he discovers are his own; he nourishes and elevates his soul; he lives at peace; he fears nothing from men, and his tender wife does not come to cut off his nose."

Full of these ideas, he retired to a country house on the banks of the Euphrates. There he did not spend his time calculating how many inches of water flowed in one second under the arches of a bridge, or whether one cubic line [1] more of rain fell in the month of the Mouse than in the month of the Sheep. He did not contrive how to make silk out of spider webs or porcelain out of broken bottles; but he studied above all the properties of animals and plants, and he soon acquired a sagacity which revealed to him a thousand differences where other men see nothing but uniformity.

One day, walking near a little wood, he saw one of the Queen's eunuchs running up to him, followed by several officers who appeared greatly worried and who were running hither and thither like distracted men looking for their most precious possession, which they have lost.

"Young man," said the chief eunuch to him, "haven't you seen the Queen's dog?"

Zadig answered modestly: "It's a bitch, not a dog."

"You are right," returned the chief eunuch.

"It's a very small spaniel," added Zadig. "She has recently had puppies, she is lame in the left forefoot, and she has very long ears."

"Then you have seen her," said the chief eunuch, quite out of breath.

"No," replied Zadig, "I have never seen her, and I never knew the Queen had a bitch."

1   One-twelfth of an inch.

At precisely the same time, by an ordinary freak of fortune, the finest horse in the King's stable had escaped from the hands of a groom into the plains of Babylon. The chief huntsman and all the other officers were running after him with as much anxiety as the chief eunuch after the bitch. The chief huntsman addressed Zadig and asked him if he had not seen the King's horse go past.

"He is the horse that gallops best," said Zadig. "He is five feet high and has a very small hoof; his tail is three and a half feet long; the studs on his bit are of twenty-three carat gold, his shoes of eleven-pennyweight [2] silver."

"What road did he take? Where is he?" asked the chief huntsman.

"I haven't seen him," said Zadig, "and I have never heard of him."

The chief huntsman and the chief eunuch had no doubt that Zadig had stolen the King's horse and the Queen's bitch; they had him brought before the Assembly of the Grand Desterham,* which condemned him to the knout and to spend the rest of his days in Siberia. Scarcely was the judgment rendered when the horse and the bitch were found. The judges were in the painful necessity of reversing their decision. But they condemned Zadig to pay four hundred ounces of gold for having said he had not seen what he had seen; first he had to pay this fine; after which Zadig was permitted to plead his cause before the Council of the Grand Desterham. He spoke in these terms:

"Stars of justice, abysses of knowledge, mirrors of truth, you who have the weightiness of lead, the hardness of iron, the brilliance of the diamond, and much affinity with gold: since I am allowed to speak before this august assembly, I swear to you by Ormuzd that I have never seen the respectable bitch of the Queen or the sacred horse of the King of kings. Here is what happened to me.

"I was walking toward the little wood where I later met the venerable eunuch and the most illustrious chief huntsman. I saw on the sand the tracks of an animal, and I easily judged that they were those of a little dog. Long shallow furrows imprinted on little rises in the sand between the tracks of the paws informed me that it was a bitch whose dugs were hanging down, and that therefore she had had

2   That is, eleven-twelfths pure silver.

puppies a few days before. Other traces in a different direction, which seemed to have always skimmed the surface of the sand beside the forepaws, taught me that she had very long ears; and since I noticed that the sand was always less furrowed by one paw than by the three others, I understood that the bitch of our august Queen was a little lame, if I may venture to say so.

"As regards the horse of the King of kings, you shall know that while walking along the roads of this wood I perceived the marks of horseshoes, all equal distances apart. 'There,' I said, 'is a horse with a perfect gallop.' The dust on the trees, along this narrow road only seven feet wide, was brushed off a little right and left three and a half feet from the middle of the road. 'This horse,' I said, 'has a three and a half foot tail, which by its movements right and left has swept off this dust.' I saw beneath the trees, which formed a bower five feet high, leaves newly fallen from the branches; and I knew that this horse had touched them, and that thus he was five feet high. As for his bit, it must be of twenty-three carat gold, for he rubbed the studs of it against a stone which I recognized as a touchstone and which I tested. Lastly I judged by the marks his shoes left on another kind of pebbles that he was shod with eleven-pennyweight silver."

All the judges marveled at Zadig's profound and subtle discernment; the news of it came even to the King, and to the Queen. The talk was of nothing but Zadig in the antechambers, the chamber, and the cabinet;[3] and although several magi opined that he should be burned as a sorcerer, the King ordered that the fine of four hundred ounces of gold, to which he had been condemned, be returned to him. The clerk of the court, the ushers, the attorneys came to his house in grand apparel to bring him back his four hundred ounces; they retained only three hundred and ninety-eight of them for the costs of justice; and their valets asked for honoraria.

Zadig saw how dangerous it sometimes was to be too knowing, and promised himself firmly, at the first opportunity, not to say what he had seen.

The opportunity soon came. A prisoner of state escaped; he passed under the windows of Zadig's house. They ques-

3   The antechambers of the hall of justice; the King's chamber; the cabinet where the King holds council.

tioned Zadig, he answered nothing; but they proved to him that he had looked out the window. For this crime he was condemned to pay five hundred ounces of gold, and he thanked his judges for their indulgence, according to the custom of Babylon.

"Good heavens!" he said to himself, "what a catastrophe it is to walk in a wood where the Queen's bitch and the King's horse have passed! How dangerous it is to look out the window! And how difficult it is to be happy in this life!"

4 *The Envious Man*

ZADIG TRIED to console himself by philosophy and by friend- ship for the repeated harm that fortune had done him. In a suburb of Babylon he had a house, tastefully decorated, where he assembled all the arts and all the pleasures worthy of a gentleman. His library was open to all the learned in the morning, his table to good company in the evening; but he soon found out how dangerous learned men are; there arose a great dispute over a law of Zoroaster which forbade the eating of griffin.

"How can griffin be forbidden," said some, "if that animal does not exist?"

"It certainly must exist," said the others, "since Zoroaster does not want it to be eaten."

Zadig tried to reconcile them by saying:

"If there are griffins, let's not eat any; if there aren't any, we will eat even less of them; and thereby we shall all obey Zoroaster."

A scholar who had composed thirteen volumes on the properties of the griffin, and who moreover was a great theurgist, hastened to accuse Zadig before an archimagus named Yebor,[1] the stupidest of the Chaldeans and hence the most fanatical. This man would have had Zadig impaled for the greater glory of the sun and would therefore have recited the breviary of Zoroaster in a more satisfied tone of voice. Friend Cador (one friend is worth more than a thousand priests) went to see old Yebor and said to him:

1   Anagram of Boyer (Jean-François), bishop of Mirepoix, an active enemy of Voltaire.

"Long live the sun and the griffins; beware of punishing Zadig, he is a saint; he has griffins in his poultry yard and does not eat them; and his accuser is a heretic who dares to maintain that rabbits have cloven feet, and are not unclean." [2]

"Well," said Yebor, wagging his bald head, "we must impale Zadig for having had bad thoughts about griffins, and the other for having said bad things about rabbits."

Cador composed the matter by means of a maid of honor who had borne him a child and who had great influence in the College of the Magi. No one was impaled; whereat several doctors murmured and predicted the decadence of Babylon. Zadig exclaimed: "On what does happiness depend? Everything persecutes me in this world, even beings that do not exist." He cursed the learned, and decided henceforth to live only in good company.

He assembled at his home the finest men and the most attractive ladies of Babylon; he gave dainty suppers, often preceded by concerts, and animated by charming conversations from which he had managed to banish eagerness to display wit, which is the surest way to have none and to spoil the most brilliant society. Neither the choice of his friends nor that of his dishes was prompted by vanity; for in all things he preferred being to seeming, and thereby he attracted true consideration, to which he did not aspire.

Across from his house lived Arimaze, a person whose wicked soul was portrayed on his gross countenance. He was corroded with gall and puffed up with pride; and to top it all, he was a tedious would-be wit. Never having been able to succeed in society, he took his revenge by slandering it. For all his riches, he had trouble assembling flatterers at his house. The sound of the chariots that came to Zadig's house in the evening annoyed him, the sound of his praises irritated him even more. He sometimes went to Zadig's and sat down to table without being asked; there he spoiled all the enjoyment of the company, just as they say the harpies infect the foods they touch.

It happened one day that he wanted to give a party for a lady who, instead of accepting, went to supper at Zadig's. Another day, as he was chatting with Zadig in the palace, they met a minister of state who asked Zadig to supper and

2   Cf. Deuteronomy 14:6–7. In verse 12 of this chapter, in the French version used by Voltaire, eating of the griffin is forbidden.

did not ask Arimaze. The most implacable hatreds often have no more important bases. This man, who was called Envious in Babylon, tried to ruin Zadig, because he was called Happy. The opportunity of doing harm comes a hundred times a day, and that of doing good once a year, as Zoroaster says.

Envious went to the house of Zadig, who was walking in his gardens with two friends and a lady to whom he often paid gallant compliments with no other intention than that of paying them. The conversation concerned a war that the King had just concluded successfully against his vassal the Prince of Hyrcania. Zadig, who had demonstrated his courage in this short war, praised the King highly and the lady even more. He took his tablets and wrote four verses which he composed on the spot and gave to this fair person to read. His friends begged him to let them see or hear them; modesty, or rather an intelligent self-esteem, prevented him. He knew that impromptu verses are never good in the eyes of anyone but the lady in whose honor they are composed; he broke in two the sheet of the tablets on which he had just written and threw the two halves into a rosebush where his friends looked for them in vain. There followed a bit of rain, they went back to the house. Envious, who remained in the garden, searched so hard that he found one piece of the sheet. It had been broken in such a way that each half verse, which filled up the line, made sense and even made a verse of shorter measure; but by an even stranger chance, these little verses turned out to have a meaning that contained the most horrible insults against the King. They read thus:

> By all the greatest crimes
> Established on the throne
> In these our peaceful times
> He is the foe alone

Envious was happy for the first time in his life. He had in his hands the means of ruining a virtuous and attractive man. Full of this cruel joy, he had this satire, written in Zadig's hand, communicated to the King himself. Zadig was put in prison, himself, his two friends, and the lady. His trial was soon over without anyone's deigning to hear him. When he came to receive sentence, Envious was near where he passed

and told him in a very loud voice that his verses were
worthless. Zadig did not plume himself on being a good poet,
but he was in despair at being condemned as guilty of *lèse-
majesté*, and at seeing a beautiful lady and two friends held
in prison, for a crime he had not committed. He was not
allowed to speak, because his tablets spoke for him. Such
was the law of Babylon. So he had to go to his execution
through a curious crowd of whom not one dared to sym-
pathize with him and who came rushing up to study his
face and see if he would die with good grace. His relatives alone were distressed, for they were inheriting nothing.
Three-quarters of his estate was confiscated to the advantage
of the King, and the other quarter to the advantage of Envious.

In the time when he was preparing for death, the King's
parrot flew away from its balcony and alighted in Zadig's
garden on a rosebush. A peach had been carried there by the
wind from a nearby tree; it had fallen on a piece of writing
tablet and had stuck to it. The bird picked up the peach
and the tablet and brought and laid them on the monarch's
knees. The prince, curious, read on it some words that made
no sense and that seemed to be the ends of verses. He loved
poetry, and princes who love verses are always resourceful;
the adventure of his parrot set him thinking. The Queen,
who remembered what had been written on one piece of
Zadig's tablet, had it brought to her. They compared the two
pieces, which fitted together perfectly; then they read the
verses as Zadig had composed them:

By all the greatest crimes the earth is racked and sore.
Established on the throne, the King controls our sphere.
In these our peaceful times, 'tis only Love makes war.
He is the foe alone whom now men have to fear.

The King immediately ordered that Zadig be brought
before him, and his two friends and the fair lady released
from prison. Zadig cast himself face down on the ground at
the feet of the King and Queen; he begged their pardon
very humbly for having written bad verse; he spoke with so
much grace, wit, and good sense that the King and Queen
wanted to see him again. He came again, and they liked him
even more. He was given all the property of Envious, who
had accused him unjustly, but Zadig gave it all back; and

Envious was touched by nothing but the pleasure of not losing his property.

The King's esteem for Zadig increased day by day. He associated him in all his pleasures and consulted him on all his affairs. From then on the Queen regarded him with a graciousness that might become dangerous for herself, for her august husband the King, for Zadig, and for the kingdom. Zadig began to think it is not so difficult to be happy.

5 *The Generous Men*

THE TIME CAME to celebrate a great festival which came around every five years. It was the custom in Babylon to declare solemnly, at the end of five years, which citizen had done the most generous deed. The grandees and the magi were the judges. The chief satrap, charged with the care of the city, would set forth the finest actions that had taken place under his government. They put it to a vote; the King pronounced judgment. People came to this solemnity from the ends of the earth. The winner received from the monarch's hands a gold cup studded with precious stones, and the King said these words to him:

"Receive this prize for generosity, and may the gods give me many subjects like you!"

This memorable day having come, the King appeared on his throne, surrounded by the grandees, the magi, and the deputies of all the nations, who came to these games where glory was acquired not by swiftness of horses, not by strength of body, but by virtue. The chief satrap in a loud voice reported the actions that might entitle their authors to this inestimable prize. He did not speak of the magnanimity with which Zadig had returned all his fortune to Envious: this was not an action that deserved to compete for the prize.

He presented first a judge who, having made a citizen lose a considerable lawsuit by a mistake for which he was not even responsible, had given him all his property, which was of the value of what the other had lost.

He then produced a young man who, being madly in love with a girl whom he was going to marry, had given her up to a friend who was ready to die of love for her, and had also paid her dowry even while giving up the girl.

Then he brought forward a soldier who in the Hyrcanian war had given an even greater example of generosity. Some enemy soldiers were carrying off his mistress and he was defending her against them; someone came and told him that some other Hyrcanians were carrying off his mother a few steps away; weeping, he left his mistress and ran to deliver his mother; then he returned to his beloved and found her dying. He wanted to kill himself; his mother pointed out to him that she had no one but him to support her, and he had the courage to endure living.

The judges leaned in favor of this soldier. The King spoke up and said:

"His deed and those of the others are fine, but they do not astonish me; yesterday Zadig did one that did astonish me. A few days before, I had disgraced my minister and favorite Coreb. I was complaining of him violently, and all my courtiers were assuring me that I was too mild; it was a question who would tell me the most evil about Coreb. I asked Zadig what he thought, and he dared to say some good about him. I admit that I have seen in our histories examples of men paying for an error with their property, giving up a mistress, preferring a mother to a beloved; but I have never read that a courtier has spoken favorably of a minister in disgrace against whom his sovereign was angry. I give twenty thousand gold pieces to each of those whose generous actions have just been related, but I give the cup to Zadig."

"Sire," said Zadig, "it is Your Majesty alone that deserves the cup, it is you who have performed the most unheard-of act in that, being King, you did not grow angry with your slave when he opposed your passion."

All marveled at the King and at Zadig. The judge who had given his property, the lover who had married his mistress to his friend, the soldier who had preferred his mother's safety to that of his mistress, received the monarch's presents; they saw their names inscribed in the Book of Generous Men. Zadig got the cup. The King acquired the reputation of a good prince, which he did not keep long. That day was consecrated by feasts longer than the law provided for. The memory of it is still preserved in Asia. Zadig said: "So at last I am happy!" But he was mistaken.

6 The Minister

THE KING HAD LOST his prime minister.[1] He chose Zadig to fill
this position. All the fair ladies of Babylon applauded this
choice, for since the foundation of the empire there had
never been so young a minister. All the courtiers were angry;
Envious had to spit blood, and his nose swelled prodigiously.
Zadig, having thanked the King and Queen, went to thank
the parrot too.

"Beautiful bird," he said to him, "it is you who saved my
life and made me prime minister; Their Majesties' bitch and
horse had done me much harm, but you have done me even
more good. So that is what the destinies of men depend on!
But," he added, "so strange a happiness perhaps will vanish
soon."

The parrot answered: "Soon."

The word struck Zadig. However, since he was a good
natural scientist and did not believe that parrots were prophets,
he was soon reassured and began to carry out his ministry as
best he could.

He made everyone feel the sacred power of the laws and
no one feel the weight of his own dignity. He did not curb
freedom of speech in the Divan,* and each vizier* could have
an opinion without displeasing him. When he judged an affair, it was not he who judged, it was the law; but when the
law was too severe he tempered it; and when laws were
lacking, his equity created some that might have been taken
for Zoroaster's.

It is from him that the nations hold this great principle,
that it is better to risk saving a guilty man than to condemn
an innocent man. He believed that laws were made to help
citizens as much as to intimidate them. His principal talent

---

1   In all the editions before 1756, the present Chapters 6 and
7 formed a single chapter, "The Judgments." Instead of the first
five paragraphs of the present text (from "The King had lost" to
"taken for Zoroaster's."), the single chapter began as follows:
"Young as he was, he was set up as supreme judge of all the
tribunals of the empire. He filled this position like a man to whom
God had given knowledge and justice."

was to bring to light the truth, which all men seek to obscure. From the first days of his administration he put this great talent to use.

A famous merchant of Babylon had died in the Indies; he had made his two sons his heirs with equal portions, after having seen their sister married; and he left a present of thirty thousand gold pieces to the one of his two sons who should be judged to love him most. The elder built him a tomb, the younger increased his sister's dowry by part of his own inheritance. Everyone said: "It is the elder who loves his father better; the younger loves his sister better; the thirty thousand pieces belong to the elder."

Zadig sent for them both one after the other. He said to the elder: "Your father is not dead, he is cured of his last illness, he is coming back to Babylon."

"God be praised," replied the young man, "but that's a tomb that cost me a lot."

Zadig then said the same thing to the younger.

"God be praised," he replied, "I shall return all I have to my father, but I wish he would leave my sister what I gave her."

"You shall return nothing," said Zadig, "and you shall have the thirty thousand gold pieces; it is you who love your father best."

A very rich girl had made a promise of marriage to two magi, and after having received instructions from both for a few months, she found herself pregnant. They both wanted to marry her. "I shall take for my husband," she said, "whichever of the two has put me in a position to present the empire with a citizen."

"It was I who performed this good work," said one.

"It was I who had that privilege," said the other.

"Well," she replied, "I will recognize as father of the child the one who can give him the better education."

She gave birth to a son. Each of the magi wants to bring him up; the case is brought before Zadig. He sends for the two magi.

"What will you teach your pupil?" he asked the first.

"I will teach him," said the doctor, "the eight parts of speech, dialectics, astrology, demonomania; what is meant by substance and accident, abstract and concrete, monads and pre-established harmony."

"I," said the second, "shall try to make him just and worthy of having friends."

"Whether you are his father or not," declared Zadig, "you shall marry his mother." [2]

2   The rest of this chapter, the story of Irax, appeared in editions from 1749 to 1756, was then suppressed by Voltaire, and was restored only in the posthumous Kehl edition of 1785–1789.

At this point in the original story *Memnon* (the first version of *Zadig*), and at the end of the present chapter after the Irax story in two editions of *Zadig* in 1748 and 1749, appeared the following story. (We have changed the name "Memnon" to "Zadig.")

"Some time after, they brought before him a man juridically convicted of having committed a murder six years before. Two witnesses attested to having seen it; they indicated the place, the day, and the hour; they had not contradicted each other under interrogation. The accused had been the declared enemy of the dead man. Several persons had seen him go past armed on the road where the assassination had been committed; never had proofs been stronger; and yet this man protested his innocence with that air of truth that can counterbalance the proofs themselves in the eyes of an enlightened judge; but he could excite pity and not avoid condemnation; he did not complain of his judges; he merely accused his destiny, and he was resigned to death. Zadig had pity on him and undertook to discover the truth; he had the two informers brought before him one after the other. He said to the first:

" 'I know, my friend, that you are a good man and an irreproachable witness. You have done our country a great service by revealing the author of the murder that was committed six years ago, in winter, at the time of the solstice, at seven o'clock in the evening, before the very eyes of the sun.'

" 'My lord,' replied the accuser, 'I don't know what the solstice is, but it was the third day of the week and it was still bright sunlight.'

" 'Go in peace,' said Zadig to him, 'and always be a good man.'

"Then he sent for the other witness and said to him:

" 'May virtue accompany you in all your ways; you have glorified truth, and you deserve rewards for having convicted a citizen of an abominable murder that was committed six years ago by the sacred rays of the full moon, at the time when it was in the same sign and the same degree as the sun.'

" 'My lord,' replied the accuser, 'I know neither signs nor degrees; but there was the most beautiful full moon in the world at the time.'

"Then Zadig brought back the first witness and said to them both:

" 'You are scoundrels who have borne false witness against an innocent man; one asserts that the murder was committed at seven o'clock before the sun had gone under the horizon; and that day it had set before six. The other affirms that the deed was done by the light of the full moon, and that day there was no moon; you shall both be hanged for having been false witnesses and bad astronomers.' "

Every day complaints came to court against the itima-doulet [3] of Media, who was named Irax. He was a great lord who was not bad at bottom but who had been corrupted by vanity and voluptuousness. He rarely allowed anyone to speak to him, and never anyone to dare to contradict him. Peacocks are no more vain, doves no more voluptuous, tortoises less lazy. He breathed in nothing but false glory and false pleasures. Zadig undertook to correct him.

He sent him on behalf of the King a music master with twelve singers and twenty-four violinists, a steward with six cooks, and four chamberlains who were not to leave him for a moment. The King's order was that the following ceremony should be inviolably observed, and this is how things happened.

The first day, as soon as the voluptuous Irax was awake, the music master entered followed by the singers and the violinists; they sang a cantata that lasted two hours, and every three minutes this was the refrain:

> How great is his merit!
> What grandeur, what graces has he!
> How can My Lord bear it?
> How pleased with himself he must be!

After the performance of the cantata, a chamberlain delivered to him a harangue of three-quarters of an hour, in which he was praised expressly for all the good qualities he lacked. The harangue over, he was conducted to table to the sound of instruments. The dinner lasted three hours; as soon as he opened his mouth to speak, the first chamberlain said: "He will be right." Hardly had he uttered four words when the second chamberlain said: "He is right." The two other chamberlains burst into loud laughter at the witticisms that Irax had uttered or must have uttered. After dinner they repeated his cantata.

This first day seemed to him delightful, he thought that the King of kings was honoring him according to his merits. The second seemed to him less agreeable, the third was tiresome, the fourth was unbearable, the fifth was a torture; finally, exhausted at always hearing the song—

> How can My Lord bear it?
> How pleased with himself he must be!

3   First minister.

—at always hearing that he was right, and at being harangued every day at the same time, he wrote to court begging the King to deign to recall his chamberlains, his musicians, his steward; he promised thenceforth to be less vain and more diligent. He had himself flattered less, had fewer feasts, and was happier; for as the Sadder* says: always pleasure is no pleasure.

7 The Disputes and the Interviews [1]

IT WAS THEN that he showed every day the subtlety of his genius and the goodness of his soul; he was admired, and yet he was loved. He passed for the most fortunate of all men; the whole empire was full of his name; all the women made eyes at him; all the citizens celebrated his justice; the learned regarded him as their oracle, even the priests admitted that he knew more than the old archimagus Yebor. They were very far from prosecuting him about griffins; they believed only what seemed to him believable.

There was a great quarrel going on in Babylon which had lasted fifteen hundred years and which split the empire into two opinionated sects: one claimed that you must never enter the temple of Mithra except left foot first; the other held this custom in abomination and never entered except right foot first. They awaited the day of the solemn festival of the sacred fire to learn which sect would be favored by Zadig. The universe had its eyes on his two feet, and the whole city was in agitation and suspense. Zadig entered the temple by jumping with his two feet together, and then proved in an eloquent speech that the God of heaven and earth, with whom there is no respect of persons,[2] sets no

1   This chapter did not appear until 1756, when it replaced the following conclusion to the chapter ("The Judgments") which was the predecessor of the present Chapters 6 and 7:
"Every day Zadig showed the subtlety of his genius and the goodness of his soul; he was adored by the people and cherished by the King; the first setbacks of his life further increased his present felicity; but every night he had a dream that gave him some anxiety."
There follows most of the last two paragraphs of the present Chapter 7, from "It seemed to him" to the end.
2   Romans 2:11.

more store by the left leg than by the right leg. Envious and
his wife claimed that there were not enough figures in his
speech, that he had not made the mountains and hills dance
enough.[3]

"He is dry and lacks genius," said they. "In him you do not
see the ocean flee, or the stars fall, or the sun melt like wax;
he does not have the good Oriental style."

Zadig was content with having a reasonable style. Everyone was for him, not because he was on the right path, not
because he was reasonable, not because he was attractive, but
because he was grand vizier.

He ended just as happily the great lawsuit between the white
magi and the black magi. The whites maintained that it was an
impiety, when praying to God, to turn toward where the sun
rises in the winter; the blacks asserted that God abhorred the
prayers of men who turned toward where the sun sets in the
summer. Zadig ordained that people should turn whichever
way they wanted.

In this way he discovered the secret of expediting his
private and public affairs in the morning; the rest of the day
he occupied himself with embellishing Babylon. He had
tragedies performed at which people wept, and comedies at
which people laughed;[4] these had been out of fashion for a
long time, and he revived them because he had taste. He did
not claim to know more about it than the performing artists;
he rewarded them with benefits and distinctions, and he was
not secretly jealous of their talents. In the evening he highly
entertained the King, and especially the Queen. The King
said: "What a great minister!" The Queen said: "What an attractive minister!" And both added: "It would have been a
great pity if he had been hanged."

Never was a man in high position obliged to give so many
interviews to ladies. Most of them came to talk to him about
affairs they did not have, so as to have one with him. Envious'
wife presented herself among the first; she swore to him by
Mithra, by the Zend-Avesta, and by the sacred fire, that she
had detested her husband's conduct; she then confided to him
that her husband was a jealous brute; she gave him to under-

3   For these and the following figures, see for example Psalms
114:3-6; Isaiah 14:12, 54:10; Judith 16:15.
4   The *comédie larmoyante* (tearful comedy) of Nivelle de
La Chaussée was extremely popular in the 1740's.

stand that the gods were punishing him by refusing him the
precious effects of that sacred fire by which alone man is like
the immortals; she finally dropped her garter; Zadig picked it
up with his usual politeness, but did not put it back on the
lady's knee; and this slight fault, if such it is, was the cause
of the most horrible misfortunes. Zadig thought nothing about
it, and Envious' wife thought about it a great deal.

Other ladies presented themselves every day. The secret
annals of Babylon claim that he succumbed once, but that he
was quite astounded that he enjoyed his mistress without
pleasure and embraced her absent-mindedly. The lady to
whom, almost unawares, he gave these tokens of his protection, was a chambermaid of Queen Astarté. This tender
Babylonian girl said to herself, for consolation:

"That man must have a prodigious amount of business on
his mind, since he still thinks about it even while making
love."

In those moments when many people say nothing and
when others utter only sacred words, these words escaped
Zadig: "The Queen." The Babylonian girl thought that he had
at last come back to himself at a good moment and was saying
to her: "My Queen." But Zadig, still absent-minded, uttered
the name Astarté. The lady, who in these happy circumstances
interpreted everything to her own advantage, imagined that
that meant: "You are more beautiful than Queen Astarté."
She left Zadig's seraglio with very handsome presents. She
went and told her adventure to Mrs. Envious, who was her
intimate friend, and who was cruelly piqued at this preference:

"He did not even deign," she said, "to put this garter back
on for me. Here it is; I no longer wish to use it."

"Oh! oh!" said the lucky girl to Mrs. Envious, "you wear
the same garters as the Queen! So you get them from the same
maker?"

Mrs. Envious thought deeply, answered nothing, and went
to consult her husband Envious.

Meanwhile Zadig noticed that he was always absent-minded
when giving interviews and judging; he did not know how to
account for this; that was the only thing that troubled him.

He had a dream. It seemed to him that at first he was lying
on dry grass, some of which pricked and made him uncom-
fortable, and that then he was resting softly on a bed of roses

from which there emerged a snake that wounded him in the heart with its sharp, poisonous tongue.

"Alas," he said, "I have lain a long time on that dry and prickly grass, I am now on the bed of roses; but who will be the snake?"

8 *Jealousy*

ZADIG'S UNHAPPINESS came from his very happiness, and especially from his merit. Every day he had talks with the King and with his august wife Astarté. The charms of his conversation were further enhanced by that desire to please which is to wit as ornament is to beauty; his youth and graces imperceptibly made an impression on Astarté which she did not at first notice. Her passion grew in the bosom of innocence. Astarté gave herself up without fear or scruple to the pleasure of seeing and hearing a man dear to her husband and to the state; she never ceased praising him to the King; she talked about him to her women, who outdid even her praises; everything served to plunge deeper into her heart the arrow of which she was not aware. She gave Zadig presents in which there was more gallantry than she supposed; she thought she spoke to him only as a Queen content with his services, and sometimes the expressions she used were those of a woman capable of love.

Astarté was much more beautiful than that Semire who so hated one-eyed men and that other woman who had tried to cut off her husband's nose. Astarté's familiarity, her tender remarks at which she was beginning to blush, her eyes, which she wanted to turn aside, and which fixed themselves on his, kindled in Zadig's heart a fire that astounded him. He struggled; he called to his aid philosophy, which had always helped him; he derived from it only enlightenment and no relief. Duty, gratitude, sovereign majesty violated: these presented themselves to his eyes like avenging gods; he fought, he triumphed; but this victory, which had to be won every moment, cost him groans and tears. No longer did he dare speak to the Queen with that sweet liberty which had had so many charms for them both; his eyes would grow clouded, his

remarks constrained and disconnected; he would lower his
gaze; and when in spite of himself his eyes turned toward
Astarté, they would meet the Queen's, wet with tears and
darting arrows of flame. They seemed to say to each other:
"We adore each other and we fear to love each other; we both
burn with a fire which we condemn."

Zadig would leave her side bewildered, distracted, his heart
overloaded with a burden he could no longer bear. In the
violence of these agitations, he let his friend Cador penetrate
his secret, like a man who, having long endured attacks of
sharp pain, finally makes known his suffering by a cry torn
from him in a moment of greater anguish and by the cold
sweat that pours over his forehead.

Cador said to him:

"I have already discerned the feelings that you wanted to
hide from yourself; passions have symptoms that cannot be
mistaken. Judge, my dear Zadig, since I have read in your
heart, whether the King will not discover there a feeling that
is an offense against him. His only defect is that of being the
most jealous of men. You are resisting your passion with more
strength than the Queen is fighting hers, because you are a
philosopher and because you are Zadig. Astarté is a woman,
she lets her eyes speak with all the more imprudence because
she does not yet believe herself guilty. Unfortunately reassured about her innocence, she neglects necessary appearances. I shall tremble for her so long as she has nothing for
which to reproach herself. If there was an understanding between you, you could deceive all eyes; a budding and resisted
passion explodes; a satisfied love knows how to hide itself."

Zadig shuddered at the suggestion of betraying the King his
benefactor, and never was he more faithful to his prince than
when he was guilty of an involuntary crime against him.
Meanwhile the Queen pronounced Zadig's name so often, her
face blushed so as she pronounced it, she was now so animated, now so dumfounded, when she spoke to him in the
presence of the King, she fell into so deep a reverie when he
had left, that the King was troubled. He believed all he saw
and imagined all he did not see. He noticed especially that his
wife's slippers were blue and Zadig's slippers were blue; that
his wife's ribbons were yellow and Zadig's cap was yellow:
these were terrible indications for a prince of delicate sensibility. Suspicions turned to certainty in his embittered mind.

All the slaves of kings and queens are so many spies on their hearts. It was soon discovered that Astarté was tender and that Moabdar was jealous. Envious persuaded his wife to send the King her garter, which resembled the Queen's. As a crowning misfortune this garter was blue. The monarch no longer thought of anything but the manner of his revenge. He resolved one night to poison the Queen, and have Zadig strangled, at daybreak. The order was given to a pitiless eunuch, executor of his vengeances.

There was in the King's room then a little dwarf who was dumb but not deaf. He was always allowed everywhere; he witnessed the most secret things that happened, like a domestic animal. This little mute was very attached to the Queen and Zadig. He heard the order for their death given, with as much surprise as horror. But what could he do to anticipate this frightful order, which would be carried out in a very few hours? He did not know how to write, but he had learned to paint, and above all he could draw a good likeness. He spent part of the night penciling what he wanted the Queen to understand. His drawing showed the King beside himself with fury, in one corner of the picture, giving orders to his eunuch; a blue cord, and a vase on a table, with blue garters and yellow ribbons; the Queen in the middle of the picture dying in the arms of her women, and Zadig strangled at her feet. The horizon showed the rising sun, to indicate that this horrible execution was to be performed at the first rays of dawn. As soon as he had finished this work, he ran to one of Astarté's women, waked her, and made her understand that she must take this picture to the Queen that very moment.

In the middle of the night someone comes knocking at Zadig's door, wakes him, gives him a note from the Queen; he wonders if it is a dream; he opens the letter with a trembling hand. What was his surprise, and who could express the consternation and despair that overwhelmed him, when he read these words:

"Flee this very moment, or your life will be taken. Flee, Zadig, I command you in the name of our love and my yellow ribbons. I was not guilty, but I feel that I am going to die a criminal!"

Zadig had scarcely strength to speak. He ordered Cador sent for, and without saying a word gave him the note. Cador forced him to obey and take the road to Memphis at once.

"If you dare go to find the Queen," he said to him, "you hasten her death; if you speak to the King, you also ruin her. I charge myself with her destiny; follow your own. I shall spread the rumor that you have taken the road to India. I will soon come to find you and tell you what has happened in Babylon."

Cador, that very moment, had two of the swiftest racing dromedaries posted by a secret door of the palace; he had Zadig mount, who had to be carried and was ready to give up the ghost. One single servant accompanied him, and soon Cador, plunged in astonishment and grief, lost sight of his friend.

This illustrious fugitive, arriving on the side of a hill from which you could see Babylon, turned his gaze to the palace of the Queen, and fainted; he regained consciousness only to shed tears and wish for death. At last, after brooding over the deplorable destiny of the most attractive of women and the greatest Queen in the world, he turned his thoughts back to himself for a moment and exclaimed:

"What then is human life? O virtue! of what use have you been to me? Two women have unworthily deceived me; the third, who is not guilty, and who is more beautiful than the others, is about to die! All the good I have done has always been a curse to me, and I have been raised to the pinnacle of greatness only to fall into the most horrible abyss of misfortune. If I had been wicked, like so many others, I would be happy like them."

Overwhelmed by these gloomy reflections, his eyes shrouded with the veil of sorrow, the pallor of death on his face, and his soul sunk in the depths of dark despair, he continued his journey toward Egypt.

9   *The Beaten Woman*

ZADIG SET HIS COURSE by the stars. The constellation of Orion and the brilliant star Sirius guided him toward the pole of Canopus.[1] He marveled at these vast globes of light which to our eyes appear to be only feeble sparks, whereas the earth,

1   Toward the south.

which is in fact only an imperceptible point in nature, appears to our cupidity as something so great and so noble. He then visualized men as they really are, insects devouring one another on a little atom of mud. This true picture seemed to annihilate his misfortunes by retracing for him the nullity of his own being and of Babylon. His soul flew up into the infinite and, detached from his senses, contemplated the immutable order of the universe. But when later, returning to himself and looking into his own heart again, he thought how Astarté was perhaps dead for his sake, the universe disappeared from before his eyes, and he saw nothing in all of nature but Astarté dying and Zadig miserable.

As he gave himself up to this ebb and flow of sublime philosophy and overwhelming grief, he was advancing toward the frontiers of Egypt; and already his faithful servant was in the first village looking for lodging. Zadig meanwhile was walking toward the gardens that bordered this village. He saw not far from the highroad a woman in tears calling on heaven and earth for help, and a furious man pursuing her. He had already caught up with her; she was clasping his knees. The man was overwhelming her with blows and reproaches. Zadig judged by the Egyptian's violence and the lady's repeated requests for pardon that the man was jealous and the woman unfaithful; but when he had contemplated this woman, who was of touching beauty and who even looked a little like the unhappy Astarté, he felt himself moved to compassion for her and horror for the Egyptian.

"Help me," she cried to Zadig amid sobs; "deliver me from the hands of the most barbarous of men; save my life."

At these cries Zadig ran and threw himself between her and this barbarian. He had some knowledge of Egyptian. He said to him in that language:

"If you have any humanity, I conjure you to respect beauty and weakness. How can you thus outrage a masterpiece of nature, who is at your feet and who has only tears for her defense?"

"Aha!" said the frenzied man, "so you love her too, and you are the man on whom I must take vengeance."

So saying, he leaves the lady, whom he was holding by the hair with one hand, and taking his lance, he tries to pierce the stranger with it. Zadig, whose head was cool, easily avoids the frenzied blow. He seizes the lance near the iron tip. One tries to pull it back, the other to take it away. It breaks between their hands. The Egyptian draws his sword, Zadig pulls out his. They attack each other. The one strikes a hundred hasty blows; the other parries them skillfully. The lady, seated on a lawn, fixes her hair and watches them. The Egyptian was more robust than his adversary, Zadig was more adroit; he fought like a man whose head directed his arm, and the other like a madman whose blind anger guided his movements at random. Zadig makes a thrust at him and disarms him; and while the Egyptian, madder than ever, tries to throw himself upon him, he seizes him, grips him tight, brings him down, holding his sword to his chest, offers to grant him his life. The Egyptian, beside himself, draws his dagger; he wounds Zadig with it at the very same time that the victor was pardoning him. Zadig, indignant, plunges his sword into his breast. The Egyptian utters a horrible cry and dies in convulsions.

Zadig then advanced toward the lady and said to her in a submissive voice:

"He forced me to kill him; I have avenged you; you are delivered from the most violent man I have ever seen. What do you want of me now, Madame?"

"I want you to die, you scoundrel," she answered, "I want you to die; you have killed my lover; I wish I could tear your heart out."

"Truly, Madame, that was a strange man you had for a lover," answered Zadig; "he was beating you with all his might and he wanted to take my life because you conjured me to help you."

"I wish he were still beating me," replied the lady, screaming. "I certainly deserved it, I had given him cause for jealousy. Would to Heaven that he were beating me and that you were in his place!"

Zadig, more surprised and more angry than he had ever been in his life, said to her:

"Madame, beautiful as you are, you are so preposterous that you really deserve to have me beat you in my turn; but I will not take the trouble."

Thereupon he mounted his camel again and advanced toward the village. Hardly had he taken a few steps when he turned around at the noise made by four couriers from Babylon. They were coming at full speed. One of them, seeing this woman, cried out: "That's the one; she looks just like the description they gave us." They did not bother about the dead man, and immediately seized the lady. She never stopped crying out to Zadig:

"Help me once more, generous stranger; I beg your pardon for having found fault with you. Help me, and I am yours until the tomb."

Zadig no longer had any desire to fight for her.

"Try someone else," he answered, "you won't catch me again."

Besides, he was wounded; his blood was flowing; he needed help; and the sight of the four Babylonians, probably sent by King Moabdar, filled him with anxiety. He advanced hastily toward the village, unable to imagine why four couriers from Babylon had come and seized this Egyptian woman, but even more astonished at the character of this lady.

10 *Slavery*

AS HE ENTERED the Egyptian village he found himself surrounded by the people. Everyone was crying out:

"There's the man who carried off the beautiful Missouf, and who has just assassinated Cletofis!"

"Gentlemen," he said, "God preserve me from ever carrying off your beautiful Missouf; she is too capricious; and as regards Cletofis, I did not assassinate him, I merely defended myself against him. He wanted to kill me because I had very humbly asked him for mercy on the beautiful Missouf, whom he was beating pitilessly. I am a foreigner coming to seek asylum in Egypt, and it is not likely that in coming to ask your protection I should have begun by carrying off a woman and assassinating a man."

At that time the Egyptians were just and humane. The people conducted Zadig to the town hall. They began by dressing his wound, and then they questioned him and his servant separately to learn the truth. They acknowledged that Zadig was not a murderer at all; but he was guilty of a man's blood; the law condemned him to be a slave. They sold his two camels for the benefit of the village. They distributed among the inhabitants all the gold he had brought; his person was exposed for sale in the public square along with that of his traveling companion.

An Arab merchant named Setoc bid for them; but the servant, better fitted for hard labor, was sold at a much higher price than the master. They found no comparison between the two men. So Zadig was a slave subordinate to his servant; they fastened them together with a chain passed around their feet, and in this state they followed the Arab merchant to his home. On the way Zadig consoled his servant and exhorted him to patience; but according to his custom, he made some reflections on human life.

"I see," he said to him, "that the misfortunes of my destiny spread over yours. Everything up to now has turned out in a very strange way for me. I was condemned to a fine for seeing a bitch pass by; I was almost impaled over a griffin; I was sent to execution because I had written verses in praise of the King; I was on the point of being strangled because the Queen had yellow ribbons; and here I am a slave with you because a brute beat his mistress. Come, let's not lose heart; perhaps all this will end; Arab merchants must necessarily have slaves, and why should I not be one just like anyone else, since I am a man just like anyone else? This merchant will not be pitiless; he must treat his slaves well if he wants to get service out of them."

He spoke thus; and at the bottom of his heart he was preoccupied with the fate of the Queen of Babylon.

Setoc, the merchant, left two days later for Arabia Deserta with his slaves and his camels. His tribe lived near the desert of Horeb. The road was long and difficult. On the way Setoc set much more store by the servant than by the master, because the former was much better at loading camels; and all the little distinctions were for him.

A camel died two days this side of Horeb; they divided its load onto the back of each of the servants; Zadig got his share. Setoc began to laugh on seeing all his slaves walk bent over. Zadig took the liberty of explaining this to him, and taught him the laws of equilibrium. The merchant, astonished, began to regard him with a different eye. Zadig, seeing that he had excited his curiosity, redoubled it by teaching him many things that were not foreign to his trade: the specific gravities of metals and goods of equal bulk, the properties of several useful animals, the way to make useful those that were not; finally he seemed to him a sage. Setoc gave him the preference over his comrade, whom he had so esteemed. He treated him well, and had no cause to repent of it.

Back among his tribe, the first thing Setoc did was to ask to have five hundred ounces of silver back from a Hebrew to whom he had lent them in the presence of two witnesses; but these two witnesses had died, and the Hebrew, who could not be convicted, was appropriating the merchant's money while thanking God for having given him the means of cheating an Arab. Setoc confided his trouble to Zadig, who had become his adviser.

"In what place," asked Zadig, "did you lend your five hundred ounces to this infidel?"

"On a big stone," replied the merchant, "near Mount Horeb."

"What is the character of your debtor?" said Zadig.

"He's a rogue," retorted Setoc.

"But I want to know whether he is quick or phlegmatic, cautious or imprudent."

"Of all men who don't pay their debts," said Setoc, "he is the hastiest man I know."

"Well," insisted Zadig, "allow me to plead your cause before the judge."

And indeed he summoned the Hebrew to the tribunal and spoke thus to the judge:

"Pillow of the throne of equity, I come to ask back from this man, in the name of my master, five hundred ounces of silver that he will not give back."

"Have you witnesses?" said the judge.

"No, they are dead; but there remains a big stone on which the money was counted out; and if it please Your Greatness to order someone to go get the stone, I hope it will bear witness. The Hebrew and I will stay here and wait for the stone to come; I will send for it at the expense of my master Setoc."

"Very well," said the judge, and he set about expediting other business.

At the end of the day's hearings, he said to Zadig:

"Well, hasn't your stone come yet?"

The Hebrew, laughing, answered:

"Your Greatness could wait here till tomorrow and the stone would still not have arrived; it is more than six miles from here, and it would take fifteen men to move it."

"Well," cried Zadig, "I told you the stone would bear witness; since this man knows where it is, he admits that it was the one on which the money was counted out."

The Hebrew, disconcerted, was soon constrained to admit everything. The judge ordered that he be bound to the stone without food or drink until he had returned the five hundred ounces, which were soon paid.

The slave Zadig and the stone were held in high esteem in Arabia.

11 *The Funeral Pyre*

SETOC, ENCHANTED, made his slave his intimate friend. He could no more get along without him than could the King of Babylon before; and Zadig was glad that Setoc had no wife. He discovered in his master a natural inclination to goodness, much uprightness and good sense. He was sorry to see that he worshiped the celestial army—that is to say the sun, moon, and stars—according to the old practice in Arabia. He talked to him about it sometimes with much discretion. Finally he said to him that they were bodies just like others, which no more deserved his homage than a tree or a rock.

"But," said Setoc, "they are eternal beings from whom we derive all our advantages; they animate nature, they regulate the seasons; moreover they are so far from us that one cannot help revering them."

"You receive more advantages," said Zadig, "from the waters of the Red Sea, which bears your merchandise to the Indies. Why should it not be as old as the stars? And if you worship what is distant from you, you should worship the land of the Ganges, which is at the ends of the world."

"No," said Setoc, "the stars are too brilliant for me not to worship them."

When evening came, Zadig lit a large number of torches in the tent where he was to sup with Setoc; and as soon as his master appeared, he threw himself on his knees before these lighted tapers and said to them:

"Eternal and shining lights, be always propitious to me."

Having uttered these words, he sat down to table without glancing at Setoc.

"What *are* you doing?" said Setoc, astonished.

"I am doing as you do," replied Zadig; "I worship these candles, and neglect their master and mine."

Setoc understood the deep meaning of this parable. The wisdom of his slave entered his soul; he no longer lavished his incense on created things, and worshiped the eternal Being who created them.

There was at that time in Arabia a frightful custom which came originally from Scythia and which, having established itself in India through the authority of the Brahmans, threatened to invade the whole Orient. When a married man had died and his well-beloved wife wanted to be holy, she burned herself in public on her husband's body. It was a solemn festival that was called The Pyre of Widowhood. The tribe in which there had been the most women burned was the most esteemed.

An Arab of Setoc's tribe having died, his widow, named Almona, who was very pious, made known the day and hour when she would throw herself into the fire to the sound of drums and trumpets. Zadig remonstrated to Setoc how contrary this horrible custom was to the good of the human race; that every day they were letting young widows be burned who could give children to the state or at least bring up their own; and he made him agree that so barbaric a practice should, if possible, be abolished. Setoc replied:

"It has been more than a thousand years now that women have had the privilege of burning themselves. Which one of us shall dare to change a law that time has consecrated? Is there anything more respectable than an ancient abuse?"

"Reason is more ancient," retorted Zadig. "Speak to the chiefs of the tribes, and I will go find the young widow."

He had himself introduced to her; and after having insinuated himself into her mind by praise of her beauty, after telling her what a pity it was to put so many charms into the fire, he praised her further for her constancy and courage.

"So you loved your husband prodigiously?" he said to her.

"I? Not at all," replied the Arab lady. "He was a jealous

brute, an unbearable man; but I am firmly resolved to throw myself on his funeral pyre."

"Apparently," said Zadig, "there must be a most delightful pleasure in being burned alive."

"Ah! it makes nature herself shudder," said the lady, "but one must go through with it. I am a pious woman; my reputation would be ruined, and everyone would laugh at me, if I did not burn myself."

Zadig, having got her to admit that she was burning herself for others and out of vanity, talked to her for a long time in such a way as to make her love life a little, and even managed to inspire in her some good will toward the man who was talking to her.

"Well, now, what would you do," he said to her, "if you were free of the vanity of burning yourself?"

"Alas!" said the lady, "I think I would ask you to marry me."

Zadig was too full of the idea of Astarté not to elude this declaration; but he went instantly to find the chiefs of the tribes, told them what had happened, and advised them to make a law whereby no widow would be allowed to burn herself until after having one full hour's tête-à-tête with a young man. From that time on no lady burned herself in Arabia. Everyone was under obligation to Zadig alone for having destroyed in one day so cruel a custom, which had lasted for so many centuries. Thus he was the benefactor of Arabia.

12 *The Supper*

SETOC, WHO COULD NOT part with this man in whom wisdom dwelt, took him to the great fair at Basra, where the greatest merchants of the habitable world were to gather. It was a palpable consolation to Zadig to see so many men from different countries gathered in the same place. It seemed to him that the universe was one big family assembling at Basra.

Already on the second day he found himself at table with an Egyptian, an Indian from the Ganges country, an inhabitant of Cathay, a Greek, a Celt, and several other foreigners, who in their frequent trips toward the Red Sea had learned enough Arabic to make themselves understood. The Egyptian seemed very angry.

"What an abominable country Basra is!" he said. "They refuse me a loan of a thousand ounces of gold here on the best security in the world!"

"How's that?" said Setoc. "On what security were you refused this sum?"

"On the body of my aunt," replied the Egyptian. "She was the finest woman in Egypt. She always accompanied me; she died on the road; I made her into one of the most beautiful mummies we have; and if I pawned her in my own country I could get anything I wanted. It is very strange that here they won't give me even a thousand ounces of gold on so solid a security."

Even as he gave vent to his anger, he was ready to eat an excellent boiled chicken, when the Indian, taking him by the hand, exclaimed sorrowfully:

"Oh! what are you going to do?"

"Eat some of this chicken," said the man with the mummy.

"Beware of doing that," said the man from the Ganges. "It might be that the soul of the dead woman has passed into the body of this chicken, and you would not want to expose yourself to eating your aunt. To cook chickens is a manifest outrage against nature."

"What do you mean with your nature and your chickens?" retorted the choleric Egyptian. "We worship a bull, but we eat beef just the same."

"You worship a bull! Is that possible?" said the man from the Ganges.

"Nothing is more possible," returned the other. "We have been doing so for a hundred and thirty-five thousand years, and no one of us finds anything wrong with it."

"Oh? A hundred and thirty-five thousand years?" said the Indian. "That count is a bit exaggerated; it is only eighty thousand years that India has been populated, and we are certainly your elders; and Brahma had forbidden us to eat oxen before it occurred to you to put them on altars and on spits."

"That Brahma of yours is a funny kind of animal to compare with Apis," said the Egyptian; "what did your Brahma do that was so fine?"

The Brahman replied: "It was he who taught men to read and write, and to whom the whole world owes the game of chess."

"You are wrong," said a Chaldean who was sitting near him, "it is the fish Oannes to whom we owe such great benefits; and it is just to pay our homage to him alone. Everyone will tell you that he was a divine Being, that he had a golden tail and a handsome human head, and that he left the water to come and preach on land for three hours every day. He had several children, who were kings, as everyone knows; I have his portrait at home, and I revere it as I should. One may eat all the beef one wants; but it is certainly a very great impiety to cook fish; moreover you are both of too common and too recent an origin to argue with me about anything. The Egyptian nation can count only a hundred and thirty-five thousand years, and the Indians boast of only eighty thousand, whereas we have almanacs for four thousand centuries. Believe me, renounce your follies, and I will give you each a handsome portrait of Oannes."

The man from Cambalu [1] spoke up and said: "I have great respect for the Egyptians, the Chaldeans, the Greeks, the Celts, Brahma, the bull Apis, the handsome fish Oannes; but perhaps Li or Tien,[2] whichever you wish to call him, is well worth the bulls and the fishes. I shall say nothing of my country; it is bigger than the land of Egypt, Chaldea, and India put together. I do not argue about antiquity, because it is enough to be happy and it is not much to be old; but if I had to speak about almanacs, I would say that all Asia takes ours and that we had very good ones before they knew arithmetic in Chaldea."

"You're a bunch of great ignoramuses, the whole lot of you," cried the Greek. "Don't you know that Chaos is the father of everything and that form and matter have put the world into its present state?"

The Greek spoke for a long time; but at last he was interrupted by the Celt, who, having drunk a good deal while they were arguing, now thought himself more learned than the others, and said with an oath that only Teutates and the oak-

---

1   The capital of Cathay, modern Peiping.
2   Author's note: "Chinese words which properly mean, *Li*, natural light, reason, and *Tien*, the heavens; and which also mean God."

mistletoe were worth talking about; that for his part he
always had some mistletoe in his pocket; that his ancestors
the Scythians were the only good people there had ever been
in the world; that they had indeed sometimes eaten men, but
that that did not mean we should not have much respect
for his nation; and finally that if anyone spoke ill of Teutates,
he would teach him how to behave.

Then the quarrel grew hot, and Setoc saw the moment
coming when the table would be covered with blood. Zadig,
who had kept silence during the whole dispute, finally rose.
He addressed the Celt first, as being the most furious; he told
him he was right, and asked him for some mistletoe; he
praised the Greek for his eloquence, and soothed all their
heated spirits. He said very little to the man from Cathay,
because he had been the most reasonable of all. Then he
said to them:

"My friends, you were about to quarrel over nothing, for
you are all of the same opinion."

At these words they all cried out in protest.

"Isn't it true," he said to the Celt, "that you do not
worship this mistletoe, but him who made the mistletoe and
the oak?"

"Assuredly," answered the Celt.

"And you, Mr. Egyptian, you apparently worship in a
certain bull him who gave you bulls?"

"Yes," said the Egyptian.

"The fish Oannes," he continued, "must give way before
him who made the sea and fish."

"Agreed," said the Chaldean.

"The Indian," he added, "and the Cathayan recognize
a First Principle as you do; I did not understand too well
the admirable things the Greek said, but I am sure that he
also admits a superior Being on whom form and matter depend."

The Greek, who was much admired, said that Zadig had
understood his thought very well.

"Then you are all of the same opinion," replied Zadig, "and
there is no reason for quarreling."

Everyone embraced him. Setoc, after selling his wares very
dear, took his friend Zadig back to his tribe. On arriving,
Zadig learned that he had been tried in his absence and was
going to be burned over a slow fire.

13 *The Assignations*

DURING HIS TRIP to Basra the priests of the stars had resolved to punish him. The precious stones and adornments of the young widows whom they sent to the funeral pyre belonged to them by right; it was certainly the least they could do to have Zadig burned for the bad turn he had done them. So they accused Zadig of having erroneous views about the celestial army; they testified against him under oath that they had heard him say that the stars did not set in the sea. This frightful blasphemy made the judges shudder; they were ready to tear their garments when they heard these impious words, and beyond doubt they would have done so if Zadig had had enough money to pay for them. But in the excess of their grief they contented themselves with condemning him to be burned over a slow fire.

Setoc, in despair, in vain used all his influence to try to save his friend; he was soon obliged to be silent. The young widow Almona, who had acquired quite a taste for life and who owed it to Zadig, resolved to deliver him from the stake, the abuse of which he had taught her. She turned over her plan in her head without speaking to anyone about it. Zadig was to be executed the next day; she had only the night in which to save him: here is how, as a charitable and prudent woman, she went about it.

She perfumed herself; she set off her beauty by the richest and most seductive attire, and went and asked a secret interview of the chief of the priests of the stars. When she was before this venerable old man, she spoke to him in these terms:

"Eldest son of the Great Bear, brother of the Bull, cousin of the Great Dog Star (these were the pontiff's titles), I come to confide to you my scruples. I am much afraid I have committed an enormous sin in not burning myself on my dear husband's funeral pyre. Indeed, what did I have to preserve? Perishable flesh, which is already all withered." As she said these words she drew from her long silk sleeves her bare arms, admirable in shape and dazzling in whiteness. "You see," she said, "how little this is worth."

The pontiff thought in his heart that this was worth a great deal. His eyes said so, and his mouth confirmed it; he swore he had never in his life seen such beautiful arms.

"Alas!" said the widow, "the arms may be a little less bad than the rest, but you will admit that the bosom is not worth my attention." Then she revealed the most charming breast that nature had ever formed. A rosebud on an ivory apple would have seemed in comparison like madder on boxwood, and lambs coming from the washing place would have seemed brownish yellow. This bosom, her great black eyes which shone softly and languishingly with a tender fire, her cheeks animated with the fairest crimson mingled with the white of the purest milk, her nose which was not like the Tower of Mount Lebanon,[1] her lips which were like two coral borders enclosing the loveliest pearls of the Arabian Sea—all this together made the old man think he was twenty. He stammered out a tender declaration. Almona, seeing him inflamed, asked him for mercy for Zadig.

"Alas!" he said, "my lovely lady, even if I granted you his pardon, my indulgence would be of no use to you; it must be signed by three others of my colleagues."

"Sign anyway," said Almona.

"Gladly," said the priest, "on condition that your favors will be the price of my complaisance."

"You do me too much honor," said Almona; "only be pleased to come to my chamber after the sun has set and as soon as the bright star Scheat is on the horizon. You will find me on a rose-colored sofa, and you will deal with your servant as you may."[2]

She then went out, taking along the signature, and left the old man full of love and of mistrust of his powers. He spent the rest of the day bathing himself; he drank a liquor composed of cinnamon from Ceylon and precious spices from Tidor and Ternate, and waited impatiently for the star Scheat to appear.

Meanwhile the beauteous Almona went to find the second pontiff, who assured her that the sun, moon, and all the fires of the firmament were but will-o'-the-wisps compared with

---

1   Cf. Song of Solomon 7:4: "thy nose is as the tower of Lebanon which looketh toward Damascus."
2   Or, "you will use it as you may with your servant." Voltaire's play on words here seems untranslatable.

her charms. She begged the same mercy of him, and he
proposed that she give the same price. She let herself be won
over, and gave the second pontiff an assignation at the rising
of the star Algenib. From there she passed to the third and
the fourth priests, each time getting a signature and giving
an assignation from star to star. Then she sent word to the
judges to come to her house on important business. They
came; she showed them the four names and told them at
what a price the priests had sold mercy for Zadig; each of
these arrived at the appointed hour. Each one was quite
astonished to find his colleagues, and even more to find the
judges, before whom their shame was manifested.

Zadig was saved. Setoc was so charmed with Almona's
ability that he made her his wife.[3]

3 The next two chapters (14, "The Dance"; 15, "Blue Eyes")
were never included in *Zadig* until the posthumous Kehl edition.
Voltaire presumably wrote them but may not have intended to include them. These chapters replaced the following ending to this
chapter, which forms a transition to the present Chapter 16 (originally 14), "The Brigand":
   "Zadig left after throwing himself at the feet of his lovely
liberator. Setoc and he parted weeping, swearing eternal friendship,
and promising each other that the first of the two to make a great
fortune would share it with the other.
   "Zadig walked in the direction of Syria, always thinking of the
unfortunate Astarté, and always reflecting on the fate that persisted in toying with him and persecuting him. 'What,' he said,
'four hundred ounces of gold for having seen a bitch pass by!
condemned to be decapitated for four bad verses in praise of the
King! ready to be strangled because the Queen had slippers the
same color as my cap! reduced to slavery for having rescued a
beaten woman! and on the point of being burned for having saved
the lives of all young Arab widows!' "

14 *The Dance*[1]

SETOC HAD TO go on business to the isle of Serendib;[2] but
the first month of marriage, which is, as we know, the honeymoon, allowed him neither to leave his wife nor to believe
he ever could leave her; he begged his friend Zadig to make
the journey for him.

"Alas!" said Zadig, "must I put another still greater dis-

1 See the preceding note.
2 Ceylon.

tance between the beautiful Astarté and me? But I must serve
my benefactors." He spoke, he wept, and he left.

He was not long in the isle of Serendib before he was
regarded as an extraordinary man. He became the arbiter of
all differences between merchants, the friend of the wise,
the adviser of the small number of people who take advice.
The King wanted to see and hear him. He soon recognized
all Zadig's worth; he put confidence in his wisdom, and made
him his friend. The King's familiarity and esteem made
Zadig tremble. Night and day he was deeply struck by the
misfortune that Moabdar's kindnesses had brought upon him.
"The King likes me," he said, "shall I not be ruined?" However, he could not escape His Majesty's favors; for it must
be admitted that Nabussan, King of Serendib, son of Nussanab, son of Nabassun, son of Sanbusna, was one of the
best princes in Asia, and that when you spoke to him it was
hard not to like him.

This good prince was always praised, deceived, and robbed;
everyone competed in pillaging his treasures. The chief tax
collector of the isle of Serendib always set this example,
which was faithfully followed by the others. The King knew
it; he had changed his treasurer many times, but he had
been unable to change the established custom of dividing
the King's revenues into two unequal parts of which the
smaller always went to His Majesty and the larger to the
administrators.

King Nabussan confided his trouble to the wise Zadig.
"You who know so many fine things," he said to him, "don't
you know a way to find me a treasurer who will not rob me?"

"Certainly," replied Zadig, "I know an infallible method of
giving you a man with clean hands."

The King, delighted, embraced him and asked him how he
should go about it.

"All you have to do," said Zadig, "is to have everyone
dance who presents himself for the dignity of treasurer, and
the one who dances most lightly will infallibly be the most
honest man."

"You are making fun of me," said the King; "that's a
queer way to choose a collector of my finances. What! You
claim that the man who can best do an *entrechat* will be the
ablest and most honest financier!"

"I do not answer for his being the ablest," returned Zadig,

"but I assure you that he will undubitably be the most honest."

Zadig spoke with so much confidence that the King thought he had some supernatural secret for knowing financiers.

"I do not love the supernatural," said Zadig; "I have never liked prodigies in people or in books. If Your Majesty will let me make the test I propose, you will be fully convinced that my secret is the simplest and easiest thing in the world."

Nabussan, King of Serendib, was much more astounded to hear that this secret was simple than if it had been given out to be a miracle.

"Very well then," he said, "do as you see fit."

"Leave it to me," said Zadig; "you will gain more than you think from this test."

That very day he had it published in the name of the King that all those who aspired to the post of High Receiver of the Pence of His Gracious Majesty Nabussan, son of Nussanab, should appear in clothes of light silk on the first day of the moon of the Crocodile in the King's antechamber. They appeared, sixty-four in number. Violinists had been brought into a neighboring drawing room; everything was ready for the ball; but the door to this drawing room was closed, and to enter it was necessary to pass through a rather dark little gallery. An usher came to get and lead each candidate, one after the other, into this passage, in which he was left alone for a few minutes. The King, who had the word, had spread out all his treasures in this gallery. When all the aspirants had arrived in the drawing room, His Majesty ordered that they be made to dance. Never did anyone dance more heavily and with less grace; they all had their heads bowed, their backs bent, their hands glued to their sides.

"What rascals!" said Zadig very low.

Only one of them executed his steps with agility, head high, glance assured, arms outstretched, body erect, legs firm.

"Ah! An honest man, a good man!" said Zadig.

The King embraced this good dancer and declared him treasurer. All the others were punished and taxed with the greatest justice in the world, for each one, in the time he had been in the gallery, had filled his pockets and could hardly walk. The King was grieved for human nature that out of these sixty-four dancers there were sixty-three thieves. The dark gallery was called The Corridor of Temptation. In Persia they would have impaled these sixty-three lords; in other countries they would have set up a chamber of justice which would have consumed in expenses three times the money stolen and would have put nothing back into the sovereign's coffers; in one other kingdom they would have fully justified themselves and had so light a dancer disgraced; in Serendib they were condemned merely to increase the public treasure, for Nabussan was very lenient.

He was very grateful; he gave Zadig a sum of money more considerable than any treasurer had ever stolen from the King his master. Zadig used it to send express couriers to Babylon to bring him information about Astarté's fate. His voice trembled as he gave the order, his blood ebbed toward his heart, his eyes were covered with shadows, his soul was ready to leave him. The courier left, Zadig saw him embark; he came back to the palace, seeing no one, thinking he was in his room, and uttering the word "love."

"Ah! love!" said the King. "That's just it; you have guessed the cause of my pain. What a great man you are! I hope you will teach me to recognize a woman whose fidelity could meet any test, just as you have led me to find a disinterested treasurer!"

Zadig, having regained his senses, promised to serve him in love as he had in finance, although the matter seemed even more difficult.

15 Blue Eyes[1]

"MY BODY and my heart . . ." said the King to Zadig.

At these words the Babylonian could not keep from interrupting His Majesty.

"How grateful I am to you," he said, "for not saying 'my mind and my heart'; for you hear nothing but those words in conversations in Babylon; you see nothing but books dealing with the heart and the mind, written by people who have neither. But I beg you, Sire, go on."

1   See note at end of Chapter 13.

Nabussan continued thus:

"My body and my heart are destined to love; the first of these two powers has every reason to be satisfied. I have here a hundred wives at my disposal, all beautiful, complaisant, eager to please, voluptuous even—or pretending to be so with me. My heart is nowhere near so happy. I have experienced only too clearly that there are many caresses for the King of Serendib and that they care very little about Nabussan. It is not that I think my wives unfaithful, but I would like to find one soul that was mine; for such a treasure I would give the hundred beauties whose charms I possess; see if among these hundred sultanas you can find me one by whom I can be sure to be loved."

Zadig answered him as he had done in the matter of the financiers: "Sire, leave it to me; but first let me dispose of what you had spread out in the Gallery of Temptation; I shall give you a good account of it, and you shall lose nothing by it."

The King left him absolute mastery. He chose in Serendib thirty-three of the ugliest little hunchbacks he could find, thirty-three of the handsomest pages, and thirty-three of the most eloquent and most robust bonzes.[2] He gave them all liberty to enter the sultanas' cells; each little hunchback had four thousand gold pieces to give away, and from the first day on all the hunchbacks were happy. The pages, who had nothing to give but themselves, triumphed only after two or three days. The bonzes had a little more trouble, but finally thirty-three pious women gave in to them. The King, through Venetian blinds that gave a view into all the cells, saw all these tests and was amazed. Of his hundred wives, ninety-nine succumbed before his eyes. There remained one, very young, brand new, whom His Majesty had never approached. They sent her one, two, three hunchbacks, who offered her as much as twenty thousand gold pieces; she was incorruptible, and could not keep from laughing at the idea these hunchbacks had that money would make them better built. They presented to her the two handsomest pages; she said she found the King even handsomer. They loosed on her the most eloquent of the bonzes, and then the most intrepid; she found the first a prattler and did not even deign to suspect the merit of the second.

2 Buddhist priests.

"The heart is all that matters," she said; "I shall never yield to a hunchback's gold, nor a youth's graces, nor a bonze's enticements; I shall love only Nabussan, son of Nussanab, and I shall wait until he deigns to love me."

The King was transported with joy, astonishment, and tenderness. He took back all the money that had made the hunchbacks successful and made a present of it to the beautiful Falide; that was the name of this young person. He gave her his heart; she well deserved it. Never was the flower of youth so brilliant; never were the charms of beauty so enchanting. Historical truth obliges me to mention that she curtsied badly, but she danced like the fairies, sang like the Sirens, and spoke like the Graces: she was full of talents and virtues.

Nabussan, loved at last, adored her; but she had blue eyes, and this was the source of the greatest misfortunes. There was an ancient law which forbade Kings to love one of those women whom the Greeks later called *boopis*.[3] The chief of the bonzes had established this law more than five thousand years before; it was to appropriate the mistress of the first King of the isle of Serendib that this first bonze had transferred this anathema on blue eyes into the fundamental constitution of the state. All the orders of the empire came to make remonstrances to Nabussan. It was said publicly that the last days of the kingdom had arrived, that this was the height of abomination, that all nature was threatened by a disastrous event—in a word, that Nabussan, son of Nussanab, loved two big blue eyes. The hunchbacks, the financiers, the bonzes, and the brunettes filled the kingdom with their complaints.

The savage races which live in the north of Serendib profited by this general discontent. They made an invasion into the states of the good Nabussan. He asked his subjects for subsidies; the bonzes, who owned half the revenues of the state, contented themselves with raising their hands to heaven, and refused to put them in their coffers to help the King. They chanted beautiful prayers to music, and left the state a prey to the barbarians.

"Oh my dear Zadig," cried Nabussan sorrowfully, "will you also get me out of this horrible mess?"

"Very gladly," replied Zadig. "You shall have as much of

3 βοῶπις: "ox-eyed."

the bonzes' money as you want. Leave the lands abandoned where their castles are, and defend only your own."

Nabussan did not fail to do this; the bonzes came and threw themselves at the King's feet and implored his assistance. The King answered them with a beautiful bit of music whose words were prayers to heaven for the preservation of their lands. The bonzes finally gave money, and the King brought the war to a happy end.

Thus Zadig, by his wise and successful advice, and by the greatest services, had drawn upon himself the irreconcilable enmity of the most powerful men in the state. The bonzes and the brunettes swore his ruin; the financiers and the hunchbacks did not spare him; he was made suspect to the good Nabussan. "Services rendered often remain in the antechamber, suspicions enter the cabinet," in the words of Zoroaster. Every day it was new accusations; the first is repulsed, the second brushes you, the third wounds, the fourth kills.

Zadig, intimidated, having done his friend Setoc's business well and got his money for him, now thought only of leaving the island, and resolved to go and seek news of Astarté himself.

"For," he said, "if I remain in Serendib, the bonzes will have me impaled. But where can I go? I shall be a slave in Egypt, in all likelihood burned in Arabia, strangled in Babylon. However, I must know what has become of Astarté; let's go and see what my sad destiny has in store for me." [4]

16 *The Brigand*

ON REACHING the frontier that separates Arabia Petraea from Syria, as he was passing near a rather strong castle, some

[4] In the Kehl edition, where this and the previous chapter first appeared, there followed this note:

"This is the end of the rediscovered manuscript of the story of Zadig. These two chapters should certainly be placed after the twelfth and before the arrival of Zadig in Syria. It is known that he suffered many other adventures that have been faithfully written down. We beg the gentlemen who interpret Oriental languages to communicate these if they come to their knowledge."

armed Arabs came out. He saw himself surrounded; they
cried out to him:

"Everything you have belongs to us, and your person
belongs to our master."

In reply, Zadig drew his sword; his valet, who had courage,
did the same. They knocked over dead the first Arabs who
laid hands on them; the number redoubled, they were not
daunted and resolved to die fighting. One could see two men
defending themselves against a multitude; such a combat
could not last long. The master of the castle, Arbogad by
name, having seen from a window the prodigies of valor
performed by Zadig, conceived an esteem for him. He came
down in haste and himself dispersed his men and delivered
the two travelers.

"Everything that passes over my lands is mine," he said,
"as well as what I find on the lands of others; but you seem
to me such a brave man that I exempt you from the common
law." He had him enter his castle, ordering his men to treat
him well; and in the evening Arbogad decided to sup with
Zadig.

The lord of the castle was one of those Arabs who are
called robbers; but he sometimes did good deeds amid a
throng of bad ones; he stole with furious rapacity, and gave
liberally; intrepid in action, rather mild in company, de-
bauched at table, gay in debauchery, and above all full of
frankness. He was much pleased with Zadig, whose conversation, which grew animated, drew the meal out. Finally Arbogad said to him:

"I advise you to enroll in my service, you could not do
better; this trade is not bad, you may someday become what
I am."

"May I ask you," said Zadig, "how long you have practiced
this noble profession?"

"From my tenderest youth," replied the lord. "I was a valet
to a rather able Arab; my position was unendurable to me.
I was in despair to see that in all the earth, which belongs
equally to all men, destiny had not reserved me my share.
I confided my troubles to an old Arab, who said to me: 'My
son, do not despair; once upon a time there was a grain of
sand which lamented that it was an unknown atom in the
deserts; after a few years it became a diamond; and now it is
the fairest ornament in the crown of the King of India.'

"These words made an impression on me; I was the grain of sand, I resolved to become a diamond. I began by stealing two horses; I took some comrades in with me; I made myself capable of robbing small caravans; thus bit by bit I abolished the disproportion there had been at first between other men and me. I got my share of the goods of this world, and I was even rewarded with interest; I was much esteemed; I became a brigand chief; I acquired this castle by assault. The satrap of Syria wanted to dispossess me of it, but I was already too rich to have anything to fear; I gave some money to the satrap, in return for which I kept this castle, and I enlarged my domains; he even named me treasurer of the tributes that Arabia Petraea paid to the King of kings. I did my job as collector, and as payer not at all.

"The Grand Desterham* of Babylon sent a little satrap here in the name of King Moabdar to have me strangled. This man arrived with his orders; I was informed of everything; I had the four persons strangled in his presence whom he had brought with him to tighten the noose; after which I asked him how much the commission of strangling me might have been worth to him. He replied that his honorarium might amount to three hundred gold pieces. I made him see clearly that there would be more to gain with me. I made him under-brigand; today he is one of my best officers, and one of the richest. If you will take my word for it, you will succeed as he has. Never has the robbing season been better, now that Moabdar is killed and all is in confusion in Babylon."

"Moabdar is killed!" said Zadig. "And what has become of Queen Astarté?"

"I know nothing about that," replied Arbogad. "All I know is that Moabdar went mad, he was killed, Babylon is one great den of cutthroats, the whole empire is desolated, there are still nice jobs to do, and for my part I've pulled off some wonderful ones."

"But the Queen?" said Zadig. "I implore you, don't you know anything about the fate of the Queen?"

"I have heard talk of a prince of Hyrcania," he returned; "she is probably among his concubines, unless she was killed in the tumult; but I'm more interested in booty than in news. I have taken many women in my raids; I don't keep any of them; I sell them dear when they are beautiful, without inquiring who they are. People don't buy rank: a Queen that was ugly wouldn't find a purchaser; maybe I sold Queen Astarté, maybe she's dead; but it matters little to me, and I don't think you are likely to worry about it any more than I do."

So saying, he kept drinking so courageously, he got all his ideas so confused, that Zadig could get no enlightenment from him.

He remained dumfounded, overwhelmed, motionless. Arbogad kept right on drinking, telling stories, continually repeating that he was the happiest of men, exhorting Zadig to make himself as happy as he was. Finally, gently lulled by the fumes of the wine, he went off to enjoy a peaceful sleep. Zadig spent the night in the most violent agitation.

"What?" said he. "The King has gone mad? He has been killed? I cannot help pitying him. The empire is torn apart, and this brigand is happy. O fortune! O destiny! A robber is happy, and the most lovable creature nature ever made has perhaps perished in a frightful manner or is living in a state worse than death. O Astarté! What has become of you?"

As soon as day broke he questioned everyone he met in the castle; but everyone was busy, no one answered him; they had made new conquests during the night, they were dividing the spoils. All he could obtain in this tumultuous confusion was permission to leave. He took advantage of it without delay, more sunk than ever in his sorrowful reflections.

Zadig walked on, worried, agitated, his mind wholly occupied with the unfortunate Astarté, the King of Babylon, his own faithful Cador, the happy brigand Arbogad, that capricious woman whom the Babylonians had carried off on the confines of Egypt—in short, with all the adversities and all the misfortunes he had undergone.

17 *The Fisherman*

A FEW LEAGUES from Arbogad's castle he found himself on the bank of a little river, still bewailing his destiny and considering himself as the model of unhappiness. He saw a fisherman lying on the bank, one listless hand barely holding his net, which he seemed ready to drop, and raising his eyes toward heaven.

"I am certainly the most unfortunate of all men," the fisherman was saying. "I was, by common agreement, the most famous cream-cheese merchant in Babylon, and I have been ruined. I had the prettiest wife that a man of my sort could possess, and she betrayed me. I still had a poor little house left, I have seen it pillaged and destroyed. Taking refuge in a shack, I have no resource but my fishing, and do not catch a single fish. O my net! I will no longer throw you in the water, I will throw myself instead."

So saying he gets up and advances in the manner of a man about to throw himself in and end his life.

"How's this?" said Zadig to himself. "So there are men as unhappy as I am?"

Ardent desire to save the fisherman's life was as prompt as this reflection. He runs to him, stops him, questions him in a sympathetic and consoling manner. It is claimed that we are less unhappy when we are not unhappy alone. But, according to Zoroaster, this is not from malice but from need. We then feel drawn to an unfortunate as to our fellow. The joy of a happy man would be an insult; but two unhappy men are like two frail little trees, which, leaning on each other, strengthen each other against the storm.

"Why are you succumbing to your misfortunes?" said Zadig to the fisherman.

"Because," he replied, "I see no way out. I was the most respected man in the village of Derlback right near Babylon, and with the help of my wife I made the best cream cheeses in the empire. Queen Astarté and the famous minister Zadig were passionately fond of them. I had supplied their houses with six hundred cheeses. I went to town one day to be paid; on arriving in Babylon I learned that the Queen and Zadig had disappeared. I ran to the house of Lord Zadig, whom I had never seen; I found the archers of the Grand Desterham, who, armed with a royal warrant, were pillaging his house lawfully and in good order. I flew to the Queen's kitchens; some of the lords of the table told me she was dead; others said she was in prison; others claimed she had taken flight; but all assured me that I would not be paid for my cheeses. I went with my wife to Lord Orcan's, who was one of my customers; we asked him for his protection in our fall from favor. He granted it to my wife and refused it to me. She was whiter than her cream cheeses, which began my unhappiness; and the splendor of Tyrian purple was no more brilliant than the crimson which animated this whiteness. That is what made Orcan keep her and drive me out of his house. I wrote my dear wife the letter of a desperate man. She said to the bearer: 'Oh, oh yes, I know who the man is who is writing me, I've heard of him; they say he makes excellent cream cheeses; have some brought to me and have him paid for them.'

"In my misery I decided to seek justice. I had six ounces of gold left; I had to give two of them to the man of law I consulted, two to the attorney who undertook my case, two to the chief judge's secretary. When all this was done, my case had not yet started, and I had already spent more money than my cheeses and my wife were worth. I went back to my village with the intention of selling my house in order to get back my wife.

"My house was well worth sixty ounces of gold, but people saw I was poor and in a hurry to sell: the first one I went to offered me thirty ounces, the second twenty, the third ten. At last I was ready to settle, so blinded was I, when a prince of Hyrcania came to Babylon and ravaged everything on his way. My house was first sacked and then burned.

"Having thus lost my money, my wife, and my house, I retired to this region where you see me now. I have tried to subsist on the fisherman's trade; the fish mock me just as the men do. I catch nothing, I am dying of hunger; and but for you, august consoler, I would have died in the river."

The fisherman did not tell this tale all at once, for at every moment, Zadig, transported with emotion, said to him:

"What! You know nothing of the Queen's fate!"

"No, my lord," replied the fisherman; "but I know that the Queen and Zadig did not pay me for my cream cheeses, that my wife has been taken away, and that I am in despair."

"I am confident," said Zadig, "that you will not lose all your money. I have heard of this Zadig; he is an honorable man; and if he returns to Babylon, as he hopes, he will give you more than he owes you; but as for your wife, who is not so honorable, I advise you not to try to get her back. Believe me, go to Babylon; I shall be there before you,

because I am on horseback and you are on foot. Go to see
the illustrious Cador; tell him that you have met his friend;
wait for me at his house. Go on, and maybe you won't
always be unhappy."

"O powerful Ormuzd!" he continued, "you use me to
console this man; whom will you use to console me?"

So saying, he gave the fisherman half of all the money he
had brought from Arabia; and the fisherman, confused and
delighted, kissed the feet of Cador's friend and said:

"You are an angel come to save me!"

Meanwhile Zadig kept asking for news and shedding tears.

"What, lord," exclaimed the fisherman, "so you are unhappy too, you who do good?"

"A hundred times more unhappy than you," replied Zadig.

"But how can it be," said the good man, "that he who
gives is more to be pitied than he who receives?"

"Because your greatest misfortune," returned Zadig, "was
need, and my misfortune is of the heart."

"Can Orcan have taken your wife?" said the fisherman.

This question recalled to Zadig's mind all his adventures;
he kept going over the list of his misfortunes, starting with
the Queen's bitch, right up to his arrival at the brigand
Arbogad's.

"Ah!" he said to the fisherman. "Orcan deserves to be
punished. But ordinarily those are the people who are destiny's
favorites. However that may be, go to Lord Cador's and wait
for me."

They parted; the fisherman walked along thanking his
destiny, and Zadig rode along still accusing his own.

18   The Basilisk

ARRIVING in a beautiful meadow, he saw there several women
looking for something with much application. He took the
liberty of approaching one of them and asking her if he might
have the honor of helping them in their search.

"Be careful that you don't," answered the Syrian girl.
"What we are seeking can be touched only by women."

"That is very strange," said Zadig. "May I venture to ask

you to tell me what it is that only women are permitted to touch?"

"It's a basilisk," said she.

"A basilisk, Madame? And why, if you please, are you looking for a basilisk?"

"It is for our lord and master Ogul, whose castle you see on the bank of that river at the end of the meadow. We are his very humble slaves; Lord Ogul is sick; his doctor has ordered him to eat a basilisk cooked in rose water; and since this is a very rare animal who never lets himself be caught except by women, Lord Ogul has promised to choose for his well-beloved wife whichever of us brings him a basilisk. Let me go on searching, please; for you see what it would cost me if my companions got ahead of me."

Zadig let this Syrian girl and the others look for their basilisk, and continued to walk through the meadow. When he was at the edge of a little stream, he found another lady lying there on the grass not looking for anything. Her stature appeared majestic, but her face was covered with a veil. She was leaning toward the stream; deep sighs issued from her mouth. She held in her hand a little rod, with which she was tracing characters on some fine sand that was between the grass and the stream. Zadig was curious to see what this woman was writing; he approached, he saw the letter Z, then an A, he was astonished; then a D appeared, he gave a start. Never was surprise equal to his when he saw the last two letters of his name. He remained for a time motionless; finally, breaking the silence in a halting voice:

"O noble lady! Forgive a stranger, an unfortunate, for daring to ask you by what astounding chance I find here the name of Zadig traced by your divine hand?"

At that voice, at those words, the lady lifted her veil with a trembling hand, looked at Zadig, uttered a cry of tenderness, surprise, and joy, and, succumbing to all the varied emotions that assailed her soul all together, fell swooning into his arms. It was Astarté herself, it was the Queen of Babylon, it was she whom Zadig adored and whom he reproached himself for adoring; it was she whose destiny he had so bewailed and so feared. For a moment he was deprived of the use of his senses; and when he had fixed his gaze on the eyes of Astarté, which were opening again with a languor mingled with confusion and tenderness:

"O immortal powers," he cried, "who preside over the destinies of frail humans, are you giving me back Astarté? At what a time, in what a place, in what a state do I see her again?"

He threw himself on his knees before Astarté and held his forehead against the dust of her feet. The Queen of Babylon raised him up and made him sit beside her on the edge of the stream; she repeatedly dried her eyes, from which the tears ever flowed afresh. Twenty times she resumed her talk, which was interrupted by her lamentations; she questioned him about the chance that brought them together, and immediately forestalled his answers with other questions. She would begin the story of her misfortunes and then want to know those of Zadig. When at last both had somewhat appeased the tumult of their souls, Zadig told her in a few words by what chance he happened to be in that meadow.

"But, O unhappy and honored Queen! How is it that I find you in this remote spot, dressed as a slave and accompanied by other women slaves who are searching for a basilisk to have it cooked in rose water by the doctor's orders?"

"While they are searching for their basilisk," said the beautiful Astarté, "I will tell you all I have suffered and all I forgive Heaven for, now that I see you again. You know that the King my husband took it ill that you were the most attractive of all men; and it was for that reason that he made the decision one night to have you strangled and to poison me. You know how Heaven allowed my little mute to warn me of the order of His Sublime Majesty. Scarcely had the faithful Cador forced you to obey me and leave, when he dared to enter my apartment in the middle of the night by a secret door. He carried me off and took me to the temple of Ormuzd, where his brother the magus shut me up in that colossal statue whose base touches the foundations of the temple and whose head reaches to the vault. I was there as if buried, but tended by the magus, and not lacking anything necessary. Meanwhile at daybreak His Majesty's apothecary entered my room with a potion compounded of henbane, opium, hemlock, black hellebore, and aconite; and another officer went to your apartment with a blue silk cord. They found no one. Cador, the better to deceive the King, pretended to come forward and accuse us both. He said that you had taken the road to India and I to Memphis; they sent satellites after you and after me.

"The couriers who were looking for me did not know me. I had almost never shown my face except to you alone, in my husband's presence and by his order. They ran in pursuit of me, basing themselves on the description they were given of my person; a woman of the same stature as I, and who had perhaps more charms, appeared to their eyes on the frontiers of Egypt. She was wandering about in tears. They had no doubt that this woman was the Queen of Babylon; they took her to Moabdar. Their mistake at first drove the King into a violent rage; but soon, having scrutinized this woman more closely, he found her very beautiful, and was consoled. Her name was Missouf. I have been told since then that this name, in Egyptian, means 'capricious beauty.' She was that indeed, but she was as artful as she was capricious. She was pleasing to Moabdar. She subjected him to the point of having herself declared his wife. Then her character revealed itself completely; she gave herself up without fear to all the follies of her imagination. She tried to force the chief of the magi, who was old and gouty, to dance before her; and on his refusal, she persecuted him violently. She ordered her master of the horse to make her a jam tart. The master of the horse pointed out to her in vain that he was no pastry cook; he had to make the tart; and he was dismissed because the tart was burned. She gave the post of master of the horse to her dwarf, and the post of chancellor to a page. That is how she governed Babylon. Everyone regretted the loss of me.

"The King, who had been a pretty good man up until the time he decided to poison me and have you strangled, seemed to have drowned his virtues in the prodigious love he had for the capricious beauty. He came to the temple on the great day of the sacred fire. I saw him implore the gods on behalf of Missouf at the feet of the statue in which I was enclosed. I raised my voice; I cried out to him: 'The gods refuse the prayers of a King turned tyrant, who tried to kill a reasonable woman, only to marry a scatterbrain.' Moabdar was confounded by these words, to such a point that his wits were troubled. The oracle I had rendered and the tyranny of Missouf were enough to make him lose his judgment. In a few days he went mad.

"His madness, which appeared a chastisement from Heaven, was the signal for revolt. People rose up and ran to take arms. Babylon, so long plunged in idle effeminacy, became the theater of a frightful civil war. They took me out of the hollow of my statue and set me at the head of one party. Cador sped to Memphis to bring you back to Babylon. The Prince of Hyrcania, learning this direful news, returned with his army to form a third party in Chaldea. He attacked the King, who fled before him with his flighty Egyptian girl. Moabdar died pierced with wounds. Missouf fell into the hands of the conqueror. My bad fortune would have it that I was captured myself by a party of Hyrcanians and brought before the prince at precisely the same time that they brought him Missouf. You will no doubt be flattered to learn that the prince found me more beautiful than the Egyptian, but you will be sorry to learn that he destined me for his harem. He told me most determinedly that as soon as he had completed a military expedition that he was about to undertake, he would come to me.

"Judge of my sorrow. My ties with Moabdar were broken, I could belong to Zadig, and I fell into the chains of a barbarian. I answered him with all the pride my rank and feelings gave me. I had always heard that Heaven imprinted on persons of my position a stamp of greatness which, by a word or a glance, reduced to the humility of the deepest respect those rash enough to depart from it. I spoke as a Queen; but I was treated as a maidservant. The Hyrcanian, without deigning even to speak to me, said to his black eunuch [1] that I was a saucy wench but that he found me pretty. He ordered him to look after me and to put me on the regimen of the favorites, so as to freshen my complexion and make me more worthy of his favors for the day when he would find it convenient to honor me with them. I told him that I would kill myself; he answered, laughing, that people did not kill themselves, that he was accustomed to such carryings-on; and he left me like a man who has just put a parrot in his menagerie. What a state of affairs for the greatest Queen in the world and, may I add, for a heart that belonged to Zadig!"

At these words he fell at her knees and bathed them with tears. Astarté raised him up tenderly and continued thus:

1   The eunuch in charge of the women.

"I saw myself in the power of a barbarian and rival to a madwoman with whom I was locked up. She told me her adventure in Egypt. I judged by her description of you, by the time, by the dromedary on which you were mounted, by all the circumstances, that it was Zadig who had fought for her. I had no doubt that you were in Memphis; I formed the resolution to get away there.

" 'Beautiful Missouf,' I said to her, 'you are much more amusing than I, you will divert the Prince of Hyrcania much better than I. Help me find the means to escape, you will reign alone, you will make me happy while you get rid of a rival.'

"Missouf arranged with me the means of my flight. So I left secretly with an Egyptian woman slave.

"I was already near Arabia when a famous robber named Arbogad carried me off and sold me to some merchants, who brought me to this castle where Lord Ogul lives. He bought me without knowing who I was. He is a voluptuous man who craves nothing but good cheer and who believes that God put him into the world to sit at table. He is excessively fat, and this is always on the point of suffocating him. His doctor, who has but little influence with him when he is digesting well, governs him despotically when he has eaten too much. He has persuaded him that he could cure him with a basilisk cooked in rose water. Lord Ogul has promised his hand to whichever of his women slaves will bring him a basilisk. You see that I am letting them vie eagerly to merit this honor, and I have never had less desire to find that basilisk than since Heaven has allowed me to see you again."

Then Astarté and Zadig told each other everything that long-repressed feelings, their misfortunes, and their love could inspire in the noblest and most passionate hearts; and the genii who preside over love carried their words all the way to the sphere of Venus.

The women returned to Ogul's castle without having found anything. Zadig had himself introduced to him, and spoke to him in these terms:

"May immortal health descend from Heaven to take care of your days! I am a doctor; I have hastened to see you on the report of your illness, and I have brought you a basilisk cooked in rose water. It is not that I aspire to be your wife. All I ask is the freedom of a young woman slave from Baby-

lon, whom you have had for a few days; and I consent to
remain in slavery in her place if I do not have the good
fortune to cure the magnificent Lord Ogul."

The proposal was accepted. Astarté left for Babylon with
Zadig's servant, promising to send him a courier at once to tell
him everything that had happened. Their farewells were as
tender as their recognition had been. The moment when we
meet again and the moment when we part are the two
greatest epochs in life, as the great book of Zend says.
Zadig loved the Queen as much as he swore he did, and
the Queen loved Zadig more than she told him.

Meanwhile Zadig spoke thus to Ogul:

"Lord, my basilisk is not to be eaten; all its virtue must
enter into you through your pores. I have put it into a little
leather bag, well blown up and covered with a fine skin. You
must hit this bag with all your might, and I must send it
back to you several times; and in a few days of treatment you
will see what my art can do."

On the first day Ogul was all out of breath and thought he
would die of fatigue. On the second he was less tired and
slept better. In a week he recovered all the strength, health,
lightness, and gaiety of his most sparkling years.

"You have played ball and you have been sober," Zadig
told him. "Learn that there are no basilisks in nature, that
people are always healthy with sobriety and exercise, and that
the art of making intemperance and health live together is
an art as chimerical as the philosopher's stone, judicial
astrology, and the theology of the magi."

Ogul's first doctor, sensing how dangerous this man was to
medicine, joined with the Apothecary for the Body to send
Zadig to seek basilisks in the other world. Thus after having
always been punished for doing good, he was about to perish
for curing a gluttonous lord. He was invited to an excellent
dinner. He was to be poisoned during the second course;
but during the first he received a courier from the beautiful
Astarté. He left the table and set out. When one is loved
by a beautiful woman, says the great Zoroaster, one always
gets out of trouble in this world.

19 *The Combats*

THE QUEEN HAD BEEN received in Babylon with the transports that are always felt for a beautiful princess who has been unfortunate. Babylon then seemed more tranquil. The Prince of Hyrcania had been killed in a battle. The victorious Babylonians declared that Astarté should marry the man they chose as sovereign. They did not want the highest position in the world, which would be that of Astarté's husband, to depend on intrigues and cabals. They swore to recognize as King the bravest and wisest man. A few leagues from town they built a great tilting ground bordered by magnificently decorated amphitheaters. The combatants were to present themselves there fully armed. Each of them had a separate suite behind the amphitheaters, where he was to remain unseen and unknown to anyone. They had to break four lances. Those who should be fortunate enough to conquer four knights were then to fight one another; so that he who remained the final master of the field would be proclaimed the winner of the games. He was to come back four days later, with the same arms, and explain the riddles propounded by the magi. If he did not explain the riddles, he was not King, and the jousting would have to begin again until they found a man who was the winner in both contests; for they absolutely insisted on having as King the bravest and wisest man. The Queen, during all this time, was to be closely guarded; she was only allowed to be present at the games, covered with a veil; but she was not permitted to speak to any of the aspirants, so that there might be neither favor nor injustice.

This was what Astarté made known to her lover, hoping that for her sake he would show more valor and wit than anyone. He left, and prayed Venus to fortify his courage and illumine his mind. He arrived on the banks of the Euphrates on the eve of this great day. He had his emblem inscribed among those of the combatants, concealing his face and his name as the law ordained, and went to rest in the suite that fell to him by lot. His friend Cador, who had come back to Babylon after searching for him vainly in Egypt, had a complete suit of armor, sent him by the Queen, brought to his dressing room. He also sent him on her behalf the finest horse in Persia. Zadig recognized Astarté in these presents; his courage and love drew from them new strength and new hope.

The next day, when the Queen had come to her seat under a jeweled canopy and the amphitheaters were filled with all the ladies and all the classes of Babylon, the combatants appeared in the arena. Each of them came and placed his emblem at the feet of the Grand Magus. These were drawn by lot, and Zadig's came last.

The first to advance was a very rich lord named Itobad, very vain, not very courageous, very clumsy, and witless. His servants had persuaded him that a man like him should be King; he had answered them: "A man like me should rule"; so they had armed him from head to foot. He wore golden armor enameled with green, a green plume, a lance adorned with green ribbons. It was noted first from the way Itobad managed his horse that it was not for a man like him that Heaven reserved the scepter of Babylon. The first horseman who rode against him unseated him; the second knocked him over backward on his horse's crupper, both legs in the air and arms outstretched. Itobad recovered his seat, but with such bad grace that the whole amphitheater started to laugh. The third did not deign to use his lance; but making a pass at him he took him by the right leg, turned him half around, and threw him in the sand. The squires of the tournament ran up to him laughing and set him back in the saddle. The fourth combatant takes him by the left leg and throws him on the other side. Amid hoots, they led him to his dressing room, where according to the law he was to spend the night; and as he walked along with difficulty he said: "What an adventure for a man like me!"

The other knights did their duty better. There were some who conquered two combatants in a row, some even got to three. Only Prince Otame beat four. Finally Zadig fought in his turn; he unseated four horsemen in a row with all possible grace. So it had to be seen who would win between Otame and Zadig. The former wore blue and gold arms, with plume the same; those of Zadig were white. Sympathies were divided between the blue knight and the white knight. The Queen, whose heart was palpitating, prayed to Heaven for the color white.

The two champions made passes and turns with such agility, they gave each other such fine blows with the lance, they were so firm in their saddles, that everyone except the Queen wished there might be two Kings in Babylon. At last, their horses being tired and their lances broken, Zadig resorted to this stunt: he passes behind the blue prince, springs onto the crupper of his horse, seizes him around the middle, throws him to the ground, seats himself in the saddle in his place, and prances around Otame who is stretched out on the field. The whole amphitheater shouts: "The white knight wins!"

Otame, indignant, gets up, draws his sword; Zadig jumps from his horse saber in hand. Here they are both on the field waging a new combat in which strength and agility triumph in turn. The plumes on their helmets, the studs on their armlets, the links of their armor, fly far afield under a thousand swift blows. They strike with point and edge, right, left, on the head, on the chest; they retreat, advance, measure each other, join combat again, seize each other, coil back like serpents, attack like lions; sparks fly at every moment from the blows they strike. Finally Zadig, regaining his spirits for a moment, stops, feints, leaps on Otame, throws him, disarms him; and Otame cries: "O white knight! it is you who are to reign over Babylon."

The Queen was in the heights of joy. They escorted the blue knight and the white knight each to his dressing room, as well as all the others, as the law provided. Mutes came to serve them and bring them food. One may judge whether the Queen's little mute was not the one who served Zadig. Then they left them to sleep alone until the next morning, the time when the victor was to bring his emblem to the Grand Magus to have it compared with the roll and to make himself known.

Although in love, Zadig slept, so tired was he. Itobad, who lay near him, did not sleep. He got up during the night, entered Zadig's quarters, took his white armor and emblem, and put his green armor in its place. When day came, he went proudly to the Grand Magus and declared that a man like him was the victor. This was unexpected; but he was proclaimed as such while Zadig was still asleep. Astarté, surprised and with despair in her heart, returned to Babylon. The whole amphitheater was already almost empty when

Zadig awoke; he looked for his arms, and found only this green armor. He was obliged to clothe himself in it, having nothing else at hand. Stunned and indignant, he put it on furiously and advanced in that garb.

Everyone left in the amphitheater and the arena received him with hoots. They surrounded him and insulted him to his face. Never did a man endure such humiliating mortification. He lost patience; with saber blows he cleared away the rabble that dared to abuse him; but he did not know what course to adopt. He could not see the Queen, he could not claim the white armor which she had sent him, that would have meant compromising her; thus while she was plunged in sorrow, he was steeped in fury and anxiety.

He walked along the banks of the Euphrates, convinced that his star destined him to be irremediably unhappy, going over all his mishaps in his mind, from the adventure of the woman who hated one-eyed men down to that of his armor.

"That is what comes," he said, "of waking too late; if I had slept less, I would be King of Babylon, I would possess Astarté. So knowledge, character, courage have never brought me anything but misfortune."

At last a murmur against Providence escaped him, and he was tempted to believe that everything was governed by a cruel destiny which oppressed the good and made green knights prosper. One of his vexations was to be wearing that green armor that had brought him so many hoots. A merchant passed, he sold it to him at a miserable price, and got from him a robe and a tall conical cap. In this garb he went along the Euphrates, filled with despair, and secretly accusing Providence for always persecuting him.

20 *The Hermit* [1]

AS HE WALKED he met a hermit, whose venerable white beard came down to his waist. He held in his hand a book which

---

1   The story that follows is very ancient, going back to the Koran (XVIII: 64–81) and popular in Europe from the thirteenth century on. Voltaire's main source appears to be Parnell's poem *The Hermit,* published in 1721.

he was reading attentively. Zadig stopped and made him a deep bow. The hermit greeted him with an air so noble and mild that Zadig was curious to talk to him. He asked him what book he was reading.

"It is the book of destinies," said the hermit; "do you want to read some of it?"

He put the book in the hands of Zadig, who, trained as he was in several languages, could not decipher a single character in the book. This further increased his curiosity.

"You seem to me very gloomy," said the good father.

"Alas! I have good reason to be!" said Zadig.

"If you will allow me to accompany you," replied the old man, "perhaps I may be useful to you. I have sometimes brought a sense of consolation to the souls of the unhappy."

Zadig felt respect for the hermit's manner, his beard, and his book. He found great illumination in his conversation. The hermit spoke of destiny, justice, morality, the sovereign good, human frailty, virtues, and vices, with an eloquence so live and touching that Zadig felt drawn to him by an invincible charm. He asked him insistently not to leave him until they were back in Babylon.

"I ask that favor of you myself," said the old man. "Swear to me by Ormuzd that you will not leave me for the next few days, whatever I do."

Zadig swore, and they set out together.

In the evening the two travelers arrived at a splendid castle. The hermit requested hospitality for himself and the young man who accompanied him. The porter, who might have been taken for a great lord, let them in with a sort of disdainful kindness. They were presented to one of the principal servants, who showed them the master's magnificent apartments. They were admitted to his table at the lower end, without the lord of the castle's honoring them with a glance; but they were served like the others, with delicacy and profusion. They were then given a gold basin, studded with emeralds and rubies, to wash in. They were taken to a beautiful suite to sleep, and the next morning a servant brought them each a gold piece, after which they were sent on their way.

"The master of the house," said Zadig on the road, "seems to me a generous man, though a little proud; he practices hospitality nobly." As he said these words he noticed that a very wide sort of pocket which the hermit wore seemed stretched and bulging; in it he saw the gold basin studded with gems, which the hermit had stolen. He did not dare show it at first, but he was strangely surprised.

Toward noon the hermit presented himself at the door of a very small house where dwelt a rich miser; there he requested hospitality for a few hours. A badly dressed old servant received him in a rough manner and showed the hermit and Zadig into the stable, where they were given a few rotten olives, some bad bread, and spoiled beer. The hermit ate and drank with as contented an air as the evening before; then, addressing this old servant, who was watching them both to see that they did not steal anything and who was urging them to leave, he gave him the two gold pieces he had received in the morning and thanked him for all his attentions.

"I pray you," he added, "let me speak to your master."

The servant, astonished, showed the two travelers in.

"Magnificent lord," said the hermit, "I cannot but render you very humble thanks for the noble way you have received us. Deign to accept this golden basin as a feeble token of my gratitude."

The miser almost fell over backward. The hermit did not give him time to recover from the shock, he left as soon as he could with his young traveling companion.

"Father," said Zadig, "what's all this I see? You seem in no way like other men: you steal a golden basin studded with precious stones from a lord who receives you magnificently, and you give it to a miser who treats you with indignity."

"My son," replied the old man, "that magnificent man, who receives strangers only out of vanity and to have his riches admired, will become wiser; the miser will learn to exercise hospitality. Be astonished at nothing, and follow me."

Zadig still did not know whether he was dealing with the maddest or the wisest of all men; but the hermit spoke with such authority that Zadig, bound moreover by his oath, could not help following him.

In the evening they arrived at a pleasantly built but simple house in which nothing savored of either prodigality or avarice. The master was a philosopher retired from society, who peacefully cultivated wisdom and virtue, and who nevertheless was not bored. He had taken pleasure in building this retreat, in which he received strangers with a nobility that had nothing ostentatious about it. He went himself to meet the two travelers, whom he first invited to rest in a comfortable suite. Some time later he came himself to invite them and take them to a clean and well-conceived meal, during which he talked to them discreetly about the latest revolutions in Babylon. He seemed sincerely attached to the Queen, and wished Zadig had appeared in the lists to fight for the crown.

"But men," he added, "do not deserve to have a King like Zadig."

Zadig blushed, and felt his sorrows redouble. In the course of conversation they agreed that things in this world did not always go as the wisest men would wish. The hermit steadfastly maintained that we do not know the ways of Providence and that men were wrong in passing judgment on a whole of which they perceived only the smallest part.

They spoke of the passions. "Ah! how harmful they are!" said Zadig.

"They are the winds that fill the sails of the vessel," retorted the hermit. "They sometimes submerge it, but without them it could not sail. Bile makes us angry and ill, but without bile man could not live. All is dangerous here below, and all is necessary."

They spoke of pleasure, and the hermit proved that it is a present from the Divinity. "For," he said, "man can give himself neither sensations nor ideas, he receives everything; pain and pleasure come to him from elsewhere, as does his being."

Zadig marveled how a man who had done such weird things could reason so well. Finally, after a talk as instructive as it was agreeable, the host took his two travelers back to their suite, blessing Heaven for having sent him two men so wise and so virtuous. He offered them money in a noble, easy way that could not offend. The hermit refused it and told him he was taking leave of him, since he planned to leave for Babylon before day. Their parting was tender; Zadig especially felt full of esteem and liking for so attractive a man.

When the hermit and he were in their suite, they sang the praises of their host at length. At daybreak the old man waked his comrade.

"We must be off," he said, "but while everyone is still asleep, I want to leave this man a token of my esteem and affection."

So saying, he took a torch and set fire to the house. Zadig cried out in horror, and tried to keep him from committing so frightful an act. The hermit dragged him along by superior force; the house was in flames. The hermit, who was already far enough away with his companion, calmly watched it burn.

"Thank God," he said, "there goes the house of my dear host, destroyed from basement to roof! The happy man!"

At these words Zadig was tempted at the same time to burst out laughing, to revile the reverend father, to beat him, and to run away. But he did nothing of all this, and, still dominated by the hermit's authority, he followed him in spite of himself to the final night's lodging.

It was at the house of a charitable and virtuous widow, who had a fourteen-year-old nephew, full of attractive qualities, and her only hope. She did the honors of her house as best she could. The next day she ordered her nephew to accompany the travelers as far as a bridge, which, having broken down recently, had become dangerous to cross. The young man most willingly walks ahead of them. When they were on the bridge, the hermit said to the youth:

"Come here, I must show my gratitude to your aunt."

Then he takes him by the hair and throws him into the river. The boy falls, reappears for a moment on the surface, and is swallowed up by the torrent.

"You monster! You wickedest of all men!" cried Zadig.

"You had promised me to be more patient," said the hermit, interrupting him. "Learn that under the ruins of that house to which Providence set fire, the master has found an immense treasure. Learn that this young man whose neck Providence has wrung would have murdered his aunt in a year and you in two."

"Who told you so, barbarian?" cried Zadig. "And even if you had read this event in your book of destinies, are you permitted to drown a child who has done you no harm?"

While the Babylonian was speaking, he noticed that the old man no longer had a beard, that his face was taking on the features of youth. His hermit's attire disappeared; four beautiful wings covered a majestic body resplendent with light.

"O Envoy from Heaven! O divine angel!" cried Zadig, falling on his face. "So you have come down from the empyrean to teach a frail mortal to submit to the eternal commands?"

"Men," said the angel Jesrad, "pass judgment on everything without knowing anything; of all men you were the one who most deserved to be enlightened."

Zadig asked his permission to speak. "I mistrust myself," he said, "but may I venture to ask you to clear up one doubt for me? Would it not have been better to have corrected that child and made him virtuous than to drown him?"

Jesrad replied: "If he had been virtuous and if he had lived, his destiny was to be assassinated himself, together with the wife he was to marry and the child that was to be born to them."

"But," said Zadig, "what? Then it is necessary that there be crimes and misfortunes? And the misfortunes fall on the good!"

"The wicked," replied Jesrad, "are always unhappy. They serve to test a small number of just men scattered over the earth, and there is no evil out of which some good is not born."

"But," said Zadig, "what if there were nothing but good, and no evil?"

"Then," replied Jesrad, "this earth would be another earth; the chain of events would be another order of wisdom; and that other order, which would be perfect, can exist only in the eternal abode of the Supreme Being, whom evil cannot approach. He has created millions of worlds, not one of which can resemble another. This immense variety is an attribute of his immense power. There are not two leaves of a tree on earth, or two globes in the infinite fields of the heavens, that are alike; and everything you see on the little atom on which you were born had to be, in its appointed place and time, according to the immutable orders of him who embraces all. Men think that this child who has just perished fell into the water by chance, that it was by a similar chance that that house burned down; but there is no chance; all is test, or punishment, or reward, or foreseeing. Remember that fisherman, who thought himself the most unhappy of all men. Ormuzd sent you to him to change his destiny. Frail mortal, cease to argue against what you must worship."

"But . . ." said Zadig.

As he was saying "But," the angel was already taking his flight toward the tenth sphere. Zadig, on his knees, worshiped

Providence and submitted. The angel cried to him from high in the air:

"Go your way to Babylon."

21 *The Riddles*

ZADIG, BESIDE HIMSELF and like a man near whom lightning has struck, walked along at random. He entered Babylon on the day when those who had fought in the lists were already assembled in the grand vestibule of the palace to explain the riddles and answer the questions of the Grand Magus. All the knights had arrived except the green armor. As soon as Zadig appeared in the city the people gathered round him; their eyes could not get enough of seeing him, their mouths of blessing him, their hearts of wishing him the empire. Envious saw him pass, shivered, and turned away. The people carried him along right to the assembly hall. The Queen, who was apprised of his arrival, was a prey to agitation by fear and hope. She was devoured with anxiety; she could not understand either why Zadig was without arms or why Itobad was wearing the white armor. A confused murmur arose at the sight of Zadig. Everyone was surprised and delighted to see him again; but only the knights who had fought were permitted to appear in the assembly.

"I fought like the others," he said, "but another here is wearing my armor; and while waiting to have the honor of proving it, I ask permission to present myself to explain the riddles."

They took a vote; his reputation for probity was still so strongly imprinted on their minds that they did not hesitate to admit him.

The Grand Magus first proposed this question:

"What, of all things in the world, is the longest and the shortest, the swiftest and the slowest, the most divisible and the most extensive, the most neglected and the most regretted, without which nothing can be done, which devours everything that is small and gives life to everything that is great?"

It was up to Itobad to speak. He replied that a man like him understood nothing about riddles and that it was enough for him to have conquered with stout thrusts of the lance.

Some said that the answer to the riddle was fortune, others the earth, others light. Zadig said it was time.

"Nothing is longer," he added, "since it is the measure of eternity; nothing is shorter, since it is lacking for all our plans; nothing is slower for him who waits, nothing swifter for him who enjoys; it extends right to infinity in greatness; it is divisible right down to infinity in smallness; all men neglect it, all regret its loss, nothing is done without it; it brings oblivion to all that is unworthy of posterity, and it makes great things immortal."

The assembly agreed that Zadig was right.

The next question was this:

"What is the thing that we receive without giving thanks, enjoy without knowing how, give to others when we don't know where we are, and lose without noticing it?"

Everyone had his say. Zadig alone guessed that it was life; he explained all the other riddles with the same facility. Itobad kept saying that nothing was simpler, that he would have figured them out just as easily if he had wanted to take the trouble. Questions were propounded on justice, on the sovereign good, on the art of ruling. Zadig's answers were judged the most solid.

"It's a great pity," people said, "that so good a mind is so bad a horseman."

"Illustrious lords," said Zadig, "I had the honor of conquering in the lists. I am the one to whom the white armor belongs. Lord Itobad took it while I slept; he apparently judged that it would be more becoming to him than the green. I am ready to prove to him first of all, before you all, with my robe and sword against all that fine armor that he took from me, that it is I who had the honor of conquering the brave Otame."

Itobad accepted the challenge with the greatest confidence. He had no doubt that in his helmet, cuirass, and armlet he would easily get the better of a champion in nightcap and dressing gown. Zadig drew his sword, saluting the Queen, who was watching him, filled with joy and fear. Itobad drew his, saluting no one. He advanced on Zadig like a man who had nothing to fear. He was about to split his head in two. Zadig managed to parry the blow, opposing what is called the strong part [1] of his sword to the weak part of his ad-

1 The strong part is that nearest the hilt.

versary's, so that Itobad's sword broke. Then Zadig, seizing his enemy round the body, threw him to the ground, and, putting the point of his sword to the chink in Itobad's cuirass, said:

"Let yourself be disarmed or I'll kill you."

Itobad, always surprised at the mishaps that befell a man like him, let Zadig do as he pleased, and he peacefully relieved him of his magnificent helmet, his superb cuirass, his fine armlets, his gleaming thigh pieces, put them on, and in this attire ran and threw himself at the knees of Astarté. Cador easily proved that the armor belonged to Zadig. He was recognized as King by unanimous consent, and especially by that of Astarté, who, after so many adversities, was tasting the sweetness of seeing her lover worthy in the eyes of the universe of being her husband. Itobad went off to have himself called "My Lord" in his own house. Zadig was King, and was happy. He kept in mind what the angel Jesrad had told him. He even remembered the grain of sand that became a diamond. The Queen and he worshiped Providence. Zadig let the capricious Missouf roam the world. He sent for the brigand Arbogad, to whom he gave an honorable rank in his army, with a promise to advance him to the highest dignities if he behaved like a true warrior, and to have him hanged if he practiced the brigand's trade.

Setoc was called from the depths of Arabia, with the beautiful Almona, to be at the head of the commerce of Babylon. Cador was placed and cherished according to his services; he was the King's friend, and the King was then the only monarch on earth who had a friend. The little mute was not forgotten. The fisherman was given a fine house; Orcan was condemned to pay him a large sum and give him back his wife; but the fisherman, grown wise, took only the money.

Neither could the beautiful Semire console herself for having thought that Zadig would be one-eyed, nor could Azora stop weeping for having tried to cut off his nose. He assuaged their sorrows with presents. Envious died of rage and shame. The empire enjoyed peace, glory, and abundance; it was the earth's finest century; it was governed by justice and love. Men blessed Zadig, and Zadig blessed Heaven.

Micromegas

A Philosophical Tale

[1752]

1 Voyage of an Inhabitant of the World of the Star Sirius to the Planet Saturn

IN ONE OF THOSE PLANETS that revolve around the star named Sirius, there was a young man of much intelligence whose acquaintance I had the honor of making on the last voyage he made onto our little anthill. His name was Micromegas,[1] a name well suited to all the great. He was eight leagues tall: by eight leagues I mean twenty-four thousand geometrical paces of five feet each.

Some mathematicians, people always useful to the public, will immediately take up their pens and find that since Monsieur Micromegas, inhabitant of the land of Sirius, is twenty-four thousand paces from head to foot, which makes a hundred and twenty thousand royal feet, and since we citizens of the earth are scarcely five feet tall and our globe is nine thousand leagues around—they will find, I say, that the globe which produced him must necessarily have a circumference just twenty-one million six hundred thousand times greater than our little earth. Nothing in nature is simpler and more ordinary. The states of certain sovereigns in Germany and Italy, which one can circle in half an hour, compared with the empire of Turkey, of Muscovy, or of China, give only a very feeble picture of the prodigious differences that nature has placed between all beings.

His Excellency's height being as I have said, all our sculptors and painters will agree without difficulty that his

1 From the Greek: "little big."

waist may be fifty thousand royal feet around; which makes
a very pretty proportion.[2]

As for his mind, it is one of the most cultivated that we
have; he knows many things, he has invented a few; he was
not yet two hundred and fifty years old, and was studying,
according to the custom, at the Jesuit school in his planet,
when, by sheer power of mind, he worked out more than
fifty propositions of Euclid; that is eighteen more than Blaise
Pascal,* who, after working out thirty-two of them just as
a game, so his sister says, later became a rather mediocre
geometrician and a very bad metaphysician.[3]

Toward the age of four hundred and fifty, just past childhood, he dissected many of those little insects which are less
than a hundred feet in diameter and escape ordinary microscopes. He composed a book about them that was very
curious but that got him into some trouble. The mufti* of
the country, a great hairsplitter and very ignorant, found in
his book statements that were suspect, ill-sounding, rash,
heretical, smacking of heresy, and prosecuted him vigorously:
the question was whether the substantial form of the fleas of
Sirius was of the same nature as that of the snails. Micromegas
defended himself wittily; he got the women on his side; the
trial lasted two hundred and twenty years. Finally the mufti
got the book condemned by some jurists who had not read it,
and the author was ordered not to appear at court for eight
hundred years.

He was only moderately afflicted at being banished from
a court that was filled with nothing but bickering and pettiness.
He wrote a very amusing song against the mufti which that
worthy troubled little about, and he set about traveling from
planet to planet to complete the formation of his mind and
heart, as the saying goes.[4] Those who travel only in post chaise
and berlin* will doubtless be astonished at the kind of carriages they use up there; for we, on our little pile of mud,

2   The 1752 edition here gave the following sentence, later
deleted: "His nose being one-third the height of his face, and his
handsome face being the seventh part of the height of his handsome body, it must be admitted that the Sirian's nose is six
thousand three hundred and thirty-three royal feet long plus a
fraction, which was to be demonstrated."
3   The earliest editions, less severe, read: ". . . later preferred
to be a fairly mediocre metaphysician rather than a great
geometrician."
4   Cf. Zadig, Chapter 15, p. 145.

can conceive nothing beyond our own practices. Our traveler
had a marvelous knowledge of the laws of gravitation and of
all the forces of attraction and repulsion. He made use of
them so aptly that, now with the help of a sunbeam, now by
the availability of a comet, he went from globe to globe, he
and his men, as a bird flits from branch to branch. In a short
time he crossed the Milky Way, and I am forced to confess
that he never saw, through the stars with which it is sown,[5]
that beautiful empyrean heaven which the illustrious Vicar
Derham * boasts of having seen at the end of his telescope.
Not that I claim that Mr. Derham did not see aright, God
forbid! but Micromegas was on the spot, he is a good observer,
and I do not want to contradict anyone.

After a good tour, Micromegas arrived in the globe of
Saturn. Accustomed though he was to see new things, he
could not at first, on seeing the smallness of that globe and
its inhabitants, refrain from that smile of superiority that
sometimes escapes even the wisest. For after all Saturn is
barely nine hundred times larger than the earth, and the
citizens of the country are dwarfs only a thousand fathoms
high or thereabouts. He laughed at them a little at first with
his men, much as an Italian musician starts laughing at Lully's
music when he comes to France. But since the Sirian was
intelligent, he understood very soon that a thinking being
may well not be ridiculous just because he is only six thousand
feet tall. After astounding the Saturnians, he grew familiar
with them. He formed a close friendship with the Secretary [6]
of the Academy of Saturn, a man of much wit, who indeed
had invented nothing but gave a very good account of the
inventions of others, and who passably produced little verses
and big calculations. I shall here report for the satisfaction of
the readers a singular conversation that Micromegas had
one day with Mr. Secretary.

5   The earliest editions and some later ones read: "with which
it is thought to be sown."
6   This person represents Fontenelle (1657–1757), distinguished popularizer of science, Perpetual Secretary of the Académie
des Sciences, noted for his *Entretiens sur la pluralité des mondes*.
It is from this work (*Dernier soir*) that Voltaire takes some of the
comparisons—blondes, brunettes, etc.—at the start of Chapter 2.

2 Conversation of the Inhabitant of Sirius with the Inhabitant of Saturn

AFTER HIS EXCELLENCY had lain down and the Secretary had approached his face:

"One must admit," said Micromegas, "that nature is very varied."

"Yes," said the Saturnian, "nature is like a flower bed, whose flowers . . ."

"Oh!" said the other, "leave off your flower bed."

"It is," the Secretary resumed, "like an assembly of blondes and brunettes, whose attire . . ."

"And what have I to do with your brunettes?" said the other.

"It is like a gallery of paintings whose features . . ."

"Oh, no!" said the traveler. "Once more, nature is like nature. Why search for comparisons?"

"To please you," answered the Secretary.

"I don't want to be pleased," said the traveler, "I want to be instructed. Start right in by telling me how many senses the men of your globe have."

"We have seventy-two," said the academician, "and we complain every day of having so few. Our imagination goes beyond our needs; we find that with our seventy-two senses, our ring, our five moons, we are too limited; and in spite of all our curiosity and the rather large number of passions that result from our seventy-two senses, we have plenty of time to be bored."

"I can well believe it," said Micromegas, "for we in our globe have nearly a thousand senses, and still there remains in us I know not what vague desire, what uneasiness, that incessantly reminds us that we are nothing much and that there are beings much more perfect. I have traveled a bit, I have seen mortals well below us, I have seen some well above us, but I have seen none who do not have more desires than real needs and more needs than satisfactions. Maybe someday I shall reach the country where nothing is lacking; but up to now no one has given me any positive news of that country."

The Saturnian and the Sirian then exhausted themselves

in conjectures; after many reasonings, very ingenious and very uncertain, they had to come back to facts.

"How long do you live?" said the Sirian.

"Oh, a very short time," replied the little man of Saturn.

"That is just as with us," said the Sirian, "we always complain how short. That must be a universal law of nature."

"Alas!" said the Saturnian, "we live for only five hundred great revolutions of the sun." (That comes to fifteen thousand years or thereabouts, counting in our way.) "You can readily see that that is dying almost at the moment we are born; our existence is a point, our duration an instant, our globe an atom. Hardly has a man begun to get a little education when death comes before he has experience. For my part I do not dare make any plans; I feel like a drop of water in an immense ocean. I am ashamed, especially in front of you, of the ridiculous figure I cut in this world."

Micromegas replied:

"If you were not a philosopher, I should fear to distress you by telling you that our life is seven hundred times longer than yours; but you know too well that when we must return our body to the elements and reanimate nature under another form, which is called dying; when that moment of metamorphosis comes, to have lived an eternity or lived a day comes to precisely the same thing. I have been in countries where they live a thousand times longer than in mine, and I have found that they still murmur about it. But everywhere there are people of good sense who know how to make the best of their lot and give thanks to the Author of nature. He has spread over the universe a profusion of varieties with a sort of wonderful uniformity. For example, all thinking beings are different, and at bottom they are all alike by the gift of thought and of desires. Matter is spread out everywhere, but in each globe it has different properties. How many different properties do you count in your matter?"

"If you are speaking of those properties," said the Saturnian, "without which we believe that this globe could not subsist as it is, we count three hundred, such as extension, impenetrability, mobility, gravitation, divisibility, and the rest."

"Apparently," replied the traveler, "that small number suffices for the plans the Creator had for your little habitation. I marvel at his wisdom in all things; I see everywhere differences, but also everywhere proportions. Your globe is small, your inhabitants are too; you have few sensations, your matter has few properties: all that is the work of Providence. What color is your sun, if you examine it carefully?"

"A very yellowish white," said the Saturnian, "and when we split up one of its rays, we find that it contains seven colors."

"Our sun is somewhat reddish," said the Sirian, "and we have thirty-nine primary colors. There is not one sun among all those I have approached that is like another, just as there is not one face among you that is not different from all the others."

After several questions of this nature, he inquired how many essentially different substances they counted in Saturn. He learned that they counted only about thirty, such as God, space, matter, beings that have extension and sensation, beings that have extension, sensation, and thought, beings that think and have no extension, those that interpenetrate, those that do not interpenetrate, and so on. The Sirian, in whose world they counted three hundred, and who had discovered three thousand others in his travels, astounded the philosopher of Saturn prodigiously. Finally, after communicating to each other a little of what they knew and much of what they did not know, after reasoning for one revolution of the sun, they resolved to make a little philosophical journey together.

3 Journey of the Two Inhabitants of Sirius and Saturn

OUR TWO PHILOSOPHERS were ready to embark into the atmosphere of Saturn with a very pretty provision of mathematical instruments, when the Saturnian's mistress, who got news of this, came in tears to make her remonstrances. She was a very pretty little brunette only six hundred and sixty fathoms tall, but who made up for her small stature by many charms.

"Ah, cruel man!" she cried, "when after resisting you for fifteen hundred years I was at last beginning to surrender, when I have spent barely a hundred years in your arms, you leave me to go traveling with a giant from another world.

Go to! you are just curious, you have never known love; if you were a real Saturnian you would be faithful. Where are you going to run to? What do you want? Our five moons are less erratic than you, our ring is less changing. That's the end of that! I shall never love anyone again."

The philosopher embraced her, wept with her, philosopher though he was; and the lady, after having swooned, went off and consoled herself with one of the country's dandies.

Meanwhile our two sight-seers left; first they jumped onto the ring, which they found rather flat, as an illustrious inhabitant [1] of our globe has very soundly conjectured; from there they went from moon to moon. A comet was passing right next to the last of these; they sprang upon it with their servants and their instruments. When they had gone about a hundred and fifty million leagues, they came upon the satellites of Jupiter. They passed on to Jupiter itself and stayed there a year, during which they learned some very fine secrets which would be going to press right now but for My Lords the Inquisitors, who found certain propositions a little hard to take. But I read the manuscript in the library of the illustrious archbishop of . . . , who let me see his books with that generosity and kindness that cannot be praised highly enough. Accordingly I promise him a long article in the next edition they publish of Moréri, and above all I shall not forget my lords his sons, who give such great hope of perpetuating the race of their illustrious father.[2]

But let us return to our travelers. Leaving Jupiter, they crossed a space of about a hundred million leagues and skirted the planet Mars, which, as is well known, is five times smaller than our little globe; they saw two moons which serve this planet, and which have escaped the observation of our astronomers. I am well aware that Father Castel* will write, even rather amusingly, against the existence of these two moons, but I leave the matter up to those who reason by analogy. Those good philosophers know how hard it would be for Mars, which is so far from the sun, to get along with less than two moons. Be that as it may, our

1   Huyghens in his *Systema saturnium* (1659).
2   This sentence is omitted in many of the later editions. Louis Moréri was the author of the *Grand Dictionnaire historique* (1674), still often reprinted and widely used in the eighteenth century.

friends found Mars so small that they feared they might
not find enough room to lie down for the night, and they
continued on their road like two travelers who disdain a
wretched village inn and push on to the nearest town. But
the Sirian and his companion soon repented; they went on
for a long time and found nothing. At last they perceived a
little glimmer; it was the earth; it was a pitiful sight to people
coming from Jupiter. However, for fear of repenting a second
time, they resolved to disembark. They passed onto the
tail of the comet and, finding an aurora borealis all ready,
they got inside, and arrived on the earth on the northern
shore of the Baltic Sea, July the fifth, 1737, new style.

4 *What Happens to Them on the Globe Earth*

AFTER RESTING awhile, they ate [1] for their breakfast two big
mountains, which their men prepared rather nicely for them.
Then they decided to reconnoiter the little country they
were in. They first went from north to south. The ordinary
steps of the Sirian and his men were about thirty thousand
royal feet; the dwarf from Saturn followed panting at a
distance; for he had to take about a dozen steps when the
other took only one stride. Picture to yourself (if it is permissible to make such comparisons) a very tiny lap dog
following a captain of the King of Prussia's guards.

Since these foreigners move pretty fast, they had gone
around the globe in thirty-six hours; true, the sun, or rather
the earth, makes a like journey in a day; but we must keep
in mind that it is much easier to turn on one's axis than
to walk on one's feet. So here they are back where they
started, after seeing that pool, almost imperceptible to
them, that is called the *Mediterranean,* and that other little
pond, which, under the name of the *Great Ocean,* surrounds
the molehill. The dwarf had never been in above his knees,
and the other had barely wet his heel. They did everything
they could as they went to and fro, up and down, to try to
see whether this globe was inhabited or not. They stooped,

1   Some editions omit the passage from "they ate" to "for
them. Then."

they lay down, they groped all over, but since their eyes and their hands were not proportioned to the little beings who crawl around here, they did not receive the slightest sensation that could make them suspect that we and our colleagues, the other inhabitants of this globe, have the honor of existing.

The dwarf, who sometimes judged a bit too hastily, at first decided that there was no one on the earth. His first reason was that he had seen no one. Micromegas politely made him sense that this was rather bad reasoning.

"For," he said, "you do not see with your little eyes certain stars of the fiftieth magnitude that I perceive very distinctly; do you conclude from this that these stars do not exist?"

"But," said the dwarf, "I have searched well."

"But," replied the other, "you have perceived badly."

"But," said the dwarf, "this globe is so badly constructed, it is so irregular, and the shape of it seems to me so ridiculous! Everything here seems to be in chaos: do you see these little streams, not one of which runs straight, these ponds, which are neither round, nor square, nor oval, nor of any regular form, all these little pointed grains with which this globe is prickly, and which have scraped the skin off my feet?" (He meant the mountains.) "Do you notice also the shape of the globe as a whole, how it is flat at the poles, how it turns around the sun at a clumsy angle, so that the polar climes are necessarily untilled? In truth, what makes me think there is no one here is that it seems to me that sensible people would not want to stay here."

"Well," said Micromegas, "maybe the people who inhabit it are not sensible. But after all, there is some suggestion that this was not made for nothing. Everything here seems irregular to you, you say, because everything is straight as a die in Saturn and Jupiter. Well, perhaps it is for that very reason that there is a little confusion here. Didn't I tell you that in my travels I have always observed variety?"

The Saturnian answered all these arguments; the dispute would never have ended if Micromegas, in the heat of discussion, had not by good fortune broken the string of his diamond necklace. The diamonds fell; they were pretty little stones, rather unequal in size, the largest ones of which weighed four hundred pounds and the smallest fifty. The dwarf picked up a few; he perceived, bringing them close to his eyes, that because of the way they were cut these diamonds were excellent microscopes. So he took a little microscope a hundred and sixty feet in diameter and applied it to his eye; and Micromegas selected one two thousand five hundred feet wide. They were excellent, but at first no one could see anything with the help of them; they had to make adjustments. Finally the inhabitant of Saturn saw something imperceptible stirring under water in the Baltic Sea: it was a whale. He picked it up very adroitly with his little finger, and, putting it on his thumbnail, he showed it to the Sirian, who burst out laughing for the second time at the excessive smallness of the inhabitants of our globe. The Saturnian, now convinced that our world was inhabited, very soon made the assumption that it was inhabited only by whales; and since he was a great reasoner, he tried to guess whence so small an atom derived [2] its movement, whether it had ideas, a will, freedom. Micromegas was much puzzled over this; he examined the animal most patiently, and the result of the examination was that it was impossible to believe there was a soul lodged there. So the two travelers were inclined to think that there is no intelligence in our dwelling place, when with the aid of the microscope they perceived something as big as a whale floating on the Baltic Sea.

It is well known that at that very time a flock of philosophers [3] were returning from the polar circle, beneath which they had made observations that no one had thought of until then. The newspapers said that their vessel was wrecked on the coast of Bothnia and that they had much difficulty escaping; but we never know the inside truth in this world. I shall relate candidly how the thing happened, without putting in anything of my own; which is no small effort for a historian.

5 *Experiences and Reasonings of the Two Travelers*

MICROMEGAS STRETCHED out his hand very gently toward the spot where the object appeared, and, putting forth two fingers

2   Here the 1752 edition added "its origin, . . ."
3   Maupertuis's expedition to Norway in 1736–1737.

and then drawing them back for fear of being mistaken, then opening and closing them, very adroitly took the vessel carrying those gentlemen and put it likewise on his nail without squeezing it too much, for fear of crushing it.

"Here is a very different animal from the first," said the dwarf from Saturn. The Sirian put the supposed animal in the hollow of his hand.

The passengers and crewmen, who had thought themselves swept up by a hurricane and thought they were on some sort of rock, all start to move about; the sailors take casks of wine, throw them overboard onto Micromegas' hand, and cast themselves after. The geometricians take their quadrants, their sectors, and some Lapland girls, and descend onto the Sirian's fingers. They made such an ado that he finally felt some moving thing tickling his fingers; it was an iron-shod stick that was being driven a foot deep into his index finger; he judged by this pricking that something had come out of the little animal he held, but at first he suspected nothing more. The microscope, which barely let them discern a whale and a ship, had no power to show a being as imperceptible as man. I have no intention here of shocking anyone's vanity, but I am obliged to beg the self-important to join me in noting one little fact. Taking men's height at about five feet, we cut no greater figure on the earth than would, on a ball ten feet round, an animal about one six hundred thousandth of a foot high. Imagine a being that could hold the earth in his hand and had organs proportionate to ours—and it may very well be that there are a great number of such beings. Now conceive, I pray you, what they would think of those battles which have won us a village that had to be surrendered later.

I have no doubt that if some captain of tall grenadiers ever reads this work, he will raise his troops' hats at least two full feet, but I warn him it will be no use, that he and his men will never be anything but infinitely small.

What marvelous skill did not our Sirian philosopher need, then, to perceive the atoms I have just been speaking of? When Leuwenhoek and Hartsoeker were the first to see, or to think they saw, the seed of which we are formed, they made nowhere near so astounding a discovery. What pleasure Micromegas felt in seeing these little machines move, examining all their tricks, following them in all their operations! How he cried out! How he joyfully put one of his microscopes in the hands of his traveling companion!

"I see them," they both said at the same time; "don't you see them carrying burdens, stooping down, getting up again?"

As they spoke thus, their hands trembled with pleasure at seeing objects so new, and with fear of losing them. The Saturnian, passing from an excess of wariness to an excess of credulity, thought he observed them engaged in the work of propagation.

"Ah," he said, *"I've caught nature in the act."* [1]

But he was deceived by appearances, which happens only too often, whether or not we use microscopes.

6 *What Happened to Them with Men*

MICROMEGAS, A MUCH BETTER OBSERVER than his dwarf, saw clearly that the atoms were speaking to each other, and pointed it out to his companion, who, ashamed at having been mistaken on the subject of generation, would not believe that such species could communicate ideas. He had the gift of tongues as well as the Sirian; he did not hear our atoms speak, and he assumed that they did not speak. Besides, how should such imperceptible beings have vocal organs, and what should they have to say? To speak, one must think, or just about; but if they thought, then they would have the equivalent of a soul. Now to attribute to this species the equivalent of a soul, that seemed to him absurd.

"But," said the Sirian, "you thought just now that they were making love; do you think anyone can make love without thinking and without uttering some word, or without at least making himself understood? Moreover, do you suppose it is harder to produce an argument than a child? To me, both seem great mysteries."

"I no longer dare either to believe or deny," said the dwarf. "I have no opinion any more. We must try to examine these insects, we will reason about them afterward."

"That is very well said," replied Micromegas; and immediately he pulled out a pair of scissors, cut his nails with

1 Fontenelle had written (*Eloge de M. de Tournefort*) that "nature . . . was, so to speak, caught in the act. . . ." The phrase had acquired wide currency.

them, and from a piece of his thumbnail he straightway made a sort of great speaking trumpet like a vast funnel, the tube end of which he put in his ear. The circumference of the funnel enveloped the ship and all the crew; the faintest voice entered the circular fibers of the nail; so that thanks to his ingenuity, the philosopher from up above heard perfectly the buzzing of our insects from down below. In a few hours he succeeded in distinguishing words, and finally in understanding French; the dwarf did the same, though with more difficulty.

The astonishment of the travelers redoubled each instant. They heard mites talking rather good sense; this sport of nature seemed to them inexplicable. You may well believe that the Sirian and his dwarf burned with impatience to join in conversation with the atoms. The dwarf feared that his voice of thunder, and especially that of Micromegas, might deafen the mites without being understood. They had to diminish its strength. They put in their mouths a sort of little toothpick whose very tapering end reached close to the ship. The Sirian held the dwarf on his knees and the ship with the crew on his nail; he bent his head down and spoke low; finally with the help of all these precautions and many others besides, he began his speech thus:

"Invisible insects, whom the hand of the Creator has been pleased to bring to birth in the abyss of the infinitely small, I thank him for having deigned to reveal to me secrets which seemed impenetrable. Maybe people at my court would not deign to look at you, but I disdain no one, and I offer you my protection."

If ever anyone was astonished, it was the people who heard these words. They could not guess where they came from. The ship's chaplain recited the prayers for exorcism, the sailors swore, and the ship's philosophers constructed a system; but no matter what system they made, they never could guess who was speaking to them. The dwarf from Saturn, who had a softer voice than Micromegas, then informed them in a few words what species they were dealing with; he told them about the journey from Saturn; let them know who Monsieur Micromegas was; and after sympathizing with them for being so little, he asked them whether they had always been in this miserable state so near to annihilation, what they were doing in a globe that appeared to belong to whales, whether they were happy, whether they multiplied, whether they had a soul, and a hundred other questions of that nature.

One reasoner in the party, bolder than the others, and shocked that someone doubted he had a soul, observed the interlocutor through the eyepiece of a quadrant from two stations, and at the third spoke thus:

"You believe, then, sir, that because you are a thousand fathoms from head to foot, you are a . . ."

"A thousand fathoms!" cried the dwarf. "Good heavens, how can he know my height? A thousand fathoms! He's not an inch off. What? This atom has measured me? He is a geometrician, he knows my size; and I, who see him only through a microscope, I do not yet know his?"

"Yes, I have measured you," said the physicist, "and I shall certainly measure your big friend too."

The proposition was accepted, His Excellency stretched out full length; for if he had remained standing, his head would have been too far above the clouds. Our philosophers planted in him a big tree in a place which Dr. Swift would name, but which I shall take good care not to call by name because of my great respect for the ladies; then by a series of interrelated triangles they concluded that what they saw was indeed a handsome young man one hundred and twenty thousand royal feet tall.

Then Micromegas uttered these words:

"I see more than ever that never must we judge anything by its apparent greatness. O God! who have given intelligence to substances which seem so contemptible, the infinitely small costs you as little as the infinitely great; and if it is possible that there are beings smaller than these, they may yet have minds superior to those of the superb animals I have seen in the sky, whose foot alone would cover the globe on which I have alighted."

One of the philosophers answered that he might believe in all certainty that there are indeed intelligent beings much smaller than man; he related to him, not all the fables that Virgil has told about the bees, but what Swammerdam discovered and what Réaumur [1] learned by his dissections. He

1   For Virgil see *Georgics* IV. Swammerdam was a seventeenth-century Dutch scientist; Réaumur's six-volume *Histoire des insectes* appeared from 1734 to 1742.

taught them finally that there are animals which are to bees what bees are to man, what the Sirian himself was to those vast animals he spoke of, and what those great animals are to other creatures compared with which they seem but atoms. Bit by bit the conversation grew interesting, and Micromegas spoke as follows.

7 Conversation with Men

"O INTELLIGENT ATOMS in whom the eternal Being has taken pleasure in manifesting his skill and his power, you must doubtless taste very pure joys on your globe; for having so little matter, and seeming to be all spirit, you must spend your lives in love and in thought; that is the true life of spirits. I have nowhere seen true happiness, but without doubt it is here."

At this speech all the philosophers shook their heads, and one of them, franker than the others, admitted candidly that with the exception of a small number of none too highly considered inhabitants, all the rest is an assemblage of madmen, wicked men, and unhappy men.

"We have more matter than we need," he said, "for doing much evil, if evil comes from matter, and only too much spirit if evil comes from spirit. Do you realize, for example, that at this moment when I am speaking to you there are a hundred thousand madmen of our species covered with hats killing a hundred thousand other animals covered with turbans, or being massacred by them, and that over almost all the earth that is how people have behaved from time immemorial?"

The Sirian shuddered and asked what could be the subject of these horrible quarrels between such puny animals.

"At stake," said the philosopher, "is some mud heap the size of your heel. Not that any one of these millions of men who are getting their throats cut has a straw's worth of claim to this mud heap. The point is to determine whether it shall belong to a certain man called Sultan or another called, I know not why, Caesar.[1] Neither one has ever seen, or will

1   Czar. Voltaire's reference is to the war waged by Austria and Russia against the Turks from 1736 to 1739.

ever see, the little spot of land at issue, and hardly one of these animals who are cutting each other's throats has ever seen the animal for whom they are cutting them."

"Ah! wretches!" cried the Sirian in indignation. "Can anyone conceive such an excess of frenzied rage? I have a mind to take three steps and stamp out this whole anthill of ridiculous assassins."

"Don't take the trouble," was the answer; "they are working hard enough at their own ruin. Know that after ten years there is never the hundredth part of these wretches left; know that even if they were not to have drawn their sword, hunger, fatigue, or intemperance carry them nearly all off. Besides, it is not they who should be punished, but those sedentary barbarians who, from the privacy of their cabinet and while busy digesting, order the massacre of a million men and then have solemn thanks given to God for it."

The traveler felt moved to pity for the little human race, in which he was discovering such astounding contrasts.

"Since you are of the small number of the wise," he said to these gentlemen, "and since you apparently do not kill anyone for money, tell me, I pray you, how you occupy yourselves."

"We dissect flies," said the philosopher, "we measure lines, we assemble numbers; we agree about two or three points that we understand, and we argue about two or three thousand that we do not understand."

Immediately the Sirian and the Saturnian took a notion to question these thinking atoms to see what things they agreed on.

"How far do you reckon it," said he, "from the Dog Star to the great star in Gemini?"

They all answered together: "Thirty-two and a half degrees."

"How far do you reckon it from here to the moon?"

"Sixty half-diameters of the earth, in round numbers."

"How much does your air weigh?" He thought he would catch them, but they all told him that air weighs approximately nine hundred times less than an equal volume of the lightest water, and nineteen thousand times less than pure gold. The little dwarf from Saturn, astounded by their answers, was tempted to take for sorcerers these same people to whom a quarter of an hour before he had refused a soul.

Finally Micromegas said to them: "Since you know so well what is outside of you, no doubt you know even better what is inside; tell me what your soul is, and how you form your ideas."

The philosophers all spoke at once as before, but they were all of different opinions. The oldest quoted Aristotle, another pronounced the name of Descartes, this one of Malebranche, that one of Leibniz, another of Locke. An old Peripatetic said loudly and confidently:

" 'The soul is an entelechy, and a reason whereby it has the power to be what it is.' That is what Aristotle declares expressly on page 633 of the Louvre edition. Ἐντελέχεια ἐστί, etc." [2]

"I don't understand Greek too well," said the giant.

"Nor do I," said the philosophic mite.

"Then why," retorted the Sirian, "do you quote a certain Aristotle in Greek?"

"Because," replied the scholar, "it is essential to quote what we do not understand at all in the language we understand the least."

The Cartesian took the floor and said: "The soul is a pure spirit which in its mother's womb has received all metaphysical ideas, and which on leaving there is obliged to go to school and learn all over again what it knew so well and will never know again."

"Then it was hardly worth while," replied the animal eight leagues tall, "for your soul to be so learned in your mother's womb only to be so ignorant when you have a beard on your chin. . . . But what do you understand by spirit?"

"What in the world are you asking me?" said the reasoner. "I have no idea; they say it is not matter."

"But do you at least know what matter is?"

"Very well indeed," replied the man. "For example, this stone is gray, is of such-and-such a form, has its three dimensions, is weighty and divisible."

"Well," said the Sirian, "this thing that appears to you divisible, weighty, and gray, how about telling me what it is? You see a few attributes, but do you know the nature of the thing?"

"No," said the other.

2   In some editions Voltaire quotes the whole passage in Greek after translating it; in one, this bit only; in others he omits it.

"Then you do not know what matter is."

Then Monsieur Micromegas, addressing another sage whom he held on his thumb, asked him what his soul was and what it did.

"Nothing at all," said the philosopher who followed Malebranche; "it is God who does all for me. I see all in him, I do all in him, it is he who does all without my meddling in it."

"You might as well not be," returned the sage from Sirius. "And you, my friend," he said to a Leibnizian who was there, "what is your soul?"

"It is a hand," replied the Leibnizian, "that points to the hours while my body chimes, or else if you like it is my soul that chimes while my body points to the hour; or else my soul is the mirror of the universe and my body is the frame of the mirror; that is clear."

A little partisan of Locke was there, right near, and when at last he was spoken to he said:

"I do not know how I think, but I know I have never thought except at the stimulation of my senses. That there are immaterial and intelligent beings I do not doubt; but that it is impossible for God to communicate thought to matter, this I strongly doubt. I revere the eternal power; it is not for me to set limits to it; I affirm nothing, I am content to believe that more things are possible than people think."

The animal from Sirius smiled; he did not consider that one the least wise; and the dwarf from Saturn would have embraced the disciple of Locke but for their extreme disproportion.

But unfortunately there was present a little animalcule in a square bonnet [3] who interrupted all the other philosophical animalcules; he said he knew the whole secret, that it was all to be found in the *Summa* of St. Thomas; he looked the two celestial inhabitants up and down and maintained that their persons, their worlds, their suns, their stars, everything was made solely for man.

At this speech our two travelers fell back on each other, choking with that inextinguishable laughter which, according to Homer, is the lot of the gods; their shoulders and their stomachs heaved; and in these convulsions the ship, which

3   A theologian of the Sorbonne.*

the Sirian had on his nail, fell into a pocket of the Saturnian's breeches. These two good people looked a long time for it; finally they found it, and readjusted it very nicely. The Sirian picked up the little mites again; he still spoke to them with much kindness, although at the bottom of his heart he was a little bit angry to see that infinitely small creatures should have a pride almost infinitely great. He promised to prepare them a fine book of philosophy, written very small for their use, and that in this book they would see the final word about things.

Indeed, he gave them this book before he left; they took it to Paris to the Academy of Sciences; but when the Secretary opened it he found nothing but a completely blank book.

"Ah!" he said, "that's just what I suspected."

The World as It Is

BABOUC'S VISION,

Written by Himself

[1748]

AMONG THE GENII who preside over the empires of the world, Ithuriel holds one of the highest ranks, and has the province of Upper Asia. He descended one morning into the dwelling of the Scythian Babouc, on the bank of the Oxus, and said to him:

"Babouc, the follies and excesses of the Persians have drawn down our wrath; an assembly was held yesterday of the genii of Upper Asia to see whether we would chastise Persepolis or destroy it. Go into that city, examine everything; you will return and give me a faithful report on it; and I shall decide, on the basis of your report, either to correct the city or exterminate it."

"But, Lord," said Babouc humbly, "I have never been in Persia; I know no one there."

"All the better," said the angel, "you will not be partial; from heaven you have received discernment, and I add to that the gift of inspiring confidence; go, look, listen, observe, and fear nothing; you shall be well received everywhere."

Babouc mounted on his camel and left with his servants. After a few days, near the plains of Sennar, he came across the Persian army on its way to fight the Indian army. He first accosted a soldier whom he found apart from the others. He spoke to him and asked him what was the reason for the war.

"By all the gods!" said the soldier, "I know nothing about it. It is none of my business; my trade is to kill and be killed to earn my living; it makes no difference whom I serve. Indeed I might well go over to the Indian camp tomorrow, for people say they give their soldiers almost a copper half drachma* a day more than we get in this cursed service of Persia. If you want to know why we are fighting, talk to my captain."

Babouc, having given the soldier a small present, entered the camp. He soon made the acquaintance of the captain, and asked him the reason for the war.

"How do you expect me to know it?" said the captain, "and what does this fine reason matter to me? I live two hundred leagues from Persepolis; I hear that war is declared; I immediately abandon my family and go, according to our custom, to seek fortune or death, seeing that I have nothing to do."

"But your comrades," said Babouc, "aren't they a little better informed than you?"

"No," said the officer, "there is hardly anyone except our chief satraps who knows very precisely why we are cutting each other's throats."

Babouc, astounded, introduced himself among the generals; he came to know them familiarly. Finally one of them said to him:

"The cause of this war, which has been desolating Asia for twenty years, came originally from a quarrel between a eunuch of one of the Great King of Persia's wives and a clerk in the office of the Great King of India. At issue was a duty which amounted to about the thirtieth part of a daric.* The Prime Minister of India and our own worthily supported their masters' rights. The quarrel grew hot. On either side they put into the field an army of a million soldiers. This army has to be reinforced every year with more than four hundred thousand recruits. Massacres, fires, ruins, devastations multiply; the universe suffers, and the fury continues. Our Prime Minister and that of India often protest that they are acting solely for the happiness of the human race; and at each protestation a few towns are always destroyed and a few provinces ravaged."

The next day, on a report being spread that peace was about to be concluded, the Persian general and the Indian general made haste to give battle; it was bloody. Babouc saw all the blunders and all the abominations of it; he witnessed the maneuvers of the principal satraps, who did all they could to make their leader lose. He saw officers killed by their own troops; he saw soldiers finishing off their dying comrades to strip them of a few bloody rags, torn and covered with mud. He entered the hospitals to which they were carrying the wounded, most of whom were dying from the inhuman negligence of the very people whom the King of Persia paid well to help them.

"Are these men," cried Babouc, "or wild animals? Ah! I clearly see that Persepolis will be destroyed."

Occupied with this thought, he crossed over to the camp of the Indians. He was as well received there as in that of the Persians, according to what had been predicted to him; but he saw there all the same excesses that had struck him with horror.

"Oh, oh," he said to himself, "if the angel Ithuriel decides to exterminate the Persians, then the angel of India must destroy the Indians too."

Having then informed himself in more detail about what had happened in both armies, he learned of acts of nobility, magnanimity, and humanity, that astounded and transported him.

"Inexplicable humans," he exclaimed, "how can you combine so much baseness and so much greatness, so many virtues and so many crimes?"

Meanwhile peace was declared. The leaders of both armies, neither of whom had won the victory, but who in their own interest alone had caused the bloodshed of so many of their fellow men, went to their courts to intrigue for rewards. The peace was celebrated in public writings which announced nothing but the return of virtue and happiness to earth.

"God be praised!" said Babouc. "Persepolis will be the abode of purified innocence; it will not be destroyed, as those nasty genii wanted; let us hasten without delay to this capital of Asia."

He arrived in that immense city by the old way in, which was wholly barbarous and whose disgusting rusticity was an offense to the eye.[1] All that part of the city smacked of the time when it was built; for in spite of men's stubbornness in praising the ancient at the expense of the modern, it must

1   Compare *Candide*, Chapter 22, p. 68, on entering Paris by the Faubourg Saint-Marceau.

be admitted that in every form of art the first essays are
always crude.

Babouc mingled in a crowd of the people composed of all
the dirtiest and ugliest of both sexes. This crowd, with a
stupefied air, was rushing into a vast dark enclosure. From
the constant hum, from the movement he noted, from the
money that some persons were giving others to have the right
to sit down, he thought he was in a market where they were
selling straw-bottomed chairs; but soon, seeing that several
women were falling down on their knees while pretending
to look straight ahead and meanwhile glancing sideways at
the men, he perceived that he was in a temple. Harsh, raucous,
wild, discordant voices made the vault resound with ill-
articulated sounds, which produced the same effect as the
voices of wild asses when, on the plains of the Pictavians,[2]
they reply to the goat horn that calls them. He stopped up
his ears; but he was ready to stop up his eyes and nose too
when he saw workmen enter the temple with crowbars and
shovels. They removed a big stone and tossed up right and
left some earth from which there exhaled a pestilential smell;
then they came and deposited a dead man in this opening
and put the stone back on top.

"What!" cried Babouc, "these people bury their dead in
the same places where they worship the Deity! What! their
temples are paved with corpses! I am no longer astonished at
those pestilential diseases which often make Persepolis desolate.
The putrefaction of the dead, and that of so many of the
living gathered and crammed into the same place, is capable
of poisoning the whole terrestrial globe. Oh! what a nasty
city is Persepolis! Apparently the angels want to destroy it in
order to rebuild a finer one and populate it with inhabitants
who are less unclean and sing better. Providence may have
its reasons; let us leave it up to Providence."

Meanwhile the sun was approaching the height of its course.
Babouc was to dine at the other end of town with a lady for
whom her husband, an officer in the army, had given him
letters. First he made several trips about in Persepolis; he saw
other temples better built and better decorated, filled with a
polite congregation and resounding with harmonious music;

2   The Poitevins, inhabitants of Poitou.

he noticed public fountains which, although badly placed,[3] struck the eye by their beauty; squares in which the best kings who had governed Persia seemed to breathe in bronze; other squares where he heard the people cry: "When shall we see here the master whom we cherish?" He admired the magnificent bridges erected over the river, the superb and convenient quays, the palaces built up right and left, an immense house where thousands of old soldiers, wounded and victorious, gave thanks each day to the god of armies. Finally he entered the house of the lady, who was expecting him for dinner with an attractive company. The house was neat and elegantly furnished, the meal delicious, the lady young, beautiful, witty, engaging, the company worthy of her; and Babouc kept saying to himself at every moment: "The angel Ithuriel is jesting about wanting to destroy so charming a city."

However, he perceived that the lady, who had begun by asking him tenderly for news of her husband, was talking even more tenderly, toward the end of the meal, with a young magus. There came a magistrate who, in the presence of his wife, was enthusiastically hugging a young widow, and this indulgent widow had one arm draped around the magistrate's neck, while she stretched out the other to a very handsome and very modest young citizen. The magistrate's wife got up first from table to go and talk in a little adjoining room with her spiritual director, who had been expected for dinner and was arriving too late; and the director, an eloquent man, talked to her in this little room with so much vehemence and unction that when the lady came back her eyes were moist, her cheeks inflamed, her step unsteady, her speech trembling.

Then Babouc began to fear that the genie Ithuriel was right. The talent he had for winning confidence let him that very day into the lady's secrets; she confided in him her taste for the young magus, and assured him that in all the houses in Persepolis he would find the equivalent of what he had seen in hers. Babouc concluded that such a society could not subsist; that jealousy, discord, vengeance must make every household desolate; that tears and blood must flow every day; that the husbands would certainly kill their wives' lovers, or be killed by them; and that, in short, Ithuriel was doing very

3   Again Voltaire has Paris in mind. The "immense house" a few lines below represents the Hôtel des Invalides.

well in destroying at one blow a city abandoned to continual disasters.

He was plunged in these gloomy thoughts when there appeared at the door a grave man in a black cloak who humbly asked to speak to the young magistrate, who, without getting up, without looking at him, gave him some papers haughtily and absently, and dismissed him. Babouc asked who that man was. The mistress of the house said to him very low:

"He is one of the best lawyers in the city; he has been studying the laws for fifty years. The young gentleman, who is only twenty-five, and who for two days has been a satrap of the law, is giving him the job of making an abstract of a case he is to judge,⁴ which he has not yet examined."

"That giddy young man does wisely," said Babouc, "to ask counsel of an old man; but why is it not the old man who is the judge?"

"You are joking," they told him; "never do those who have grown old in toilsome and subordinate employments attain high dignities. That young man has a great post because his father is rich and because the right of dispensing justice is bought here like a farm."

"O mores! O unhappy city!" cried Babouc; "that is the height of disorder. No doubt those who have thus bought the right to judge sell their judgments; I see nothing here but abysses of iniquity."

As he was thus marking his sorrow and surprise, a young warrior, who had that very day come from the army, said to him:

"Why would you not have people buy judicial employments? For myself, I certainly bought the right to confront death at the head of two thousand men whom I command; it cost me forty thousand gold darics this year to sleep on the ground thirty nights in a row in a red uniform and then to receive two good arrow wounds which I still feel. If I ruin myself to serve the Persian emperor, whom I have never seen, My Lord the satrap of the law may well pay something to have the pleasure of giving a hearing to litigants."

Babouc, indignant, could not keep from condemning a country where they put up for auction the high dignities of peace and war; he concluded precipitately that here they

4   Here the Kehl edition adds: "tomorrow."

must be absolutely ignorant of war and of laws, and that even
if Ithuriel should not exterminate this people they would
perish through their detestable administration.

His bad opinion increased further on the arrival of a fat
man who, having greeted the whole company with great
familiarity, approached the young officer and said to him:

"I can lend you only fifty thousand gold darics, for in
truth the empire's customs duties have brought me in only
three hundred thousand this year."

Babouc inquired who this man was who complained of
earning so little; he learned that there were in Persepolis forty
plebeian kings [5] who held a lease on the Persian empire and
who paid something out of what they made to the monarch.

After dinner he went into one of the grandest temples in
the city; he sat down in the middle of a crowd of men and
women who had come there to pass the time. A magus appeared in an elevated contrivance and talked a long time about
vice and virtue. This magus divided into many parts what did
not need to be divided; he proved methodically all that was
clear, he taught all that they already knew. He coolly grew
impassioned, and went out sweating and out of breath. The
whole assembly then awoke and thought they had attended an
instructive talk. Babouc said:

"There is a man who has done his best to bore two or three
hundred of his fellow citizens; but his intention was good,
and here is not reason enough for destroying Persepolis."

On leaving this assembly he was taken to see a public
entertainment which was given every day of the year; it was
in a sort of basilica in the depths of which a palace was seen.
The most beautiful townswomen of Persepolis, the most important satraps, arranged in order, formed so fine a spectacle
that Babouc thought at first that this was the whole entertainment. Two or three persons, who appeared to be kings and
queens, soon appeared in the vestibule of this palace; their
language was very different from that of the people; it was
measured, harmonious, and sublime. No one slept, people
listened in deep silence, which was interrupted only by the
manifestations of the public's sensibility and admiration. The
duty of kings, the love of virtue, the dangers of the passions,

5   An allusion to the French farmers-general (*fermiers-
généraux*).

were expressed by such vivid and moving touches that Babouc shed tears. He had no doubt that these heroes and heroines, these kings and queens that he had just heard were the preachers of the empire; he even purposed to persuade Ithuriel to come to hear them, quite sure that such a spectacle would reconcile him forever to the city.

As soon as this entertainment was finished, he wanted to see the principal Queen, who in that handsome palace had recited so noble and pure a morality; he got himself admitted to Her Majesty's abode; he was taken up a narrow staircase to the third floor, into a badly furnished apartment, where he found a badly dressed woman who said to him with a noble and pathetic air:

"This profession does not give me a living; one of those princes you saw has got me with child; I shall soon be delivered; I lack money, and without money you can't be delivered."

Babouc gave her a hundred gold darics, saying:

"If that were the only evil in the town, Ithuriel would be wrong to be so angry."

From there he went to spend his evening at the stores of the merchants of useless magnificences. An intelligent man whose acquaintance he had made took him there; he bought what he liked, and they sold it to him politely for much more than it was worth. His friend, back at his house, made him see how much he was being cheated. Babouc put down the merchant's name on his tablets in order to have Ithuriel single him out on the day of the city's punishment. As he was writing, someone knocked on his door; it was the merchant himself coming to bring him back his purse, which Babouc had left on his counter by mistake.

"How can it be," exclaimed Babouc, "that you are so honest and generous, after having no shame at selling me some trinkets for four times more than their value?"

"There is no businessman of any note in this city," replied the merchant, "who would not have come to bring you back your purse; but someone deceived you when he told you that I had sold you what you bought at my store for four times more than it is worth; I sold it to you for ten times more, and that is so true that if in a month you want to sell it again, you won't even get that one tenth. But nothing is more just: it is men's fancy that sets the price on these frivolous things; it is that fancy which provides a living for a hundred workmen whom I employ; it is that which gives me a fine house, a comfortable carriage, and horses; it is that which stimulates industry, which maintains taste, traffic, and abundance. I sell the same trifles to the neighboring nations at a higher price than to you, and thereby I am useful to the empire."

Babouc, after reflecting a bit, scratched the man's name from his tablets.[6]

Babouc, very uncertain about what he should think of Persepolis, resolved to see the magi and the men of letters; for the latter study wisdom, the others religion; and he flattered himself that these men would obtain mercy for the rest of the people. The next morning he went to a college of the magi. The archimandrite admitted to him that he got a hundred thousand crowns of income for having taken a vow of poverty, and that he exercised a rather extensive rule by virtue of his vow of humility; after which he left Babouc in the hands of a lowly friar who did him the honors.

While this friar was showing him the magnificences of this house of penitence, a rumor spread that he had come to reform all these houses. Immediately he received memoranda from each of them; and the memoranda all said in substance: "Preserve us, and destroy all the others." To hear their apologies, these societies were all necessary. To hear their mutual accusations, they all deserved to be annihilated. He marveled how there was not one of them that, in order to edify the universe, did not want dominion over it. Then a little man presented himself who was a demi-magus and who said to him:

"I clearly see that the work is going to be accomplished; for Zerdust has returned to earth; little girls prophesy, having themselves pinched with tongs in front, and whipped behind.[7] So we ask you for your protection against the Grand Lama."

---

6   Here the 1749 edition added: " 'For after all,' he said, 'the arts of luxury are in great number in an empire only when all the necessary arts are practiced and when the nation is populous and opulent. Ithuriel seems to me a bit severe.' "

7   An allusion to the convulsionaries.* The demi-magus represents a Jansenist,* and the Grand Lama the Pope.
Here instead of the present passage "So we ask you . . . against him which he does not read," the 1749 edition had the following:

"What!" said Babouc, "against that pontiff-king who resides in Tibet?"

"Against his very self."

"Then you are making war on him, and raising armies against him?"

"No, but he says that man is free, and we do not believe a word of it; we write little books against him which he does not read; he has hardly heard of us; he has only had us condemned as a master orders to have the caterpillars cleared from the trees in his gardens."

Babouc shuddered at the folly of these men who made a profession of wisdom, the intrigues of those who had renounced the world, the ambition and arrogant covetousness of those who taught humility and disinterestedness; he concluded that Ithuriel had good reasons for destroying this whole breed.

Returned home, he sent for some new books to relieve his gloom, and he asked a few men of letters to dinner to cheer him up. There came twice as many as he had asked, like wasps attracted by honey. These parasites were eager to eat and to talk; they praised two sorts of persons, the dead and themselves, and never their contemporaries, except the master of the house. If one of them made a clever remark, the others lowered their eyes and bit their lips in anguish at not having said it. There was less dissimulation in them than in the magi, because the objects of their ambition were not so great. Each of them was intriguing for a valet's position and a great man's reputation; they said to each other's face insulting things which they thought were flashes of wit. They had gained some knowledge of Babouc's mission. One of them besought him in a low voice to exterminate an author who had not praised him enough five years before. Another requested the

---

" 'It is evident that the world is about to end; could you not, before that lovely time, protect us against the Grand Lama?'

" 'What balderdash,' said Babouc; 'against the Grand Lama? against that pontiff-king who resides in Tibet?'

" 'Yes,' said the little demi-magus with a stubborn air, 'against his very self.'

" 'Then you are making war on him, then you have armies?' said Babouc.

" 'No,' said the other, 'but we have written against him three or four thousand fat books that no one reads and as many pamphlets that we get women to read.' "

destruction of a citizen who had never laughed at his comedies. A third asked for the extinction of the Academy, because he had never succeeded in being admitted. When the
meal was over, each of them went off alone; for in the whole
crowd there were not two men who could stand each other,
or even speak to each other anywhere but at the houses of
the rich who invited them to their table. Babouc judged that
there would be no great harm if all this vermin perished in
the general destruction.

As soon as he was rid of them, he began to read some of
the new books. In them he recognized the spirit of his guests.
He saw with especial indignation those gazettes of slander,
those archives of bad taste, which envy, baseness, and hunger
dictate; those cowardly satires that humor the vulture and
tear the dove to pieces; those novels devoid of imagination,
where you see so many portraits of women whom the author
does not know.

He threw all these detestable writings in the fire and went
out to take an evening walk. He was introduced to an old
man of letters who had not come to swell the number of the
parasites. This man of letters always shunned the crowd, knew
men, made use of them, and communicated his ideas with
discretion. Babouc spoke to him with grief of what he had
read and what he had seen.

"You have read some very despicable things," the wise
man of letters told him; "but at all times, and in all countries,
and in all genres, the bad teems and the good is rare. You
have received at your house the scum of pedantry, because in
all professions what is most unworthy to appear is always what
presents itself with the most impudence. The true sages live
among themselves, withdrawn and tranquil; there are still
among us men and books worthy of your attention."

In the time he was speaking thus another man of letters
joined them; their talk was so agreeable and so instructive,
so far above prejudice and so conformable to virtue, that
Babouc admitted he had never heard anything like it.

"Here are men," he whispered to himself, "whom the angel
Ithuriel will not dare to touch, or else he will be most pitiless."

Reconciled with the men of letters, he was still angry with
the rest of the nation.

"You are a foreigner," said the judicious man who was talking to him; "abuses come to your eyes in a crowd, and the good, which is hidden and which sometimes results from these very abuses, escapes you."

Then he learned that among men of letters there were some who were not envious, and that even among the magi there were some who were virtuous.[8] He finally understood that these great bodies, which in clashing seemed to prepare their common ruin, were at bottom salutary institutions; that each society of magi was a check upon its rivals; that if these competitors differed in some opinions, they all taught the same morality; that they instructed the people and lived submissive to the laws, like the tutors who watch over the son of the house while the master watches over them. He made the acquaintance of several and found celestial souls. He learned that even among the madmen who aspired to make war on the Grand Lama there had been some very great men. Finally he suspected that it might be with the morals of Persepolis as with the buildings, some of which had seemed to him worthy of pity while others had transported him with admiration.

He said to his man of letters:

"I know very well that these magi whom I had thought so dangerous are in fact very useful, especially when a wise government keeps them from making themselves too necessary; but you will grant me at least that your young magistrates, who buy a judge's seat as soon as they have learned to mount a horse, must display in the courts the most ridiculous impertinence and the most perverse inequity; it would undoubtedly be better to give those positions free to those old jurists who have spent their whole lives weighing the pros and cons."

The man of letters replied to him:

"You saw our army before you arrived in Persepolis; you know that our young officers fight very well, although they

8   Instead of this sentence, the editions before 1756 carried the following:

"Then they took him to visit the principal magus whom they called the surveillant. Babouc saw in this magus a man worthy of being at the head of the just; he learned that there were many who were like him."

The "surveillant" (Greek ἐπίσκοπος, bishop) refers to Christophe de Beaumont, Archbishop of Paris. Voltaire's removal of this praise was occasioned by the archbishop's support of the *billets de confession* in 1750. (Cf. *Candide*, p. 69.)

bought their posts; maybe you will see that our young magistrates do not judge badly, although they have paid to judge."

He took him the next day to the high court, where an important verdict was to be rendered. The case was known to everyone. All the old lawyers who talked about it were wavering in their opinions: they cited a hundred laws, not one of which was applicable to the heart of the question; they looked at the affair from a hundred angles, not one of which showed it in its true light; the judges were quicker to decide than the lawyers to raise doubts. Their judgment was almost unanimous; they judged well, because they followed the light of reason, and the others had given bad opinions, because they had consulted only their books.

Babouc concluded that there was often much good in abuses. He saw that very day that the riches of the financiers, which had so revolted him, could produce an excellent effect; for when the Emperor needed money, he found in an hour by their means what he would not have got in six months by ordinary channels; he saw that these fat clouds, swollen with the dew of the earth, gave back to the earth in rain more than they received from it. Moreover, the children of these newly risen men, often better brought up than those of the older families, were sometimes much better people; for nothing prevents a man from being a good judge, a brave warrior, an able statesman, when he has had a father who was good at figures.

Imperceptibly Babouc was coming to forgive the greed of the financiers, who at bottom are not more greedy than other men and who are necessary. He excused the folly of ruining oneself in order to judge or to fight, a folly which produces great magistrates and heroes. He pardoned the envy of men of letters, among whom there were men who enlightened the world; he became reconciled with the ambitious and intriguing magi, in whom there were even more great virtues than petty vices. But he had many grievances left; and above all the love affairs of the ladies, and the havoc that must ensue, filled him with anxiety and fear.

Since he wanted to gain insight into all the conditions of men, he had himself taken to visit a minister of state; but he was trembling all the time on the way lest some wife should be assassinated by her husband in his presence. On arriving

at the statesman's house, he remained two hours in the antechamber without being announced, and two hours more after
he had been. He fully promised himself, in this interval, to
recommend to the angel Ithuriel both the minister and his
insolent ushers. The antechamber was filled with ladies of all
levels, magi with robes of all colors, judges, merchants, officers, pedants; all were complaining about the minister. The
miser and the usurer were saying: "Undoubtedly that man
plunders the provinces." The capricious man reproached him
with being eccentric; the voluptuous man said: "He thinks
only of his pleasures." The intriguer flattered himself he would
soon see him ruined by a cabal. The women hoped they
would soon be given a younger minister.

Babouc heard their remarks; he could not help saying:

"There is a very happy man; he has all his enemies in his
antechamber, he crushes with his power those who envy him;
he sees those who detest him at his feet."

At last he went in; he saw a little old man bent under the
weight of years and affairs, but still lively and full of wit.

He liked Babouc, and Babouc thought him an estimable
man. The conversation became interesting. The minister admitted to him that he was a very unhappy man; that he passed
for rich, and was poor; that he was thought all-powerful, and
was constantly contradicted; that he had obliged hardly anyone but ingrates; and that in the continual labors of forty
years he had had hardly a moment of solace. Babouc was
touched and thought that if this man had faults and if the
angel Ithuriel wanted to punish him, he should not exterminate him but merely leave him his post.

While he was talking to the minister, enter suddenly the
beautiful lady at whose house Babouc had dined. You could
see in her eyes and on her forehead the symptoms of grief and
anger. She burst into reproaches against the statesman; she
shed tears; she complained bitterly that her husband had been
refused a position to which his birth allowed him to aspire and
which his services and his wounds merited; she expressed
herself with so much force, she put so much grace into her
complaints, she annihilated objections with so much skill, she
enhanced her arguments with so much eloquence, that she did
not leave the room until she had made her husband's fortune.

Babouc gave her his hand. "Is it possible, Madame," he said

to her, "that you have given yourself all this trouble for a man you do not love and from whom you have everything to fear?"

"A man I do not love?" she cried. "Know that my husband is the best friend I have in the world; that there is nothing I would not sacrifice for him, except my lover; and that he would do anything for me, except leave his mistress. I want to have you meet her; she is a charming woman, full of wit and with the best character in the world; we are having supper together this evening with my husband and my little magus: come and share our joy."

The lady took Babouc to her house. The husband, who had at last arrived plunged in grief, saw his wife again with transports of delight and gratitude; he embraced in turn his wife, his mistress, the little magus, and Babouc. Unity, gaiety, wit, and the graces were the soul of the meal.

"Learn," said the fair lady at whose house he was supping, "that those who are sometimes called dishonorable women almost always have as much merit as a very honorable man; and to convince yourself of it, come and dine with me tomorrow at the beautiful Teona's.[9] There are a few old vestals who pick her to pieces, but she does more good than all of them together. She would not commit even a slight injustice for the greatest of interests; she gives her lover only magnanimous advice; she is occupied solely with his glory; he would blush to face her if he had let slip any occasion of doing good; for nothing encourages virtuous actions more than having as witness and judge of one's conduct a mistress whose esteem one wants to deserve."

Babouc did not fail to keep the appointment. He saw a house where all pleasures reigned; Teona reigned over them; she knew how to talk to everyone in his own language. Her natural wit set the wit of the others at ease; she was attractive almost without wanting to be; she was as lovable as she was kind; and, what enhanced the value of all her good qualities, she was beautiful.

Babouc, Scythian though he was and envoy of a genie, perceived that if he stayed any longer in Persepolis he would forget Ithuriel for Teona. He was growing fond of the city, the people of which were polite, gentle, and kind, although frivolous, slanderous, and full of vanity. He feared to see

9   Teona is generally taken to represent Madame du Châtelet.

Persepolis condemned; he even feared the report he was going to give.

Here is how he went about giving this report. He had the best metalworker in the city make a little statue composed of all the most precious and all the basest metals, earth, and stones; he took it to Ithuriel.

"Will you break this pretty statue," he said, "because it is not all gold and diamonds?"

Ithuriel took the hint; he resolved not even to think of correcting Persepolis, and to leave *the world as it is*. "For," he said, *"if all is not well, all is passable."*

So they let Persepolis subsist, and Babouc was very far from complaining like Jonah, who grew angry that Nineveh was not destroyed. But when a man has been three days in the body of a whale, he is not as good-humored as when he has been to the opera or the theater, and when he has supped in good company.

Memnon

or HUMAN WISDOM

[1749]

MEMNON ONE DAY conceived the insane plan of being perfectly wise. There are few men through whose heads this mad idea has not at some time passed. Memnon said to himself:

"In order to be very wise, and consequently very happy, one has only to be without passions; and nothing is easier, as everyone knows. In the first place, I will never love a woman; for when I see a perfect beauty I will say to myself: 'Those cheeks will grow wrinkled one day; those beautiful eyes will be rimmed with red; that round bosom will become flat and dangling; that beautiful head will become bald.' Now, all I have to do is to see her at present with the same eyes as I will then; and assuredly that head of hers will not turn mine.

"In the second place, I will always be sober. However much I may be tempted by good cheer, delicious wines, the seductions of society, I shall have only to picture to myself the consequences of excesses, a heavy head, a congested stomach, the loss of reason, health, and time: then I shall eat only because of need; my health will be always uniform, my ideas always pure and luminous. All that is so easy that there is no merit in achieving it.

"Next," said Memnon, "I must think a bit about my fortune. My desires are moderate; my wealth is solidly invested with the Receiver General of Finances of Nineveh; I have enough to live independently; that is the greatest wealth of all. I shall never be under the cruel necessity of courting favor; I shall envy no one, and no one will envy me. That too is very easy.

"I have friends," he continued, "I shall keep them, since they will have nothing to dispute with me for. I shall never be

bad-humored with them, nor they with me. There is no difficulty in that."

Having thus made his little plan of wisdom in his room,
Memnon put his head out the window. He saw two women
walking under some plane trees near his house. One was old
and seemed to be thinking of nothing. The other was young
and pretty, and seemed much preoccupied. She sighed, she
wept, and had only the more charms for it. Our sage was
touched, not by the beauty of the lady (he was quite sure
of not feeling any such weakness), but by the distress he saw
her in. He went down, he accosted the young Ninevite, de-
signing to console her with wisdom. This lovely person related
to him with the most natural and touching air all the evil
being done her by an uncle she did not have: with what
artifices he had taken from her some property she had never
possessed, and all that she had to fear from his violence.

"You seem to me a man of such good counsel," she said
to him, "that if you were to condescend to come all the way
to my house and examine my affairs, I am sure you would
pull me out of the cruel embarrassment I am in."

Memnon did not hesitate to follow her in order to examine
her affairs wisely and give her good counsel.

The afflicted lady took him into a perfumed room and had
him sit down with her politely on a wide sofa, where they
both sat with their legs crossed opposite each other. The lady
spoke with downcast eyes, from which sometimes tears
escaped, and which when raised always met those of the
wise Memnon. Her remarks were full of a tenderness which
redoubled every time they looked at each other. Memnon
took her affairs very much to heart, and more and more felt
the greatest desire to oblige a person so honorable and so
unhappy. Imperceptibly, in the heat of conversation, they
stopped being opposite each other. Their legs were no longer
crossed. Memnon advised her so closely, and gave her coun-
sels so tender, that neither of them could talk business, and
they no longer knew what point they were at.

As they were at this point, enter the uncle, as one may
well suppose; he was armed from head to foot; and the first
thing he said was that he was going to kill, as was reasonable,
the wise Memnon and his niece; the last thing that escaped
him was that he was capable of forgiveness for much money.
Memnon was obliged to give all he had. One was fortunate

at that time to be quit so cheap; America was not yet discovered, and ladies in distress were nowhere near so dangerous as they are today.[1]

Memnon, ashamed and in despair, went back home; there
he found a note inviting him to dinner with some of his
intimate friends.

"If I stay home alone," he said, "my mind will be busy
with my sad adventure, I shall not eat, I shall fall ill. It is
better to go and make a frugal meal with my intimate friends.
I shall forget, in the sweetness of their company, the stupid
thing I did this morning."

He goes to the rendezvous; they find him a bit gloomy.
They get him to drink to dissipate his sadness. A little wine
taken in moderation is a remedy for the soul and for the
body. Thus reasons the wise Memnon; and he gets drunk.
They propose a game after the meal. A well-ordered game
with friends is a respectable pastime. He plays; they win all
he has in his purse, and four times as much on his word. A
dispute arises over the game, it grows heated; one of his
intimate friends throws a dice box at his head and puts out
one of his eyes. The wise Memnon is carried back home
drunk, with no money, and minus an eye.

He sleeps off the wine a bit; and as soon as his head is
clear he sends his valet to the Receiver General of Finances
of Nineveh to get some money to pay off his intimate friends;
they tell him that that morning his debtor managed a fraud-
ulent bankruptcy which places a hundred families in dire
alarm. Memnon, out of patience, goes to court with a plaster
over his eye and a petition in his hand to ask the King for
justice against the bankrupt. He meets in a drawing room
several ladies who were all nonchalantly wearing hoops
twenty-four feet in circumference. One of them, who knew
him slightly, said, looking at him sidewise:

"Oh! what a horrible man!"

Another, who knew him better, said to him:

"Good evening, Monsieur Memnon;[2] really, Monsieur Memnon, I am very glad to see you. By the way, Monsieur Mem-

---

1   An allusion to syphilis, which came to Europe only after
the discovery of America.
2   The form "Monsieur" alone would be polite; the form
"Monsieur Memnon" is impolite, condescending if not contemp-
tuous.

non, why did you lose an eye?" And she passed on without waiting for an answer.

Memnon hid in a corner and waited for the moment when he could cast himself at the feet of the monarch. This moment arrived. He kissed the ground three times and presented his petition. His Gracious Majesty received him very favorably and gave the memorandum to one of his satraps to report to him on. The satrap draws Memnon aside and says to him with a lofty air and a bitter sneer:

"You impress me as a one-eyed joker to address yourself to the King rather than to me, and even more of a joker to dare to ask justice against an honest bankrupt whom I honor with my protection and who is the nephew of a chambermaid of my mistress. Abandon this affair, my friend, if you want to keep the eye you have left."

Memnon, having thus in the morning renounced women, excesses at table, gaming, all quarreling, and above all the court, had before night been duped and robbed by a beautiful lady, got drunk, gambled, had a quarrel, had an eye put out, and been to court, where they had laughed at him.

Petrified with astonishment and stricken with grief, he goes back home with death in his heart. He wants to go in, he finds bailiffs stripping his house of furniture on behalf of his creditors. He remains under a plane tree, almost unconscious; there he meets the beautiful lady of that morning, who was walking with her dear uncle and who burst out laughing on seeing Memnon with his plaster. Night came; Memnon lay down on some straw near the walls of his house. A fever seized him; in the fit he fell asleep; and a celestial spirit appeared to him in a dream.

He was all resplendent with light. He had six wings, but neither feet nor head nor tail, and he bore no resemblance to anything.

"Who are you?" Memnon said to him.

"Your good genie," the other answered.

"Then give me back my eye, my health, my wealth, my wisdom," said Memnon. Then he told him how he had lost all that in one day.

"Those are adventures that never happen to us in the world we inhabit," said the spirit.

"And what world do you inhabit?" said the afflicted man.

"My country," he replied, "is five hundred million leagues

from the sun, in a little star near Sirius, which you can see from here."

"What a fine country!" said Memnon. "What! where you come from you have no rascally women who dupe a poor fellow, no intimate friends who win his money from him and put one of his eyes out, no bankrupts, no satraps who laugh at you while refusing you justice?"

"No," said the inhabitant of the star, "none of all that. We are never duped by women, because we have none; we never commit excesses at table, because we do not eat; we have no bankrupts, because with us there is neither silver nor gold; no one can put out our eyes, because we do not have bodies fashioned like yours; and satraps never do us injustice, because in our little star everyone is equal."

Memnon said to him then: "My lord, without women and dining, how do you spend your time?"

"In watching," said the genie, "over the other globes that are entrusted to us; and I come to console you."

"Alas!" returned Memnon, "why didn't you come last night to keep me from committing so many follies?"

"I was with Hassan, your older brother," said the celestial being. "He is more to be pitied than you. His Gracious Majesty the King of India, at whose court he has the honor to be, has had both his eyes put out for a petty indiscretion, and right now he is in a dungeon, his feet and hands in irons."

"It is certainly worth while," said Memnon, "to have a good genie in a family, so that one of two brothers may be one-eyed, the other blind, one lying on straw, the other in prison."

"Your lot will change," returned the animal from the star. "It is true that you will always have only one eye; but except for that you will be happy enough, provided you never form the stupid plan of being perfectly wise."

"Then that is something impossible to attain?" cried Memnon with a sigh.

"As impossible," replied the other, "as to be perfectly able, perfectly strong, perfectly powerful, perfectly happy. We ourselves are very far from it. There is a globe where all that is found; but in the hundred thousand millions of worlds that are dispersed in extensive space, everything goes by degrees. There is less wisdom and pleasure in the second of these than in the first, less in the third than in the second.

And so for the rest down to the last, in which everyone is completely mad."

"I am much afraid," said Memnon, "that our little terraqueous globe may be precisely that madhouse of the universe that you do me the honor of telling me about."

"Not quite," said the spirit; "but it comes close; everything must be in its proper place."

"But then," said Memnon, "certain poets, certain philosophers are very wrong to say that *all is well*." [3]

"They are very right," said the philosopher from on high, "considering the arrangement of the whole universe."

"Ah! I shall believe that only," replied poor Memnon, "when I have two eyes again."

[3]   Especially Pope, Shaftesbury, Bolingbroke, Leibniz, Wolff. Cf. *Candide*.

Bababec and the Fakirs[1]

[1750]

WHEN I WAS in the city of Benares on the banks of the Ganges, the ancient land of the Brahmans, I strove to learn. I understood Hindi fairly well; I listened much and noted everything. I was staying with my correspondent Omri; he was the worthiest man I have ever known. He was of the religion of the Brahmans, I have the honor to be a Moslem: never have we had one word louder than the other on the subject of Mohammed and Brahma. We performed our ablutions, each his own; we drank of the same lemonade, we ate of the same rice, like two brothers.

One day we went together to the pagoda of Gavani. There we saw several bands of fakirs, some of whom were yogis, that is to say contemplative fakirs, and the others disciples of the ancient gymnosophists, who led an active life. As is well known, they have a learned language, which is that of the most ancient Brahmans, and in this tongue a book they call the Veda. It is assuredly the oldest book in all Asia, not excepting the Zend-Avesta. I passed in front of a fakir who was reading this book.

"Oh! wretched infidel!" he cried. "You have made me lose the number of the vowels I was counting; and because of this incident, my soul will pass into a hare's body instead of going into a parrot's, as I had every reason to flatter myself it would do."

I gave him a rupee to console him. A few steps from there I had the misfortune to sneeze, and the noise I made awakened a fakir who was in ecstasy.

"Where am I?" he said. "What a horrible fall! I no longer

---

1   First published under the title *Letter from a Turk about the Fakirs and His Friend Bababec.*

see the end of my nose: the celestial light has disappeared." [2]

"If I am the cause," I said to him, "of your seeing at last farther than the end of your nose, here is a rupee to repair the harm I have done; go back to your celestial light."

Having thus got out of trouble discreetly, I passed on to the other gymnosophists: there were several who brought me some very pretty little nails to drive into my arms and thighs in honor of Brahma. I bought their nails and nailed down my rugs with them. Others were dancing on their hands; others were performing on the slack rope; others always went about on one foot. There were some who bore chains, others a pack-saddle; some had their heads in a bushel: in other respects the best people in the world.[3]

My friend Omri took me into the cell of one of the most famous of them; his name was Bababec: he was naked as a monkey and around his neck had a great chain that weighed more than sixty pounds. He was sitting on a wooden chair appropriately furnished with little points of nails that penetrated into his buttocks, and you would have thought he was on a bed of satin. Many women came to consult him; he was the oracle of every family; and it may be said that he enjoyed a very great reputation. I was witness to the long talk that Omri had with him.

"Do you believe, father," he said to him, "that after passing through the test of the seven metempsychoses I may reach the abode of Brahma?"

"That depends," said the fakir. "How do you live?"

"I strive," said Omri, "to be a good citizen, a good husband, a good father, a good friend; I lend money without interest to the rich upon occasion, I give it to the poor; I maintain peace among my neighbors."

"Do you sometimes put nails in your ass?" asked the Brahman.

"Never, reverend father."

"I am sorry about that," replied the fakir; "you will certainly not go beyond the nineteenth heaven; and that's a pity."

2   Author's note: "When the fakirs want to see the celestial light, which happens very often among them, they turn their eyes toward the end of their nose."
3   From a famous verse by Clément Marot (1496–1544).

"What!" said Omri. "That's very decent; I am very content with my lot. What do I care whether it's the nineteenth or the twentieth, provided I do my duty on my pilgrimage and am well received at the last resting place? Is it not enough to be a decent man in this land, and then to be happy in the land of Brahma? Into what heaven then do you expect to go, you, Monsieur Bababec, with your nails and your chains?"

"Into the thirty-fifth," said Bababec.

"I think you are very comical," replied Omri, "to expect to be lodged higher than I: assuredly that can be only the effect of excessive ambition. You condemn those who seek honors in this life, why do you want such great ones in the other? And besides, on what grounds do you expect to be treated better than I? Learn that I give more in alms in ten days than all the nails you stick in your behind cost you in ten years. Much it matters to Brahma that you spend the day stark naked with a chain around your neck! That is a fine service you render your country! I set a hundred times more store by a man who sows vegetables or plants trees than by all your comrades who gaze at the end of their nose or carry a pack-saddle out of excessive nobility of soul."

Having spoken thus, Omri became gentle again, cajoled him, persuaded him, at last pledged him to leave behind his nails and his chain and come and lead a decent life at his house. They scoured him, they rubbed him with perfumed ointments, they dressed him decently; he lived two weeks in a very wise manner and admitted that he was a hundred times happier than before. But he was losing his authority among the people; the women no longer came to consult him; he left Omri, and resumed his nails in order to have consideration.

History of Scarmentado's Travels

Written by Himself

[1756]

I WAS BORN in the city of Candia [1] in 1600. My father was the governor; and I remember that a mediocre poet named Iro, [2] who was not mediocrely harsh, composed some bad verses in my praise, in which he made me a direct descendant of Minos; but when my father fell into disfavor, he composed some other verses in which I descended only from Pasiphae [3] and her lover. This Iro was a very wicked man, and the most boring knave on the island.

At the age of fifteen my father sent me to study at Rome. I arrived in the hope of learning all truths; for until then I had been taught just the opposite, according to the custom of this poor world of ours from China to the Alps. Monsignor Profondo, to whom I was recommended, was a singular man and one of the most terrible erudites in the world. He tried to teach me Aristotle's categories and was on the point of placing me in the category of his darling boys; I barely escaped. I saw processions, exorcisms, and a few pillages. It was said, but very falsely, that Signora Olimpia, [4] a person of

1   A city of Crete, now called Herakleion in Greek.
2   The anagram represents Pierre-Charles Roy (1683–1764), poet, author of plays, operas, and ballets, satirist, and enemy of Voltaire.
3   Wife of Minos, a legendary King of Crete. When Minos refused to sacrifice to Poseidon, as he had promised, a beautiful bull sent him by the god, Poseidon punished him by making Pasiphae fall in love with the bull and in time give birth to their son the Minotaur, part bull and part man.
4   Olimpia Maldachini, sister-in-law and favorite of Innocent X.

great prudence, sold many things that people should not sell.
I was at an age when all that seemed to me very amusing.
A young lady with very sweet ways, named Signora Fatelo,[5]
took it into her head to love me. She was being courted by
the Reverend Father Poignardini and the Reverend Father
Aconiti, young votaries of an order that no longer exists: she
reconciled them by granting her good graces to me; but at
the same time I ran the risk of being excommunicated and
poisoned. I left very pleased with the architecture of St.
Peter's.

I traveled in France; it was during the reign of Louis the
Just.[6] The first thing I was asked was whether I wanted for
breakfast a little piece of Marshal d'Ancre,[7] whose flesh the
people had roasted, and who was being distributed at a very
reasonable price to those who wanted any of him.

This state was continually a prey to civil wars, sometimes
for a place in the Council, sometimes for two pages of controversy. For more than sixty years this fire, now covered
and now violently blown on, had been devastating these lovely
climes. These were all freedoms of the Gallican church.

"Alas!" I said, "yet this people was born gentle; what can
have drawn it so far out of character? It makes jokes, and
it makes Saint Bartholomew's Day Massacres. Happy the
time when it will make nothing but jokes!"

I crossed over to England: there the same quarrels were
exciting the same furies. Some holy Catholics had resolved,
for the good of the Church, to blow sky-high with gunpowder [8]
the King, the royal family, and the entire Parliament, and
to deliver England from these heretics. They showed me the
square where the Blessed Queen Mary, daughter of Henry
VIII, had had more than five hundred of her subjects burned.
A Hibernian priest assured me that this was a very good
action: firstly, because those who had been burned were
English; in the second place, because they never took holy
water and did not believe in Saint Patrick's Purgatory.[9] He
was especially astonished that Queen Mary was not yet

5   In Italian, "Do it."
6   Louis XIII (1601–1643), who reigned from 1610 to 1643.
7   Concino Concini, Marquis, like his wife a favorite of Queen
Marie de Médicis, assassinated in 1617 by order of the King.
8   The Gunpowder Plot (1605) of Guy Fawkes and others.
9   The cave of Lough Derg, a place of pilgrimage, from the
early Middle Ages reputed to be a gate to Purgatory.

canonized; but he hoped that she would be soon, when the cardinal nephew [10] had a little leisure.

I went to Holland, where I hoped to find more tranquillity among more phlegmatic peoples. They were cutting off the head of a venerable old man when I arrived at the Hague. It was the bald head of Prime Minister Barneveldt,[11] the man who had deserved the best from the republic. Touched with pity, I asked what was his crime, and whether he had betrayed the state.

"He did much worse," answered a black-cloaked preacher; "he is a man who believes that one can be saved by good works as well as by faith. You can well sense that if such opinions became established, a republic could not subsist, and that severe laws are needed to repress such scandalous horrors."

A profound political theorist of that country told me, sighing:

"Alas! sir, good times will not last forever; it is only by chance that the people is so zealous; the depths of their character lean toward the abominable dogma of tolerance; one day they will come to it; it makes a man shudder."

As for me, while waiting for the fatal day of moderation and indulgence to arrive, I very quickly left a country where severity was relieved by no amenity, and I embarked for Spain.

The court was at Seville; the galleons had arrived; everything breathed abundance and joy in the fairest season of the year. I saw at the end of an alley of orange and lemon trees a sort of immense tilting ground surrounded by stands covered with precious fabrics. The King, the Queen, the infantes, the infantas, were under a superb canopy. Facing this august family was another but loftier throne. I said to one of my traveling companions: "Unless that throne is reserved for God, I do not see what use it can be." These indiscreet words were overheard by a grave Spaniard and cost me dear. Meanwhile I was imagining that we were going to see some tournament or some bullfight, when the Grand Inquisitor appeared on this throne, from which he blessed the King and the people.

---

10   Presumably Ludovico Ludovisi, right-hand man to his uncle, Pope Gregory XV, who made him a cardinal in 1621.

11   Johan van Oldenbarneveldt (1547–1619), known as Barneveldt, Land's Advocate of Holland, supporter of religious tolerance.

Then came an army of monks filing past two by two, white, black, gray, shod, unshod, with beard, without beard, with pointed cowl, and without cowl; next marched the executioner; then, amid alguazils [12] and grandees, one could see about forty persons covered with sacks on which devils and flames had been painted. They were Jews who had not been willing to renounce Moses absolutely, they were Christians who had married their godsons' godmothers, or who had not worshiped Our Lady of Atocha,[13] or who had not been willing to rid themselves of their ready money in favor of the Hieronymite friars.[14] Some very beautiful prayers were piously sung, after which all the culprits were burned in a slow fire; at which the entire royal family appeared extremely edified.

In the evening, at the time when I was about to go to bed, there arrived in my room two familiars of the Inquisition together with the Holy Hermandad: [15] they embraced me tenderly, and without saying a word to me took me into a very cool dungeon, furnished with a bed of straw and a handsome crucifix. I stayed there six weeks, at the end of which the Reverend Father Inquisitor sent to ask me to come and talk with him: he clasped me in his arms for some time with an affection quite paternal; he told me he was sincerely distressed to have learned that I was so ill lodged, but that all the apartments in the house were full, and that another time he hoped I would be more comfortable. Then he asked me cordially whether I did not know why I was there. I told the Reverend Father that it was apparently for my sins. "Well, my dear child, for what sin? Speak to me with confidence." I used my imagination to no avail, I did not guess; he charitably set me on the right track.

At last I remembered my indiscreet words. I got off with a whipping and a fine of thirty thousand reales.[16] They took me to make a bow to the Grand Inquisitor: he was a polite man, who asked me what I had thought of his little festivities.

12   Police officers.
13   A wooden image of the Virgin in Madrid, supposedly brought from Antioch by an apostle, said to weep each year on her feast day.
14   Members of hermit orders of Saint Jerome.
15   The Holy Brotherhood, an association formed in Spain with a police force to track down criminals.
16   Spanish silver coins.

I told him that they were delightful, and I went and urged my traveling companions to leave this country, beautiful as it is. They had had time to learn about all the great things the Spaniards had done for religion. They had read the memoirs of the famous bishop of Chiapa,[17] from which it appears that in America ten million infidels had been slaughtered or burned or drowned in order to convert them. I thought this bishop was exaggerating; but even if these sacrifices were reduced to five million victims, that would still be admirable.

The desire to travel still impelled me. I had planned to end my tour of Europe with Turkey; we set out for it. I fully intended to speak my mind no longer about the festivities I would see.

"These Turks," I said to my companions, "are unbelievers, who have not been baptized, and who consequently will be much more cruel than the Reverend Father Inquisitors. Let us keep silence when we are among the Mohammedans."

So I went to their country. I was strangely surprised to see in Turkey many more Christian churches than there were in Candia. I even saw large troops of monks who were allowed freely to pray to the Virgin Mary and curse Mohammed, some in Greek, some in Latin, a few others in Armenian. "Fine people, the Turks!" I exclaimed.

The Greek Christians and the Latin Christians were mortal enemies in Constantinople; these slaves persecuted each other, like dogs who bite each other in the street and whom their masters beat with sticks to separate them. The Grand Vizier* was then protecting the Greeks. The Greek patriarch accused me of having had supper at the Latin patriarch's, and I was condemned by the whole Divan* to a hundred strokes with a lathe on the soles of my feet, redeemable for five hundred sequins.* The next day the Grand Vizier was strangled; the day after that his successor, who was for the party of the Latins, and who was not strangled until a month later, condemned me to the same fine for having had supper at the Greek patriarch's. I was in the sad necessity of no longer attending either the Greek or the Latin church. To

17 The *Brevissima relacion de la destruycion de las Indias occidentales* (c. 1554) by Bartolomé de Las Casas (1474–1566), Dominican missionary, at one time (1544–1547) bishop of Chiapa in Mexico.

console myself, I rented a beautiful Circassian woman, who was the most tender of persons in a tête-à-tête and the most pious in the mosque. One night, in the sweet transports of her love, she cried out as she embraced me: *"Allah illah allah."* [18] Those are the sacramental words of the Turks; I thought they were those of love; I also exclaimed most tenderly: *"Allah illah allah."* "Ah!" she said to me. "Merciful God be praised, you are a Turk." I told her that I blessed him for having given me the strength to be, and I thought myself only too happy. In the morning the imam* came to circumcise me; and since I offered some objection, the district cadi,* an upright man, proposed to me that he impale me; I saved my foreskin and my behind with a thousand sequins, and quickly fled to Persia, resolved nevermore to hear either a Greek or a Latin Mass in Turkey, and nevermore to exclaim *"Allah illah allah"* at a rendezvous.

Arriving at Ispahan, I was asked whether I was for the black sheep or for the white sheep. I answered that that was quite indifferent to me provided the mutton was tender. The reader must know that the factions of the White Sheep and the Black Sheep [19] still divided the Persians. It was thought that I was making fun of the two parties, so that already at the gates of the city I found myself with violent trouble on my hands; it cost me another large number of sequins to get rid of the sheep.

I pushed on all the way to China with an interpreter who assured me that that was the country where people lived freely and gaily. The Tartars had made themselves masters of it after having put everything to fire and the sword; and the Reverend Jesuit Fathers on the one hand, like the Reverend Dominican Fathers on the other, said that they were winning souls to God without anyone's knowing anything about it. Such zealous converters have never been seen: for they took turns persecuting one another; they wrote volumes of calumnies to Rome; they called one another infidels, and prevaricators for the sake of a soul. Above all there was a horrible quarrel between them over the way to make a bow. The Jesuits wanted the Chinese to greet their

18   An English corruption of Arabic *la ilāha illa allāh,* there is no God but Allah.
19   Persia was torn by these rival factions in the fifteenth century.

fathers and mothers Chinese fashion, and the Dominicans wanted them to greet them Roman fashion.

It happened that I was taken for a Dominican by the Jesuits. I was brought before His Tartar Majesty as a spy for the Pope. The Supreme Council instructed a prime mandarin, who ordered a sergeant, who commanded four of the country's myrmidons, to arrest me and bind me ceremoniously. After a hundred and forty genuflexions I was led before His Majesty. He had me asked whether I was the Pope's spy and whether it was true that that prince was due to come in person to dethrone him. I answered that the Pope was a seventy-year-old priest; that he lived four thousand leagues away from His Sacred Tartaro-Chinese Majesty; that he had about two thousand soldiers, who went on guard with a parasol; that he dethroned nobody, and that His Majesty could sleep in security. This was the least disastrous adventure of my life. I was sent to Macao, whence I embarked for Europe.

My ship had to go into dry dock near the coasts of Golconda. I took this time to go to see the court of the great Aurangzeb,[20] about which wonders were told around the world; it was then in Delhi. I had the consolation of beholding it on the day of the pompous ceremony in which he received the celestial present sent him by the Sherif of Mecca. It was the broom with which they had swept the holy house, the Kaaba, the Beth Allah.[21] This broom is the symbol that sweeps away the refuse of the soul. Aurangzeb did not appear to need it; he was the most pious man in all Hindustan. It is true that he had cut the throat of one of his brothers and poisoned his father. Twenty rajas and as many omrahs[22] had died under torture; but that was nothing, and men spoke only of his piety. The only man compared to him was the Sacred Majesty of the Most Serene Emperor of Morocco, Mulai Ismail,[23] who cut off heads every Friday after prayers.

I said not a word; my travels had shaped me, and I felt that it was not for me to decide between these two august

---

20   Alamgir I (1619–1707), Emperor of Hindustan from 1658 to 1707.

21   The house of Allah.

22   Raja: an Indian prince or chief. Omrah: a lord of a Mohammedan court in India.

23   Mulai (or Muley) Ismail (1646–1727), known as "The Bloodthirsty," Sultan of Morocco from 1672 to 1727.

sovereigns. A young Frenchman with whom I was lodging failed, I admit, to show respect for the Emperors of India and Morocco. He took it into his head to say very indiscreetly that in Europe there were some very pious sovereigns who governed their states well and who even attended church, without therefore killing their fathers and their brothers and without cutting off the heads of their subjects. Our interpreter passed on in Hindi the impious remarks of my young friend. Having learned from the past, I quickly had my camels saddled; we left, the Frenchman and I. I have since learned that that very night, when the officers of the great Aurangzeb came to get us, they found only the interpreter. He was executed in a public square, and all the courtiers admitted without flattery that his death was a very just thing.

It remained for me to see Africa, to enjoy all the amenities of our earth. Indeed I did see it. My vessel was captured by Negro corsairs. Our master made vehement complaints; he asked them why they were thus violating the laws of nations. The Negro captain answered him:

"Your nose is long, and ours is flat; your hair is quite straight, and our wool is curly; your skin is of the color of ashes, and ours of the color of ebony; consequently, by the sacred laws of nature, we must always be enemies. You buy us at the fairs on the Guinea coast, like beasts of burden, to make us work at some sort of labor as arduous as it is ridiculous. With strokes of a bull's pizzle you make us dig in the mountains to get out a kind of yellow earth which of itself is good for nothing and is nowhere near worth a good Egyptian onion; and so when we come upon you and we are the stronger, we make slaves of you, we make you till our fields, or else we cut off your nose and ears."

No one had any reply to so wise a speech. I went and tilled an old Negress's field to preserve my ears and nose. After a year I was ransomed. I had seen everything beautiful, good, and admirable on earth: I resolved to see nothing more but my penates.[24] I married in my own country: I became a cuckold, and I saw that that was life's sweetest estate.

24 Household gods.

Plato's Dream

[1756]

PLATO DREAMED A LOT, and people have dreamed no less since. It had seemed to him that human nature was once double, and that as a punishment for its faults it was divided into male and female.

He had proved that there can be only five perfect worlds, because there are only five regular bodies in mathematics. His *Republic* was one of his great dreams. He had also dreamed that sleep is born out of waking and waking out of sleep, and that we are sure to lose our eyesight if we look at an eclipse elsewhere than in a pool of water. In those days dreams gave a man a great reputation.

Here is one of his dreams, which is not one of the least interesting. It seemed to him that the great Demiurge, the eternal Geometrician, having populated infinite space with innumerable globes, decided to test the knowledge of the genii who had been witnesses of his works. He gave each of them a little piece of matter to arrange, much as Phidias and Zeuxis might have given their disciples statues and pictures to make, if it is permissible to compare small things with great.

Demogorgon [1] had as his share the bit of mud that is called *Earth;* and, having arranged it in the manner that we see today, he claimed to have made a masterpiece. He thought he had triumphed over envy, and was expecting praise, even from his colleagues; he was quite surprised to be received by them with hoots.

One of them, who was a very bad joker, said to him:

"Truly, you have worked very well: you have separated your world in two, and you have put a great space of water between the two hemispheres, so that there should be no

1   A mysterious, terrible, and evil divinity.

communication between the two. They will freeze with cold at your two poles, they will die of heat at your equinoctial line. You have prudently established great deserts of sand, so that those who cross them may die of hunger and thirst. I am fairly content with your sheep, cows, and hens; but frankly I am none too much so with your snakes and spiders. Your onions and artichokes are very good things; but I don't see what your idea was in covering the earth with so many venomous plants, unless you had the intention of poisoning the inhabitants. Moreover it seems to me that you have formed about thirty kinds of monkeys, many more kinds of dogs, and only four or five kinds of men: it is true that you have given this last animal what you call *reason;* but in all conscience, that reason of his is too ridiculous and comes too close to madness. Moreover it appears to me that you set no great store by that two-footed animal, since you have given him so many enemies and so little defense, so many maladies and so few remedies, so many passions and so little wisdom. Apparently you do not want many of those animals to remain on earth; for, without counting the dangers to which you expose them, you have done your calculating so well that someday the smallpox will carry off regularly every year the tenth part of this species, and the sister of this smallpox [2] will poison the source of life in the remaining nine-tenths; and as if that were still not enough, you have so arranged things that half the survivors will be occupied in pleading suits, the other half in killing each other; no doubt they will be very much obliged to you, and that's a fine masterpiece you have made."

Demogorgon blushed: he fully sensed that there was moral evil and physical evil in the work he had done, but he maintained that there was more good than evil.

"It is easy to criticize," said he; "but do you think it is so easy to make an animal that is always reasonable, that is free, and that never abuses its liberty? Do you think that when a person has nine or ten thousand plants to cause to multiply, he can so easily keep some of these plants from having harmful qualities? Do you imagine that with a certain quantity of water, sand, mud, and fire, one can have neither sea nor desert? You, sir, who like to laugh, you have just arranged the planet Mars; we shall see how you made out

2   The pox, or syphilis.

with your two great bands, and what a fine effect your moonless nights make; we shall see whether among your people there is neither madness nor illness."

Indeed, the genii examined Mars, and they fell roughly upon the mocker. The serious genie who had molded Saturn was not spared; his colleagues, the makers of Jupiter, Mercury, Venus, each had reproaches to take.

They wrote fat volumes and pamphlets; they said witty things; they composed songs; they made each other look ridiculous; the factions grew bitter; finally the eternal Demiurge imposed silence on them all:

"You have made," he said to them, "some things good and some bad, because you have much intelligence and because you are imperfect; your works will last only a few hundreds of millions of years, after which, having learned more, you will do better: it belongs to me alone to make things perfect and immortal."

That is what Plato was teaching his disciples. When he had finished speaking, one of them said to him: "And then you awoke."

Account of the Sickness, Confession, Death, and Apparition of the Jesuit Berthier

[1759 ¹]

IT WAS ON OCTOBER 12, 1759, that Father Berthier* went, for his misfortune, from Paris to Versailles, with Friar Coutu, who ordinarily accompanies him. Berthier had put in the carriage a few copies of the *Journal de Trévoux* to present to his protectors and protectresses, such as the maid of My Lady the Nurse, an officer of the table, one of the King's apprentice apothecaries, and several other lords who set store by talents. On the road Berthier felt several attacks of nausea; his head grew heavy, he gave frequent yawns.

"I don't know what's the matter with me," he said to Coutu, "I have never yawned so much."

"Reverend Father," replied Friar Coutu, "it is only a fair return."

"What? What do you mean by your fair return?" said Friar Berthier.

"The point is," said Friar Coutu, "that I am yawning too, and I don't know why, for I have read nothing all day, and

---

1   In 1760 Voltaire added another part, not included here, the "Account of the Trip of Friar Garassise, Nephew of Friar Garasse, Successor to Friar Berthier, and What Follows, While Waiting for What Will Follow." Berthier lived until 1782.
  This story is not listed among Voltaire's tales, and appears in his *Mélanges*.

you haven't spoken to me since I have been on the road with you."

While saying these words, Friar Coutu yawned more than ever. Berthier replied with yawns that never ended. The coachman turned around and, seeing them yawn so, started yawning too; the malady attacked all the passers-by, everyone yawned in all the neighboring houses: so great an influence does the mere presence of a learned man sometimes have upon other men.

Meanwhile a slight cold sweat came over Berthier.

"I don't know what's the matter with me," he said, "I feel like ice."

"I should think so," said his friar companion.

"What? You should think so?" said Berthier. "What do you mean by that?"

"I mean I am frozen too," said Coutu.

"I'm falling asleep," said Berthier.

"I am not surprised a bit," said the other.

"Why not?" said Berthier.

"Because I'm falling asleep too," said the companion.

So there they were both seized by a soporific and lethargic ailment; and in this state they stopped before the carriage gate at Versailles. The coachman, opening the door for them, tried to draw them out of this deep sleep; he could not accomplish it; help was sent for. The companion, who was more robust than Friar Berthier, finally gave some signs of life; but Berthier was colder than ever. A few court doctors, coming back from dinner, passed by the carriage; they were asked to take a look at the sick man: one of them, having taken his pulse, went off, saying that he no longer meddled with medicine since he had been at court; another, having looked at him more attentively, declared that the trouble came from the gall bladder, which was always too full; a third asserted that the whole thing came from the brain, which was too empty.

While they were reasoning the patient was getting worse; convulsions were beginning to give sinister signs, and already the three fingers that hold a pen were drawn back, when a chief doctor, who had studied under Mead and Boerhaave and who knew more about it than the others, opened Berthier's mouth with a baby's bottle and, having reflected attentively on the odor exhaled, declared that he was poisoned.

At this word everyone protested.

"Yes, gentlemen," he continued, "he is poisoned; all you have to do is feel his skin to see that the exhalations of a cold poison have made their way into him through the pores; and I maintain that this poison is worse than a mixture of hemlock, black hellebore, opium, solanum, and henbane. Coachman, mightn't you have put into your carriage some package for our apothecaries?"

"No, sir," replied the coachman, "here is the only bundle, which I placed there by order of the Reverend Father."

Then he fumbled in the chest and drew out two dozen copies of the *Journal de Trévoux*.

"Well, gentlemen, was I wrong?" said this great doctor.

All those present marveled at his prodigious sagacity; everyone recognized the origin of the disease: they burned the pernicious package on the spot under the patient's nose, and, the heavy particles having been lightened by the action of the fire, Berthier was relieved a little; but since the disease had made great progress and attacked the head, the danger still persisted. The doctor thought of having him swallow a page of the *Encyclopédie** in white wine, to restore the flow of the humors of the thickened bile; there resulted a copious evacuation; but the head was still horribly heavy, spells of vertigo continued, the few words he was able to articulate made no sense. He remained two hours in this state, after which it was necessary to have him given confession.

Two priests were then walking along the Rue des Récollets:* they accosted them. The first refused.

"I do not want," he said, "to make myself responsible for the soul of a Jesuit, that's too ticklish; I want nothing to do with those people, either for the affairs of this world or for those of the next; let him who will confess a Jesuit, it won't be me."

The second one was not so difficult. "I will undertake this operation," said he; "advantage may be derived from anything."

Immediately he was taken into the room to which the patient had just been transported; and since Berthier still could not speak distinctly, the confessor decided to question him.

"Reverend Father," he said to him, "do you believe in God?"

"That's a strange question," said Berthier.

"Not so strange," said the other; "there is believing and believing; to be sure of believing as we should, it is necessary to love God and our neighbor; do you love them sincerely?"

"I make a distinction," said Berthier.

"No distinctions, if you please," returned the confessor; "no absolution if you do not begin with these two duties."

"Very well, yes," said the confessant, "since you force me to it, I love God, and my neighbor as I can."

"Haven't you often read bad books?" said the confessor.

"What do you mean by bad books?" said the confessant.

"I do not mean," said the confessor, "simply boring books, like the Roman history of Friars Catrou and Rouillé, and your school tragedies, and your books entitled *Of Belles Lettres*, and the *Louisiade** of your man Le Moyne, and the verses of your Du Cerceau* on herb sauce, and his noble stanzas on the messenger from Le Mans, and his thanks to the Duke of Maine for liver patties, and your *Think Well on It,** and all the subtleties of monkish wit. I mean the writings of Friar Bougeant,* condemned by the Parlement and by the Archbishop of Paris; I mean the prettinesses of Friar Berruyer,* who changed the Old and New Testaments into a bluestocking novel in the style of *Clélie,** so justly stigmatized in Rome and in France; I mean the theology of Friar Busenbaum [2] and Friar La Croix, who have gone so far beyond everything that Friar Guignard and Friar Guéret had written, and Friar Garnet and Friar Oldcorn, and so many

2   Author's note: "These two honest Jesuits say, in this fine book, recently reprinted, that a citizen proscribed by a prince may be lawfully assassinated only in that prince's territory; but that a prince proscribed by the Pope may be assassinated anywhere in the whole world, because the Pope is sovereign of the whole world; that a man entrusted with killing an excommunicate may give this commission to another; that it is an act of charity to accept this commission, etc.; pages 101, 102, 103."

The book in question is the *Theologia moralis* of the German Father Hermann Busenbaum (1600–1668), as enlarged by Father Claude La Croix (1652–1714).

All the men that follow except Harlay are of course Jesuits. Guignard, a teacher in Paris, was executed in 1595 for moral complicity in the unsuccessful attempt by Jean Châtel on the life of Henry IV. Guéret (Abbé Louis-Gabriel) is a Jesuit contemporary of Voltaire. Garnet and Oldcorn, English, were executed in 1606 for complicity in the Gunpowder Plot. Harlay was a loyalist president of the Parlement of Paris at the time of Châtel's attempt. Jouvency, a historian, ranks Guignard among the martyrs.

others; I mean Friar Jouvency, who delicately compares President de Harlay to Pilate, the Parlement to the Jews, and Friar Guignard to Jesus Christ, because a citizen, too carried away, but filled with just horror at a professor of parricide, decided to spit in the face of Friar Guignard, assassin of Henry IV, at the time when that impenitent monster was refusing to ask pardon of the King and of justice; I mean finally that innumerable crowd of your casuists, whom the eloquent Pascal* let off too easily, and especially your Sanchez, who, in his book *De Matrimonio,* made a collection of everything that Aretino and *The Carthusians' Gate-Keeper* would have trembled to say.[3] If you have read any such things, your salvation is in great danger."

"I make a distinction," replied the questionee.

"Once more, no distinctions," returned the questioner. "Have you read all these books, yes or no?"

"Sir," said Berthier, "I have the right to read everything, in view of the eminent position I occupy in the Society."

"Ah! Then what is this great position?" said the confessor.

"Well," replied Berthier, "since you must know, it is I who am the author of the *Journal de Trévoux.*"

"What! You are the author of that work that damns so many people?"

"Sir, sir, my book damns no one; into what sin could it make anyone fall, if you please?"

"Ah, brother," said the confessor, "don't you know that whoever calls his brother *Raca*[4] is liable to hell fire? Now you have the misfortune to lead anyone who reads you into

---

3 Pascal satirized Jesuit casuistry in his *Lettres provinciales.* Pietro Aretino (1492–1557) was noted for his licentious verse. The *Histoire de Dom B . . . , portier des chartreux, écrite par lui-même* is a pornographic novel, published in 1745 or earlier, by Jean-Charles Gervaise de Latouche.
Author's note: "This Friar Sanchez examines 'utrum femina quae nondum seminavit, possit, virili membro extracto, se tactibus ad seminandum provocare?' Lib. IX, disp. xvii, no. 8. 'Semen ubi femina effudit, an teneatur alter effundere, sive inter uxores, sive inter fornicantes? Utrum liceat intra vas praeposterum, aut in os feminae, membrum intermittere, animo consummandi intra vas legitimum, etc.' Lib. IX, disp. xvii, from no. 1, 2, 3, 4 on. This same Sanchez pushes his abomination to the point of seriously examining 'An virgo Maria semen emiserit in copulatione cum Spiritu Sancto?' Lib. II, disp. xxi, no. 11. And he holds for the affirmative."
4 Fool. See Matthew 5:22.

immediate temptation to call you *Raca*. How many decent men I have seen who, having read just two or three pages of your book, threw it in the fire, transported with anger! 'What an impertinent author!' they would say. 'The ignoramus! the dolt! the pedant! the ass!' It would never end; the spirit of charity was totally extinguished in them, and they were evidently in danger of their salvation. Judge of how many evils you have been the cause! There are perhaps about fifty persons who read you, and they are fifty souls whom you place in peril every month; what especially excites anger among the faithful is that confidence with which you decide about everything you do not understand. This vice manifestly has its source in two mortal sins: one is pride and the other covetousness. Isn't it true that you write your book for money, and that you are smitten with haughtiness when you inappropriately criticize Abbé Velly, and Abbé Coyer, and Abbé d'Olivet,[5] and all our good authors? I cannot give you absolution unless you make a firm resolution never again in your life to work on the *Journal de Trévoux*."

Friar Berthier did not know what to reply; his head was not very clear, and he clung furiously to his two favorite sins.

"What's this! You hesitate?" said the confessor. "Consider that in a few hours everything will be finished for you: can a man still cherish his passions when he must renounce satisfying them forever? Will you be asked on Judgment Day whether or not you succeeded in writing the *Journal de Trévoux*? Is that what you were born for? Was it to bore us that you took a vow of chastity, humility, and obedience? Dry tree, stunted tree, who are going to be reduced to ashes, profit by the moment you have left, bear the fruits of penitence yet; above all, detest the spirit of calumny that has possessed you up to now; try to have as much religion as those whom you accuse of being without religion. Know, Friar Berthier, that piety and virtue do not consist in believing that when your Francis Xavier [6] dropped his crucifix in the sea a crab came humbly and brought it back to him. One may be a good man and still doubt that the same Xavier was in two

5   Paul-François Velly (1709–1759) wrote a *Histoire de France . . . jusqu'au règne de Louis XIV*. Gabriel-François Coyer (1707–1782) wrote widely on economics. Pierre-Joseph Thorellier d'Olivet (1682–1768) was a former teacher of Voltaire.
6   Author's note: "Miracles reported in the life of St. Francis Xavier."

places at the same time; your books may say so; but, my brother, it is permissible to believe nothing of what is in your books.

"By the way, brother, didn't you perhaps write to Friar Malagrida* and his accomplices? Really I was forgetting that peccadillo. So you think that because it once cost Henry IV only a tooth and today it costs the King of Portugal only an arm, you can save yourself with the direction of intention? [7] You think that those are venial sins, and provided the *Journal de Trévoux* sells, you care little about the rest."

"I make a distinction, sir," said Berthier.

"More distinctions!" said the confessor. "Well, for my part I make no distinctions, and I flatly refuse you absolution."

As he was saying these words, Friar Coutu arrives on the dead run all out of breath, all sweating, all puffing, all stinking; he had found out who it was that had the honor of confessing his Reverend Father.

"Stop, stop," he cried; "no sacraments, my dear Reverend Father, no sacraments, I implore you, my dear Reverend Father Berthier, die without sacraments; it is the author of the *Nouvelles ecclésiastiques* [8] that you are with, it is the fox confessing to the wolf: you are lost if you have told the truth."

Then astonishment, shame, pain, anger, rage revived the patient's spirits for a moment.

"You, the author of the *Nouvelles ecclésiastiques?*" he exclaimed. "And you have caught a Jesuit?"

"Yes, my friend," replied the confessor with a bitter smile.

"Give me back my confession, rogue," said Berthier, "give me back my confession right now. Ah! so it is you, the enemy of God, of kings, and even of Jesuits, it is you who come to take advantage of the state I am in. Traitor, why aren't you having apoplexy and why can't *I* give *you* extreme unction? So you think you are less boring and less fanatical than I? Yes, I have written stupid things, I admit it; but you, aren't you the lowest and most execrable of all the smearers of paper in whose hands insanity has put a pen? Just tell me whether your convulsion* business is not fully a match for our *Curious and Edifying Letters.** We want to dominate

7   Theory advanced by some Jesuit authors that sins could be nullified if pious motives could be assigned to them.
8   The journal of the Jansenists, arch-rivals of the Jesuits.

everywhere, I confess; and you, you would like to throw everything into confusion: we would like to seduce all the powers; and you, you would like to excite sedition against them. Justice has had our books burned, but hasn't it had yours burned too? We are all in prison in Portugal, it is true; but hasn't the police prosecuted you and your accomplices a hundred times? If I have had the stupidity to write against enlightened men who have thus far disdained to crush me, haven't you had the same impertinence? Aren't we both made to look ridiculous? and mustn't we admit that in this century, the sewer of the centuries, we are both the vilest insects of all the insects that buzz in the middle of the filth of this mire?"

That is what the power of truth wrested from the mouth of Friar Berthier. He was speaking like a man inspired; his eyes, filled with a somber fire, rolled wildly; his mouth twisted, foam covered it; his body was stiffening, his heart palpitating: soon a general collapse followed these convulsions, and in this collapse he tenderly squeezed the hand of Friar Coutu.

"I admit," he said, "that there are many poor things in my *Journal de Trévoux;* but we must excuse human weakness."

"Ah! Reverend Father, you are a saint," said Friar Coutu; "you are the first author who ever admitted he was boring; go, die in peace, snap your fingers at the *Nouvelles ecclésiastiques;* die, Reverend Father, and be sure that you will do miracles."

Thus passed from this life to the next Friar Berthier, October 12, at half past five in the evening.

Apparition of Friar Berthier to Friar Garassise, Continuator of the Journal de Trévoux

ON OCTOBER 14, I, Ignace Garassise, grandnephew of Friar Garasse,[9] being awake around two hours after midnight, had a vision, and saw coming toward me the ghost of Friar Berthier, whereupon I was seized with the longest and most terrible yawn I have ever experienced.

9 Chronology to the contrary notwithstanding, this is a reference to Father François Garasse (1585–1631), Jesuit, a vehement foe of freethinkers. Ignace is of course the French form of Ignatius (Loyola).

"So you are dead, Reverend Father?" I said to him.

Yawning, he gave a nod that meant yes.

"All the better," I said to him, "for no doubt Your Reverence is numbered among the saints; you must occupy one of the foremost places; what a pleasure to see you in Heaven with all our brethren, past, present, and future! Is it not true that that makes about four million haloed heads from the foundation of our Society down to our day? I do not believe there are as many among the Fathers of the Oratory.* Speak, Reverend Father, do not yawn any more, and tell me the news of your joys."

"Oh my son!" said Friar Berthier in a lugubrious voice, "how wrong you are! Alas! The *Paradise Open to Philagia* [10] is closed to our Fathers!"

"Is it possible?" said I.

"Yes," he said, "beware of the pernicious vices that damn us; and above all, when you work on the *Journal de Trévoux*, do not imitate me, be neither a calumniator, nor a bad reasoner, nor above all a bore, as I have had the misfortune to be, which is the most unpardonable of sins."

I was seized with a holy horror at this terrible statement of Friar Berthier.

"So you are damned?" I exclaimed.

"No," he said; "I fortunately repented at the last moment; I am in purgatory for three hundred and thirty-three thousand three hundred and thirty-three years, three months, three weeks, and three days, and I shall be taken out only when one of our brothers shall be found who will be humble and peaceful, who will not wish to go to the court, who will not spread calumny about anyone to princes, who will not meddle in the affairs of the world, who, when he writes books, will not make anyone yawn, and who will assign all his merits to me."

"Ah! brother," I said to him, "your purgatory will last long. Well, tell me, I pray you, what is your penance in this purgatory?"

"I am obliged," he said, "to make a Jansenist's chocolate

10   The Jesuit Father Paul de Barry's book *Le Paradis ouvert à Philagie par cent dévotions à la Mère de Dieu, aisées à pratiquer* was satirized already a century earlier by Pascal in the ninth of his *Lettres provinciales*.

every morning; they make me read aloud during dinner a *Lettre provinciale*,* and the rest of the time they keep me busy mending the blouses of the nuns of Port-Royal."*

"You make me tremble," I said; "then what has become of our Fathers, for whom I had such great veneration? Where is the Reverend Father Le Tellier,[11] that leader, that apostle of the Gallican church?"

"He is damned without mercy," replied Friar Berthier, "and he richly deserved it: he had duped his King; he had lit the torch of discord, fabricated letters from bishops, and persecuted in the most cowardly and fiery way the worthiest archbishop that the capital of France ever had. He was irremissibly condemned as a forger, a calumniator, and a disturber of the public peace. It was he above all who ruined us, it was he who redoubled in us that mania that makes us go to hell by the hundreds and the thousands. We believed, because Father Le Tellier had influence, that we all should; we imagined, because he had duped his penitent, that we should dupe all ours; we believed, because one of his books had been condemned in Rome, that we should write only books that should also be condemned; and finally, we created the *Journal de Trévoux*."

While he was speaking to me, I was turning onto my left side, then on my right side, then on my backside; then I exclaimed:

"O my dear purgatorian! What must one do to avoid the state you are in? What is the sin most to be feared?"

Berthier then opened his mouth and said:

"Passing by hell to go to purgatory, I was made to enter the cavern of the seven capital sins, which is at the left of the vestibule: I first accosted Lust; she was a plump wench, fresh and appetizing; she was lying on a bed of roses, with Sanchez' book at her feet and a young abbé by her side; I said to her:

" 'Madame, apparently it is not you who are damning our Jesuits?'

" 'No,' she said, 'I do not have that honor; to be sure, I

---

11   Father Michel Le Tellier (1643–1719) gained great influence as confessor to the aged Louis XIV, brought the Cardinal Archbishop de Noailles into disfavor, and helped induce the Pope to condemn Jansenism in 1713.

have a little brother who had taken possession of the Abbé Desfontaines [12] and a few others of his kind, while they wore the frock; but in general I do not meddle in your affairs: sensual pleasure is not made for everyone.'

"Covetousness was in a corner, weighing out herbs from Paraguay [13] against gold.

" 'Is it you, Madame, who have the most influence with us?'

" 'No, Reverend Father; I damn only a few of your Fathers in charge of business matters.'

" 'Could it be you?' I said to Anger.

" 'Talk to someone else, I am a transient; I enter every heart, but I do not remain; my sisters soon take my place.'

"I then turned toward Gluttony, who was at table.

" 'As for you, Madame,' I said to her, 'I know full well, thanks to our brother cook, that you are not the cause of the perdition of our souls.'

"She had her mouth full and could not answer me, but she signaled to me by shaking her head that we were not worthy of her.

"Sloth was resting on a sofa half asleep; I did not want to wake her; I fully suspected the aversion she has for people who, like ourselves, roam all over the world.

"I perceived Envy in a corner gnawing at the hearts of three or four poets, a few preachers, and a hundred writers of pamphlets.

" 'You certainly look,' I said to her, 'as though you had a great hand in our sins.'

" 'Ah,' she said, 'Reverend Father, you are too kind; how could people who have so good an opinion of themselves have recourse to a poor wretch like me, who am nothing but skin and bones? Go talk to His Lordship my father.'

"Indeed her father was beside her in a sedan chair, dressed in an ermine-lined suit, head high, glance disdainful, cheeks red, full, and hanging; I recognized Pride; I prostrated myself; he was the only being to whom I could pay these respects.

" 'Your pardon, my father,' I said to him, 'if I did not address you first; you have always been in my heart; yes, it

12   Voltaire had helped save this abbé, Pierre-François-Guyot Desfontaines (1685–1745), from capital punishment for homosexuality, and the abbé in reply had contributed to slandering Voltaire in the *Voltairomanie.*

13   A reference to the Jesuit rule in Paraguay. Cf. *Candide,* Chapters 14–15.

is you who govern us all. The most ridiculous writer, even if he were the author of the *Année Littéraire,** is inspired by you. O magnificent devil! It is you who rule over the mandarin and the peddler, the Grand Lama and the Capuchin, the sultana and the bourgeoise; but our Fathers are your prime favorites; your divinity bursts forth in us through the veils of politics; I have always been the proudest of your disciples, and I even feel that I still love you.'

"He replied to my hymn with a protective smile, and immediately I was transferred into purgatory."

Here ends the vision of Father Garassise. He gave up the *Journal de Trévoux,* went to Lisbon, where he had long conferences with Friar Malagrida, and then went to Paraguay.[14]

14   The Kehl edition adds: "The account of these two trips of Friar Garasse [it lists Garassise as Garasse throughout] will be given to the public forthwith."

Story of a Good Brahman

[1761]

I MET ON MY TRAVELS an old Brahman, a very wise man, full of wit and very learned; moreover he was rich, and consequently even wiser; for, lacking nothing, he had no need to deceive anyone. His family was very well governed by three beautiful wives who schooled themselves to please him; and when he was not entertaining himself with his wives, he was busy philosophizing.

Near his house, which was beautiful, well decorated, and surrounded by charming gardens, lived an old Indian woman, bigoted, imbecilic, and rather poor.

The Brahman said to me one day: "I wish I had never been born."

I asked him why. He replied:

"I have been studying for forty years, which is forty years wasted; I teach others, and I know nothing; this situation brings into my soul so much humiliation and disgust that life is unbearable to me. I was born, I live in time, and I do not know what time is; I find myself in a point between two eternities, as our sages say, and I have no idea of eternity. I am composed of matter; I think, and I have never been able to find out what produces thought; I do not know whether my understanding is a simple faculty in me like that of walking or of digesting, and whether I think with my head, as I take with my hands. Not only is the principle of my thinking unknown to me, but the principle of my movements is equally hidden from me. I do not know why I exist. However, people every day ask me questions on all these points; I have to answer; I have nothing any good to say; I talk much, and I remain confounded and ashamed of myself after talking.

"It is much worse yet when they ask me whether Brahma was produced by Vishnu or whether they are both eternal.

God is my witness that I don't know a thing about it, and it certainly shows in my answers. 'Ah! Reverend Father,' they say to me, 'teach us how it is that evil inundates the whole world.' I am as much at a loss as those who ask me that question; I sometimes tell them that all is for the very best, but those who have been ruined and mutilated at war believe nothing of it, and neither do I; I retreat to my house overwhelmed with my curiosity and my ignorance. I read our ancient books, and they redouble the darkness I am in. I talk to my companions: some answer that we must enjoy life and laugh at men; the others think they know something, and lose themselves in absurd ideas; everything increases the painful feeling I endure. I am sometimes ready to fall into despair, when I think that after all my seeking I know neither where I come from, nor what I am, nor where I shall go, nor what shall become of me."

The state of this good man caused me real pain; no one was either more reasonable or more honest than he. I perceived that the greater the lights of his understanding and the sensibility of his heart, the more unhappy he was.

That same day I saw the old woman who lived in his vicinity: I asked her whether she had ever been distressed not to know how her soul was made. She did not even understand my question: she had never reflected a single moment of her life over a single one of the points that tormented the Brahman; she believed with all her heart in the metamorphoses of Vishnu, and, provided she could sometimes have some water from the Ganges to wash in, she thought herself the happiest of women.

Struck by the happiness of this indigent creature, I returned to my philosopher and said to him:

"Aren't you ashamed to be unhappy at a time when right at your door there is an old automaton who thinks of nothing and who lives happily?"

"You are right," he answered; "I have told myself a hundred times that I would be happy if I was as stupid as my neighbor, and yet I would want no part of such a happiness."

This answer of my Brahman made a greater impression on me than all the rest. I examined myself and saw that indeed I would not have wanted to be happy on condition of being imbecilic.

I put the matter up to some philosophers, and they were of my opinion.

"There is, however," I said, "a stupendous contradiction in this way of thinking."

For after all, what is at issue? Being happy. What matters being witty or being stupid? What is more, those who are content with their being are quite sure of being content; those who reason are not so sure of reasoning well.

"So it is clear," I said, "that we should choose not to have common sense, if ever that common sense contributes to our ill-being."

Everyone was of my opinion, and yet I found no one who wanted to accept the bargain of becoming imbecilic in order to become content. From this I concluded that if we set store by happiness, we set even greater store by reason.

But, upon reflection, it appears that to prefer reason to felicity is to be very mad. Then how can this contradiction be explained? Like all the others. There is much to be said about it.

Jeannot and Colin

[1764]

SEVERAL TRUSTWORTHY PERSONS have seen Jeannot and Colin at school in the town of Issoire in Auvergne, a town famous throughout the universe for its school and for its caldrons. Jeannot was the son of a very renowned dealer in mules, and Colin owed his origin to a worthy plowman of the neighborhood, who cultivated the land with four mules, and who, after paying the taille, the *taillon,* the *aides* and salt taxes, the sou per franc, the poll tax and the five percents,[1] found himself not overpoweringly rich at the end of the year.

Jeannot and Colin were very nice-looking for Auvergnats; they were very fond of each other, and they had their own private little familiarities which people always remember with pleasure when they meet later in society.

The time of their studies was on the point of ending when a tailor brought Jeannot a three-colored velvet suit, with a jacket made in Lyons, in very good taste; all this was accompanied by a letter to Monsieur de la Jeannotière. Colin admired the suit and was not jealous; but Jeannot assumed an air of superiority that distressed Colin. From that moment on Jeannot stopped studying, looked at himself in the mirror, and despised everyone. Some time later a valet arrives by the post and brings a second letter to My Lord the Marquis de la Jeannotière; it was an order from My Lord his father to bring My Lord his son to Paris. Jeannot climbed into the carriage holding out his hand to Colin with a rather noble protective smile. Colin felt his own nonentity and wept. Jeannot left in all the pomp of his glory.

The readers who like to learn are to know that Monsieur Jeannot the father had rather rapidly acquired immense riches in business. You ask how people make these great fortunes?

1   These are all taxes.

It is because they are happy. Monsieur Jeannot was good-looking, his wife too, and she was still fresh. They went to Paris over a lawsuit that was ruining them, when fortune, which raises and lowers men at will, introduced them to the wife of a contractor for army hospitals, a man of great talent who could boast of having killed more soldiers in one year than the cannon slays in ten. Madame liked Jeannot, Monsieur liked Jeannot's wife. Jeannot soon had a share in the enterprise; he went into other affairs. As soon as a man is moving with the current, all he has to do is let himself go; with no trouble he can make an immense fortune. Rogues, who from the banks watch you go full sail, are wide-eyed with astonishment; they do not know how you have been able to succeed; they envy you at random, and write pamphlets against you which you do not read. This is what happened to Jeannot Senior, who was very soon Monsieur de la Jeannotière, and who, having bought a marquisate after six months, took My Lord the Marquis his son out of school to launch him in high society in Paris.

Colin, still affectionate, wrote a letter of compliments to his former comrade to congratulate him. The little Marquis made no reply. Colin was sick with grief over it.

The father and mother first gave the young Marquis a tutor; this tutor, who was a man of fashion and who knew nothing, could teach his pupil nothing. Monsieur wanted his son to learn Latin, Madame did not. They took as their arbiter an author who was then famous for his pleasant works. He was asked to dinner. The master of the house began by saying to him first of all:

"Sir, since you know Latin and are a man of the court . . ."

"I, sir, Latin! I don't know a word of it," replied the wit, "and a good thing too! It is clear that a man speaks his own language much better when he does not divide his attention between it and foreign languages. Look at all our ladies: they have a more charming wit than the men, their letters are written with a hundred times more grace; they have this superiority over us only because they do not know Latin."

"Well! wasn't I right?" said Madame. "I want my son to be a witty man, to succeed in the world; and you see full well that if he knew Latin he would be lost. Do they perform plays and operas, if you please, in Latin? Do they plead in Latin when you have a lawsuit? Do they make love in Latin?"

Monsieur, dazzled by these arguments, passed sentence of condemnation, and it was concluded that the young Marquis would not waste his time learning Cicero, Horace, and Virgil.

"But what shall he learn then? For he still has to know something; couldn't he be exposed to a little geography?"

"What use will that be to him?" replied the tutor. "When My Lord the Marquis visits his estates, won't the postilions know the roads? They will certainly not get him lost. You don't need a quadrant to travel, and you can go very comfortably from Paris to Auvergne without knowing what your latitude is."

"You are right," replied the father; "but I have heard of a fine science which I think is called astronomy."

"How pitiful!" retorted the tutor. "Do people guide themselves by the stars in this world? And will My Lord the Marquis have to kill himself calculating an eclipse when he can find it on the dot in the almanac, which also teaches him the movable holidays, the age of the moon, and that of all the princesses of Europe?"

Madame was entirely of the tutor's opinion. The little Marquis was at the heights of joy; the father was very undecided.

"Then what should my son be taught?" he said.

"To be attractive," replied the friend they were consulting; "and if he knows how to please, he will know everything; that is an art he will learn from My Lady his mother without the slightest effort on her part or on his."

Madame, at this statement, embraced the gracious ignoramus and said to him:

"It is clear to see, sir, that you are the most learned of men of fashion; my son will owe you his whole education. I imagine, however, it would not be bad for him to know a little history."

"Alas! Madame, what good is that?" he replied. "There is certainly no pleasant and useful history but that of the present moment. All ancient history, as one of our wits [2] used to say, is only accepted fables; and as for modern, it is a chaos that no one can disentangle. What does it matter to My Lord your son that Charlemagne instituted the twelve peers of France and that his successor stammered?" [3]

2   Fontenelle.
3   Not his immediate successor Louis I, but Louis II.

"You couldn't have said it better!" exclaimed the tutor. "They stifle children's wits under a pile of useless knowledge; but of all sciences the most absurd, in my opinion, and the one most capable of stifling any sort of genius, is geometry. This ridiculous science has as its subject surfaces, lines, and points which do not exist in nature. In your mind you make a hundred thousand curved lines pass between a circle and its tangent, although in reality you can't even make a straw pass. Truly, geometry is only a bad joke."

Monsieur and Madame did not understand any too well what the tutor meant, but they were entirely of his opinion.

"A nobleman like My Lord the Marquis," he continued, "must not dry out his brain in these fruitless studies. If someday he needs a sublime geometrician to draw a plan of his lands, he will have them surveyed for his money. If he wants to unravel the antiquity of his nobility, which goes back to the most remote times, he will send for a Benedictine. It is the same with all the arts. A young lord born to good fortune is neither painter, musician, architect, nor sculptor; but he makes all these arts flourish by encouraging them through his magnificence. Beyond doubt it is better to protect them than to practice them; it is enough for My Lord the Marquis to have taste; it is up to the artists to work for him; and this is why it is very rightly said [4] that people of quality (I mean those who are very rich) know everything without having learned anything, because in fact they know in the long run how to judge all the things they order and pay for."

The amiable ignoramus then spoke up and said:

"You have very well observed, Madame, that the great goal of man is to succeed in society. In all good faith, is it by knowledge that men obtain this success? Did anyone in good company ever take a notion to talk about geometry? Does anyone ever ask a gentleman what star rises with the sun today? Does anyone inquire at supper whether Clodion the Hairy* crossed the Rhine?"

"Undoubtedly not," exclaimed the Marquise de la Jeannotière, whose charms had initiated her into high society; "and my noble son must not extinguish his genius by the study of all this trash; but after all what shall he be taught? For as my noble husband says, it is good for a young lord to

4 By Mascarille in Molière's *Les Précieuses ridicules* (1659), Scene X.

be able to shine upon occasion. I remember having heard an abbé say that the most agreeable of the sciences was something the name of which I've forgotten but which begins with a *b*."

"With a *b*, Madame? Mightn't it be botany?"

"No, it wasn't botany he was telling me about; it began, as I said, with a *b*, and ended in *on*."

"Oh, I understand, Madame, it is blazon. That is indeed a very deep science, but it is no longer in fashion since people have lost the habit of having their coats of arms painted on the doors of their carriages; it was the most useful thing in the world in a really civilized state. Besides, this would be an infinite study; there is no barber today who does not have his coat of arms; and you know that everything that becomes common is made little of."

Finally, after examining the strengths and weaknesses of the sciences, it was decided that My Lord the Marquis would learn to dance.

Nature, which does everything, had given him one talent which soon developed with prodigious success: that of singing vaudevilles [5] pleasantly. The graces of youth, combined with this superior gift, made him regarded as the most promising of young men. The women loved him; and, having his head all full of songs, he wrote some for his mistresses. He plundered *Bacchus and Cupid* in one vaudeville, *The Night and the Day* in another, *Charms and Alarms* in a third. But since in his verses there were always a few syllables more or less than there should have been, he had them corrected in consideration of twenty louis d'or per song; and in the *Année Littéraire* * he was reckoned among the La Fares, the Chaulieus, the Hamiltons, the Sarrasins, and the Voitures.[6]

My Lady the Marquise then thought she was the mother of a wit, and gave a supper for the wits of Paris. The young man's head was soon turned; he acquired the art of speaking without understanding himself, and perfected himself in the habit of being good for nothing. When his father saw him so eloquent, he keenly regretted not having had him learn Latin, for he would have bought him a fine position in the judiciary. The mother, who had nobler sentiments, took it

5   Variety songs, satiric and usually topical.
6   Popular vaudeville writers of the seventeenth and eighteenth centuries.

upon herself to solicit a regiment for her son; in the meantime he made love. Love is sometimes more expensive than a regiment. He spent a lot, while his parents were exhausting their means even more in living as great nobles.

A young widow of quality, their neighbor, who had only a modest fortune, was willing to bring herself to place in security the great riches of Monsieur and Madame de la Jeannotière, by appropriating them and marrying the young Marquis. She attracted him to her house, let herself be loved, let him glimpse that he was not just anybody to her, led him on by degrees, bewitched him, subjugated him without difficulty. She gave him now praise, now advice; she became the best friend of the father and mother. An old lady neighbor suggested marriage; the parents, dazzled at the splendor of this alliance, accepted the suggestion with joy: they gave their only son to their intimate friend. The young Marquis was about to marry a woman he adored and by whom he was loved; the friends of the family congratulated him; they were about to draw up the articles, while working on the marriage garments and the epithalamium.

One morning he was at the knees of the charming widow whom love, esteem, and friendship were about to give him; they were tasting, in a tender and animated conversation, the first fruits of their happiness; they were making arrangements to lead a life of delight, when a valet of My Lady the mother arrives thoroughly frightened:

"Here is very different news," he says; "bailiffs are unfurnishing Monsieur and Madame's house; everything is seized by creditors: there is talk of imprisonment, and I am going to make all possible haste to be paid my wages."

"Let's just see," says the Marquis, "what this is all about, what this adventure is."

"Yes," says the widow, "go punish those rascals, go quick."

He runs there, he arrives at the house; his father was already imprisoned; all the servants had fled in all directions, carrying off everything they could. His mother was alone, without help, without consolation, drowned in tears; she had nothing left but the memory of her fortune, of her beauty, of her mistakes, and of her mad expenditures.

After the son had wept at length with the mother, he finally said to her:

"Let's not despair; this young widow loves me to distraction; she is even more generous than rich, I'll answer for her; I will fly to her and bring her back to you."

So he returns to his mistress's, he finds her tête-à-tête with a very attractive young officer.

"What! it's you, Monsieur de la Jeannotière? What are you doing here? Does a person abandon his mother thus? Go to that poor woman and tell her that I still wish her well: I need a lady's maid, and I will give her first chance."

"My boy, you look to me pretty well built," said the officer; "if you want to enter my company, I'll give you a good enlistment."

The Marquis, stupefied, rage in his heart, went to find his former tutor, laid his griefs in his lap, and asked him for advice. His proposal was to become a children's tutor like himself.

"Alas! I don't know anything, you didn't teach me anything, and you are the first cause of my misfortune"; he was sobbing as he spoke to him thus.

"Write novels," said a wit who was there, "that's an excellent resource in Paris."

The young man, more desperate than ever, ran to see his mother's confessor: he was a well-accredited Theatine,* who took under his direction only women enjoying the highest consideration; as soon as he saw him he rushed to him.

"Oh, Heavens! My Lord the Marquis, where is your carriage? How is My respectable Lady the Marquise your mother?"

The poor unfortunate told him his family's disaster. As he explained himself, the Theatine put on a countenance more grave, more indifferent, more imposing:

"My son, this is where God willed you to be; riches serve only to corrupt the heart; so God has granted your mother the grace of reducing her to beggary?"

"Yes, sir."

"All the better, she is sure of salvation."

"But, Father, in the meantime, would there be no way of obtaining some help in this world?"

"Farewell, my son, there is a lady in the courtyard waiting for me."

The Marquis was ready to faint; he was treated in about the same way by his friends, and gained more knowledge of the world in half a day than in all the rest of his life.

As he remained plunged in overwhelming despair, he saw approaching an old-fashioned one-horse shay, a sort of covered tumbrel with leather curtains, followed by four enormous carts fully loaded. In the shay there was a rustically dressed young man; his was a fresh round face that breathed sweetness and gaiety. His little wife, brunette, and attractive in a rustic way, was being jolted up and down beside him. The carriage did not ride like that of a dandy. The traveler had plenty of time to contemplate the Marquis, immobile, swallowed up in his grief.

"Hey, good Lord!" he cried, "I think that's Jeannot."

At that name the Marquis raises his eyes, the carriage stops.

"It's Jeannot himself, it's Jeannot!"

The chubby little man takes one jump and runs to embrace his former comrade. Jeannot recognized Colin; shame and tears covered his face.

"You abandoned me," said Colin, "but even if you are a great lord, I shall always love you."

Jeannot, confounded and touched, told him, sobbing, part of his story.

"Come to the hotel where I am staying and tell me the rest," said Colin, "give my little wife a kiss, and let's go and have dinner together."

They all three go on foot, followed by the baggage.

"Why, what's all this paraphernalia? Does it belong to you?"

"Yes, it is all my wife's and mine. We're just arriving from back home; I am at the head of a good business manufacturing tin plate and copper. I married the daughter of a rich dealer in utensils necessary to great and small; we work very hard; God is good to us; we have not changed our status, we are happy, we will help our friend Jeannot. Don't be a Marquis any more; all the grandeurs of this world are not worth a good friend. You will come back home with me, I'll teach you the trade, it's not very hard; I'll give you a share in the profits, and we will live gaily in the patch of land where we were born."

Jeannot, distraught, felt himself divided between grief and joy, tenderness and shame; and he whispered to himself:

"All my fashionable friends have betrayed me, and Colin, whom I despised, alone comes to my rescue. What a lesson!"

Colin's goodness of soul fostered in Jeannot's heart the seed of natural goodness that society had not yet stifled. He felt that he could not abandon his father and mother.

"We will take care of your mother," said Colin; "and as for that innocent father of yours, who is in prison, I understand business a bit; his creditors, seeing that he has nothing left, will settle for very little; I'll take charge of everything."

Colin worked to such good purpose that he got the father out of prison. Jeannot returned to his home region with his parents, who resumed their former profession. He married a sister of Colin, who, being of the same temperament as her brother, made him very happy. And Jeannot the father, and Jeannotte the mother, and Jeannot the son, saw that happiness does not lie in vanity.

An Indian Adventure

Translated by the Ignoramus

[1766]

PYTHAGORAS, DURING HIS STAY in India, learned, as everyone knows, at the school of the gymnosophists, the language of the animals and that of the plants. Walking one day in a meadow rather near the seashore, he heard these words:

"How unhappy I am at being born grass! Hardly have I grown two inches tall when along comes a devouring monster, a horrible animal, who tramples me with his broad feet; his maw is armed with a row of slicing scythes with which he cuts me, tears me, and engulfs me. Men call this monster a *sheep*. I do not believe there is a more abominable creature in the world."

Pythagoras advanced a few steps; he found an oyster yawning on a little rock; he had not yet embraced that admirable rule by which we are forbidden to eat our fellow animals. He was about to swallow the oyster when it uttered these touching words:

"O nature! how happy is the grass, which is your handiwork like me! When it has been cut it is reborn, it is immortal; and we poor oysters are protected in vain by a double cuirass; villains eat us by the dozens for breakfast, and we are finished forever. What a frightful destiny is that of an oyster, and how barbarous men are!"

Pythagoras shuddered; he felt the enormity of the crime he had been about to commit; weeping, he asked the oyster's pardon, and replaced it very nicely on its rock.

As he was meditating deeply upon this adventure on his way back to town, he saw spiders eating flies, swallows eating spiders, sparrow hawks eating swallows.

"All those folk," he said, "are not philosophers."

Entering the town, Pythagoras was jostled, bruised, knocked down by a multitude of scoundrels and scoundrellesses who were laughing as they ran:

"Well done, well done, they certainly deserved it."

"Who? What?" said Pythagoras, picking himself up; and the people kept running and saying:

"Ah! what a pleasure it will be to see them cooked!"

Pythagoras thought they were talking about lentils or some other vegetables; not at all, it was about two poor Indians.

"Ah!" said Pythagoras, "no doubt they are two great philosophers who are tired of life; they are very glad to be reborn under another form; there is pleasure in changing from one house to another, although we are always badly lodged; we must not argue over tastes."

He advanced with the crowd as far as the public square, and it was there that he saw a great pyre lit, and opposite this pyre a bench that they called a "tribunal," and on this bench judges, and these judges each had a cow's tail in his hand and on his head a cap exactly resembling the two ears of the animal [1] who carried Silenus when he came to this country once with Bacchus, after crossing the Erythrean Sea* dry-shod and stopping the sun and moon, as is related faithfully in the Orphic poems.

Among these judges there was an honorable man well known to Pythagoras. The sage from India explained to the sage from Samos what was at issue in the entertainment that was about to be given to the Hindu people.

"The two Indians," said he, "have no desire to be burned; my grave colleagues have condemned them to this torture, one for having said that the substance of Xaca is not the substance of Brahma, and the other for having suspected that it was possible to please the supreme Being by virtue, without holding a cow by the tail while dying; because, he said, one can be virtuous at any time, and one does not always find a cow just when wanted. The good women of the town were so frightened by these two so heretical propositions that they gave the judges no peace until they ordered the torture and death of these two unfortunates."

Pythagoras judged that all along the line from grass to

1   The ass.

man there were many reasons for sorrow. Nevertheless, he made the judges, and even the pious women, see reason; and that is something that has happened only that one time.

Then he went to preach tolerance at Croton; but an intolerant man set fire to his house: he, who had rescued two Indians from the flames, was burned. *Escape if you can!*

Ingenuous

A TRUE STORY

Drawn from the Manuscripts of
FATHER QUESNEL[1]

[1767]

1 How the Prior of Our Lady of the Mountain and His Noble Sister Met a Huron

ONE DAY ST. DUNSTAN, an Irishman by nation and a saint by profession, left Ireland on a little mountain that sailed toward the shores of France, and arrived by this conveyance in the bay of Saint-Malo. When he landed he gave a benediction to his mountain, which bowed deeply to him and went back to Ireland by the same way it had come.

Dunstan founded a small priory in that neighborhood and gave it the name of Priory of the Mountain, which it still bears, as everyone knows.

In the year 1689, on the evening of July 15, the Abbé de Kerkabon, Prior of Our Lady of the Mountain, was walking along the seashore with his sister Mademoiselle de Kerkabon to take the air. The prior, already a little on in years, was a very good clergyman, well loved by the people of the neighborhood, as he had formerly been by the women. What had most of all given him great consideration was that he was the only benefice holder in that part of the country

---

1 Early Paris editions bore the title: "The Huron, or Ingenuous." Voltaire's habit of attributing his potentially dangerous works to others is familiar. Father Pasquier Quesnel (1634–1719), Jansenist leader, raised great disputes by his *Réflexions morales sur le Nouveau Testament;* this was the main target of the Pope's condemnation in 1713.

255

who did not have to be carried to bed when he had supped with
his colleagues. He knew a decent amount of theology; and
when he was tired of reading St. Augustine, he enjoyed
himself with Rabelais; and so everyone spoke well of him.

Mademoiselle de Kerkabon, who had never been married
although she wanted very much to be, preserved a certain
freshness at the age of forty-five; she combined sensibility
with a good character; she loved pleasure, and was pious.

The prior was saying to his sister, looking at the sea:

"Alas! it was here that our poor brother embarked with
our dear sister-in-law Madame de Kerkabon his wife on the
frigate *Swallow* in 1669 to go and serve in Canada. If he
had not been killed, we might hope to see him again."

"Do you believe," said Mademoiselle de Kerkabon, "that
our sister-in-law was eaten by the Iroquois, as we were told?
It is certain that if she had not been eaten, she would have
come back to her country. I shall weep for her all my life;
she was a charming woman; and our brother, who was very
intelligent, would assuredly have made a great fortune."

As they were both moved by this memory, they saw a small
ship enter the bay of the Rance, coming in with the tide;
it was some Englishmen coming to sell some goods of their
country. They leaped ashore without looking at the reverend
prior or his noble sister, who was very shocked at the little
attention shown her.

It was not the same with a very well-built young man who
sprang with one jump over the heads of his companions and
found himself face to face with the lady. He nodded to her,
not being in the habit of making a bow. His face and ac-
couterment attracted the glances of the brother and sister.
He was bareheaded and barelegged, his feet shod with little
sandals, his head adorned by long hair in plaits, with a small
doublet tightly girding a slim neat waist; his air was martial
and gentle. He held in his hand a little bottle of Barbados
water,* and in the other a sort of wallet in which was a
goblet and some very good sea biscuit. He spoke French very
intelligibly. He offered some of his Barbados water to
Mademoiselle de Kerkabon and to her reverend brother; he
drank some with them; he had them drink some more, and
all this with an air so simple and so natural that the brother
and sister were charmed. They offered him their services,
asking him who he was and where he was going. The young

man answered them that he knew nothing about that, that
he was curious, that he had wanted to see what the shores of
France were like, that he had come and was going to go back.

His Reverence the Prior, judging by his accent that he was
not English, took the liberty of asking him what country he
was from.

"I am a Huron," replied the young man.

Mademoiselle de Kerkabon, astonished and enchanted to
see a Huron who had paid her courtesies, asked the young
man to supper; he did not need to be asked twice, and all
three went together to the priory of Our Lady of the
Mountain.

The short round lady kept looking at him, her little eyes
wide, and from time to time said to the prior:

"That tall lad has a lily-and-rose complexion! What a
beautiful skin he has for a Huron!"

"You are right, sister," said the prior.

She asked a hundred questions one on top of the other,
and the traveler always answered very soundly.

The report soon spread that there was a Huron at the
priory. The good society of the district hastened to come
to supper there. The Abbé de Saint-Yves came with his
sister, a very pretty and very well-bred young woman of
Lower Brittany. The magistrate, the tax collector, and their
wives were at the supper. The foreigner was placed between
Mademoiselle de Kerkabon and Mademoiselle de Saint-Yves.
Everyone looked at him with wonder; everyone talked to him
and questioned him at the same time; the Huron was not
disturbed. It seemed as if he had taken for his motto that of
My Lord Bolingbroke: *nil admirari*. But finally, out of
patience with so much noise, he said to them somewhat gently
but somewhat firmly:

"Gentlemen, in my country people talk one after the other;
how do you expect me to answer you when you keep me from
hearing you?"

Reason always brings people to their senses for a few
moments. There was a deep silence. Sir Magistrate, who
always took over foreigners no matter what house he was in
and who was the greatest questioner of the province, said
to him, opening his mouth a half a foot:

"Sir, what is your name?"

"I have always been called Ingenuous," returned the Huron,

"and this name was confirmed in England, because I always spontaneously say what I think, just as I do everything I want."

"How were you able, sir, born a Huron, to come to England?"

"The fact is I was brought there; I was taken prisoner in a battle by the English after defending myself pretty well; and the English, who love bravery, because they are brave and as honorable as we are, having proposed to return me to my parents or have me come to England, I accepted the latter course, because by my nature I am passionately fond of seeing the world."

"But, sir," said the magistrate in his imposing tone, "how could you thus abandon your father and mother?"

"Because I have never known either father or mother," said the foreigner.

The company was touched, and everyone kept repeating: "Neither father nor mother!"

"We will fill their place," said the mistress of the house to her brother the prior. "How interesting this Huron gentleman is!"

Ingenuous thanked her with a noble and proud cordiality, and gave her to understand that he needed nothing.

"I perceive, Mr. Ingenuous," said the grave magistrate, "that you speak French better than befits a Huron."

"A Frenchman," he said, "whom we had captured in Huronia in my extreme youth, and for whom I felt much friendship, taught me his language; I learn very fast what I want to learn. On arriving in Plymouth I found one of your French refugees whom you call Huguenots, I know not why; he helped me make some progress in the knowledge of your language; and as soon as I was able to express myself intelligibly I came to see your country, because I rather like the French when they do not ask too many questions."

The Abbé de Saint-Yves, in spite of this little hint, asked him which of the three languages he liked best, Huron, English, or French?

"Huron, incontestably," replied Ingenuous.

"Is it possible?" exclaimed Mademoiselle de Kerkabon. "I had always supposed that French was the most beautiful of all languages after Lower Breton."

Then they were all competing in asking Ingenuous how

they said "tobacco" in Huron, and he answered *taya*, how they said "eat," and he answered *essenten*. Mademoiselle de Kerkabon absolutely insisted on knowing how they said "make love"; he replied *trovander*,[2] and maintained, not without plausibility, that those words were just as good as the French and English words that correspond to them. All the guests considered *trovander* very pretty.

His Reverence the Prior, who had in his library the Huron grammar which the Reverend Father Sagard-Théodat,[3] a famous Recollect* missionary, had given him, left the table for a moment to go and consult it. He returned quite out of breath with tenderness and joy. He acknowledged Ingenuous for a real Huron. There was a short discussion about the multiplicity of languages, and there was agreement that but for the incident of the Tower of Babel all the world would have spoken French.

The interrogative magistrate, who up to then had been a little mistrustful of the man, conceived a deep respect for him; he spoke to him with more civility than before, which Ingenuous did not notice.

Mademoiselle de Saint-Yves was most curious to know how they made love in the land of the Hurons.

"By doing fine deeds," he replied, "to please persons who are like you."

All the guests applauded in astonishment, Mademoiselle de Saint-Yves blushed and was very pleased. Mademoiselle de Kerkabon also blushed, but she was not so pleased; she was a little piqued that this gallantry was not addressed to her, but she was such a good person that her affection for the Huron was not a bit altered for all that. She asked him very kindly how many mistresses he had in Huronia.

"I have never had any but one," said Ingenuous; "that was Mademoiselle Abacaba, my dear nurse's good friend; the reeds are no straighter, the ermine is no whiter, lambs are less gentle, eagles less proud, and stags not as light-footed, as was Abacaba. One day she was chasing a hare in our neighborhood, at about fifty leagues from where we lived. An ill-bred Algonquin who lived a hundred leagues farther away came and

2   Author's note: "All these words are really Huron."
3   Voltaire owned his work entitled *Grand Voyage au pays des Hurons situé en Amérique . . . avec un dictionnaire de la langue huronne* (Paris, 1632).

took her hare from her; I learned of it, I ran there, I
knocked down the Algonquin with a blow of my club, I
brought him to the feet of my mistress bound hand and foot.
Abacaba's parents wanted to eat him, but I never had much
taste for that sort of feast; I gave him back his freedom, I
made a friend of him. Abacaba was so touched by my conduct that she preferred me to all her lovers. She would still
love me if she had not been eaten by a bear. I punished the
bear, I long wore his skin, but that did not console me."

Mademoiselle de Saint-Yves, hearing this story, felt a
secret pleasure in learning that Ingenuous had had only one
mistress and that Abacaba was no more; but she did not
discern the cause of her pleasure. Everyone fixed his eyes
on Ingenuous; all praised him greatly for having kept his
comrades from eating an Algonquin.

The relentless magistrate, who could not repress his mania
for questioning, finally pushed his curiosity to the point of
inquiring to what religion the Huron gentleman belonged;
whether he had chosen the Anglican religion, or the Gallican,
or the Huguenot.

"I am of my own religion," said he, "as you are of yours."

"Alas!" cried la Kerkabon, "I can easily see that those
hapless English did not even think of baptizing him."

"Why, good Lord," said Mademoiselle de Saint-Yves,
"how can it be that the Hurons are not Catholics? Didn't the
reverend Jesuit Fathers convert them all?"

Ingenuous assured her that in his country no one converted anybody; that never had a true Huron changed his
opinion; and that in his language there was not even a term
to signify inconstancy. Mademoiselle de Saint-Yves liked these
last words very much.

"We'll baptize him, we'll baptize him," said la Kerkabon
to His Reverence the prior, "you shall have the honor, my
dear brother, I absolutely insist on being his godmother; the
Reverend Abbé de Saint-Yves shall present him at the font:
it will be a most brilliant ceremony, it will be talked about
all over Lower Brittany, and it will do us infinite honor."

All the company seconded the mistress of the house; all
the guests were exclaiming: "We'll baptize him!"

Ingenuous replied that in England they let people live as
they fancied. He intimated that he did not like the proposition at all and that the law of the Hurons was at least as good

as the law of the Lower Bretons; finally he said that he was going back the next day. They finished emptying his bottle of Barbados water, and everyone went to bed.

When they had taken Ingenuous back to his room, Mademoiselle de Kerkabon and her friend Mademoiselle de Saint-Yves could not keep from looking through a large keyhole to see how a Huron slept. They saw that he had stretched the bedding on the floor and that he was resting in the handsomest posture in the world.

2 The Huron Named Ingenuous Recognized by His Relatives

INGENUOUS, according to his custom, awoke with the sun at cock-crow, which in England and in Huronia is called "the trumpet of the day." He was not like people of good society, who languish in a bed of idleness until the sun has done half its course, who can neither sleep nor get up, who lose so many precious hours in this intermediate state between life and death, and who still complain that life is too short.

He had already gone two or three leagues, he had killed thirty head of game with bullets alone, when on his return he found the reverend prior of Our Lady of the Mountain and his discreet sister walking in their little garden in their nightcaps. He presented them with all his game, and, drawing out of his shirt a sort of little talisman that he always wore around his neck, he begged them to accept it in acknowledgment of their kind reception.

"It is the most precious thing I have," he said to them. "I have been assured that I should always be happy so long as I wore this little trinket on me, and I give it to you so that you may always be happy."

The prior and Mademoiselle smiled with emotion at the naïveté of Ingenuous. This present consisted of two little portraits, rather poorly done, attached together with a very greasy thong.

Mademoiselle de Kerkabon asked him whether there were painters in Huronia.

"No," said Ingenuous, "this curio comes to me from my nurse; her husband had got it by conquest, in stripping a few

Frenchmen from Canada who had made war on us; that is all
I ever learned about it."

The prior was looking attentively at these portraits; he
changed color, he was moved, his hands trembled.

"By Our Lady of the Mountain," he cried, "I believe that
these are the faces of my brother the captain and his wife!"

Mademoiselle, after considering them with the same emotion, judged likewise. Both were seized with astonishment
and a joy mingled with sorrow, both were deeply moved,
both wept, their hearts beat fast, they uttered cries, they
snatched the portraits from each other, each one took them
and gave them back twenty times a second; they devoured the
portraits and the Huron with their eyes; they asked him one
after the other, and both at once, at what place, at what
time, and how these miniatures had fallen into his nurse's
hands; they compared and computed the times since the
captain's departure; they remembered having had news
that he had been as far as the land of the Hurons, and that
since that time they had never heard of him.

Ingenuous had told them that he had known neither father
nor mother. The prior, who was a man of sense, noticed that
Ingenuous had a bit of beard; he knew very well that the
Hurons have none.

"His chin is downy, so he is the son of a man from Europe.
My brother and sister-in-law never appeared again after the
expedition against the Hurons in 1669. My nephew must then
have been a babe at the breast; the Huron nurse saved his
life and was a mother to him."

Finally, after a hundred questions and a hundred answers,
the prior and his sister concluded that the Huron was their
own nephew. They embraced him, shedding tears; and Ingenuous laughed, unable to imagine that a Huron could be
the nephew of a Lower Breton prior.

All the company came down; Monsieur de Saint-Yves, who
was a great physiognomist, compared the two portraits with
Ingenuous' face; he pointed out very ably that he had his
mother's eyes, the forehead and nose of the late Captain
de Kerkabon, and cheeks that took after both.

Mademoiselle de Saint-Yves, who had never seen the
father or the mother, asserted that Ingenuous looked exactly
like them. They all admired Providence and the concatenation
of the events of this world. At last they were so persuaded, so

convinced about Ingenuous' birth, that he himself consented to be the reverend prior's nephew, saying that he was as glad to have him for an uncle as anyone else.

They went to give thanks to God in the church of Our Lady of the Mountain, while the Huron, with an air of indifference, amused himself in the house by drinking.

The Englishmen who had brought him, and who were ready to set sail, came to tell him it was time to leave.

"Apparently," he said to them, "you have not rediscovered your uncles and aunts here. I am staying here; go on back to Plymouth; I give you all my clothes; I no longer need anything in the world, since I am the nephew of a prior."

The Englishmen set sail, caring very little whether or not Ingenuous had relatives in Lower Brittany.

After the uncle, the aunt, and the company had sung the *Te Deum,* after the magistrate had again overwhelmed Ingenuous with questions, after they had exhausted everything that astonishment, joy, tenderness can make people say, the Prior of the Mountain and the Abbé de Saint-Yves decided to have Ingenuous baptized as fast as possible. But it was not the same with a grown Huron of twenty-two as with an infant who is regenerated without knowing a thing about it. He had to receive instruction, and that appeared difficult; for the Abbé de Saint-Yves supposed that a man who had not been born in France did not have common sense.

The prior pointed out to the company that even if indeed Mr. Ingenuous his nephew had not had the good fortune to be born in Lower Brittany, he had no less intelligence for all that; that this could be judged by all his answers, and that surely nature had greatly favored him, on his father's as well as on his mother's side.

First they asked him whether he had ever read any book? He said he had read Rabelais translated into English, and a few fragments of Shakespeare which he knew by heart; that he had found these books in the cabin of the captain of the ship which had brought him from America to Plymouth, and that he was very pleased with them. The magistrate did not fail to question him about these books.

"I admit," said Ingenuous, "that I thought I guessed some of their meaning, and that I did not understand the rest."

At this statement the Abbé de Saint-Yves reflected that

that was how he had always read, and that most people read hardly any differently.

"No doubt you have read the Bible," said he to the Huron.

"Not at all, Mr. Abbé; it was not among my captain's books; I have never heard of it."

"That's the way those accursed English are," cried Mademoiselle de Kerkabon; "they will set more store by a Shakespeare play, a plum pudding, and a bottle of rum, than by the Pentateuch. Accordingly they have never converted anyone in America. Certainly they are accursed of God; and we shall take Jamaica and Virginia from them before long."

However that may be, they sent for the ablest tailor in Saint-Malo to dress Ingenuous from toe to crown. The company broke up, the magistrate went to ask his questions elsewhere. Mademoiselle de Saint-Yves, on leaving, turned around several times to look at Ingenuous, and he made her deeper bows than he had ever made to anyone in his life.

The magistrate, before taking his leave, introduced to Mademoiselle de Saint-Yves a great booby of a son of his, who was just out of school; but she hardly looked at him, so occupied was she with the Huron's politeness.

3 *The Huron Named Ingenuous Converted*

HIS REVERENCE the prior, seeing that he was a little on in years and that God was sending him a nephew for his consolation, took it into his head that he would be able to resign his benefice in his favor if he succeeded in baptizing him and having him enter holy orders.

Ingenuous had an excellent memory. The strong constitution of a child of Lower Brittany, fortified by the climate of Canada, had made his head so vigorous that if you hit him on it he hardly felt it; and when anything was engraved on it, nothing was effaced; he had never forgotten anything. His conception was all the more lively and clear because, his childhood not having been burdened with the futilities and stupidities that overwhelm ours, things entered his brain unclouded. The prior finally resolved to have him read the

New Testament. Ingenuous devoured it with much pleasure; but knowing neither at what time nor in what country all the adventures related in this book had happened, he did not doubt that the scene was located in Lower Brittany; and he swore that he would cut the nose and ears off Caiaphas and Pilate if ever he met those scoundrels.

His uncle, charmed with these good dispositions, set him right in a short time; he praised his zeal, but he taught him that this zeal was useless, seeing that those people had died about sixteen hundred and ninety years before. Ingenuous soon knew almost the whole book by heart. He sometimes proposed difficulties that gave the prior much embarrassment. He was often obliged to consult the Abbé de Saint-Yves, who, not knowing what to reply, sent for a Lower Breton Jesuit to complete the Huron's conversion.

Finally grace operated; Ingenuous promised to become a Christian. He did not doubt that he must begin by being circumcised.

"For," he said, "I do not see in the book they had me read a single person who was not; so it is evident that I must make the sacrifice of my foreskin; the sooner the better."

He did not deliberate. He sent for the village surgeon and asked him to perform the operation, counting on giving Mademoiselle de Kerkabon and the whole company infinite joy when once the thing should be done. The sawbones, who had never performed this operation, informed the family, who uttered loud cries. The good lady Kerkabon trembled lest her nephew, who appeared resolute and expeditious, might perform the operation very clumsily upon himself with sad resultant effects, in which ladies always take an interest out of the goodness of their souls.

The prior corrected the Huron's ideas; he pointed out to him that circumcision was no longer in fashion, that baptism was much pleasanter and more salutary, that the law of grace was not like the law of rigor. Ingenuous, who had much good sense and rectitude, argued, but recognized his error, which is rather rare in Europe in people who argue; finally he promised to have himself baptized whenever they should wish.

Before that, he had to go to confession; and that was the most difficult thing. Ingenuous always had in his pocket the book his uncle had given him. He could not find there that a single apostle had gone to confession, and that made him very balky. The prior shut his mouth by pointing out to him, in the Epistle of St. James the Less, these words that give heretics so much grief: "confess your sins one to another." [1] The Huron was silent, and made his confession to a Recollect friar. When he had finished he pulled the Recollect from the confessional, and seizing his man with a vigorous arm, set himself in his place and had the other get on his knees before him:

"Come on, my friend, it is written: 'confess one to another.' I have told you my sins, you shall not leave here until you have told me yours."

So saying, he pressed his big knee against the chest of his adversary. The Recollect utters howls that make the church resound. They run up at the noise, they see the catechumen pummeling the monk in the name of St. James the Less. The joy of baptizing a Huron and English Lower Breton was so great that they passed over these singularities. There were even many theologians who considered that confession was not necessary, since baptism took the place of everything.

They set a date with the Bishop of Saint-Malo, who, flattered, as one may well believe, at baptizing a Huron, arrived in a pompous carriage followed by his clergy. Mademoiselle de Saint-Yves, blessing God, put on her most beautiful dress and sent for a hairdresser from Saint-Malo so as to shine at the ceremony. The interrogative magistrate hurried up with everyone in the region. The church was magnificently decorated. But when it was time to take the Huron up to the baptismal font, he was not to be found.

The uncle and aunt looked for him everywhere. They thought he was out hunting according to his custom. All the guests at the ceremony scoured the neighboring woods and villages: no news of the Huron.

They were beginning to fear that he had gone back to England. They remembered having heard him say that he liked that country very much. The reverend prior and his sister were persuaded that they never baptized anyone there, and they trembled for their nephew's soul. The bishop was disconcerted and ready to go back home; the prior and the

1   The King James Version (James 5:16) reads "faults," not "sins."

Abbé de Saint-Yves were in despair; the magistrate was questioning all the passers-by with his usual gravity. Mademoiselle de Kerkabon was weeping. Mademoiselle de Saint-Yves was not weeping, but she was uttering deep sighs that seemed to testify to her taste for sacraments. The two women were walking sadly beside the willows and reeds that border the little river Rance when they perceived in the middle of the river a large, rather white figure with both hands crossed on its chest. They uttered a loud scream and turned their heads away. But, curiosity soon overcoming every other consideration, they slipped gently in among the reeds, and when they were quite sure of not being seen, they decided to see what this was all about.

4 *Ingenuous Baptized*

THE PRIOR and the abbé, having rushed to the scene, asked Ingenuous what he was doing there.

"Why, forsooth, gentlemen, I am awaiting baptism. For an hour now I have been in the water up to my neck, and it is not civil to let me get a chill."

"My dear nephew," said the prior to him tenderly, "this is not the way we baptize in Lower Brittany; put your clothes back on and come with us."

Mademoiselle de Saint-Yves, hearing these words, whispered to her companion: "Mademoiselle, do you think he will put his clothes back on so soon?"

Meanwhile the Huron retorted to the prior:

"You won't take me in this time like the other time; I have been studying carefully since then, and I am quite certain that people are not baptized in any other way. Queen Candace's eunuch [1] was baptized in a stream; I defy you to show me in the book you gave me that they ever went about it in another way. I will either not be baptized at all or else be baptized in the river."

In vain they pointed out to him that customs had changed. Ingenuous was headstrong, for he was a Breton and a Huron. He kept always coming back to Queen Candace's eunuch.

1   See Acts 8:27–39.

And although Mademoiselle his aunt and Mademoiselle de Saint-Yves, who had observed him between the willows, were in a position to tell him that it was not for him to cite such a man, yet they did nothing of the sort, so great was their discretion. The bishop himself came to talk to him, which is quite a thing, but he gained nothing; the Huron argued with the bishop.

"Show me," he said to him, "in the book my uncle gave me, a single man who was not baptized in the river, and I'll do anything you want."

His despairing aunt had noticed that the first time her nephew had made a bow he had made a deeper one to Mademoiselle de Saint-Yves than to any other person in the company, that he had not even greeted my lord the bishop with that respect mingled with cordiality which he had shown to this beautiful young lady. She decided to apply to her in this great embarrassment; she besought her to bring her influence to bear in order to induce the Huron to have himself baptized in the same way as the Bretons, not believing that her nephew could ever be a Christian if he persisted in wanting to be baptized in running water.

Mademoiselle de Saint-Yves blushed at the secret pleasure she felt at being charged with so important a commission. She modestly approached Ingenuous and, squeezing his hand in a wholly noble manner, said to him:

"Won't you do anything for me?"

And as she uttered these words she lowered her eyes and raised them again with touching grace.

"Ah! Whatever you want, Mademoiselle, whatever you order me, baptism by water, baptism by fire, baptism in blood, there is nothing I would refuse you."

Mademoiselle de Saint-Yves had the glory of doing in two words what neither the assiduities of the prior, nor the reiterated interrogations of the magistrate, nor even the arguments of my lord the bishop had been able to do. She felt her triumph, but she did not yet feel the full extent of it.

The baptism was administered and received with all possible decency, magnificence, and charm. The uncle and aunt yielded to the Reverend Abbé de Saint-Yves and his sister the honor of holding Ingenuous upon the font. Mademoiselle de Saint-Yves was radiant with joy at seeing herself a godmother. She did not know to what this great title was enslaving her; she accepted this honor without knowing its fatal consequences.

As there has never been a ceremony that was not followed by a great dinner, they sat down to table on leaving the baptism. The wags of Lower Brittany said that no one must baptize his wine.[2] His Reverence the Prior said that wine, according to Solomon,[3] rejoices the heart of man. My lord the bishop added that the patriarch Judah had to bind his ass's colt unto the vine, and wash his clothes in the blood of grapes,[4] and that it was very sad that they could not do as much in Lower Brittany, to which God had denied vines. Everyone was trying to say something witty about Ingenuous' baptism and something gallant to the godmother. The magistrate, still interrogative, asked the Huron whether he would be faithful to his promises.

"How can you expect me to fail to keep my promises," replied the Huron, "since I made them in the hands of Mademoiselle de Saint-Yves?"

The Huron grew excited; he drank a lot to his godmother's health.

"If I had been baptized by your hand," he said, "I feel that the cold water they poured over the nape of my neck would have burned me."

The magistrate found this too poetic, not knowing how familiar a figure allegory is in Canada. But the godmother was very pleased with it.

The name of Hercules had been given to the baptized man. The Bishop of Saint-Malo kept asking who was this patron saint whom he had never heard of. The Jesuit, who was very learned, told him this was a saint who had performed twelve miracles. There was a thirteenth that was worth the twelve others, but of which it did not befit a Jesuit to speak: that of changing fifty girls into women in a single night.[5] A comic who was there extolled this miracle energetically. All the ladies lowered their eyes, and judged by the figure of Ingenuous that he was worthy of the saint whose name he bore.

2   Dilute it with water; a current expression in French.
3   Ecclesiasticus 40:20: "Wine and musick rejoice the heart."
4   See Genesis 49:11.
5   The fifty daughters of Thestius.

5 *Ingenuous in Love*

IT MUST BE ADMITTED that from the time of that baptism and that dinner, Mademoiselle de Saint-Yves passionately wished that my lord the bishop would again make her a participant in some fine sacrament with Mr. Hercules Ingenuous. However, as she was well-bred and very modest, she did not dare completely admit her tender feelings to herself; but if a glance, a word, a gesture, a thought escaped her, she enveloped all that in an infinitely attractive veil of modesty. She was tender, lively, and well behaved.

As soon as my lord the bishop had left, Ingenuous and Mademoiselle de Saint-Yves met without having recognized that they were looking for each other. They spoke to each other without having imagined what they would say. Ingenuous first told her that he loved her with all his heart, and that the beauteous Abacaba, whom he had been mad about in his own country, did not come near to her. Mademoiselle answered him, with her ordinary modesty, that he must speak about it as soon as possible to the reverend prior his uncle and Mademoiselle his aunt, and that for her part she would say a few words about it to her dear brother the Abbé de Saint-Yves, and that she flattered herself on the prospect of common consent.

Ingenuous answered her that he needed no one's consent, that it seemed to him extremely ridiculous to go ask others what one should do; that when two parties are agreed there is no need of a third to bring them together.

"I consult no one," he said, "when I want to have breakfast, or hunt, or sleep; I am well aware that in love it is not a bad thing to have the consent of the person in question; but since it is neither my uncle nor my aunt that I am in love with, it is not to them that I must apply in this affair; and if you will take my advice, you will also do without the Reverend Abbé de Saint-Yves."

One may well judge that the Breton beauty employed all the delicacy of her mind to reduce her Huron to the terms of propriety. She even grew angry, and soon grew mild again. Finally, there is no knowing how this conversation would

have ended if toward sundown the abbé had not brought
his sister back to his abbey. Ingenuous let his uncle and
aunt, who were a little tired from the ceremony and their
long dinner, go to bed. He spent part of the night writing
verses in the Huron language to his dearly beloved; for it
should be known that there is no country on earth where
love has not made lovers into poets.

The next day his uncle spoke to him thus after breakfast
in the presence of Mademoiselle de Kerkabon, who was deeply
moved:

"Heaven be praised that you have the honor, my dear
nephew, to be a Christian and a Lower Breton; but that is
not enough; I am a bit on in years; my brother left only a
little patch of land which doesn't amount to much; I have a
good priory; if you will merely become a subdeacon, as I
hope you will, I will resign my priory to you, and you will
live very comfortably after being the consolation of my
old age."

Ingenuous replied: "Uncle, may it do much good for you;
live as long as you can. I do not know what it is to be a
subdeacon or to resign; but everything will seem good to me
provided I have Mademoiselle de Saint-Yves at my disposal."

"Why, Good Lord, nephew, what is that you are saying? So
you are madly in love with that beautiful young lady?"

"Yes, uncle."

"Alas! nephew, it is impossible for you to marry her."

"It is very possible, uncle; for not only did she squeeze my
hand on leaving me, but she promised me that she would
ask to marry me; and assuredly I shall marry her."

"That is impossible, I tell you, she is your godmother; it
is a frightful sin for a godmother to squeeze her godson's
hand; it is not permissible to marry one's godmother; the
laws, human and divine, oppose it."

"By Heaven, uncle, you are making fun of me; why should
it be forbidden to marry your godmother when she is young
and pretty? I never saw in the book you gave me that it was
bad to marry girls who have helped people to be baptized.
I perceive every day that people here do an infinity of things
which are not in your book, and that they do nothing at all
of what it says to do. I admit that this astounds and angers
me. If I am to be deprived of the fair Saint-Yves on the

pretext of my baptism, I warn you that I will carry her off and get unbaptized."

The prior was confounded; his sister wept.

"My dear brother," said she, "our nephew must not damn himself; Our Holy Father the Pope can give him a dispensation, and then he can be Christianly happy with the one he loves."

Ingenuous embraced his aunt.

"Then who," he said, "is this charming man who so kindly favors boys and girls in their amours? I want to go talk to him right away."

They explained to him what the Pope was, and Ingenuous was even more astonished than before.

"There is not a word of all that in your book, my dear uncle; I have traveled, I know the sea; we are here on the shore of the Atlantic Ocean; and I should leave Mademoiselle de Saint-Yves to go ask permission to love her of a man who lives near the Mediterranean, four hundred leagues from here, and whose language I do not understand! This is incomprehensibly ridiculous. I am going straight to see the Reverend Abbé de Saint-Yves, who lives only a league away from you, and I warrant you I'll marry my mistress this very day."

As he was still speaking, the magistrate entered and, according to his custom, asked him where he was going.

"I am going to get married," said Ingenuous as he ran; and in a quarter of an hour he was already at the house of his dear Lower Breton beauty, who was still asleep.

"Ah! my brother," said Mademoiselle de Kerkabon to the prior, "never will you make a subdeacon of our nephew."

The magistrate was very unhappy about this trip; for he aspired to have his son marry la Saint-Yves; and this son was even more stupid and unbearable than his father.

6   Ingenuous Runs to See His Mistress, and Becomes Furious

HARDLY HAD Ingenuous arrived when, having asked an old womanservant where his mistress's bedroom was, he had pushed hard on the badly closed door and sprung toward the bed. Mademoiselle de Saint-Yves, waking with a start, had cried:

"What! It's you? Ah! It's you! Stop, what are you doing?"

He had answered: "I am marrying you."

And indeed he would have married her if she had not fought back with all the decency of a person of education.

Ingenuous was very much in earnest; he considered all those ways of acting very inappropriate.

"That was not the way Mademoiselle Abacaba, my first mistress, behaved; you have no probity, you promised to marry me, and you will not act married; that is failing the first laws of honor; I will teach you to keep your word and put you back on the path of virtue."

Ingenuous possessed an intrepid male virtue worthy of his patron Hercules whose name they had given him at his baptism; he was about to exercise it to its fullest extent, when at the piercing cries of the more discreetly virtuous young lady there hurried up the wise Abbé de Saint-Yves with his house-keeper, a pious old manservant, and a priest of the parish. This sight moderated the courage of the assailant.

"Why, Good Lord! my dear neighbor," said the abbé to him, "what's that you're doing?"

"My duty," replied the young man; "I am fulfilling my promises, which are sacred."

Mademoiselle de Saint-Yves readjusted her clothes, blushing. They took Ingenuous into another apartment. The abbé pointed out to him the enormity of his conduct. Ingenuous defended himself on the grounds of the privileges of the natural law, which he knew perfectly. The abbé tried to prove that the positive law must have all the advantage, and that without the conventions adopted among men, natural law would almost never be anything but a natural brigandage.

"There must," he said to him, "be notaries, priests, witnesses, contracts, dispensations."

Ingenuous answered him with the observation that savages have always made:

"Then you must be very dishonest people, since you need so many precautions against one another."

The abbé had some trouble in resolving this difficulty.

"There are," he said, "I admit, many unreliables and knaves among us; and there would be as many among the Hurons if they were assembled in a big city; but also there

are wise, decent, enlightened souls, and those are the men who
made the laws. The more righteous a man is, the more he
must submit to them; he sets an example to the vicious, who
respect a curb that virtue has given to itself."

This reply struck Ingenuous. It has already been noted
that he was fair-minded. They mollified him with flattering
words; they gave him some hopes; those are the two traps
in which men of both hemispheres are caught. They even
brought in Mademoiselle de Saint-Yves to see him when
she had performed her toilet. Everything went off with the
greatest propriety. But in spite of this decorum, the sparkling
eyes of Hercules Ingenuous always made his mistress lower
hers and the company tremble.

They had the utmost difficulty in sending him back to
his relatives. Again they had to use the influence of the fair
Saint-Yves; the more she felt her power over him, the more
she loved him. She made him leave, and was very distressed
about it; finally, when he had left, the abbé, who not only
was Mademoiselle de Saint-Yves's much older brother, but
was also her tutor, determined to withdraw his ward from
the assiduities of this terrifying lover. He went and consulted
the magistrate, who, still destining his son for the abbé's sister,
advised him to put the poor girl into a convent. This was
a terrible blow; an uninvolved girl put in a convent would
utter loud cries, but being in love, and as honorably as tenderly in love, it was enough to drive her to despair.

Ingenuous, back at the prior's, related everything with his
usual naïveté. He bore the same remonstrances, which had
some effect on his mind and none on his senses; but the next
day, when he wanted to go back to his beautiful mistress
to reason with her upon the laws of nature and the laws of
convention, Mr. Magistrate informed him with insulting joy
that she was in a convent.

"Very well," he said, "I'll go and reason in this convent."

"That cannot be," said the magistrate; he explained to him
at great length what a convent was, that this word came from
the Latin *conventus,* which means assembly; and the Huron
could not understand why he could not be admitted to the
assembly. As soon as he was informed that this assembly
was a kind of prison in which girls were kept shut up, a
horrible thing unknown among the Hurons and the English,
he became as furious as was his patron Hercules when

Eurytus King of Oechalia, no less cruel than the Abbé de
Saint-Yves, refused him the beautiful Iole, his daughter,
no less beautiful than the abbé's sister. He wanted to go set
fire to the convent, and carry off his mistress, or be burned
with her. Mademoiselle de Kerkabon, terrified, more than
ever renounced all hopes of seeing her nephew a subdeacon,
and said, weeping, that he had the devil in the flesh since he
had been baptized.

7 Ingenuous Repulses the English

INGENUOUS, plunged in deep and gloomy melancholy, walked
toward the seashore, his double-barreled gun over his shoulder,
his big cutlass at his side, firing from time to time at some
birds, and often tempted to fire at himself; but he still loved
life because of Mademoiselle de Saint-Yves. Now he would
curse his uncle, his aunt, and all Lower Brittany and his
baptism; now he would bless them, since they had brought
him to know the one he loved. He would make a resolution
to go burn the convent, and stop short for fear of burning
his mistress. The waves of the Channel are not more
agitated by the winds from east and west than was his
heart by so many conflicting emotions.

He was walking with long strides without knowing where,
when he heard the sound of a drum. He saw from a distance
a great multitude of people, half of whom were running to
the shore, the other half fleeing.

A thousand cries arise from all sides; curiosity and courage
instantly send him headlong toward the place these noises
were coming from; he flies there in four bounds. The commander of the militia, who had supped with him at the
prior's, recognized him immediately; he runs to him with
open arms:

"Ah! it's Ingenuous, he will fight for us."

And the militiamen, who were dying with fear, were
reassured, and also cried:

"It's Ingenuous, it's Ingenuous."

"Gentlemen," he said, "what's up? Why are you so
frightened? Have they put your mistresses into convents?"

Then a hundred confused voices exclaimed:

"Don't you see the English landing?"

"Well!" replied the Huron. "They are good folk; they have never proposed to make me a subdeacon; they have not carried off my mistress."

The commander gave him to understand that the English were coming to pillage the Abbey of the Mountain, drink his uncle's wine, and perhaps carry off Mademoiselle de Saint-Yves; that the little ship on which he had landed in Brittany had come only to reconnoiter the coast, that they committed acts of hostility without having declared war on the King of France, and that the province was exposed.

"Ah! if that is so, they are violating the law of nature; leave it to me; I have lived a long time among them, I know their language, I will speak to them; I do not believe their designs can be so wicked."

During this conversation the English squadron was approaching; now the Huron runs toward it, flings himself into a little boat, arrives, climbs into the flagship, and asks whether it is true that they are coming to ravage the countryside without having declared war honestly. The admiral and all on board burst into great roars of laughter, had him drink some punch, and sent him back.

Ingenuous, piqued, now thought of nothing but fighting well against his former friends for his compatriots and for the reverend prior. The gentlemen of the neighborhood were running up from all directions, he joins them; they had a few cannon, he loads them, aims them, fires them one after the other. The English land, he runs to meet them, he kills three with his own hand, he even wounds the admiral who had laughed at him. His valor animates the courage of the whole militia; the English re-embark, and all the coast resounds with cries of victory:

"Long live the King! Long live Ingenuous!"

Everyone was embracing him, everyone was trying eagerly to stanch the blood from a few light wounds he had received.

"Ah!" said he. "If Mademoiselle de Saint-Yves were here, she would put on a compress."

The magistrate, who had hidden in his cellar during the combat, came to compliment him like the others. But he was much surprised when he heard Hercules Ingenuous say to a dozen young men of good will who were around him:

"My friends, it is nothing to have delivered the Abbey of the Mountain, we must deliver a girl."

All this ebullient youth took fire at these words alone. Already they were following him in a body, they were running to the convent. If the magistrate had not instantly warned the commander, if they had not run after the joyous troop, the thing would have been done. They brought Ingenuous back to the house of his uncle and aunt, who bathed him in tears of tenderness.

"I see very well that you will never be either a subdeacon or a prior," said the uncle to him; "you will be an even braver officer than my brother the captain, and probably just as poor."

And Mademoiselle de Kerkabon still kept weeping as she embraced him and said: "He will get himself killed just like my brother; it would be much better for him to be a subdeacon."

In the combat Ingenuous had picked up a fat purse full of guineas, which probably the admiral had dropped. He did not doubt that with this purse he could buy all Lower Brittany, and above all make Mademoiselle de Saint-Yves a great lady. Everyone exhorted him to make the trip to Versailles to receive the reward for his services. The commander, the chief officers heaped him with certificates. The uncle and aunt approved the nephew's trip. He was to be presented to the King without any difficulty. That alone would give him prodigious distinction in the province. These two good people added to the English purse a considerable present out of their savings. Ingenuous said to himself:

"When I see the King, I will ask him for Mademoiselle de Saint-Yves in marriage and certainly he will not refuse me."

So he left amid the acclamation of the whole district, smothered with embraces, bathed in his aunt's tears, blessed by his uncle, and recommending himself to the fair Saint-Yves.

8 Ingenuous Goes to Court. He Sups on the Road with Some Huguenots

INGENUOUS TOOK the road for Saumur by public coach, because there was then no other transportation. When he was

at Saumur, he was astounded to find the town almost deserted,
and to see several families moving out. He was told that six
years before, Saumur contained more than fifteen thousand
souls, and that at present there were not six thousand. He
did not fail to speak about this at supper in his inn. Several
Protestants were at table; some were complaining bitterly,
others were trembling with rage, others, weeping, were
saying: *"Nos dulcia linquimus arva, nos patriam fugimus."* [1]

Ingenuous, who did not know Latin, had these words explained to him, which mean: "We are abandoning our sweet
fields, we are fleeing from our native land."

"And why are you fleeing from your native land, gentlemen?"

"Because they want us to acknowledge the Pope."

"And why shouldn't you acknowledge him? Then you
don't have any godmothers that you wanted to marry? For
I have been told that it is he who gives permission for that."

"Ah! Sir, this Pope says he is the master of the King's
dominions."

"But, gentlemen, what is your profession?"

"Sir, for the most part we are drapers and manufacturers."

"If your Pope says he is master of your cloths and
your factories, you do very well not to recognize him; but
as for kings, that is their affair; what business is that of yours?"

Then a little man in black [2] spoke up and very learnedly
expounded the company's grievances. He spoke of the Revocation of the Edict of Nantes with so much energy, he
deplored in so pathetic a manner the fate of fifty thousand
fugitive families and of fifty thousand others converted by
the dragoons, that Ingenuous shed tears in turn.

"How does it come to pass," said he, "that so great a King,
whose glory extends even among the Hurons, thus deprives
himself of so many hearts that would have loved him and
so many arms that would have served him?"

"Because he was duped, like other great kings," replied
the man in black. "He was made to believe that as soon as
he had said a word all men would think like him, and that
he would make us change our religion as his musician Lully
changes in a moment the decorations of his operas. Not only
is he already losing five or six hundred thousand very use-

1   Virgil: *Eclogues* I, verse 3.
2   A Protestant minister.

ful subjects, but he is making enemies of them; and King
William, who is now master of England, has formed several
regiments of these same Frenchmen who would have fought
for their own monarch.

"Such a disaster is all the more astounding because the
reigning Pope,[3] to whom Louis XIV is sacrificing a part of
his people, is his declared enemy. They have both even been
having a violent quarrel for the last nine years. It has been
carried so far that France has at last hoped to see the yoke
broken which has subjected her for so many years to this
foreigner, and above all not to give him any more money,
which is the prime mover of the affairs of this world. So it
seems evident that this great King has been duped about his
own interests as well as about the extent of his power, and
that injury has been done to the magnanimity of his heart."

Ingenuous, more and more touched, asked who were the
Frenchmen who were thus deceiving a monarch so dear to
the Hurons.

"It is the Jesuits," was the reply, "and above all Father
de La Chaise,[*] His Majesty's confessor. It is to be hoped
that God will punish them someday, and that they will be
driven out just as they are driving us out. Is there any
misfortune equal to ours? Monsieur de Louvois [4] sends us
Jesuits and dragoons from all directions."

"Well, gentlemen," replied Ingenuous, who could contain
himself no longer, "I am going to Versailles to receive the
reward due to my services; I will speak to this Monsieur de
Louvois; I have been told that it is he who makes war from
his study. I shall see the King, I shall let him know the
truth. It is impossible for a man not to yield to this truth when
he feels it. I shall soon return to marry Mademoiselle de
Saint-Yves, and I invite you to the wedding."

These good people now took him for a great lord traveling
incognito by the public coach. Some took him for the King's
fool.

There was at table a Jesuit in disguise who was serving
as a spy for the Reverend Father de La Chaise. He would
give him an account of everything, and Father de La Chaise

3   Innocent XI.
4   An influential public servant (1641–1691) under Louis
XIV, who suggested the dragonnades which led to many forced
conversions of Protestants.

would inform Monsieur de Louvois of it. The spy wrote. Ingenuous and the letter arrived almost at the same time at
Versailles.

9 *Arrival of Ingenuous at Versailles. His Reception at Court*

INGENUOUS GETS OUT of the *pot-de-chambre* [1] into the kitchen
courtyard. He asks the sedan-chair porters at what time the
King can be seen. The porters laugh in his face just as the
English admiral had done. He treated them in the same way,
he beat them; they tried to give it back to him, and the scene
would have become bloody if there had not come past a
member of the King's bodyguard, a Breton gentleman, who
scattered the rabble.

"Sir," said the traveler, "you seem to me a good man. I am
the nephew of His Reverence the Prior of Our Lady of
the Mountain. I have killed some Englishmen, I am coming
to speak to the King. I beg you to take me to his chamber."

The guardsman, delighted to find a brave man from his
province who did not seem up on the customs of the court,
informed him that you did not speak to the King that way,
and that you had to be presented by My Lord de Louvois.

"Well, then, take me to this Lord de Louvois, who will
doubtless take me to His Majesty."

"It is even more difficult," replied the guardsman, "to speak
to My Lord de Louvois than to His Majesty. But I am going
to take you to Monsieur Alexandre, the chief clerk in the
War Office; that is just as though you were speaking to the
minister."

So they go to see this Monsieur Alexandre, chief clerk, and
they could not gain admittance; he was in conference with
a lady of the court, and there were orders not to let anyone in.

"Well, then," said the guardsman, "there is nothing lost, let's
go to see Monsieur Alexandre's chief clerk; that is just as
though you were speaking to Monsieur Alexandre himself."

The Huron, quite astonished, follows him; together they
remain half an hour in a little antechamber.

1   Author' note: "This is a carriage from Paris to Versailles,
which looks like a little covered tumbrel."

"What in the world is all this?" said Ingenuous. "Is everyone invisible in this country? It is much easier to fight against Englishmen in Lower Brittany than to meet people you have business with at Versailles."

He relieved his boredom by relating his love affair to his compatriot. But the hour struck, calling the guardsman back to his post. They promised to see each other again on the morrow; and Ingenuous stayed yet another half hour in the antechamber, thinking of Mademoiselle de Saint-Yves and of the difficulty of speaking to kings and chief clerks.

Finally the master appeared.

"Sir," said Ingenuous, "if I had waited as long to repulse the English as you have made me wait for my audience, they would right now be ravaging Lower Brittany quite at their ease."

These words struck the chief clerk. Finally he said to the Breton: "What are you requesting?"

"A recompense," said the other; "here are my titles to it."

He spread out all his certificates before him. The clerk read, and told him he would probably be granted permission to buy a lieutenancy.

"Me? I should pay money for having repulsed the English? I should pay for the right to get myself killed for you, while you tranquilly give your audiences here? I think you are saying this for a laugh. I want a cavalry company for nothing. I want the King to have Mademoiselle de Saint-Yves released from the convent and to give her to me in marriage. I want to speak to the King on behalf of fifty thousand families whom I propose to restore to him. In a word, I want to be useful; let me be employed and advanced."

"What is your name, sir, you who take such a high tone?"

"Oho!" retorted Ingenuous, "so you didn't read my certificates? So that's how they are treated! My name is Hercules de Kerkabon; I am baptized, I am lodging at the Blue Dial, and I shall complain of you to the King."

The clerk concluded, like the people of Saumur, that he was not quite right in the head, and did not pay much attention.

That same day the Reverend Father de La Chaise, confessor to Louis XIV, had received his spy's letter, which accused the Breton Kerkabon of favoring the Huguenots in his heart and condemning the conduct of the Jesuits. Monsieur de

Louvois, on his side, had received a letter from the interrogative magistrate, which depicted Ingenuous as a scapegrace who wanted to burn down convents and carry off girls.

Ingenuous, after walking in the gardens of Versailles, in which he grew bored, after having supper like a Huron and a Lower Breton, had gone to bed in the sweet hope of seeing the King the next day, obtaining Mademoiselle de Saint-Yves in marriage, getting at least a cavalry company, and making the persecution of the Huguenots stop. He was lulling himself with these flattering ideas when the mounted police entered his bedroom. First they seized his double-barreled gun and his big saber.

They took an inventory of his ready money and took him to the castle [2] constructed by order of King Charles V, son of John II, near the Rue Saint-Antoine, at the Porte des Tournelles.

What Ingenuous' astonishment was along the way I leave to your imagination. At first he thought it was a dream. He remained stupefied; then suddenly, transported with a fury that redoubled his strength, he seizes by the throat two of his conductors who were in the carriage with him, throws them out the door, throws himself after them, and drags along the third, who was trying to hold him back. He falls down from the effort, he is tied up, he is put back in the carriage.

"So this," he said, "is what you gain for driving the English out of Lower Brittany? What would you say, beautiful Saint-Yves, if you saw me in this state?"

At last they reach his destined resting place. He is carried up in silence into the room where he was to be locked up, like a dead man being carried into a cemetery. This room was already occupied by an old solitary from Port-Royal* named Gordon, who had been languishing there for two years.

"Look," said the chief myrmidon, "here is some company that I'm bringing you."

And immediately they shot home again the enormous bolts of the thick door, covered with great bars. The two captives remained shut off from the entire universe.

2   The Bastille.

10 *Ingenuous Locked Up in the Bastille with a Jansenist*

MONSIEUR GORDON was a fresh, serene old man who knew two great things: how to bear adversity and how to console the unhappy. He advanced toward his companion with an open and compassionate air and said, as he embraced him:

"Whoever you are who come to share my tomb, be assured that I shall always forget myself in order to soften your torments in the infernal abyss into which we are plunged. Let us worship the Providence that has brought us here. Let us suffer in peace, and have hope."

These words had, on the soul of Ingenuous, the effect of drops of English cordial,* which bring a dying man back to life and make him half open his astonished eyes.

After the first compliments, Gordon, without pressing him to teach him the cause of his misfortune, inspired in him, by the sweetness of his talk and by that interest which two unfortunates take in each other, a desire to open his heart and lay down the burden that was oppressing him, but he could not guess the reason for his misfortune; it seemed to him an effect without a cause, and that good man Gordon was as astonished as himself.

"It must be," said the Jansenist to the Huron, "that God has great designs upon you, since he has led you from Lake Ontario to England and to France, has had you baptized in Lower Brittany, and has placed you here for your salvation."

"Faith," replied Ingenuous, "I believe that the devil alone has taken a hand in my destiny. My compatriots in America would never have treated me with the barbarity I am enduring; they have no idea of it. They are called savages; they are crude good men, and the men of this country are refined scoundrels. I am, in truth, quite surprised to have come from another world to be locked up in this one behind four bolts with a priest; but then I reflect on the prodigious number of men who leave one hemisphere to go and get themselves killed in the other, or who are shipwrecked on the way and eaten by the fishes. I do not see God's gracious design upon all those people."

They were brought dinner through a grating. The conversation turned on Providence, on *lettres de cachet*,* and on the art of not succumbing under the mishaps to which every man is exposed in this world.

"I have been here for two years," said the old man, "with no other consolation than myself and some books. I have not had a moment of bad humor."

"Ah! Monsieur Gordon," exclaimed Ingenuous, "then you are not in love with your godmother! If you knew Mademoiselle de Saint-Yves, as I do, you would be in despair."

At these words he could not restrain his tears, and then he felt a little less oppressed.

"But," said he, "then why do tears give relief? It seems to me they should have an opposite effect."

"My son, everything in us is physical," said the good old man; "every secretion does the body good, and everything that relieves it relieves the soul; we are the machines of Providence."

Ingenuous, who, as we have several times remarked, had a great fund of intelligence, reflected deeply on this idea, the seeds of which he seemed to have in himself. After which he asked his companion why his machine had been for two years behind four bolts.

"By effectual grace," answered Gordon. "I pass for a Jansenist, I have known Arnauld and Nicole;[1] the Jesuits have persecuted us. We believe that the Pope is only a bishop just like any other, and it was for this that Father de La Chaise obtained from the King his penitent an order to snatch from me, without any formality of justice, man's most precious possession, liberty."

"This is very strange," said Ingenuous; "all the unfortunates I have met are so only because of the Pope. As regards that effectual grace of yours, I confess to you that I don't understand a thing about it; but I regard it as a great grace that God has caused me to find in my misfortune a man like you, who pours into my heart consolations of which I thought myself incapable."

Each day the conversation became more interesting and more instructive. The souls of the two captives were growing attached to each other. The old man knew much, and the

1 Jansenist leaders.

young man wanted to learn much. After a month he studied geometry; he devoured it. Gordon had him read Rohault's* *Physics*, which was still in vogue, and he had the wit to find in it nothing but uncertainties.

Then he read the first volume of *The Quest for Truth*.[2] This brought him new light.

"What!" he said, "our imagination and our senses deceive us to this extent! What! objects do not form our ideas, and we ourselves cannot give ourselves ideas?"

When he had read the second volume, he was no longer so content with it, and he concluded that it is easier to destroy than to build.

His colleague, astounded that a young ignoramus should make that reflection, which belonged only to practiced minds, conceived a great notion of his intelligence, and grew more attached to him.

"Your Malebranche," said Ingenuous to him one day, "appears to me to have written half his book with his reason, and the other half with his imagination and his prejudices."

A few days afterward Gordon asked him: "Then what do you think about the soul, the way we receive our ideas? About our will, about grace, about free will?"

"Nothing," retorted Ingenuous. "If I thought anything, it is that we are under the power of the eternal Being, like the stars and the elements; that he does all things in us, that we are little wheels in the immense machine of which he is the soul, that he acts by general laws and not from particular views. This alone appears intelligible to me, all the rest is for me an abyss of darkness."

"But, my son, that would be making God the author of sin!"

"But, my father, your effectual grace would also make God the author of sin; for it is certain that all who were refused this grace would sin; and is not he who delivers us into evil the author of evil?"

This naïveté greatly embarrassed the good man; he felt that he was making vain efforts to pull himself out of this quagmire; and he kept piling up so many words that seemed

2   *La Recherche de la vérité* (2 vols., 1674–1675) by Nicolas Malebranche, Oratorian, who stresses the pitfalls of imagination and of the senses.

to make sense and that did not (in the style of "physical premotion"),[3] that Ingenuous pitied him. This question obviously depended on the origin of good and evil; and then poor Gordon had to pass in review Pandora's box, the egg of Ormuzd pierced by Ahriman, the enmity between Typhon and Osiris, and finally original sin; and they both kept racing around in this deep darkness without ever meeting one another. But after all, this romance of the soul diverted their eyes from the contemplation of their own misery; and by a strange charm the host of calamities spread over the universe diminished the sensation of their own troubles; they dared not complain when everything suffered.

But in the repose of night the picture of the fair Saint-Yves effaced from her lover's mind all ideas about metaphysics or morality. He would wake with his eyes wet with tears, and the old Jansenist would forget his effectual grace, and the Abbé de Saint-Cyran,* and Jansenius,* to console a young man whom he believed to be in mortal sin.

After their readings, after their reasonings, they still talked of their adventures; and after talking uselessly about them, they read together or apart. The young man's mind grew stronger and stronger. He would have gone very far in mathematics especially but for the distractions caused him by Mademoiselle de Saint-Yves.

He read histories; they made him sad. The world seemed to him too wicked and too wretched. Indeed history is only the picture of crimes and misfortunes. The crowd of innocent and peaceful men always disappears on these vast stages. The characters are nothing but perverse, ambitious men. It appears that history gives pleasure only like tragedy, which languishes if it is not animated by passions, crimes, and great misfortunes. Clio must be armed with a dagger like Melpomene.

Although the history of France is filled with horrors like all the others, yet it appeared to him so disgusting in its beginnings, so arid in its middle, finally so petty, even in the time of Henry IV; always so destitute of great monuments, so foreign to those beautiful discoveries that have made other nations illustrious, that he was obliged to struggle against

3   God's immediate co-operation with his creatures, a theory advanced by Laurent-François Boursier (1679–1749) in his *Action de Dieu sur les créatures, ou la prémotion physique.*

boredom in order to read all those details of obscure calamities concentrated in one corner of the world.

Gordon thought as he did. Both laughed with pity when they read about the sovereigns of Fezensac, Fezensaguet, and Astarac.[4] This study indeed would be good only for their heirs, if they had any. The noble periods of the Roman Republic made him for a while indifferent toward the rest of the earth. The spectacle of Rome, victorious and lawgiver to the nations, occupied his entire soul. He glowed as he contemplated this people which was governed for seven hundred years by enthusiasm for liberty and glory.

Thus passed the days, the weeks, the months; and he would have thought himself happy in the abode of despair if he had not been in love.

His natural goodness was also moved to compassion over the good prior of Our Lady of the Mountain and over the tender Kerkabon.

"What will they think," he often repeated, "when they get no news from me? They will think me an ingrate."

This idea tormented him; he pitied those who loved him much more than he pitied himself.

11   *How Ingenuous Develops His Genius*

READING ENLARGES the soul, and an enlightened friend consoles it. Our captive was enjoying these two advantages, which he had never even suspected before.

"I would be tempted," he said, "to believe in metamorphoses, for I have been changed from a brute into a man."

He built himself up a selected library with a part of his money that he was allowed to dispose of. His friend encouraged him to put his reflections in writing. Here is what he wrote about ancient history:

"I imagine that nations were long like me, that they became educated only very late, that they were occupied for centuries only with the present moment as it flowed by, very little with the past, and never with the future. I have traveled over five or six hundred leagues in Canada, I have not found a

4   Tiny counties in the Armagnac region.

single monument; no one there knows anything about what
his great-grandfather did. Isn't that probably the natural
state of man? The species on this continent seems to me
superior to that on the other. For several centuries it has
enlarged its being by the arts and sciences. Is that because
they have a beard on their chin and because God has refused
a beard to the Americans? I do not think so; for I see that the
Chinese have almost no beard, and that they have been
cultivating the arts for more than five thousand years. Indeed,
if they have more than four thousand years of annals, the
nation must certainly have been brought together and flourish-
ing for more than five hundred centuries.

"One thing above all strikes me in the ancient history of
China: that almost everything there is plausible and natural.
I admire it because there is nothing marvelous about it.

"Why have all the other nations given themselves fabulous
origins? The ancient chroniclers of the history of France, who
are not very ancient, make the French come down from one
Francus, son of Hector. The Romans said that they were
the issue of a Phrygian, although there was not a single word
in their language that had the slightest connection with the
language of Phrygia. The gods had dwelt ten thousand years
in Egypt, and the devils in Scythia, where they had engendered the Huns. I see nothing before Thucydides but
romances like the *Amadises*, and much less amusing. Everywhere it is apparitions, oracles, prodigies, sorcery, metamorphoses, dreams that are explained and that shape the
destiny of the greatest empires and the smallest states: here
talking beasts, there beasts worshiped, gods transformed into
men, and men transformed into gods. Ah! if we must have
fables, let these fables be at least emblematic of the truth! I
love the fables of philosophers, I laugh at those of children,
and I hate those of impostors."

One day he chanced upon a history of the Emperor
Justinian. In it one read that the Apedeutes [1] of Constantinople
had delivered, in very bad Greek, an edict against the greatest
captain [2] of his day, because that hero had uttered these

1   Ignorant, untaught; from the Greek ἀπαίδευτος, and more
directly from Rabelais (Book V, Chapter 16), who calls them
Apedeftes.
2   Belisarius. The quotation from him is taken from Jean-
François Marmontel's novel *Bélisaire*, censured by the Sorbonne
in the same year (1767) it appeared.

words in the heat of conversation: "Truth shines by its own light, and minds are not enlightened by the flames of the stake." The Apedeutes asserted that this proposition was heretical, smacking of heresy; and that the contrary axiom was Catholic, universal, and Greek: "Minds are enlightened only by the flames of the stake, and truth cannot shine by its own light." Thus these Linostoles [3] condemned several speeches of the captain and delivered an edict.

"What!" exclaimed Ingenuous, "edicts rendered by those people!"

"They are not edicts," replied Gordon, "they are con-tradicts,[4] which everyone in Constantinople laughed at and the Emperor first of all; he was a wise prince who had managed to reduce the Linostole Apedeutes to inability to do anything but good. He knew that those gentlemen and many other Pastophores [5] had exhausted the patience of the Emperors his predecessors by their contradictions in more serious matters."

"He did very well," said Ingenuous; "one must support the Pastophores and constrain them."

He put into writing many other reflections which appalled old Gordon.

"What!" he said to himself, "I have consumed fifty years in learning, and I fear I may never attain the natural good sense of this almost savage lad! I tremble lest I may have laboriously strengthened my prejudices; he listens only to the voice of pure nature."

The good man had some of those little books of criticism, those periodical pamphlets in which men incapable of pro-ducing anything insult the publications of others, in which the Visés [6] insult the Racines* and the Faydits the Fénelons. Ingenuous ran through a few of them.

"I compare them," he said, "to certain gnats who go and lay

3   Linen-clad, from the Greek λινόστολος; in Voltaire's vo-cabulary designating the doctors of the Sorbonne. Compare Rabe-lais (Book V, Chapter 4): *linostolies* or *linoscolies*.
4   Properly, "contradictions." The French is *édits, contredits*.
5   From the Greek παστοφόρος: priests carrying small shrines; in Voltaire's vocabulary designating any priests. Voltaire is again indebted to Rabelais, Book III, Chapter 48.
6   Jean Donneau de Visé (1640–1710), enemy of Racine, Molière, and Boileau, founder of the *Mercure galant*, later to be the *Mercure de France*. Faydit attacked Fénelon in his *Télé-machomanie* (1700).

their eggs in the backsides of the finest horses; that does not stop the horses from running."

Hardly did the two philosophers deign to cast their eyes on these excrements of literature.

Soon they read together the elements of astronomy; Ingenuous sent for some spheres: this great spectacle enchanted him.

"How hard it is," he said, "to be starting to know the heavens only when I am robbed of the right to contemplate them! Jupiter and Saturn revolve in those immense spaces; millions of suns light up billions of worlds; and in the patch of land where I am cast there are beings who deprive me, a seeing and thinking being, of all those worlds which my vision could reach and of the one in which God had me born! The light made for the whole universe is lost for me. No one hid it from me in the northern clime where I spent my childhood and my youth. Without you, my dear Gordon, I would be in nothingness here."

12 *What Ingenuous Thinks of Plays*

YOUNG INGENUOUS was like one of those vigorous trees which, born in sterile soil, spread out their roots and branches in a short time when they are transplanted into favorable terrain; and it was quite extraordinary that a prison should be that terrain.

Among the books that occupied the leisure of the two captives there was poetry, translations of Greek tragedies, and some French plays. The poetry which spoke of love brought pleasure and pain into Ingenuous' soul at the same time. It all spoke to him of his dear Saint-Yves. The fable of "The Two Pigeons" [1] pierced his heart; he was very far from being able to return to his own dovecote.

Molière enchanted him. He made him know the morals of Paris and of the human race.

"To which of his comedies do you give the preference?"

"To *Tartuffe*, easily."

"I think as you do," said Gordon; "it was a Tartuffe who plunged me into this dungeon, and perhaps it is Tartuffes

1   La Fontaine, *Fables*, IX, "Les Deux Pigeons."

who have caused your misfortune. . . . How do you like
these Greek tragedies?"

"Good for Greeks," said Ingenuous.

But when he read the modern *Iphigénie, Phèdre, Andromaque, Athalie,*[2] he was in ecstasy, he sighed, he shed tears,
he learned them by heart without trying to memorize them.

"Read *Rodogune,*"[3] said Gordon, "they say it is the
masterpiece of the drama; the other plays that have given you
so much pleasure are not much by comparison."

The young man, after the first page, said to him:

"This is not by the same author."

"How can you see that?"

"I know nothing about it yet, but these verses go neither
to my ear nor to my heart."

"Oh! The verses are nothing," replied Gordon.

Ingenuous answered: "Then why write them?"

After reading the play very attentively with no other purpose than pleasure, he looked at his friend with dry astonished
eyes and knew not what to say. Finally, urged to report what
he had felt, here is what he replied:

"I hardly understood the beginning; I was revolted by the
middle; the last scene greatly touched me, although it seems to
me very implausible; I did not become involved on behalf of
anybody, and I did not retain twenty lines, I who retain them
all when I like them."

"Yet this play passes for the best one we have."

"If that is so," he replied, "perhaps it is like many people
who do not deserve their positions. After all, this is a matter
of taste, mine must not be formed yet; I may be mistaken; but
you know that I am accustomed to say what I think, or rather
what I feel. I suspect that there is often illusion, vogue,
caprice in men's judgments. I have spoken according to
nature; it may be that in me nature is very imperfect; but it
may also be that sometimes she is consulted little by most
men."

Then he recited some verses from *Iphigénie,* of which he
was full; and though his declamation was not good, he put
into it so much truth and unction that he made the old
Jansenist weep. He then read *Cinna;* he did not weep, but
he admired.

2   All tragedies by Jean Racine.
3   By Pierre Corneille,* as is *Cinna.*

13 *The Fair Saint-Yves Goes to Versailles*

WHILE OUR UNFORTUNATE was gaining more enlightenment than consolation; while his genius, so long stifled, was unfolding with so much rapidity and power; while nature, which was perfecting itself in him, was avenging him for the outrages of fortune—what became of the reverend prior and his good sister, and the beautiful recluse Saint-Yves? For the first month they were anxious, and by the third they were plunged in grief. False conjectures, ill-founded rumors gave alarm. After six months they believed him dead. Finally, Monsieur and Mademoiselle de Kerkabon learned by an old letter which one of the King's guards had written to Brittany, that a young man resembling Ingenuous had arrived one evening at Versailles, but that he had been carried off during the night, and that since that time no one had heard of him.

"Alas!" said Mademoiselle de Kerkabon, "our nephew must have done something foolish and gotten into some pretty bad trouble. He is young, he is a Lower Breton, he cannot know how to behave at court. My dear brother, I have never seen Versailles or Paris, here is a fine opportunity, perhaps we will find our poor nephew; he is our brother's son, our duty is to rescue him. Who knows whether we will not finally be able to succeed in making him a subdeacon when the fire of youth has died down? He had much inclination for learning. Do you remember how he used to argue over the Old and New Testaments? We are responsible for his soul; we are the ones who had him baptized; his dear mistress Saint-Yves spends her days weeping. In truth we must go to Paris. If he is hidden in one of those nasty houses of pleasure that I have heard so many stories about, we will get him out."

The prior was touched by his sister's words. He went and found the Bishop of Saint-Malo, who had baptized the Huron, and asked him for his protection and advice. The prelate approved of the trip. He gave the prior letters of recommendation to Father de La Chaise, confessor to the King, who was the highest dignitary in the kingdom; to Harlay,* Archbishop of Paris, and to Bossuet,* Bishop of Meaux.

At last the brother and sister left; but when they had reached Paris, they found themselves lost as if in a vast labyrinth, without a thread or a way out. Their means were modest; they needed carriages every day to go in quest of discovery, and they discovered nothing.

The prior presented himself at the house of the Reverend Father de La Chaise; he was with Mademoiselle du Tron, and could not give audience to priors. He went to the archbishop's door; the prelate was in closed conference with the beautiful Madame de Lesdiguières on Church affairs. He hastened to the country house of the Bishop of Meaux; he was examining, with Mademoiselle de Mauléon, the mystical love of Madame Guyon. However, he did succeed in getting a hearing from these two prelates; both declared that they could not concern themselves with his nephew, seeing that he was not a subdeacon.

At last he saw the Jesuit, who received him with open arms and, never having known him, protested that he had always had a particular esteem for him. He swore that the Society had always been strongly attached to Lower Bretons.

"But," said he, "doesn't your nephew have the misfortune of being a Huguenot?"

"Assuredly not, Reverend Father."

"Mightn't he be a Jansenist?"

"I can assure Your Reverence that he is barely a Christian. It was about eleven months ago that we baptized him."

"That's fine, that's fine, we'll take care of him. Is yours a considerable benefice?"

"Oh, a very small matter; and our nephew costs us a lot."

"Are there any Jansenists in your neighborhood? Take good care, my dear Mr. Prior, they are more dangerous than the Huguenots and the atheists."

"Reverend Father, we have none; they do not know what Jansenism is at Our Lady of the Mountain."

"So much the better; go, there is nothing I will not do for you."

He dismissed the prior affectionately, and thought no more about it.

Time was flowing by; the prior and his good sister were growing desperate.

Meanwhile the accursed magistrate was urging the marriage of his great booby of a son with the fair Saint-Yves, who had

been taken out of the convent for that purpose. She still
loved her dear godson just as much as she detested the
husband offered her. The affront of having been put into a
convent increased her passion. The order to marry the
magistrate's son capped it all. Regrets, tenderness, and horror
quite upset her soul. Love, as we know, is much bolder and
more ingenious in a young girl than is friendship in an old
prior and an aunt past forty-five. Moreover, she had had a
good education in her convent from the novels she had read
on the sly.

The fair Saint-Yves remembered the letter that a guardsman had written to Lower Brittany and that had been talked
about in the province. She resolved to go herself to get information at Versailles, to throw herself at the feet of the
ministers if her husband was in prison as they said, and to
obtain justice for him. Something, I know not what, secretly
told her that at court nothing is refused to a pretty girl. But
she did not know what it cost.

Her resolution once taken, she is consoled, she is tranquil,
she no longer rebuffs her stupid suitor; she welcomes the
detestable father-in-law, caresses her brother, spreads gladness
throughout the house; then on the day destined for the
ceremony she leaves secretly at four o'clock in the morning
with her little wedding presents and everything she could gather
together. Her measures were so well taken that she was already
more than ten leagues away when they went into her room
around noon. Great was the surprise and consternation. The
interrogative magistrate asked more questions that day than he
had asked all week; the groom remained more stupid than
he had ever been. The Abbé de Saint-Yves in his anger
decided to pursue his sister. The magistrate and his son insisted on accompanying him. Thus destiny led to Paris almost
that whole district of Lower Brittany.

The fair Saint-Yves fully suspected that she would be
followed. She was on horseback; she cleverly inquired of
the passing couriers whether they had not encountered a fat
abbé, an enormous magistrate, and a young booby racing
along the roads to Paris. Having learned on the third day
that they were not far off, she took a different route, and
had cleverness and luck enough to arrive in Versailles while
they were searching for her vainly in Paris.

But how was she to proceed in Versailles? Young, beautiful,

without advice, without support, unknown, exposed to everything, how could she dare to go in search of one of the King's
guardsmen? She thought of applying to a low-level Jesuit;
they had them for all conditions of life, just as God, they
said, has given different foods to the different kinds of
animals. God had given the King his confessor, whom all the
solicitors of benefices called "the head of the Gallican
church"; then came the confessors of princesses; the ministers
had none, they were not so stupid. There were the Jesuits
for the general public, and especially the Jesuits for house-
maids, from whom they learned their mistresses' secrets, and
that was no petty occupation. The fair Saint-Yves addressed
herself to one of these last, whose name was Father Tout-à-
tous.[1] She made her confession to him, exposed to him her
adventures, her situation, her danger, and conjured him to
get her lodging with some good pious woman who would
shelter her from temptation.

Father Tout-à-tous put her in the house of the wife of an
officer of the wine cellar, one of his most trusty penitents.
As soon as she was there, she worked assiduously to gain the
confidence and friendship of this woman; she inquired
about the Breton guardsman, and had him invited to come
to the house. Having learned from him that her lover had been
carried off after talking with a chief clerk, she ran to see
this clerk; the sight of a beautiful woman softened him, for it
must be admitted that God made women only to tame men.

The quill driver, moved to tenderness, admitted everything
to her.

"Your lover has been in the Bastille for almost a year, and
without you he might be there all his life."

The tender Saint-Yves swooned. When she had regained
her senses, the quill driver said to her:

"I have no influence to do good, all my power is limited
to doing evil sometimes. Believe me, go to see Monsieur de
Saint-Pouange,* who does both good and evil, cousin and
favorite of Monseigneur de Louvois. That minister has two
souls: Monsieur de Saint-Pouange is one, Madame du Belloy
the other, but she is not at Versailles at present; the only
thing left for you to do is to soften the protector I am
mentioning to you."

The fair Saint-Yves, divided between a little joy and ex-

1   All things to all men.

treme sorrows, between some measure of hope and sad fears, pursued by her brother, adoring her lover, drying her tears and shedding yet more, trembling, weakened, and taking fresh courage, sped to the house of Monsieur de Saint-Pouange.

14 *Progress of Ingenuous' Mind*

INGENUOUS WAS MAKING rapid progress in all kinds of knowledge, and especially in the knowledge of man. The cause of the rapid development of his mind was due to his savage education almost as much as to the temper of his soul. For having learned nothing in his childhood, he had learned no prejudices. His understanding, not having been warped by error, had remained in all its rectitude. He saw things as they are, whereas the ideas we are given in childhood make us see things all our lives as they are not.

"Your persecutors are abominable," he said to his friend Gordon. "I pity you for being oppressed, but I pity you for being a Jansenist. Every sect appears to me a rallying point for error. Tell me whether there are any sects in geometry?"

"No, my dear lad," said the good Gordon with a sigh, "all men are agreed on the truth when it is demonstrated, but they are all too divided over obscure truths."

"Say rather over obscure falsehoods. If there had been one single truth hidden in your piles of arguments that have been repeated over and over for so many centuries, without a doubt it would have been discovered, and the universe would have been agreed at least on that point. If that truth were necessary, as the sun is to the earth, it would shine like the sun. It is an absurdity, it is an outrage against the human race, it is a felonious assault against the infinite and supreme Being to say: There is a truth essential to man, and God has hidden it."

Everything said by this young ignoramus, taught by nature, made a deep impression on the mind of the unfortunate old scholar.

"Could it really be true," he exclaimed, "that I have made

Father de La Chaise, who will have him put into the abode where at present lies the dear person whom you are to marry."

The poor girl, after long embarrassment and great irresolution, finally gave him the name of Saint-Pouange.

"My Lord de Saint-Pouange!" cried the Jesuit. "Ah! my daughter, that's quite another matter; he is a cousin of the greatest minister we have ever had, a worthy man, protector of the good cause, a good Christian; he cannot have had such a thought, you must have misunderstood."

"Ah! Father, I understood only too well; I am lost whatever I do; I have only the choice between misery and shame; either my lover must remain buried alive, or I must make myself unworthy to live. I cannot let him perish, and I cannot save him."

Father Tout-à-tous tried to calm her with these sweet words:

"In the first place, my daughter, never use the term 'my lover'; there is something worldly about it that might offend God. Say 'my husband'; for although he is not that yet, you regard him as such, and there is nothing more honorable.

"Secondly, although he is your husband in your mind, in your hopes, he is not so in fact: thus you would not be committing adultery, an enormous sin that one must always avoid as far as possible.

"Thirdly, actions are not maliciously guilty when the intention is pure; and nothing is purer than to deliver your husband.

"Fourthly, you have examples in sacred antiquity which can be wonderfully helpful for your conduct. St. Augustine reports [1] that in the proconsulate of Septimius Acindynus, in the year 340 of our salvation, a poor man, unable to render unto Caesar the things that were Caesar's, was condemned to death, as is just, in spite of the maxim: *Where there is nothing, the King loses his rights.* At issue was a pound of gold; the condemned man had a wife in whom God had set both beauty and prudence. A rich old man promised to give the lady a pound of gold and even more on condition that he would commit the filthy sin with her. The lady did not think she did evil in saving her husband's life. St. Augustine strongly approves her generous resigna-

[1] *The Lord's Sermon on the Mount*, Book I, Chapter xvi.

tion. It is true that the rich old man cheated her, and maybe even her husband was hanged none the less; but she had done all that was in her to save his life.

"Be sure, my daughter, that when a Jesuit quotes you St. Augustine, that saint must certainly be fully right. I give you no advice; you are wise; it is to be presumed that you will be useful to your husband. Monseigneur de Saint-Pouange is an honorable man, he will not cheat you, that is all I can say to you; I shall pray God for you; and I hope that everything will come out to his greater glory."

The fair Saint-Yves, no less terrified by the Jesuit's remarks than by the assistant minister's propositions, went back, frantic, to her friend's house. She was tempted to deliver herself by death from the horror of leaving in frightful captivity the lover she adored and from the shame of delivering him at the cost of the most precious thing she had, which ought to belong only to that unfortunate lover.

17   *She Succumbs out of Virtue*

SHE KEPT BEGGING her friend to kill her; but this woman, no less indulgent than the Jesuit, spoke to her more clearly still.

"Alas!" she said. "Business is hardly conducted in any other way in this court which is so charming, so gallant, and so renowned. The most mediocre and the most considerable positions have often been given only at the price that is being exacted of you. Listen! You have inspired friendship and trust in me; I will admit to you that if I had always been as difficult as you are, my husband would not enjoy the little position that keeps him alive; he knows it, and far from being angry about it, he sees in me his benefactress; and he regards himself as my creature. Do you think that all those who have been at the head of provinces or even armies have owed their honors and their good fortune to their services alone? There are some who are indebted to my ladies their wives. The dignities of war were solicited by love, and the position was given to the husband of the fairest.

"You are in a much more interesting situation: it is for you to restore your lover to the light of day, and to marry

him; it is a sacred duty that you must fulfill. People did
not blame the beautiful and great ladies I am speaking to
you of; they will applaud you; they will say that you allowed
yourself a frailty only through an excess of virtue."

"Ah! what a virtue!" cried the fair Saint-Yves. "What a
labyrinth of iniquities, what a country, and how I am learning
to know men! A Father de La Chaise and a ridiculous
magistrate have my husband put in prison; my family persecutes me, a hand is stretched out to me in my disaster only
to dishonor me. A Jesuit has ruined a good man, another
Jesuit wants to ruin me; I am surrounded by nothing but
snares, and I am at the point of falling into misery! I must
either kill myself or speak to the King; I will throw myself
at his feet when he passes on his way to Mass or to the
theater."

"They won't let you get near him," said her good friend;
"and if you had the misfortune to speak, Monsieur de Louvois
and the Reverend Father de La Chaise might bury you in the
depths of a convent for the rest of your days."

While this good person was thus increasing the perplexities
of this despairing soul and plunging the dagger into her
heart, there arrives a special messenger from Monsieur de
Saint-Pouange with a letter and two beautiful earrings. Saint-
Yves, weeping, rejected everything, but her friend took
charge of it.

As soon as the messenger had left, our confidante reads
the letter, which proposes a private supper that evening for
the two friends. Saint-Yves swears she will not go. Her pious
friend wants to try the diamond earrings on her; Saint-Yves
could not endure it, she fought against it all day. Finally,
having nothing in mind but her lover, vanquished, dragged
along, not knowing where she is being taken, she lets herself
be brought to the fatal supper. Nothing had been able to
persuade her to adorn herself with her earrings; the confidante brought them along and put them on her in spite
of her before they sat down to table. Saint-Yves was so
confused, so troubled, that she let herself be tormented thus;
and the master took it for a very favorable omen. Toward
the end of the meal the confidante discreetly withdrew. The
master then displayed the revocation of the *lettre de cachet*,
the letters patent for a considerable reward and for the command of a company, and he did not spare the promises.

"Ah!" said Saint-Yves to him, "how I would love you if you didn't insist on being loved so much!"

Finally after a long resistance, after sobs, cries, tears, weakened by the struggle, frantic, drooping, she had to surrender. Her only resource was to promise herself to think only of Ingenuous while her cruel persecutor took pitiless advantage of the necessity to which she was reduced.

18 She Delivers Her Lover and a Jansenist

AT DAYBREAK she flies to Paris armed with the minister's order. It is hard to depict what went on in her heart during this trip. Imagine a virtuous and noble soul, humiliated by its own opprobrium, intoxicated with tenderness, torn with remorse for having betrayed her lover, thrilled with the pleasure of delivering the one she adores. Her bitterness, her struggles, her success divided all her thoughts. She was no longer the simple girl whose ideas had been narrowed by a provincial education. Love and unhappiness had molded her. Feeling had made as much progress in her as had reason in the mind of her unfortunate lover. Girls learn to feel more easily than men learn to think. Her adventure had taught her more than would four years in a convent.

Her dress was of extreme simplicity. She viewed with horror the attire in which she had appeared before her baneful benefactor; she had left her diamond earrings to her friend without even looking at them. Abashed and charmed, idolizing Ingenuous and hating herself, she arrives at last at the gate

> Of that grim fort where vengeance has its seat,
> Where crime and innocence imprisoned meet.[1]

When she had to get out of the carriage her strength failed; she was helped down; she entered, heart palpitating, eyes moist, consternation on her face. She is introduced to the governor; she tries to speak to him, her voice dies; she displays her order, barely articulating a few words. The governor

[1] Verses 456–457 of Canto IV of Voltaire's *Henriade*, slightly altered to fit the present context.

liked his prisoner; he was very glad of his deliverance. His heart was not hardened like that of some of his honorable fellow jailers, who, thinking only of the compensation attached to the custody of their captives, founding their incomes on their victims, and living off the misery of others, secretly took a frightful joy in the tears of the unfortunate.

He has the prisoner brought to his apartment. The two lovers see each other, and both swoon. The fair Saint-Yves remained long motionless and inanimate; the other soon recovered his spirits.

"Apparently this lady is your wife," said the governor to him; "you had not told me you were married. I am informed that it is to her generous efforts that you owe your deliverance."

"Ah! I am not worthy to be his wife," said the fair Saint-Yves in trembling voice, and she fell back into her swoon.

When she had regained her senses she presented, still trembling, the letters patent for the reward and the written promise of a company. Ingenuous, as astounded as he was touched, awoke from one dream only to fall back into another.

"Why was I locked up here? How were you able to get me out? Where are the monsters who plunged me in here? You are a divinity come down from heaven to my rescue."

The fair Saint-Yves lowered her gaze, looked at her lover, blushed, and the next moment turned away her eyes wet with tears. At last she told him all she knew and all she had been through except what she would have wished to hide from herself forever and what another man than Ingenuous, more accustomed to the ways of the world and more versed in the practices of the court, would easily have guessed.

"Is it possible that a wretch like that magistrate had the power to rob me of my liberty! Ah! I see clearly that it is with men as with the vilest animals: all can do harm. But is it possible that a monk, a Jesuit who is confessor to the King, contributed to my misfortune as much as that magistrate, without my being able to imagine under what pretext this detestable rogue persecuted me? Did he make me pass for a Jansenist? Finally, how did you remember me? I didn't deserve it, I was only a savage then. What! You managed, without advice, without help, to undertake the trip to Versailles! You appeared there, and they broke my chains! So

there is, in beauty and virtue, an invincible charm that makes
gates of iron fall and softens hearts of bronze!"

At that word "virtue," sobs escaped the fair Saint-Yves.
She did not know how virtuous she was in the crime for
which she reproached herself.

Her lover continued thus:

"Angel who have broken my chains, if you had (which
I do not yet understand) enough influence to have justice
done to me, have it done also to an old man who was the
first to teach me to think, as you have taught me to love.
Calamity has united us; I love him like a father, I cannot live
either without you or without him."

"I, solicit the same man who . . . !"

"Yes, I want to owe everything to you, and I never want
to owe anything except to you: write to this powerful man,
overwhelm me with your good deeds, complete what you have
begun, complete your miracles."

She felt that she should do all that her lover demanded. She
tried to write, her hand would not obey. She began her letter
three times, tore it up three times; finally she wrote, and the
two lovers left after embracing the old martyr to effectual
grace.

The happy and desolate Saint-Yves knew what house her
brother was lodging in; she went there; her lover took an
apartment in the same house.

Hardly had they arrived there than her protector sent her
the order for the release of that good man Gordon and asked
her for a rendezvous the next day. Thus with every honorable
and generous deed she did her dishonor was the price. She
looked with execration on this practice of selling the unhappiness and happiness of men. She gave her lover the
order for release and refused the rendezvous with a benefactor whom she could no longer see without dying of grief
and shame. Ingenuous could not leave her except to go deliver a friend. He flew to it. He fulfilled this duty while reflecting on the strange events of this world and marveling
at the courageous virtue of a young girl to whom two unfortunates owed more than life.

19 Ingenuous, the Fair Saint-Yves, and Their Relatives Are Reunited

THE GENEROUS, respectable, unfaithful girl was with her brother the Abbé de Saint-Yves, the good Prior of the Mountain, and the Lady de Kerkabon. All were equally astonished, but their situations and their feelings were quite different. The Abbé de Saint-Yves was weeping at the feet of his sister for the wrongs he had done, and she was forgiving him. The prior and his tender sister were weeping too, but for joy; the vile magistrate and his insufferable son were not there to trouble this touching scene. They had left at the first news of their enemy's release, they were hastening to bury in their own province their stupidity and their fear.

The four people, agitated by a hundred diverse emotions, were waiting for the young man to come back with the friend he was to deliver. The Abbé de Saint-Yves did not dare raise his eyes in front of his sister; the good Kerkabon was saying:

"So I shall see my dear nephew again."

"You will see him again," said the charming Saint-Yves, "but he is no longer the same man; his bearing, his tone, his ideas, his mind, all is changed; he has become as impressive as he used to be naïve and foreign to everything. He will be the honor and the consolation of your family; would that I could also be the honor of mine!"

"You are not the same either," said the prior; "what happened to you, then, that made so great a change in you?"

In the midst of this conversation Ingenuous arrives holding his Jansenist by the hand. The scene then became more novel and interesting. It began with the tender embraces of the uncle and aunt. The Abbé de Saint-Yves almost went on his knees to Ingenuous, who was no longer Ingenuous. The two lovers talked to each other by glances expressing all the feelings which penetrated their hearts. Satisfaction and gratitude could be seen bursting out over the face of one, embarrassment was depicted in the tender and somewhat distracted eyes of the other. There was astonishment that with so much joy she mingled grief.

Old Gordon within a few moments became dear to the whole family. He and the young prisoner had been unhappy together, and that was a great claim. He owed his deliverance to the two lovers, that alone reconciled him with love; the harshness of his former opinions was leaving his heart, he was changed into a man, just like the Huron. Each one related his adventures before supper. The two abbés and the aunt listened like children hearing ghost stories and like people who were all interested in all these disasters.

"Alas!" said Gordon. "There are perhaps more than five hundred virtuous people who are at present in the same chains that Mademoiselle de Saint-Yves has broken; their misfortunes are unknown. You find plenty of hands that strike the multitude of the unfortunate, and rarely one to help."

This reflection, so true, increased his emotion and his gratitude; everything redoubled the triumph of the fair Saint-Yves, everyone admired the greatness and firmness of her soul. The admiration was mingled with that respect which people feel in spite of themselves for a person they believe to have influence at court. But the Abbé de Saint-Yves sometimes said:

"How could my sister manage to obtain this influence so soon?"

They were going to sit down to table very early. Up comes the good friend from Versailles, knowing nothing of all that had happened; she was in a six-horse carriage, and it is easy to see to whom the carriage belonged. She enters with the imposing air of a court person who has important business, offers a scanty greeting to the company, and, drawing the fair Saint-Yves aside:

"Why keep people waiting? Follow me. Here are your diamonds that you forgot."

She could not say these words so low as not to be heard by Ingenuous; he saw the diamonds; the brother was dumfounded; the uncle and aunt experienced only the surprise of simple folk who have never seen such magnificence. The young man, who had formed himself by a year's reflections, made some now in spite of himself, and appeared troubled for a moment. His mistress perceived it; a mortal pallor overspread her beautiful face, a tremor seized her, she could barely stand:

"Ah! Madame," she said to the fatal friend, "you have ruined me! You bring me death."

These words pierced Ingenuous' heart; but he had already learned self-possession; he did not pick them up, for fear of worrying his mistress in front of her brother, but he turned as pale as she.

Saint-Yves, frantic at the alteration she perceived in her lover's face, drags this woman out of the room into a little passage, throws the diamonds on the ground in front of her.

"Ah! it was not those that seduced me, you know that; but the man who gave them shall never see me again."

The friend picked them up and Saint-Yves added:

"Let him take them back or give them to you. Go; don't make me ashamed of myself any more."

Finally the ambassadress went back, unable to understand the remorse she was witnessing.

The fair Saint-Yves, oppressed, feeling in her body a revolt that was suffocating her, was obliged to put herself to bed, but in order not to alarm anyone she did not speak of what she was suffering; and using only her exhaustion as a pretext, she asked permission to take some rest; but this was after reassuring the company by consoling and encouraging words and after casting glances at her lover which kindled a fire in his soul.

The supper, which she was not there to animate, was sad at the beginning, but with that interesting sadness which produces engaging and useful conversations, so superior to the frivolous joy that people seek and that is ordinarily only a tedious noise.

Gordon told in a few words the story of Jansenism and Molinism,* of the persecutions with which one sect over-whelmed the other, and the stubbornness of both. Ingenuous criticized them and pitied men who, not content with all the discord kindled by their interests, make new troubles for themselves for the sake of chimerical interests and unin-telligible absurdities. Gordon narrated, the other judged; the guests listened with emotion and were illumined by new light. They talked of the length of our misfortunes and the shortness of life. They observed that each profession has attached to it one vice and one danger; and that from the prince on down to the lowest of beggars everything seems to accuse nature. How do there come to be so many men who for so little money make themselves the persecutors, the satellites, the executioners of other men? With what inhuman indifference a man in high position signs an order for the destruction of a family, and with what still more barbaric joy mercenaries carry it out!

"I saw in my youth," said the good Gordon, "a relative of Marshal de Marillac,* who, being pursued in his own province on account of that illustrious unfortunate, was hiding in Paris under an assumed name. He was an old man of seventy-two. His wife, who accompanied him, was about his age. They had had a libertine son who at fourteen had run away from the home of his father; becoming a soldier, then a deserter, he had passed through all the stages of debauch and misery; finally, having assumed a noble name, he was one of the guards of Cardinal Richelieu (for this priest, just like Mazarin, kept guards); he had obtained an adjutant's baton in this company of satellites. This adventurer was given the task of arresting the old man and his wife, and acquitted himself with all the harshness of a man who wanted to please his master. As he was taking them in, he heard these two victims deploring the long sequence of calamities that they had undergone since the cradle. The father and mother counted among their greatest misfortunes the transgressions and the loss of their son. He recognized them; he took them to prison none the less, assuring them that His Eminence must be served in preference to everything. His Eminence rewarded his zeal.

"I have seen a spy of Father de La Chaise betray his own brother in the hope of a small benefice which he did not get; and I saw him die, not of remorse, but of grief at having been duped by the Jesuit.

"The office of confessor, which I long exercised, has made me know families from the inside; I have seen hardly any that were not plunged in bitterness, while outwardly, covered with the mask of happiness, they seemed to be swimming in joy; and I have always observed that great vexations were the fruit of our unrestrained greed."

"As for me," said Ingenuous, "I think that a noble, grateful, and tender soul can live happily; and I certainly count on enjoying unmixed felicity with the beautiful and generous Saint-Yves. For I flatter myself," he added, addressing her brother with the smile of friendship, "that you will not refuse me as you did last year, and that I will go about things in a more decent manner."

The abbé was profuse in excuses for the past and in protestations of eternal attachment.

Uncle Kerkabon said that would be the happiest day of his life. The good aunt, ecstatic and weeping for joy, exclaimed:

"I always told you you would never be a subdeacon; this sacrament is much better than the other; would God I had been honored by it! But I shall be a mother to you."

Then they all vied in singing the praises of the tender Saint-Yves.

Her lover's heart was too full of what she had done for him, he loved her too much, for the incident of the diamonds to have made a dominating impression on his heart. But those words that he had heard only too well, "you bring me death," still secretly frightened him and spoiled all his joy, while the eulogies of his beautiful mistress further increased his love. Finally no one any longer thought of anything but her; they talked only of the happiness that these two lovers deserved; they made arrangements all to live together in Paris, they made plans for fortunes and aggrandizement, they gave themselves up to all those hopes that the slightest glimmer of happiness so easily engenders. But Ingenuous at the bottom of his heart had a secret feeling that repelled this illusion. He read once again those promises signed Saint-Pouange and the letters patent signed Louvois; these two men were depicted to him as they were, or as they were thought to be. Everyone spoke of the ministers and the ministry with that mealtime freedom that is regarded in France as the most precious freedom that can be savored on earth.

"If I were the King of France," said Ingenuous, "here is the Minister of War [1] I would choose: I would want a man of the highest birth, because he gives orders to the nobility. I would require him to have been an officer himself, to have come up through all the ranks, to be at least Lieutenant-General of the Armies and worthy to be a Marshal of France. For is it not necessary for him to have served in person, the better to know the details of the service? And won't the officers obey a hundred times more cheerfully a man of

1 What follows is a eulogy of the Duke of Choiseul, Minister of War at the time Voltaire was writing this.

war who like themselves has manifested his courage than an
armchair strategist who can at most only guess at the operations of a campaign, however good a mind he may have?
I would not be sorry to see my minister generous, although
my guardian of the royal treasury might sometimes be
embarrassed by this. I would like him to have a facility for
work, and even to distinguish himself by that gaiety of spirit,
the quality of a man superior to business, which the nation
likes so much and which makes all duties less irksome."

He wanted a minister to have this character because he had
always observed that this good humor is incompatible with
cruelty. Monsieur de Louvois would perhaps not have been
satisfied with Ingenuous' wishes; he had a different sort of
merit.

But while they were at table, the illness of this unfortunate
girl took on a deadly character; her blood had caught fire,
a devouring fever had broken out, she suffered and did not
complain, careful not to disturb the joy of the guests.

Her brother, knowing that she was not asleep, went to her
bedside; he was surprised at the state she was in. Everyone
came running up; the lover appeared on the brother's heels.
He was beyond doubt the most alarmed and distressed of
all; but he had learned to add discretion to all the happy gifts
that nature had lavished on him, and a prompt sense of
propriety was beginning to prevail in him.

They immediately sent for a neighborhood doctor. He was
one of those who visit their patients on the run, who confuse
the illness they have just seen with the one they see now,
who blindly practice a science from which all the maturity
of sound and thoughtful discernment cannot remove its
uncertainty and its dangers. He made the illness twice as
bad by his precipitancy in prescribing a remedy then in
fashion. Fashion even in medicine! This mania was all too
common in Paris.

The sad Saint-Yves contributed even more than her doctor
to make her illness dangerous. Her soul was killing her body.
The multitude of thoughts which agitated her sent into her
veins a poison more dangerous than that of the most burning
fever.

20 The Fair Saint-Yves Dies, and What Comes of It

THEY CALLED another doctor; this one, instead of assisting nature and letting it act in a young person all of whose organs were trying to bring life back, was concerned only with counteracting his colleague. The illness became mortal in two days. The brain, which is thought to be the seat of the understanding, was attacked as violently as the heart, which is, they say, the seat of the passions.

What incomprehensible mechanism has subjected the organs to feeling and thought? How does a single painful idea disturb the bloodstream, and how does the blood in turn carry its disorders into the human understanding? What is that unknown fluid, whose existence is certain, which, more prompt and active than light, flies in less than a wink into all the channels of life, produces sensations, memory, sadness or joy, reason or vertigo, recalls with horror what we would like to forget, and of a thinking animal makes either an object of admiration or a subject for pity and tears?

That was what the good Gordon was saying; and this most natural reflection, which men rarely make, took away none of his sympathy; for he was not one of those unhappy philosophers who strive to be insensible. He was touched by the fate of this girl, like a father who sees his beloved child slowly dying. The Abbé de Saint-Yves was in despair; the prior and his sister poured out streams of tears. But who could depict the state of her lover? No language has expressions to correspond with this acme of sorrows; languages are too imperfect.

The aunt, almost lifeless, was holding the dying girl's head in her feeble arms, her brother was on his knees at the foot of the bed. Her lover was squeezing her hand, bathing it with tears, and bursting into sobs; calling her his benefactress, his hope, his life, half of himself, his mistress, his wife. At that word "wife" she sighed, looked at him with inexpressible tenderness, and suddenly uttered a cry of horror; then in one of those intervals in which the prostration of the oppressed senses and a suspension of suffering leave the soul its freedom and its strength, she cried:

313

"I, your wife! Ah! dear lover, that name, that happiness, that prize were no longer made for me; I am dying, and I deserve it. O God of my heart! O you whom I have sacrificed to infernal demons, it is all over, I am punished, live and be happy."

These tender and terrible words could not be understood; but they brought fright and compassion into all hearts; she had the courage to explain herself. Each word caused a shudder of astonishment, pain, and pity in all those present. All joined in detesting the powerful man who had repaired a horrible injustice only by a crime, and who had forced the most respectable innocence to be his accomplice.

"What! You guilty!" said her lover to her. "No, you are not; crime can exist only in the heart, and yours belongs to virtue and to me."

He supported this sentiment by words which seemed to bring the fair Saint-Yves back to life. She felt consoled, and was astonished to be still loved. Old Gordon would have condemned her in the time when he was only a Jansenist; but having become wise, he esteemed her and he wept.

In the midst of so many tears and fears, while the danger to so dear a girl filled every heart, while everything was in consternation, a courier from the court is announced. A courier? And from whom? And why? His letter was from the King's confessor, for the Prior of the Mountain; it was not Father de La Chaise who was writing, it was his valet Friar Vadbled, a very important man at that time, he who communicated to the archbishops the wishes of the Reverend Father, he who gave audiences, he who promised benefices, he who sometimes had *lettres de cachet* issued. He wrote to the Abbé of the Mountain "that His Reverence was informed of the adventures of his nephew, that his imprisonment was just a mistake, that these little mishaps occurred frequently, that one should pay no attention to them, and that finally it behooved him, the prior, to come and present his nephew to him the next day, that he should bring the good man Gordon with him, that he, Friar Vadbled, would take them to see His Reverence and Monsieur de Louvois, who would have a word to say to him in his antechamber."

He added that the story of Ingenuous and his battle with the English had been told to the King, that His Majesty would certainly deign to notice him when he passed along the gallery and perhaps would even nod to him. The letter ended on the hope, with which they flattered him, that all the ladies of the court would be eager to invite his nephew to their morning toilets, that several of them would say to him "Good morning, Mr. Ingenuous," and that assuredly he would be a subject of conversation at the King's supper. The letter was signed "Your Affectionate Vadbled, Jesuit Friar."

The prior having read the letter aloud, his nephew, furious, and mastering his anger for a moment, said nothing to the bearer; but, turning toward the companion of his misfortunes, he asked him what he thought of that style. Gordon replied:

"So that is how they treat men like monkeys? They beat them and they make them dance!"

Ingenuous, resuming his character, which always comes back when the soul is deeply moved, tore the letter into bits and threw them in the courier's face:

"Here is my answer."

His uncle, terrified, thought to see the thunder and twenty *lettres de cachet* fall upon him. He went quickly to write and excuse as best he could what he took for a young man's transport of anger, and what was really the outburst of a great soul.

But more painful cares took possession of all hearts. The fair and unfortunate Saint-Yves felt her end already approaching; she was calm, but with that frightful calm of exhausted nature which no longer has the strength to fight.

"O my dear lover," she said, in a failing voice, "death is punishing me for my frailty, but I die with the consolation of knowing you are free. I adored you when I betrayed you, and I adore you as I bid you an eternal farewell."

She did not put on any vain fortitude; she had no conception of that wretched glory of making a few neighbors say: "She died with courage." Who can lose, at twenty, her lover, her life, and what people call honor, without regrets and without being torn? She felt all the horror of her state and made it felt by those words and by those dying looks which speak with such authority. In fine, she wept like the others in the moments when she had the strength to weep.

Let others praise the ostentatious deaths of those who enter into destruction with insensibility. This is the lot of all the animals. We die the way they do only when age or illness makes us like them by the stupefaction of our organs. Whoever suffers a great loss has great regrets; if he stifles them, it is because he is carrying vanity even into the arms of death.

When the fatal moment arrived, all those present broke into tears and cries. Ingenuous lost the use of his senses. Strong souls have much more violent feelings than others, when they are tender. The good Gordon knew him well enough to fear that when he came to he might kill himself. They removed all weapons; the unhappy young man noticed it; he said to his relatives and Gordon, without a tear, without a moan, without emotion:

"Then do you think there is anyone on earth who has the right and the power to prevent me from ending my life?"

Gordon took good care not to parade those tedious commonplaces by which people try to prove that it is not permissible to use our liberty in order to cease to be when we are in a horribly bad way, that we must not leave our house when we can no longer remain in it, that man is on earth like a soldier at his post: as if it mattered to the Being of beings whether the collection of a few particles was in one place or another; impotent reasons to which a firm and considered despair disdains to listen, and to which Cato replied only by a dagger thrust.

The bleak and terrible silence of Ingenuous, his somber eyes, his trembling lips, the quiverings of his body, induced in the souls of all those who looked at him that mixture of compassion and fright which fetters all the powers of the soul, which precludes all connected speech, and which manifests itself only by broken words. The hostess and her family had hastened up, everyone trembled at his despair, they kept their eye on him, they watched all his movements. Already the ice-cold body of the fair Saint-Yves had been carried into a downstairs room far from the eyes of her lover, who still seemed to look for her although he was no longer in condition to see anything.

In the midst of this spectacle of death, while the body is exposed at the door of the house, while two priests beside a holy-water basin recite prayers with an absent-minded air, while passers-by idly sprinkle a few drops of holy water on the bier, while others continue on their way with indifference, while the relatives weep and lovers believe they will not

survive their loss,[1] the Saint-Pouange arrives with the lady
friend from Versailles.

His passing taste, having been satisfied only once, had
become love. The refusal of his gifts had piqued him. Father
de La Chaise would never have thought of coming into this
house; but Saint-Pouange, having every day before his eyes
the picture of the fair Saint-Yves, burning to assuage a passion which by one single enjoyment had plunged the goad
of desires into his heart, did not hesitate to come himself to
seek the woman whom he would perhaps not have wanted
to see three times if she had come of herself.

He gets out of his carriage; the first object that appears to
him is a bier; he turns away his eyes with the simple disgust
of a man brought up on pleasures who thinks he should be
spared any sight that might bring him back to the contemplation of human misery. He wants to go upstairs. The woman
from Versailles asks, out of curiosity, who is going to be
buried; the name of Mademoiselle de Saint-Yves is spoken.
At that name she turns pale and utters a frightful scream;
Saint-Pouange turns around; surprise and grief fill his soul.
The good Gordon is there, his eyes filled with tears. He
interrupts his sad prayers to inform the man from court
about this whole horrible catastrophe. He speaks to him
with that authority which grief and virtue give. Saint-Pouange
had not been born wicked; the torrent of affairs and amuse-
ments had carried away his soul, which did not yet know
itself. He was not yet reaching old age, which ordinarily
hardens ministers' hearts; he listened to Gordon with downcast eyes, and it made him wipe away some tears that he was
astonished to shed; he came to know repentance.

"I absolutely insist," he said, "on seeing this extraordinary
man you have told me about; he arouses my sympathy almost
as much as this innocent victim whose death I have caused."

Gordon follows him into the bedroom, where the prior,
la Kerkabon, the Abbé de Saint-Yves, and a few neighbors were
calling back to life the young man, who had again fallen into
a faint.

"I have brought about your unhappiness," said the assistant minister to him. "I shall use my life to make repara-
tion."

The first idea that came to Ingenuous was to kill him and

1   Some editions read: "a lover is ready to take his own life."

to kill himself afterward. Nothing was more in order; but he was without arms and closely watched. Saint-Pouange was not rebuffed by the refusals, accompanied by the reproach, scorn, and horror that he had deserved and that were lavished on him. Time softened everything. Monsieur de Louvois finally managed to make an excellent officer of Ingenuous, who appeared under another name in Paris and in the armies, with the approbation of all good people, and who was an intrepid warrior and philosopher at the same time.

He never spoke of this adventure without a moan; and yet his consolation was in speaking about it. He cherished the memory of the tender Saint-Yves until the last moment of his life. The Abbé de Saint-Yves and the prior each got a good benefice; the good Kerkabon preferred to see her nephew in military honors rather than in the subdeaconate. The pious woman from Versailles kept the diamond earrings and received still another handsome present. Father Tout-à-tous got packages of chocolate, coffee, sugar candy, candied lemons, together with the *Meditations* of the Reverend Father Croiset* and the *Flower of the Saints,** bound in morocco. The good Gordon lived with Ingenuous in the most intimate friendship until his death; he got a benefice too, and forever forgot effectual grace and concomitant concurrence. He took as his motto: *misfortune is good for something.* How many good people in the world have been able to say: *misfortune is good for nothing!*

The One-Eyed Porter

[1774 [1]]

OUR TWO EYES do not make our lot better; one serves us to see the good things, the other the evils, of life. Many people have the bad habit of closing the first, and very few close the second; that is why there are so many people who would rather be blind than see all they see. Happy the one-eyed people who are deprived only of that bad eye which spoils everything we look at! Mesrour is an example.

One would have had to be blind not to see that Mesrour was one-eyed. He was so from birth; but he was so content with his one-eyed state that it had never occurred to him to wish for another eye. It was not fortune's gifts that consoled him for nature's wrongs, for he was a mere porter and had no treasure other than his shoulders; but he was happy, and he showed that one eye more, and of hardship less, contribute very little to happiness. Money and appetite always came to him in proportion to the exercise he took; he worked in the morning, ate and drank in the evening, slept at night, and regarded all days as so many separate lives, so that care for the future never troubled him in the enjoyment of the present. He was (as you see) at the same time a man with one eye, a porter, and a philosopher.

By chance he saw, passing by in a brilliant chariot, a great princess who had one eye more than he; which did not keep him from finding her most beautiful; and since one-eyed men differ from other men only in that they have one eye less, he fell madly in love with her. Perhaps it will be said that when a man is a porter and one-eyed he should not be

1 First published in 1774 in the *Journal des Dames;* not included by Voltaire in his collected works, and first appearing under his name in the posthumous Kehl edition. It seems to have been written rather early, probably around 1746.

in love, especially with a great princess and, what is more, with a princess who has two eyes; I admit he has good reason to fear he will not be found attractive; however, since there is no love without hope, and since our porter loved, he hoped.

Since he had more legs than eyes, and his legs were good, for a distance of four leagues he followed his goddess's chariot, which was drawn with great rapidity by six great white horses. The fashion at that time among the ladies was to travel without lackey and without coachman and to drive themselves; the husbands, so as to be surer of their virtue, wanted them always to be all alone; which is directly contrary to the sentiment of those moralists who say that there can be no virtue in solitude.

Mesrour kept running beside the wheels of the chariot, turning his good eye in the direction of the lady, who was astonished to see a one-eyed man of such agility. While he was thus proving that a man is indefatigable for what he loves, a tawny wild beast, pursued by hunters, crossed the highway and frightened the horses, who, taking the bit in their teeth, were sweeping the fair lady toward a precipice. Her new lover, even more frightened than she (although she was very frightened), cut the traces with marvelous dexterity; the six horses alone took the perilous leap, and the lady, who was no less white than they, got off with a fright.

"Whoever you are," she said to him, "I shall never forget that I owe you my life; ask of me what you will; all I have is yours."

"Ah! with far more reason," replied Mesrour, "I can offer you as much; but in offering it to you I shall still offer you less: for I have only one eye, and you have two; but one eye that looks at you is better than two eyes that do not see yours."

The lady smiled; for the gallantries of a one-eyed man are still gallantries, and gallantries always bring a smile.

"I wish I could give you another eye," she said, "but your mother alone could make you that present; follow me still."

With these words she descends from her chariot and continues her way on foot; her little dog got down too and walked along beside her, barking at the strange figure of her squire. I am wrong to give him the title of squire, for he offered his arm in vain, the lady never would accept it, on the pretext that it was too dirty; and you shall see that she was the victim of her cleanliness. She had very small feet, and shoes even smaller than her feet, so that she was neither fashioned nor shod in such a way as to endure a long walk.

Pretty feet are a consolation for having weak legs, when you spend your life on a chaise longue in the midst of a crowd of fops; but what is the use of spangled embroidered shoes on a stony road where they can be seen only by a porter, and at that by a porter who has only one eye?

Mélinade (that is the lady's name, which I have had my reasons for not telling until now, because it was not yet made up) went ahead as best she could, cursing her shoemaker, tearing her shoes, scraping her feet, and spraining her ankles at every step. She had been walking about an hour and a half at a great lady's pace, which is to say that she had already gone nearly a quarter of a league, when she fell in her tracks from fatigue.

Mesrour, whose help she had refused while she was on her feet, hesitated to offer it to her for fear of dirtying her by his touch; for he knew very well that he was not clean; the lady had given him to understand that clearly enough, and the comparison he had made along the road between himself and his mistress had made him see it even more clearly. She had on a dress of a light silver fabric, strewn with garlands of flowers, which allowed the beauty of her figure to shine through; and he had on a brown smock spotted in a thousand places, full of holes, and patched in such a way that the patches were next to the holes and not over them, where after all they would have been more in place. He had compared his muscular hands, covered with calluses, with two tiny hands whiter and more delicate than lilies. Finally he had seen Mélinade's beautiful blond hair, which shone through a light gauze veil, gathered up in tresses and curls; and to put beside that he had nothing but a shaggy, kinky black mane with a torn turban as its only ornament.

Meanwhile Mélinade tries to get up, but she soon falls back, and so unfortunately that what she let Mesrour see took away the little reason that the sight of the princess's face had managed to leave him. He forgot that he was a porter, that he was one-eyed, and he no longer thought of the distance that fortune had set between Mélinade and him; hardly did he remember that he was a lover, for he failed in the delicacy which is said to be inseparable from true love, and which constitutes sometimes its charm and more often its boredom; he used the rights to brutality that his porter's estate gave him, he was brutal—and happy. The princess then was doubtless in a swoon, or else she was bemoaning her lot; but since she was just, she assuredly blessed destiny that every misfortune carries with it its consolation.

Night had spread its veils over the horizon, and with its shadow it hid the true happiness of Mesrour and the so-called unhappiness of Mélinade; Mesrour tasted the pleasures of perfect lovers, and he tasted them like a porter, that is to say (to the shame of humanity) in the most perfect manner; Mélinade's faintness came over her anew every moment, and every moment new strength came over her lover.

"Mighty Mohammed," he said once like a man transported but like a bad Catholic, "all that my felicity lacks is to be felt by her who causes it. While I am in thy paradise, divine prophet, grant me one favor more: to be in Mélinade's eyes what she would be in my eye if it were light."

He finished praying and went on enjoying. Aurora, always too diligent to suit lovers, surprised Mesrour and Mélinade in the posture in which she might have been surprised herself a moment before with Tithonus.[2] But what was Mélinade's astonishment when, opening her eyes to the dawn's first rays, she saw herself in an enchanted place with a young nobleman of noble stature, whose face resembled that daystar whose return the earth was awaiting! He had rosy cheeks, coral lips; his large eyes, tender and sparkling at the same time, expressed and inspired voluptuousness; his golden quiver, adorned with gems, hung from his shoulders, and pleasure itself, alone, made his arrows ring; his long hair, held back by a diamond clasp, floated freely over his back, and a transparent fabric, embroidered with pearls, served him as clothing and concealed nothing of the beauty of his body.

"Where am I, and who are you?" exclaimed Mélinade in the extremity of her surprise.

"You are," he replied, "with the wretch who had the happiness of saving your life, and who has repaid himself so well for his trouble."

2   Aurora, goddess of the dawn, arises each morning from the couch of Tithonus.

Mélinade, as pleased as she was astonished, was sorry that Mesrour's metamorphosis had not begun earlier. She approaches a gleaming palace that struck her gaze, and reads this inscription on the door: "Away, outsiders; these doors will open only to the master of the ring." Mesrour approaches in turn to read the same inscription; but he saw other characters and read these words: "Knock without fear."

He knocked, and immediately the doors opened of themselves with a great noise. The two lovers, to the sound of a thousand voices and a thousand instruments, entered a vestibule of Parian marble; from there they passed into a superb hall, where a delicious feast had been awaiting them for twelve hundred and fifty years without any of the dishes having yet grown cold; they sat down to table, and were each served by a thousand slaves of the greatest beauty; the meal was intermingled with concerts and dances; and when it was finished, all the genii came in the greatest order, divided into different groups, with garments as magnificent as they were unusual, to take an oath of fidelity to the master of the ring and to kiss the sacred finger on which he wore it.

Meanwhile in Bagdad there was a very devout Moslem who, being unable to go and wash in the mosque, had water brought to his home from the mosque for a small remuneration that he paid to the priest. He had just performed his fifth ablution, to make ready for the fifth prayer; and his servant, a giddy young girl, not at all devout, got rid of the holy water by throwing it out the window. It fell on an unfortunate who was sound asleep against the edge of a boundary stone that served him as a bolster. He was inundated, and awoke. It was poor Mesrour, who, returning from his enchanted sojourn, had lost Solomon's ring on the way. He had doffed his magnificent clothing and put on his smock again; his beautiful golden quiver was changed into a wooden hook, and to cap his misfortune he had left one of his eyes along the way.

He then remembered that the night before he had drunk a great quantity of brandy, which had lulled his senses and heated his imagination. Until then he had loved that drink for its taste; he began to love it for gratitude, and he gaily returned to his work, firmly resolved to use the wages of it to buy the means of finding his dear Mélinade again. Another man would have grieved at being ugly and one-eyed after having had two handsome eyes, at suffering the refusals of the women who swept the palace after having enjoyed the favors of a princess more beautiful than the mistresses of the caliph, and at being at the service of all the bourgeois of Bagdad after having ruled over all the genii; but Mesrour did not have the eye that sees the bad side of things.

Memory's Adventure

[1775]

THE THINKING HUMAN RACE, that is to say at most the hundred-thousandth part of the human race, had long believed, or at least had often repeated, that we had ideas only through our senses, and that memory is the only instrument by which we can put two ideas and two words together.

That is why Jupiter, representing nature, was in love with Mnemosyne, goddess of memory, from the first moment he saw her; and of this marriage were born the nine Muses, who were the inventors of all the arts.

This dogma, on which all our knowledge is founded, was universally accepted, and even the Nonsober [1] embraced it as soon as it was born, although it was a truth.

Some time later along came an arguer, [2] half geometrician, half chimerical, who argued against the five senses and against memory; and he said to the small numbers of the thinking human race:

"You have been wrong up to now, for your senses are useless; for ideas are inborn in you before any of your senses can act, for you had all the necessary notions when you came into the world; you knew everything without having sensed anything; all your ideas, born with you, were present to your intelligence, named *soul*, without the help of memory. That memory of yours is good for nothing."

The Nonsober condemned this proposition, not because it was ridiculous, but because it was new; however, when later on an Englishman [3] had set himself to prove, and even at length, that there were no innate ideas, that nothing was more necessary than the five senses, that memory helped greatly to

1 Non-sober: anagram of Sorbonne.*
2 Descartes.
3 Locke.

325

retain the things received by the five senses, the Nonsober condemned her own sentiments, because they had become those of an Englishman. Consequently she ordered the human race henceforth to believe in innate ideas and no longer to believe in the five senses and the memory. The human race, instead of obeying, laughed at the Nonsober, who flew into such a rage that she tried to have a philosopher burned. For this philosopher had said that it is impossible to have a complete idea of a cheese unless you have seen and eaten one; and the villain even dared put forth the idea that men and women would never have been able to work in tapestry if they had not had needles, and fingers to thread them with.

The Lioloists [4] joined with the Nonsober for the first time in their life; and the Sejanists, mortal enemies of the Lioloists, united with them for a moment. They called to their aid the ancient Dicasterics, who were great philosophers; and all together, before they died, they proscribed memory and the five senses, and the author who had said something good about these six things.

A horse happened to be present at the judgment which these gentlemen pronounced, although he was not of the same species and there were several differences between him and them such as that of height, voice, smoothness of coat, and ears; this horse, I say, who had sense as well as senses, spoke to Pegasus about it one day in my stable; and Pegasus went and told this story to the Muses with his usual vivacity.

The Muses, who for a hundred years had singularly favored the country, long barbarous, where this scene was taking place, were extremely scandalized; they tenderly loved Memory, or Mnemosyne, their mother, to whom these nine daughters are obligated for everything they know. The ingratitude of men irritated them. They did not compose a satire against the ancient Dicasterics, the Lioloists, the Sejanists, and the Nonsober, because satires correct no one, irritate fools, and make them even more wicked. They imagined a way to enlighten them while punishing them. Men had blasphemed memory; the Muses deprived them of this gift of the gods so that they might learn once and for all what it is like to be without its aid.

4   Anagram of Loyolists: Jesuits. The Sejanists just below are the Jansenists; the Dicasterics, members of the dicastery, the Parlement of Paris.

So it happened in the middle of one fine night that all brains grew heavy, so that the next morning everyone awoke without having the slightest memory of the past. A few Dicasterics, sleeping with their wives, tried, by a remnant of instinct independent of memory, to make advances to them. The wives, since wives only very rarely have an instinct to embrace their husbands, bitterly rejected their disgusting caresses. The husbands grew angry, the wives screamed, and most of the couples came to blows about it.

The gentlemen, finding a square bonnet,[5] used it for certain needs which neither memory nor good sense can relieve. The ladies employed their cosmetic jars for the same uses. The servants, no longer remembering the bargain they had made with their masters, entered their rooms without knowing where they were; but since man is born curious, they opened all the drawers; and since man naturally loves the brilliance of silver and gold without needing memory for that, they took all of it that they found at hand. The masters wanted to cry: "Stop thief!" But since the idea of thief had gone out of their head, the word could not come to their tongue. Each one, having forgotten his own language, articulated formless sounds. It was much worse than at Babel, where each man invented a new language on the spot. The feeling, inborn in the sense of young valets, for pretty women acted so powerfully that these impudent fellows threw themselves recklessly upon the first women or girls they found, whether barmaids or wives of chief justices; and these ladies, no longer remembering the lessons of shame, let them go ahead with complete freedom.

People had to have dinner; no one knew how to go about it any more. No one had been to market either to sell or to buy. The servants had taken the masters' clothes, and the masters those of the servants. Everybody looked at each other with vacant eyes. Those who had the greatest genius for pro-curing necessities (and they were of the people) found a little to live on; the others lacked everything. The chief pre-siding judge and the archbishop went about stark naked, and their grooms were some in red robes, the others in dalmatics; everything was confused, everyone was about to perish of misery and hunger, for lack of communication.

After a few days the Muses took pity on this poor race: they are good, although they sometimes make the wicked

5   The mark of a doctor of the Sorbonne.*

feel their wrath; so they besought their mother to return to these blasphemers the memory that she had taken from them. Mnemosyne came down into this region of contraries in which she had been so rashly insulted, and spoke to them in these words:

"Imbeciles, I forgive you; but this time remember that without the senses there is no memory, and without memory there is no mind."

The Dicasterics thanked her rather dryly, and decreed that they would address remonstrances to her. The Sejanists put this whole adventure in their gazette; it was noted that they were not yet cured. The Lioloists started up a court intrigue about it. Doctor Coger, quite dumfounded by the adventure and understanding nothing about it, pronounced to his eighth-grade schoolboys this fine axiom: *Non magis musis quam hominibus infensa est ista quae vocatur memoria.*[6]

6   "She who is called Memory is no more inimical to muses than to men." This is a parody of the subject proposed in 1772 by the University of Paris, of which Coger was rector, for the prize in Latin eloquence: *"Non magis Deo quam regibus infensa est ista quae vocatur hodie philosophia."* Voltaire was convinced that Coger meant *minus* instead of *magis.*

Count Chesterfield's Ears
and Chaplain Goudman

[1775]

CHAPTER 1

A H! FATALITY irremissibly governs all the things of this
world. So I judge, as is reasonable, by my adventure.

My Lord Chesterfield, who was very fond of me, had
promised to do me some good. A great *preferment*[1] was
vacant and he had power to nominate. I hasten from far off
in the country to London; I present myself to My Lord; I re-
mind him of his promises; he shakes my hand in friendship
and tells me in effect that I am looking very badly. I answer
him that my greatest trouble is poverty. He replies to me that
he wants to have me cured, and gives me on the spot a letter
for Monsieur Sidrac, near Guildhall.

I have no doubt that Monsieur Sidrac is the one to dispatch
me what I need for my curacy. I fly to his office. Monsieur
Sidrac, who was My Lord's surgeon, immediately prepares to
probe me, and assures me that if I have the stone he will cut
me open very successfully.

It should be known that My Lord had understood me to
say that I had a great pain in the bladder, and had wanted,
with his usual generosity, to have me cut open at his expense.
He was deaf, as was My Lord his brother, and I was not yet
informed of that.

During the time I lost defending my bladder against
Monsieur Sidrac, who wanted to probe me in spite of all opposition, one of the fifty-two competitors who aspired to the

1   Author's note: "*Preferment* means *benefice* in English."

same benefice arrived at My Lord's house, asked for my curacy, and went off with it.

I was in love with Miss Fidler, whom I was to marry as soon as I should be a curate; my rival got my place and my mistress.

The count, having heard of my disaster and his mistake, promised me to mend everything. But he died two days later.

Monsieur Sidrac made me see, clear as day, that my good protector could not have lived a minute longer, in view of the present condition of his organs, and proved to me that his deafness came merely from the extreme dryness of the auditory nerve and the eardrum. He even offered to toughen my two ears with spirits of wine so as to make me deafer than any peer in the kingdom.

I understood that Monsieur Sidrac was a very learned man. He inspired in me a taste for the science of nature. Moreover I saw that he was a charitable man who would cut me open for nothing if the occasion arose, and who would give me relief in case of any accidents that might happen to me around the neck of the bladder.

So I set about studying nature under his direction to console myself for the loss of my curacy and of my mistress.

CHAPTER 2

AFTER MANY OBSERVATIONS of nature made with my five senses, telescopes, microscopes, I said to Monsieur Sidrac one day:

"They are making fun of us; there is no nature, all is art. It is by an admirable art that all the planets dance regularly around the sun, while the sun turns cartwheels upon itself. Surely someone as learned as the Royal Society of London must have arranged things in such a way that the square of the revolutions of each planet is always proportionate to the cube root of their distance from their center; and one must be a sorcerer even to guess it.

"The ebb and flow of our Thames seems to me the constant effect of an art no less profound and no less difficult to understand.

"Animals, vegetables, minerals, everything appears to me arranged with weight, measure, number, movement. Everything is spring, lever, pulley, hydraulic machine, chemical laboratory, from the grass to the oak, from the flea to man, from a grain of sand to our storm-clouds.

"Certainly there is nothing but art, and nature is a chimera."

"You are right," Monsieur Sidrac answered me, "but you're not dressed for the part; that has already been said by a dreamer [1] from across the Channel, but no one has paid any attention to it."

"What astounds me, and pleases me most, is that by this incomprehensible art, two machines always produce a third; and I am very sorry not to have made one with Miss Fidler; but I clearly see that it was arranged from all eternity that Miss Fidler would employ another machine than me."

"What you say," replied Monsieur Sidrac, "has also been said, and so much the better; it is a probability that you are thinking aright. Yes, it is very amusing that two beings produce a third; but that is not true of all beings. Two roses do not produce a third rose by a fond embrace. Two pebbles, two metals do not produce a third, and yet a metal and a stone are things that all human ingenuity could not make. The great and beautiful continual miracle is that a boy and a girl make a child together, a nightingale makes a little nightingale with his female nightingale and not with a warbler. We ought to spend half our life in imitating them and the other half in blessing him who invented this method. There are a thousand utterly curious secrets about generation. Newton says that nature is everywhere like itself: *Natura est ubique sibi consona.* In love that is false: the fish, the reptiles, the birds do not make love like us: the variety is infinite. The fabrication of feeling and acting beings enchants me. The vegetables have their value too. I am always amazed that one grain of wheat cast into the earth should produce many others."

"Ah!" I said to him like the fool I still was, "that is because the wheat must die in order to be born, as the Schoolmen have said."

Monsieur Sidrac took me up, laughing with great circumspection.

"That was true in the time of the School," he said, "but the humblest plowman knows very well today that the thing is absurd."

1   Author's note: *"Questions encyclopédiques,* article 'Nature.'" This is a work of 1771 by Voltaire.

"Ah! Monsieur Sidrac, I beg your pardon; but I have been a theologian, and a man cannot get rid of his habits all at once."

CHAPTER 3

SOME TIME after these conversations between the poor priest Goudman and the excellent anatomist Sidrac, this surgeon came upon him in St. James Park lost in thought, in meditation, and looking more embarrassed than an algebraist who has just made a false calculation.

"What's the matter with you?" said Sidrac; "is it the bladder or the colon that is tormenting you?"

"No," said Goudman, "it's the gall bladder. I have just seen going past in a good carriage the Bishop of Gloucester, who is a loquacious and insolent pedant. I was on foot, and that irritated me. The thought occurred to me that if I wanted to have a bishopric in this kingdom, it would be ten thousand to one that I would not get it, seeing that there are ten thousand of us priests in England. I am without any protector since the death of My Lord Chesterfield, who was deaf. Let's assume that the ten thousand Anglican priests each have two protectors, in that case it would be twenty thousand to one that I would not get the bishopric. It makes you angry when you put your mind to it.

"I remembered that it had once been proposed to me that I go to India as a cabin boy; I was assured that I would make a great fortune there, but I did not feel myself fitted to become an admiral one day. And, after having examined all the professions, I remained a priest without being good for anything."

"Don't be a priest any more," said Sidrac, "and become a philosopher. That trade neither demands nor gives riches. What is your income?"

"I have only thirty guineas a year, and after the death of my old aunt I shall have fifty."

"Come now, my dear Goudman, that is enough to live in freedom and to think. Thirty guineas make six hundred and thirty shillings, that's almost two shillings a day. Philips [1] wanted only one. One may, with that assured revenue, say all one thinks about the East India Company, the parliament, our

1   Ambrose Philips (c. 1675–1749), one of whose poems is called "Splendid Shilling."

colonies, the King, being in general, man, and God; which is a great amusement. Come and dine with me, that will save you money; we shall talk, and your thinking faculty will have the pleasure of communicating with mine by means of speech, which is a marvelous thing that men do not admire enough."

CHAPTER 4

Conversation between Dr. Goudman and the Anatomist Sidrac on the Soul and on Something Else

GOUDMAN But, my dear Sidrac, why do you always say *my thinking faculty?* Why not just say *my soul?* That would be quicker said, and I would understand you just as well.

SIDRAC And I would not understand myself. I clearly feel, I clearly know that God has given me the faculty of thinking and speaking, but I neither feel nor know whether he has given me a being that people call *soul.*

GOUDMAN Truly, when I think about it, I see that I know nothing about it either and that for a long time I have been rash enough to believe I did. I have noted that the Oriental peoples called the soul by a name that signified *life.* Following their example, the Latins at first understood by *anima* the life of the animal. Among the Greeks they said: respiration is the soul. This respiration is a breath. The Latins translated the word breath by *spiritus;* whence the word that corresponds to "spirit" among almost all modern nations. Since no one has ever seen this breath, this spirit, they have made of it a being that no one can either see or touch. They have said that it dwelt in our body without taking up any room, that it set our organs in motion without touching them. What have they not said? All our reasonings, it seems to me, have been based on ambiguities. I see that the wise Locke has rightly perceived into what chaos these ambiguities in all languages had plunged human reason. He did not write any chapter on the soul in the only reasonable book on metaphysics that has ever been written.[1] And if by chance he uses this word in a few places, the word in him means nothing but our intelligence.

Indeed, everyone clearly feels that he has an intelligence,

1 *Essay Concerning Human Understanding* (1690).

that he receives ideas, that he puts some of them together, that he takes some of them apart; but no one feels that there is in him another being that gives him movement, sensations, and thoughts. It is ridiculous, after all, to pronounce words that we do not understand, and to recognize beings of which we cannot have the slightest knowledge.

SIDRAC   Then here we are already agreed about a thing that has been a subject of dispute for so many centuries.

GOUDMAN   And I marvel that we are agreed.

SIDRAC   It is not astonishing, we are seeking the truth in good faith. If we were on the benches of the School, we would argue like the characters in Rabelais.[2] If we were living in the periods of frightful darkness that enveloped England so long, perhaps one of us would have the other burned. We are in a century of reason; we easily find what seems to us to be the truth, and we dare to speak it.

GOUDMAN   Yes, but I am afraid the truth may be a very small thing. In mathematics we have performed prodigies that would astound Apollonius and Archimedes and make them our pupils; but in metaphysics, what have we discovered? Our ignorance.

SIDRAC   And is that nothing? You agree that the great Being has given you a faculty of feeling and thinking, as he has given your feet the faculty of walking, your viscera the power of digesting, your heart the power of pushing your blood into your arteries. We hold everything from him; we have not been able to give ourselves anything; and we shall be forever ignorant of the way the master of the universe goes about it to guide us. For my part, I give thanks to him for having taught me that I know nothing about first principles.

Men have always sought to learn how the soul acts on the body. We should have learned first whether we had a soul. Either God has made us this present, or he has communicated the equivalent to us. However he may have gone about it, we are in his hand. He is our master, that is all I know.

GOUDMAN   But at least tell me what you suspect about this. You have dissected brains, you have seen embryos and fetuses: in all this have you discovered any semblance of soul?

SIDRAC   Not the slightest, and I have never been able to

2   Probably an allusion to Baisecul and Humevesne, whose lawsuit occupies Chapters 10–13 of *Pantagruel*.

understand how an immaterial, immortal being could dwell for nine months uselessly hidden in a stinking membrane between our urine and our excrement. It seemed to me difficult to conceive that this supposed plain soul existed before the formation of its body; for what use would it have been for centuries when it was not a human soul? And then, how can one imagine a plain being? A metaphysical being which for an eternity awaits the moment to animate some matter for a few minutes? What becomes of this unknown being if the fetus it is to animate dies in its mother's womb?

It seemed to me even more ridiculous that God should create a soul at the moment when a man is lying with a woman. It seemed to me blasphemous that God should await the consummation of an act of adultery or incest to reward these turpitudes by creating souls on their behalf. It is even worse when they tell me that God draws immortal souls out of nothingness to make them eternally suffer incredible torments. What! Burn plain beings, beings that have nothing burnable about them! How would we go about it to burn the sound of a voice, a wind that has just gone past? Moreover that sound, that wind were material at the little moment when they passed; but a pure spirit, a thought, a doubt? I am lost. Whatever direction I turn, I find nothing but obscurity, contradiction, impossibility, ridiculousness, daydreams, irrelevance, chimeras, absurdity, stupidity, charlatanry.

But I am at ease when I say to myself: God is the master. He who makes innumerable stars gravitate toward one another, he who created light is certainly powerful enough to give us sensations and ideas without our needing some little foreign invisible atom called *soul*.

God has certainly given all animals sensation, memory, ingenuity. He has given them life, and it is just as fine to give the gift of life as to give the gift of a soul. It is fairly well accepted that animals live; it is demonstrated that they have sensation, since they have the organs of sensation. Now if they have all that without a soul, why do we insist at all costs on having one?

GOUDMAN Perhaps it is out of vanity. I am persuaded that if a peacock could speak, he would boast of having a soul, and he would say his soul is in his tail. I feel very much inclined to suspect as you do that God made us eaters, drinkers, walkers, sleepers, capable of feeling and thought, full of passions, pride, and misery, without telling us one word of his secret. We know no more about this subject than those peacocks I am speaking about. And he who said that we are born, live, and die without knowing how, said a great truth.[8]

The man who calls us the marionettes of Providence seems to me to have defined us well. For after all, an infinity of motions is needed for us to exist. Now we did not create motion; it is not we who established its laws. There is someone who, having created light, makes it move from the sun to our eyes and arrive there in seven minutes. It is only by motion that my five senses are stirred; it is only through my five senses that I have ideas: so it is the author of motion who gives me my ideas. And when he tells me in what manner he gives me them, I shall offer in return most humble thanksgiving. I already offer him much thanks for having allowed me for a few years to contemplate the magnificent spectacle of this world, as Epictetus used to say. It is true that he could have made me happier and let me have a good benefice and my mistress Miss Fidler; but after all, such as I am with my six hundred and thirty shillings a year, I am still under great obligation to him.

SIDRAC   You say that God could have given you a good benefice and that he could have made you happier than you are. There are people who will not grant you that proposition. So! don't you remember that you yourself have complained of fatality? A man who has wanted to be a curate is not allowed to contradict himself. Don't you see that if you had had the curacy and the wife that you were asking for, it would have been you that would have given Miss Fidler a child, and not your rival? The child she would have borne might have been a cabin-boy, become an admiral, won a naval battle at the mouth of the Ganges, and completed the dethroning of the Grand Mogul. That alone would have changed the constitution of the universe. A world entirely different from ours would have been necessary in order for your competitor not to get the curacy, not to marry Miss Fidler, for you not to be reduced to six hundred and thirty shillings while waiting for the death of your aunt. All is part of a chain, and God will not go and break the eternal chain for my friend Goudman.

GOUDMAN   I was not expecting this reasoning when I

8   Voltaire in his *Questions sur l'Encyclopédie* (1774), article
"

was speaking about fatality; but then after all, if that is so, God is a slave just like me?

SIDRAC He is the slave of his will, of his wisdom, of the very laws that he has made, of his necessary nature. He cannot infringe them, because he cannot be weak, inconstant, and flighty like us, and because the necessarily eternal being cannot be a weathervane.

GOUDMAN Monsieur Sidrac, that could lead to irreligion. For if God can change nothing in the affairs of this world, what is the use of singing his praises, what is the use of addressing prayers to him?

SIDRAC Well! Who tells you to pray God and praise him? A lot of good your praises and your petitions are to him! We praise a man because we think he is vain; we pray to him when we think he is weak, and hope to make him change his mind. Let us do our duty toward God, worship him, be just: those are our true praises and our true prayers.

GOUDMAN Monsieur Sidrac, we have covered a lot of ground; for without counting Miss Fidler, we are examining whether we have a soul, whether there is a God, whether he can change, whether we are destined to two lives, whether . . . Those are deep studies, and perhaps I would never have thought about them if I had been a curate. I must go more deeply into these necessary and sublime things, since I have nothing to do.

SIDRAC Well! tomorrow Doctor Grou is coming to dine with me; he is a very learned physician; he has been around the world with Messrs. Banks and Solander; he must certainly know God and the soul, truth and falsehood, justice and injustice, much better than those who have never been outside Covent Garden. Moreover Doctor Grou in his youth saw nearly all Europe; he witnessed five or six revolutions in Russia; he was a friend of Pasha* Count de Bonneval, who, as is well known, had become a perfect Mohammedan in Constantinople. He was intimately acquainted with the papist priest MacCarthy, an Irishman, who had his foreskin cut off in honor of Mohammed, and with our Scottish Presbyterian Ramsay, who did the same, and who then served in Russia and was killed in a battle against the Swedes in Finland. Finally, he conversed with the Reverend Father Malagrida,* who was since burned in Lisbon because the Holy Virgin had revealed to him all she had done when she was in the womb

of her mother St. Anne. You fully perceive that a man like
Monsieur Grou, who has seen so many things, must be the
greatest metaphysician in the world. So until tomorrow at
my house for dinner.

GOUDMAN   And day after tomorrow too, my dear Sidrac,
for it takes more than one dinner to learn.

CHAPTER 5

THE NEXT DAY the three thinkers dined together; and as they
were becoming a little gayer toward the end of the meal, after
the fashion of philosophers at dinner, they amused themselves
by talking about all the miseries, all the stupidities, all the
horrors that afflict the animal race from the southern lands to
near the arctic pole and from Lima to Meaco.[1] This diversity
of abominations never fails to be very amusing. It is a pleasure
unavailable to bourgeois stay-at-homes and parish vicars, who
know only their own bell tower and who think that all the
rest of the universe is made like Exchange Alley in London
or the Rue de la Huchette in Paris.

"I note," said Dr. Grou, "that in spite of the infinite variety
that is spread over this globe, nevertheless all the men I have
seen, whether woolly black, black with hair, tanned, red, or
beige and calling themselves white, have uniformly two legs,
two eyes, and one head on their shoulders, no matter what St.
Augustine said, who, in his thirty-seventh sermon, asserts that
he has seen Acephali, that is, headless men, monoculi, who
have only one eye, and monopodes, who have only one leg.
As for anthropophagi, I admit we have an oversupply, and
that everyone was that way once.

"I have often been asked whether the inhabitants of that
immense country named New Zealand, who are today the
most barbaric of all barbarians, were baptized. I replied that I
knew nothing about it, that this might be; that the Jews, who
were more barbaric than they, had had two baptisms instead of
one, the baptism of justice and the home baptism."

"Indeed, I know them," said Monsieur Goudman, "and I
have had great disputes about that with those who think that
we invented baptism. No, gentlemen, we invented nothing, we
did nothing but patch together. But tell me, I pray you,
Monsieur Grou, out of eighty or a hundred religions you have

1   Kyoto.

seen on your travels, which one seemed to you the most agreeable? Was it that of the New Zealanders or that of the Hottentots?"

MONSIEUR GROU   It was that of the isle of Tahiti, beyond all comparison. I have gone all over the two hemispheres, I have seen nothing like Tahiti and its religious Queen. It is in Tahiti that nature dwells. Elsewhere I have seen nothing but masqueraders; I have seen nothing but rogues duping fools, charlatans filching other people's money to get authority, and filching authority to get money with impunity; selling you cobwebs so as to eat your partridges; promising you riches and pleasure when there will be no one there so that you will turn the spit while they exist.

By heaven! it is not that way in the isle of Otaiti or Tahiti. This island is much more civilized than that of New Zealand or the country of the Kaffirs, and, I venture to say, than our England, because nature has favored it with a more fertile soil, and has given it the breadfruit tree, a present as useful as it is admirable, which it has given only to a few islands of the South Seas. Tahiti possesses also many fowl, vegetables, and fruits. There is no need in such a country to eat one's neighbor; but there is a more natural, sweeter, more universal need, which the religion of Tahiti orders people to satisfy in public. Of all religious ceremonies it is beyond doubt the most respectable; I have witnessed it, as well as the entire crew of our ship. These are no missionaries' fables, such as you sometimes find in the *Curious and Edifying Letters** of the reverend Jesuit Fathers. Dr. John Hawkesworth is right now completing the printing of our discoveries in the Southern Hemisphere. I have always accompanied Mr. Banks, that most estimable young man, who has dedicated his time and his money to observing nature near the antarctic pole, while Messrs. Dawkins and Wood were returning from the ruins of Palmyra and Baalbek, where they had excavated the oldest monuments of the arts, and while Mr. Hamilton was teaching the astonished Neapolitans the natural history of their Mount Vesuvius. Finally, together with Messrs. Banks, Solander, Cook, and a hundred others, I have seen what I am about to relate to you.

Princess Obeira, Queen of the island of Tahiti . . .

Then they brought coffee, and as soon as all three had had it, Monsieur Grou continued his story thus.

CHAPTER 6

"PRINCESS OBEIRA, I say, after having overwhelmed us with presents with a politeness worthy of a Queen of England, was curious to attend our Anglican service one morning. We celebrated it with as much pomp as we could. She invited us to her service after dinner; it was May 14, 1769. We found her surrounded by about a thousand persons of both sexes, arranged in a semicircle, and in respectful silence. A very pretty girl, simply adorned by a seductive state of undress, was lying on a platform that served as an altar. Queen Obeira ordered a handsome boy of about twenty to go and sacrifice. He uttered a sort of prayer and went up on the platform. The two sacrificers were half naked. The Queen, with a majestic air, taught the young victim the most suitable way to consummate the sacrifice. All the Tahitians were so attentive and so respectful that not one of our sailors dared to disturb the ceremony by an indecent laugh.

"This is what I have seen, I tell you, this is what our whole crew has seen. It is up to you to draw the conclusions."

"This sacred festival does not astonish me," said Dr. Goudman. "I am persuaded that that is the first festival that men ever celebrated; and I do not see why people should not pray to God when they are about to create a being in his image, as we pray to him before the meals that serve to sustain our body. To work to bring forth a reasonable creature is the noblest and holiest of actions. This is how the first Indians thought, who revered the Lingam, symbol of generation; the ancient Egyptians, who bore the phallus in procession; the Greeks, who erected temples to Priapus. If it is permissible to cite the miserable little Jewish nation, crude imitator of all its neighbors, it is said in their books that this people worshiped Priapus, and that the Queen mother of the Jewish King Asa was his high priestess.[1]

"However that may be, it is very likely that no people ever established or could establish a cult out of libertinage. Debauch sometimes slips in with the passage of time; but the original institution is always innocent and pure. Our first agapes, in which the boys and girls kissed one another

[1] Author's note: "Third Kings, Chapter xiii; and Paralipomena, Chapter xv." (See I Kings 15 and II Chronicles 15.)

modestly on the mouth, degenerated only rather late into
assignations and infidelities; and would God I might sacrifice
with Miss Fidler in front of Queen Obeira in all conscience
and honor! That would assuredly be the finest day and the
finest action of my life."

Monsieur Sidrac, who had kept silence until then because
Messrs. Goudman and Grou had been talking all the time,
finally came out of his taciturnity and said:

"All I have just heard transports me with admiration.
Queen Obeira seems to me the finest Queen in the Southern
Hemisphere—I do not venture to say of both hemispheres.
But amid so much glory and happiness, there is one item
that makes me shudder, and about which Mr. Goudman
said something to you that you did not answer. Is it
true, Monsieur Grou, that Captain Wallis, who dropped
anchor at this happy isle before you, brought there the earth's
two most horrible scourges, the two poxes?"

"Alas!" returned Monsieur Grou, "it is the French who
accuse us of that, and we accuse the French of it. Monsieur
Bougainville says it was those accursed Englishmen who
gave Queen Obeira the pox; and Mr. Cook claims that this
Queen got it from none other than Monsieur Bougainville
himself. However that may be, the pox is like the fine
arts: no one knows who was their inventor; but in due course
of time they go all over Europe, Asia, Africa, and America."

"I have been practicing surgery for a long time," said
Sidrac, "and I admit I owe to this pox the greater part of my
fortune; but I detest it none the less. Madame Sidrac communicated it to me on our wedding night; and since she is
a woman excessively delicate about any possible breach in
her honor, she announced in all the public journals in London
that she was indeed afflicted with the filthy disease, but that
she had brought it from her mother's womb, and that it
was an old family habit.

"What was that which we call 'nature' thinking about
when it poured this poison into the sources of life? It has
been said,[2] and I repeat it, that it is the most enormous and
detestable of all contradictions. What! man was made, they
say, in the image of God, *finxit in effigiem moderantum cuncta
deorum,*[3] and it is in the seminal vesicles of this image that

2   By Voltaire in *Candide* (Chapter 4, p. 23) and elsewhere.
3   Ovid, *Metamorphoses,* I, verse 83.

pain, infection, and death have been placed! What is to become of that fine verse of Milord Rochester: Love would cause God to be worshiped in a country of atheists?" [4]

"Alas!" then said the worthy Goudman, "perhaps I should thank Providence for my not having married my dear Miss Fidler, for who knows what would have happened? We are never sure of anything in this world. In any case, Monsieur Sidrac, you have promised me your help in anything that concerned my bladder."

"I am at your service," replied Sidrac; "but we must drive out these bad thoughts."

Goudman, in speaking thus, seemed to foresee his destiny.

CHAPTER 7

THE NEXT DAY the three philosophers debated the great question: what is the prime motive of all the actions of men? Goudman, who always had on his heart the loss of his benefice and of his beloved, said that the principle of everything was love and ambition. Grou, who had seen more countries, said it was money; and the great anatomist Sidrac asserted that it was the closestool. The two guests remained utterly astounded; and here is how the learned Sidrac proved his thesis:

"I have always observed that all the affairs of this world depended on the opinion and the will of one principal personage, whether king, or prime minister, or chief clerk. Now this opinion and this will are the immediate result of the way in which the animal spirits filter into the cerebellum and from there into the medulla oblongata; these animal spirits depend on the circulation of the blood; this blood depends on the formation of chyle; this chyle is elaborated in the network of the mesentery; this mesentery is attached to the intestines by very fine filaments; these intestines, if I may be permitted to say so, are full of shit. Now in spite of the three strong tunics in which each intestine is clad, it is riddled like a sieve; for everything is in the open in nature, and there is

4   In one of his *Satires,* "A Letter from Artemisa in the Town to Cloe in the Country" (lines 46–47), John Wilmot, Earl of Rochester, wrote of love:
    "On which one only blessing God might raise,
    In Lands of Atheists, Subsidies of Praise . . ."

no grain of sand so imperceptible as not to have more than five hundred pores. You could pass a thousand needles through a cannonball if you could find any thin enough and strong enough. So what happens to a constipated man? The most tenuous and delicate elements of his shit mingle with the chyle in the veins of Asellius, go to the portal vein and into the reservoir of Pecquet; they pass into the subclavian vein; they enter the heart of the most gallant man, the most coquettish woman. It is dew of dried turd that runs through the whole body. If this dew floods the parenchyma, the vessels, and the glands of a black-biled man, his bad humor becomes ferocity; the white of his eyes is a dark flame color, his lips are glued to each other, his complexion is mottled. He seems to threaten you; don't go near him; and if he is a minister of state, be sure you don't present a request to him. He looks on any paper only as an aid that he would like to use according to the ancient and abominable practice of the people of Europe. Find out adroitly from his favorite valet whether My Lord had a movement this morning.

"This is more important than people think. Constipation has sometimes produced the bloodiest scenes. My grandfather, who died a centenarian, was Cromwell's apothecary; he has often told me that Cromwell had not been to the toilet for a week when he had his King's head cut off.

"Everyone who knows anything about Continental affairs knows that the Duke of Guise, the Scar-faced, was often warned not to anger Henry III in winter when there was a northeast wind. This monarch went to the toilet then only with extreme difficulty. His matters rose to his head; he was capable, at those times, of every sort of violence. The Duke of Guise did not believe such wise advice; what happened to him? His brother and he were assassinated.

"Charles IX, his predecessor,[1] was the most constipated man in his kingdom. The passages from his colon and his rectum were so stopped up that finally his blood burst out of his pores. It is only too well known that this parched temperament was one of the principal causes of the St. Bartholomew.

"On the contrary, persons who have flesh on their bones, velvety entrails, flowing bile, an easy and regular peristaltic

1 Predecessor, that is (1560–74), of Henry III (1574–1589), who had Guise assassinated in December, 1588. The St. Bartholomew's Day Massacre of French Protestants was in 1572.

movement, who discharge themselves every morning, as soon as they have had breakfast, of a good stool just as easily as you spit; these persons favored by nature are gentle, affable, gracious, obliging, compassionate, serviceable. A 'no' in their mouth has more grace than a 'yes' in the mouth of a constipated man.

"The toilet has so much power that diarrhea often makes a man pusillanimous. Dysentery takes away courage. Do not propose to a man weakened by insomnia, by a slow fever, and by fifty putrid evacuations, to go and attack a demilune in broad daylight. That is why I cannot believe that our whole army had dysentery at the battle of Agincourt, as it is said, and that they won the victory pants down. A few soldiers had diarrhea, no doubt, for having gorged themselves on bad grapes along the road; and so the historians said that the whole army, sick, fought bare-ass, and that, so as not to show their behinds to the French dandies, they *beat the tar out of them*, in the words of the Jesuit Daniel.

And that is just how men write history.[2]

"It is thus that the French have all repeated, one after the other, that our great Edward III had six burghers of Calais delivered up to him with ropes around their necks to hang them with, because they had dared to sustain the siege with courage, and that his wife finally obtained their pardon with her tears.[3] These romancers do not know that it was the custom in those barbarous times for the burghers to present themselves before their conqueror with ropes around their necks whenever they had held him up too long before some shanty. But certainly the generous Edward had no desire to wring the neck of these six hostages, whom he loaded with presents and honors. I am weary of all the nonsense with which so many self-styled historians have stuffed their chronicles and of all the battles they have so badly described. I would just as soon believe that Gideon won a signal victory with three hundred pitchers.[4] Thank God, I no longer read anything but natural history, provided that a Burnet, a

2   The verse is Voltaire's, from the play *Charlot* (1767), I, vii. He had already criticized Daniel's style for vulgar clichés in the *Gazette littéraire de l'Europe*, September 30, 1764.
3   Du Belloy's tragedy *Le Siège de Calais* (1765) had followed this account and exploited patriotic sentiments with great success.
4   For Israel over the Midianites; see Judges 7:15–23.

*Pedagogue** while the Saint-Pouange and the fair Saint-Yves were in the inner room.

"Would you believe it," he said to her first, "that your brother came to ask me for a *lettre de cachet* against you? In truth I would rather draw one up to send him back to Lower Brittany."

"Alas! sir, then they must be very free with *lettres de cachet* in your offices, since people come from the far corners of the kingdom to solicit them like pensions. I am very far from asking for one against my brother. I have much reason to complain against him, but I respect the liberty of men; I ask for that of a man I want to marry, a man to whom the King owes the preservation of a province, who can serve him usefully, and who is the son of an officer killed in his service. What is he accused of? How could he be treated so cruelly without a hearing?"

Then the assistant minister showed her the letter of the Jesuit spy and that of the perfidious magistrate.

"What! There are such monsters on earth! And they want to force me in this way to marry the ridiculous son of a ridiculous and wicked man! And it is on such information that they here decide the destiny of citizens!"

She threw herself on her knees, she asked with sobs for the freedom of the worthy man who adored her. Her charms in this state appeared to their greatest advantage. She was so beautiful that the Saint-Pouange, losing all shame, insinuated to her that she would succeed if she began by giving him the first fruits of what she was reserving for her lover. The fair Saint-Yves, terrified and confused, for a long time feigned not to understand him; he had to express himself more clearly. A word uttered at first with restraint led to another stronger one, followed by another more expressive. He offered not only the revocation of the *lettre de cachet*, but rewards, money, honors, establishments; and the more he promised, the more his desire grew not to be refused.

Saint-Yves was weeping, suffocating, half reclining on a sofa, hardly believing what she saw, what she heard. The Saint-Pouange in turn threw himself on his knees. He was not without attractions, and might not have alarmed a less committed heart. But Saint-Yves adored her lover and believed it was a horrible crime to betray him in order to serve him. Saint-Pouange redoubled his prayers and promises.

Finally his head was so turned that he declared to her that
this was the only way to release from his prison the man
in whom she took so violent and tender an interest. This
strange interview went on and on. The pious woman in the
antechamber, reading her *Christian Pedagogue,* kept saying:

"Good Lord! What can they be doing for two hours now?
Never has Monseigneur de Saint-Pouange given such a long
audience; perhaps he has refused this poor · girl everything,
since she is still beseeching him."

Finally her companion came out of the inner room quite
frantic, unable to speak, reflecting deeply on the character
of the great and the half-great, who so lightly sacrifice the
liberty of men and the honor of women.

She said not a word all the way home. Back at her friend's
house she burst and told her everything. The pious woman
made great signs of the cross.

"My dear friend, promptly tomorrow you must consult
Father Tout-à-tous, our director; he has much influence with
My Lord de Saint-Pouange; he confesses several women-
servants of his house, he is a pious and accommodating
man, who also directs women of quality. Put yourself entirely
in his hands, that's the way I do; I have always come out
well; we poor women need to be guided by a man."

"Well then, my dear friend, tomorrow I will go and see
Father Tout-à-tous."

16 *She Consults a Jesuit*

AS SOON AS the beautiful and desolate Saint-Yves was with
her good confessor, she confided to him that a powerful
and voluptuous man was proposing to get the man out of
prison whom she was to marry lawfully, and that he was
asking a great price for his service; that she had a horrible
repugnance for such an infidelity, and that if it were a question
only of her own life she would sacrifice it rather than
succumb.

"That is an abominable sinner," said Father Tout-à-tous.
"You really should tell me the name of this vile man; surely
he is some Jansenist; I will denounce him to His Reverence

myself miserable over chimeras? I am much more sure of
my unhappiness than of effectual grace. I have consumed
my days in reasoning about the freedom of God and of
the human race, but I have lost my own; neither St.
Augustine nor St. Prosper* will pull me out of the abyss I am
in."

Ingenuous, giving way to his character, said at last:

"Do you want me to speak to you with bold frankness?
Those who get themselves persecuted for these vain scholastic
disputes appear to me none too wise; those who persecute
appear to me monsters."

The two captives were strongly agreed on the injustice of
their captivity.

"I am a hundred times more to be pitied than you," said
Ingenuous. "I was born free as the air; I had two lives—liberty
and the object of my love; I am deprived of both. We are
both in irons, without knowing who put us here and without
even being able to ask.[1] I lived as a Huron for twenty years;
people say they are barbarians because they take vengeance
on their enemies; but they have never oppressed their friends.
Hardly had I set foot in France when I shed my blood for
her; I may have saved a province, and as a reward I am
swallowed up in this tomb of the living where I would have
died of rage but for you. Then there are no laws in this
country! Men are condemned without a hearing! It is not
so in England. Ah! it was not the English I should have
fought against."

Thus his nascent philosophy could not subdue nature
outraged in the first of her rights, and gave free rein to his
just anger.

His companion did not contradict him. Absence always
increases unsatisfied love, and philosophy does not diminish
it. He spoke as often of his dear Saint-Yves as of morals
and metaphysics. The purer his feelings grew the more he
was in love. He read a few new novels; he found few that
portrayed for him the situation of his soul. He felt that his
heart always went beyond what he read.

"Ah!" he said, "almost all these authors have nothing but
wit and art."

1   Instead of these two phrases ("without knowing . . . able
to ask") some editions read: "without knowing the reason and
without being able to ask it."

Finally, the good Jansenist priest was imperceptibly becoming the confidant of his tender feelings. Until then he
knew love only as a sin to accuse oneself of at confession.
He learned to know it for a feeling as noble as it is tender,
which can elevate the soul quite as much as soften it, and
even sometimes produce virtues. Lastly, for a final prodigy,
a Huron was converting a Jansenist.

15 The Fair Saint-Yves Resists Some Delicate Propositions

SO THE FAIR Saint-Yves, even more tender than her lover,
went to the house of Monsieur de Saint-Pouange accompanied
by the friend with whom she was lodging, both with faces
hidden in their hoods. The first thing she saw at the door was
her brother the Abbé de Saint-Yves going out. She was
intimidated, but her pious friend reassured her.

"It is precisely because he has spoken against you that
you must speak. Be assured that in this country the accusers
are always right unless you are quick to confound them.
Moreover, your presence, unless I am much mistaken, will
have more effect than your brother's words."

With the slightest encouragement, a woman passionately in
love is intrepid. The fair Saint-Yves presents herself at the
audience. Her youth, her charms, her tender eyes wet with
a few tears attracted every glance. Every courtier of the
assistant minister forgot for a moment the idol of power to
contemplate that of beauty. The Saint-Pouange had her
come into a private room; she spoke with emotion and
grace. Saint-Pouange felt touched. She trembled, he reassured
her.

"Come back this evening," he said to her, "your business
deserves to be thought about and talked about at leisure.
There are too many people here. Interviews are expedited too
rapidly. I must talk with you thoroughly about all that
concerns you."

Then, having praised her beauty and her feelings, he recommended that she come at seven in the evening.

She did not fail to; her pious friend again accompanied
her, but remained in the waiting room and read the *Christian*

Whiston, and a Woodward do not bore me any more with their accursed systems; that a Maillet no longer tells me that the Irish Sea produced the Caucasian Mountains and that our globe is made of glass; provided that they do not present me little aquatic rushes as voracious animals, and coral as insects, provided that charlatans do not insolently present me their daydreams as truths. I set more store by a good regimen that maintains my humors in balance and procures me a commendable digestion and a sound sleep. Drink hot when it freezes, drink cool in the dog days; in everything, neither too much nor too little; digest, sleep, have pleasure, and snap your fingers at the rest of it."

CHAPTER 8

AS MONSIEUR SIDRAC was proffering these wise words, news was brought to Monsieur Goudman that Count Chesterfield's steward was at the door in his carriage and was asking to speak to him on very urgent business. Goudman runs to receive the orders of the lordly steward, who, having asked him to get in, says to him:

"Sir, no doubt you know what happened to Monsieur and Madame Sidrac on their wedding night?"

"Yes, sir, he was just telling me about that little adventure."

"Well! the very same thing happened to the beautiful Miss Fidler and to the honorable curate, her husband. The next day they fought, the day after that they separated, and the curate's benefice was taken away from him. I love the Fidler girl, I know that she loves you; she does not hate me. I am above the little disgrace that is the cause of her divorce. I am in love and intrepid. Give me up Miss Fidler, and I will see that you have the curacy, which is worth a hundred and fifty guineas a year. I give you just ten minutes to think it over."

"Sir, the proposition is delicate, I am going to consult my philosophers Sidrac and Grou; I'll be with you without delay."

He flies back to his two advisers.

"I see," he said, "that digestion alone does not decide the affairs of this world, and that love, ambition, and money play a large part."

He expounds the case to them and entreats them to decide on the spot. Both conclude that with a hundred and fifty guineas he could have all the girls in the parish, and also Miss Fidler into the bargain.

Goudman felt the wisdom of this decision; he got the curacy, he had Miss Fidler in secret, which was much sweeter than having her as a wife. Monsieur Sidrac lavished his good offices upon him when the occasion arose. He has become one of the most terrible priests in England; and he is more persuaded than ever of the fatality that governs all the things of this world.

Anabaptist: member of a Christian sect that rejected infant baptism in favor of baptism on confession of faith.

Année Littéraire: see Fréron.

auto-da-fé: from the Portuguese, "act of the faith": the ceremony attendant to a judgment by the Inquisition; hence the burning of heretics as a result of such a judgment.

Barbados water: a cordial flavored with orange peel and lemon peel.

berlin: a four-wheeled, two-seated, covered carriage.

Berruyer: Isaac-Joseph Berruyer (1681-1758), author of *L'Histoire du peuple de Dieu* (1728, 7 vols.).

Berthier: Guillaume-François Berthier (1704-1782), editor of the Jesuit *Journal de Trévoux,* opponent of Voltaire, the *Encyclopédie,* and the *philosophes* in general.

Bossuet: Jacques-Bénigne Bossuet (1627-1704), outstanding preacher, writer, and spokesman for the religious policy of Louis XIV.

Bougeant: Guillaume-Hyacinthe Bougeant (1690-1743), who argues in his *Amusement philosophique sur le langage des bêtes* (1739) that fallen angels live in the bodies of animals.

cadi: a minor Mohammedan judge or magistrate.

Castel: Louis-Bertrand Castel (1688-1757), anti-Newtonian scientist, whose works include a *Traité de physique sur la pesanteur universelle* (1724, 2 vols.) and *L'Optique des couleurs* (1740).

Christian Pedagogue: Pédagogue chrétien (1634 or earlier), French translation of a popular Latin work by Father Philippe d'Outreman (1585-1652).

Clélie: a tremendously popular novel (1654-1661, 10 vols.) by Mlle Madeleine de Scudéry, famous for its "Carte de Tendre," an allegorical map of the country of love.

Clodion the Hairy: a fifth-century Frankish chief.

convulsion(s) (convulsionary, convulsionaries): manifestations of religious ecstasy or mania, like those of the Holy Rollers today. The Jansenists were noted for them.

Corneille: Pierre Corneille (1606–1684), the first great French tragedian, author of *Le Cid, Horace, Cinna, Polyeucte, Rodogune,* many other tragedies, and a few comedies.

Croiset: Father Jean Croiset (died 1738), author of many collections of *Méditations* (*Retraite spirituelle pour un jour de chaque mois*) published from 1694 on.

Curious and Edifying Letters: Lettres édifiantes et curieuses, a collection of reports by Jesuit missionaries published from 1702 on.

daric: a gold coin of ancient Persia.

Derham: William Derham (1657–1735), author of *Astrotheology* (1715).

dervish: a member of a Mohammedan religious order.

Desterham: Voltaire's version of *defterdar,* a Turkish superintendent of finance.

Divan: Turkish council of state.

drachma: a Greek coin, once used also in Egypt.

Du Cerceau: Jean-Antoine Du Cerceau (1670–1730), Jesuit poet and dramatist.

effendi: Turkish title of respect used especially of state officials.

Encyclopédie: or *Dictionnaire raisonné des sciences, des arts, et des métiers,* a vast secular *summa* published (1751–1765) despite many obstacles, edited by Diderot with the collaboration of most of the *philosophes,* including Voltaire.

English cordial: a cordial containing spirits of ammonia.

Erythrean Sea: the Red Sea.

Flower of the Saints: Flos Sanctorum, o Libro de las vidas de los Santos (1599, 2 vols.) by the Spanish Jesuit Pedro de Ribadeneira (1526–1611), popular in French translation.

Fréron: Élie Fréron (1719–1776), publisher of the *Année Littéraire,* enemy of Voltaire and the *philosophes* and a favorite target for Voltaire's wit.

Gaeta: an Italian port northwest of Naples.

Gauchat: Gabriel Gauchat (1709–1774 or 1779), enemy of
    Voltaire and the Encyclopedists.
Harlay (Archbishop de): François de Harlay de Champ-
    vallon (1625–1695), Archbishop of Paris from
    1670, a leader in the persecution of Protestants and
    Jansenists.
imam: a Mohammedan priest.
Imaus, Mount: ancient name for an Asian mountain range,
    probably the Himalayas.
Jansenism, Jansenists, Jansenius: Jansenism is a Christian
    sect stressing predestination and asceticism, founded
    by Cornelius Jansen or Jansenius (1585–1638),
    Dutch Bishop of Ypres, author of the *Augustinus*
    (1640). It spread rapidly and widely in France,
    notably through the efforts of Saint-Cyran and
    Arnauld, and established its center near Paris in the
    religious community of Port-Royal. Opposed vio-
    lently by the Sorbonne and the Jesuits, persecuted
    by Louis XIV, and condemned by Pope Clement XI
    in 1713, Jansenism still retained some strength in
    France until about the mid-eighteenth century.
Japan: To discourage trade with the Christians, the Japanese
    required European merchants to stamp on the cross
    as a sign of rejection of Christianity.
Journal de Trévoux: the Jesuit journal, founded in 1701
    and edited for many years by Guillaume-François
    Berthier.
Kroust: Father Antoine Kroust, Jesuit, rector at Colmar
    from 1753 to 1763, hostile to Voltaire and the
    philosophes.
La Chaise: François de La Chaise (1624–1709), Jesuit
    father, from 1675 on the very influential confessor
    to Louis XIV.
lettre(s) de cachet: letters bearing the King's seal; in Vol-
    taire's time, arbitrary warrants of imprisonment.
Lettre(s) provinciale(s): see Pascal.
Louisiade: an epic poem formally entitled *Saint Louis, ou
    le héros chrétien* (1653) by Father Pierre Le Moyne
    (1602–1671).
Maeotian Marsh: ancient name for the Sea of Azov.
Malagrida: Gabriel Malagrida (1689–1761), Portuguese
    Jesuit, who pronounced it no sin to kill his King,

Joseph I, was compromised in a plot against the King's life which led to the expulsion of the Jesuits from Portugal in 1759, and was executed in 1761.

Manichean: a follower of Mani or Manicheus, a third-century Persian who believed in two nearly equal forces, of good and of evil. The sect flourished in St. Augustine's time.

maravedi: a small Spanish copper coin.

Marillac: Louis de Marillac (1573–1632), Marshal of France, who conspired against Richelieu and was executed by his orders.

Meknes: a town in Morocco.

moidore: a gold coin of Portugal and Brazil.

Molinism, Molinists: Jesuits, from the name of Luis Molina (1535–1600), Spanish Jesuit, author of a widely influential theory reconciling predestination with free will.

mufti: an official expounder of Mohammedan law.

Oratory: a preaching order (Oratorians, or Fathers of the Oratory) founded in Italy in 1564 and established in France in 1611.

Pascal: Blaise Pascal (1623–1662), eminent French mathematician, physicist, and religious writer, spokesman for the Jansenists against the Jesuits in his *Lettres provinciales* (1656–1657), Christian apologist in his unfinished *Pensées* (1670). His sister Gilberte told of his rediscovery of the first thirty-two propositions of Euclid at the age of twelve. Voltaire enjoyed his satire of the Jesuits but criticized his view of the misery of fallen man in his *Remarques sur les Pensées de M. Pascal* (1734).

pasha: a Turkish governor or military leader.

patacón (or pataca): a Portuguese and Brazilian silver coin.

piaster: a coin, usually silver, of Turkey and Egypt; also used to signify the Spanish peso.

pistole: a Spanish gold coin.

Port-Royal: *see* Jansenism.

Propontis: the Sea of Marmora, between the Bosporus and the Dardanelles.

Prosper, St.: Prosper of Aquitaine or Prosper Tiro (c. 390–c. 465), a disciple of St. Augustine.

Racine: Jean Racine (1639–1699), great French tragedian,

Voltaire's model in that genre, whose tragedies include *Andromaque, Britannicus, Bérénice, Bajazet, Mithridate, Iphigénie, Phèdre, Esther,* and *Athalie.*

Recollects (Récollets): a strict branch of the Franciscans, rivals of the Jesuits.

Rohault: Jacques Rohault (1620–1675), author of a *Traité de physique* (1671).

Sadder: an extract from the Zend-Avesta, the sacred book of Zoroastrianism.

Saint-Cyran: *see* Jansenism.

Saint-Pouange: a name probably representing Louis Phélypeaux, Count of Saint-Florentin (1705–1777), minister under Louis XV and under Louis XVI, who dismissed him in 1775. He was criticized for prodigality, loose morality, and overuse of *lettres de cachet* (q.v.).

Salé: a Moroccan port on the Atlantic near Rabat, once a headquarters for pirates.

sanbenito: a yellow robe worn by heretics condemned to the stake by the Inquisition.

sequin: a Venetian gold coin.

Socinian: a religious rationalist, denying the Trinity and the personality of Christ.

Sorbonne: a college of the University of Paris whose name is now used for the university itself and was used in Voltaire's day for the university's Faculty of Theology, a stronghold of conservative opposition to the new philosophical ideas.

Tetuan: a town in Morocco.

Theatine: a member of a Catholic order founded in 1524 to combat Protestantism.

Think Well on It: Pensez-y bien, a popular religious work by the Jesuit Father Paul de Barry (1585–1661).

Trublet: Nicolas-Charles-Joseph Trublet (1697–1770), bitter critic of Voltaire and the *Encyclopédie,* author of *Essais de littérature.*

Tucuman: a province in northern Argentina.

vizier: a high Mohammedan executive or judicial officer.

SELECTED BIBLIOGRAPHY

Works by VOLTAIRE

Philosophical Letters (or *Letters Concerning the English Nation*), 1734.
Zadig, 1748 (Signet Classic 0-451-524268)
The Century of Louis XIV, 1751
Essay on the Manners and the Spirit of Nations, 1756
Candide, 1759 (Signet Classic 0-451-524268)
Treatise on Tolerance, 1763
Philosophical Dictionary, 1764

Selected Biography and Criticism

Aldridge, Alfred O. *Voltaire and the Century of Light*. Princeton, N.J.: Princeton University Press, 1975.

Besterman, Theodore, *Voltaire*. New York: Harcourt, Brace & World, 1969.

Bottiglia, William F. "Voltaire's *Candide:* Analysis of a Classic," 2nd ed. *Studies on Voltaire and the Eighteenth Century*. Geneva: Institut et Musee Voltaire, 1964.

———, ed. *Voltaire: A Collection of Critical Essays*. Englewood Cliffs, N.J.: Prentice-Hall, 1968.

Brailsford, Henry N. *Voltaire*. New York: Holt, Rinehart & Winston, 1935.

Brandes, George. *Voltaire*. 2 vols. New York: Tudor, 1930.

Foster, Milton P., ed. *Voltaire's* Candide *and the Critics*. Belmont, Cal.: Wadsworth, 1964.

Gay, Peter. *Voltaire's Politics: The Poet as Realist*. Princeton, N.J.: Princeton University Press, 1959.

Havens, George R. *The Ages of Ideas*. New York: Henry Holt & Co., 1955.

Lanson, Gustave, *Voltaire*. Trans. Robert A. Wagoner. New York: John Wiley & Sons, 1966.

Morley, John. *Voltaire*. London: Macmillan. 1913.

Richter, Peyton and Ilona Ricardo. *Voltaire*. Twayne's World Authors Series. Boston: Twayne, 1980.

Ridgway, Ronald S. *Voltaire and Sensibility*. Montreal and London: McGill-Queen's University Press, 1973.

Topazio, Virgil W. *Voltaire: A Critical Study of His Major Works*. New York: Random House, 1967.

Torrey, Norman L. *The Spirit of Voltaire*. New York: Columbia University Press, 1938.

Wade, Ira O. *The Intellectual Development of Voltaire*. Princeton, N.J.: Princeton University Press, 1969.

———. *Voltaire and "Candide": A Study of the Fusion of History, Art, and Philosophy*. Princeton, N.J.: Princeton University Press, 1959.